...IBRARIES N...
...DRAWN FROM...

Mrs Tim of the Regiment

D. E. Stevenson

ISIS

LARGE PRINT

Oxford

LIBRARIES NI	
C900208126	
ULV	29.2.12
SAGA	£15.95
CHICHESTER	

Copyright 973

First ....

Published in Large Print 2010 by ISIS Publishing Ltd.,
7 Centremead, Osney Mead, Oxford OX2 0ES
by arrangement with
Bloomsbury Publishing Plc

All rights reserved

The moral right of the author has been asserted

British Library Cataloguing in Publication Data
Stevenson, D. E. (Dorothy Emily), 1892–1973
    Mrs. Tim of the regiment.
    1. Army spouses - - Scotland - - Fiction.
    2. Scotland - - Social life and customs - - 20th
    century - - Fiction.
    3. Great Britain - - History - - George V,
    1910–1936 - - Fiction.
    4. Diary fiction.
    5. Large type books.
    I. Title
    823.9'12–dc22

ISBN 978–0–7531–8608–4 (hb)
ISBN 978–0–7531–8609–1 (pb)

Printed and bound in Great Britain by
T. J. International Ltd., Padstow, Cornwall

EX LIBRIS

Author's Foreword
to the Story of the Christie Family
by D. E. STEVENSON

The four books about Mrs. Tim and her family were republished during 1973 and early 1974, and the author was asked to write a foreword.

The books consist of:

1. *Mrs. Tim Christie*
2. *Mrs. Tim Carries On*
3. *Mrs. Tim Gets a Job*
4. *Mrs. Tim Flies Home*

The first "Mrs. Tim" was written many years ago (in 1934). It was written at the request of the wife of a professor of English history in a well-known university who was a personal friend. Their daughter was engaged to be married to an officer in a Highland Regiment. Naturally enough they wanted to know what it would be like and what she would be expected to do.

There was nothing secret in my diary so I gave it to Mrs. Ford to read. When she handed it back, Mrs. Ford was smiling. She said, "I read it aloud to Rupert and we laughed till we cried. You could make this into a very amusing book and call it *Leaves from the Diary of an Officer's Wife*. It just needs to be expanded, and you could pep it up a little, couldn't you?"

At first I was doubtful (it was not my idea of a book), but she was so persuasive that I decided to have a try. The result was *Mrs. Tim of the Regiment* (now being reissued as *Mrs. Tim Christie*). By this time I had got into the swing of the story and had become so interested in Hester that I gave her a holiday in the Scottish Highlands with her friend Mrs. Loudon and called it *Golden Days*.

The two books were accepted by a publisher and published in an omnibus volume. It was surprisingly successful. It was well reviewed and the sales were eminently satisfactory; the fan-mail was astonishing. People wrote from near and far saying that Mrs. Tim was a real live person; they had enjoyed her adventures immensely — and they wanted more.

But it was not until the outbreak of the Second World War in 1939 that I felt the urge to write another book about Hester Christie.

Mrs. Tim Carries On was easily written, for it is just a day-to-day account of what happened and what we did — and said and felt. The book was a comfort to me in those dark days; it helped me to carry on, and a sort of pattern emerged from the chaos.

Like its predecessor, the book was written from my own personal diary but this time there was no need to expand the story nor to "pep it up" for there was enough pep already in my diary for half a dozen books.

It is all true. It is true that a German plane came down on the moor in the middle of a shooting party and the two airmen were captured. It is true that German planes came down to low level in Norfolk, and elsewhere, and used machine guns to kill pedestrians on the roads. Sometimes they circled over the harvest fields and killed a few farm labourers and horses. Why they did so is a mystery. There could not have been any military objective in these maneuvers. People soon got used to it and were not even seriously alarmed but just took cover in a convenient ditch like dear old Uncle Joe. Perhaps the German airmen did it for fun? Perhaps it amused them to see old gentlemen rolling into ditches?

An American friend wrote to me as follows: "Your Mrs. Tim has made us *think*. We have been trying to imagine what it would be like to have a man-eating tiger prowling around in *our* back-yard."

She had hit the nail on the head for, alas, the strip of water which had kept Britain safe from her enemies for hundreds of years had become too narrow: The tiger was in our backyard.

To me this book brings back the past so vividly that even now — thirty years later — I cannot read it without laughter and tears. Laughter? Yes, for in spite of the sadness and badness of Total War, the miseries we suffered, and the awful anxieties we endured, cheerfulness broke through at unexpected moments — and we laughed.

When they were first published, these four books about Mrs. Tim were all very popular. Everybody loved Mrs. Tim (everybody except the good citizens of Westburgh who disliked her intensely). Everybody wanted to know more about her and her friends. But the books have been out of print and unobtainable for years. I was pleased to hear that they were to be republished and that they would all be available again. I was particularly glad because together they contain the whole history of the Christie family and its friends. Taken in their proper sequence, readers will be able to appreciate the gradual development of Hester's character and the more rapid development of Tim's. As the years pass by there is a difference in the children; Annie and Fred Bollings become more adult; Jack and Grace McDougall, having weathered serious trouble, settle down peacefully together. The Christies' friends are very varied but all are interesting and unusual. We are introduced to the dignified Mrs. Loudon; we meet Pinkie, an attractive young lady whose secret trouble is that (although seventeen years old) she does not feel "properly grown up, inside." But, in spite of this, Pinkie makes friends wherever she goes. Her circle of friends includes all the young officers who are quartered at the depot and is enlarged by the arrival of Polish officers who have escaped from their war-shattered country and are billeted in Donford while they reorganise their forces and learn the language. There is a mysterious lady, swathed in Egyptian scarves, who is convinced that in a previous existence she helped to build the Great Pyramid. There is Erica Clutterbuck whose rude manners conceal a heart of gold, and two elegant American ladies who endeavour to persuade Mrs. Tim to go home with them to America so that they may exhibit her to their friends as "The Spirit of English Womanhood."

Several picnics take place. Some are enjoyable, others not, according to the weather conditions and the feelings of the assembled company.

But the chief interest is to be found in the curious character of Tony Morley and his relationship with the Christie family. At first he seems to Tim and Hester a somewhat alarming personage. (To Tim, because he is a senior officer and fabulously wealthy: he drives a large and powerful car, owns a string of racehorses, and hunts several days a week. To Hester, because he talks irresponsibly and displays an impish sense of humour so that she never knows whether or not he means what he says.) Soon, however, they discover that beneath the surface he is a true friend and can be relied upon whenever the services of a friend are urgently needed. We find out how he uses his tact and diplomacy to smooth the feathers of a disgruntled cook and show her how to measure out the ingredients for a cake with insufficient weights. We learn how he helps Hester to save a naval officer from making a disastrous marriage and how he consoles and advises a young husband whose wife has deserted him. We are told of Colonel Morley's success with a battalion of raw recruits, how he wins their devotion, licks them into shape, and welds them into a satisfactory fighting machine by imbuing them with the necessary *esprit de corps*. We see him salute smartly and march off at the head of his battalion en route for the Middle East. Knowing his reputation for reckless courage, Hester wonders sadly if she will ever see him again. But apparently Tony is indestructible. He has survived countless dangers and seems none the worse. He pops in, out of the blue, at Rome (where Hester, on her way home from Africa, is seriously embarrassed by her ignorance of the language). Tony Morley arrives in his usual sudden and unexpected manner. By this time he has become a full-blown general and, having learnt to speak Italian from an obliging enemy, is able to deal adequately with the situation. He also deals adequately with a little misunderstanding at the War Office where he sees a friend and pulls a string or two for Tim.

Meanwhile the Christie children, Bryan and Betty, are growing up rapidly. In fact they are "almost grown up," and, although they are still amusing and full of high spirits, it is obvious that they will soon become useful members of the post-war world.

We meet them at Old Quinings where their mother has managed to find a small house for the summer holidays. Here, also, we meet Annie and Fred Bollings, Grace McDougall and her boys, an old-fashioned squire with a pretty daughter, a school teacher whose unconventional views about free love are somewhat alarming, and a very good-looking young man who is studying medicine but is not too busy to open gates for a fair equestrienne. We meet the amiable Mrs. Daulkes and the far from amiable Miss Crease whose sharp eyes and caustic tongue cause a good deal of trouble to her neighbours. Another unpleasant visitor is Hester Christie's landlady, the wily Miss Stroude, who tries to bounce Hester and almost succeeds, but once again

Tony comes to the rescue in the nick of time to defeat Miss Stroude and send her away "with her tail between her legs."

Betty says, joyfully, "This is the best holidays, ever" but Hester's pleasure is not complete until the arrival of Colonel Tim Christie from Africa. Now, at last, she is happy with all her beloved family under one roof.

I cannot finish this foreword without voicing the grateful thanks of Mrs. Tim to her many kind friends in America, South Africa, Australia, and New Zealand who sent her parcels to augment her war-rations. The parcels contained tins of fat, packets of tea and sugar and dried fruit, bars of chocolate, and boxes of candy for the children. These generous presents were shared with friends and were worth their weight in gold.

January

First January

Tim wakes up very peevish after last night's celebrations in mess (how strange the after-effects of enjoyment on the human frame!). He reminds me that his Aunt Ethel is coming to dinner and to spend the night on her way to Dover and the Riviera. Reminder quite unnecessary, as Aunt Ethel's visit has been a cloud on my horizon ever since it was arranged in November.

Tim enjoins me to "give the old girl a decent dinner," but is not helpful as regards details. When passed he suggests lamb, which, I point out, is unprocurable at present, except in frozen form.

Tim replies that "all that" is my job, and that he can't think of food in any form this morning, as his head is like a boiler room, and what on earth are the children doing — there might be half a dozen of them from the noise.

Rush downstairs and try to keep the children quiet at breakfast, which is difficult owing to a fall of snow, and the thrilling prospect of a snowman in the Square Gardens. Betty says it is going to be as big as a real man, and Bryan — with his mouth full of bacon — tries to say "Bigger" with disastrous consequences.

Miss Hardcastle has gone away for a fortnight's holiday, which adds to the hilarity. Reflect on the annoying habit of governesses in general, and Miss H. in particular, insisting on holidays at inopportune moments.

Pack the children off as soon as possible, shod with Wellington boots and armed with a broom and a large coal shovel.

Tim — as yet unshaven and clad in a dressing gown, but somewhat soothed with strong coffee — is embarking on toast and marmalade when Mrs. Benson is seen approaching the hall door. He mutters maledictions on colonels' wives and disappears upstairs (looking like the Hatter, with a piece of toast in one hand and a cup of coffee in the other).

After an hour of Mrs. Benson I feel inclined to agree with Tim, that colonels should be celibate. The more so as I find I have consented to take charge of the Women's and Children's Christmas Tree and Tea Party, which is to take place on the fourteenth, Mrs. Benson being obliged to go to a matinée in town on that day with her father-in-law, recently returned from Australia.

Accompany Mrs. Benson to the door and find that Bryan and Betty have brought in four friends who have been helping to make the snowman, and they are all eating Golden Sovereign Oranges (at threepence each), which I had intended for dessert tonight. Smile and say that I hope they are nice, while making a mental note to speak tactfully to the children about it after the visitors have gone. Difficult subject, as it clashes somewhat with tenets of hospitality, generosity, and unselfishness which I have endeavoured to inculcate.

Aunt Ethel arrives at teatime in Rolls Royce and is conducted to the spare room, which really looks exceedingly cosy with curtains drawn and a bright fire. Feel that my efforts for her comfort deserve a word of recognition, but none is forthcoming. Remark brightly that Richard is dining with us tonight, "so we shall be a nice little family party." Aunt Ethel replies that she remembers seeing my brother at the wedding, in a tone that leaves me in some doubt as to whether her recollections of him are entirely pleasant.

Bryan and Betty appear and kiss Aunt Ethel dutifully, and accept a popgun and a jigsaw puzzle (belated Christmas presents) with ill-concealed disappointment; Tim having raised their hopes (in my opinion unwisely) of more acceptable gifts. Can sympathise with their feelings when I am presented with a pink silk pincushion — very hard — which I cannot help considering an unfair return for a flat black morocco handbag with zipper fastening. Remind myself that it is impossible to live for ever, even if you spend every winter upon the Riviera and am able to thank Aunt Ethel for her gift with appropriate enthusiasm.

Dinner is a somewhat trying meal. Annie loses her head, and hands the potatoes to Aunt Ethel minus a spoon. She realises her mistake, rushes to the sideboard, and returns with the necessary utensil which she presses into Aunt Ethel's nerveless hand muttering, "'Ere it is."

Talk feverishly about the weather, which wireless has prophesied will "continue unsettled and stormy," quite forgetting in my excitement that Aunt Ethel is crossing the Channel on Monday.

Meanwhile, Annie, who is completely demoralised by her mistake, proceeds to denude the table of cruets and mats before she has served the plum pudding.

Can see Tim looking at me in an imploring manner, but feel it best to take no notice of Annie's unusual procedure.

Richard, on whom I was depending for dash and sparkle, is in his gloomiest mood, his best story having been completely spoiled by Aunt Ethel's inability to see its point.

We retire to the drawing room, and find the fire in the last stages of dissolution. A rubber of bridge passes a difficult hour, but it is not an unqualified success in the way of entertainment, as Aunt Ethel can never remember what is trumps and Richard revokes twice from sheer boredom.

Richard now produces a flat box, which he gives me, saying it is my Christmas present, and he is sorry it is a week late. I open it, and find a large diary bound in red leather with a lock and key. Am overjoyed at the prospect of being able to record my secret thoughts without fear of detection. Joy somewhat dampened by Richard remarking that in his opinion we ought all to keep a record of our doings, *however unimportant they may be*. Aunt Ethel tries to soften this remark by saying she is sure that dear Hester does her best, and, after all, we can't all be indispensable, and at any rate she would be much missed by the dear children if anything were to happen to her.

Damned with faint praise I remove myself and my diary to the privacy of my bedroom, where I proceed to write up the first day of the New Year.

Second January

Aunt Ethel breakfasts in bed — a fortunate dispensation of providence, as the children are very full of life this morning. Remind myself that high spirits is a sign of health which enables me to bear with them, in spite of a slight headache, doubtless due to a large helping of plum pudding last night.

Visit Aunt Ethel to see if she has all she requires, and find that she has brought her own eiderdown, pillow, and sandbags for door and window. Also that the mysterious sounds heard by Tim and self during the night, and at first attributed to burglars, and afterwards (doubtfully) to the next-door cat, must have been Aunt Ethel moving her bed into a less draughty corner. Express much sorrow and solicitude for lack of amenities in the spare bedroom. Aunt Ethel replies that it is high time that Timothy and I had a comfortable home of our own. Agree fervently and hopefully, but nothing more is said on the subject.

Aunt Ethel then Rises and Descends (only capital letters can adequately describe her movements), and

7

announces her intention of departing southwards directly after luncheon, instead of at twelve o'clock, as previously arranged. Rush frantically to the kitchen to counter order hash and milk pudding, and to substitute cutlets and mashed potatoes, tinned peas and banana fritters for our midday meal. Katie, decidedly annoyed at the alteration in menu, says that the butcher has been, and I shall have to telephone if I want cutlets.

Children come in with wet stockings, which they declare are perfectly dry. Both exceedingly naughty when I insist on stockings being changed. No time to bring them to a better frame of mind, as Aunt Ethel is sitting alone in the drawing room.

Shortly after this Aunt Ethel goes upstairs to pack, and rings her bell three times for Annie to come and strap her boxes. Am told on enquiry, that Annie is "washing her face," so the only thing to be done is to go upstairs and strap boxes myself. Whilst I am engaged on this Herculean task, Aunt Ethel regales me with details of the ménage of a certain Mrs. Hunter, who lives near her at Greenvale and runs her house perfectly with one maid.

It is all a matter of organisation, Aunt Ethel says. Mrs. Hunter arranges every detail herself and plans every moment of the day. Mrs. Hunter never glosses over mistakes, she expects things to be perfect, and they are perfect. (Feel convinced that if I expected anything of the kind it would merely lead to disappointment.) Discover that Mrs. Hunter is — as I thought — a childless widow with unlimited means.

Rolls Royce drives up to the door after lunch and waits for half an hour while we all hunt for Aunt Ethel's bag, which is unaccountably missing. Aunt quite frantic, as her passport and money are contained therein. She pins Tim in a corner and asks in a penetrating whisper how long we have had the servants, and whether he is quite certain they are honest. At last she says in despair, "I can't go until the bag is found." Everyone immediately redoubles efforts to locate bag. It is eventually run to earth beneath Aunt Ethel's pillow, where she now remembers she put it last night for safety.

Annie has had no time nor opportunity to "make down" bed this morning, but considers this a blot on her character, and is heard announcing audibly to Katie that she "*does believe* the old lady done it on purpose to show her up."

In the midst of all this turmoil Tim whispers to me that he has just seen the doctor's car pass, and that he is sure to charge double in his bill after seeing the Rolls standing at the gate. Murmur something soothing.

We all go out and watch Aunt Ethel being hoisted into her car by her efficient chauffeur, and wave enthusiastically as she glides off down the road.

"Thank God!" says Tim devoutly.

Betty enquires in an interested voice why Daddy is thanking God, to which Tim replies with admirable presence of mind that it is because the wind has gone down and Aunt Ethel will have a calm passage.

9

Third January

Decide to take the children to church. Bryan, slightly aggrieved, says he "thought it was the holidays." Best to pretend I have not heard this remark, but must remember to speak seriously to him at a more leisure and opportune moment. Betty fidgets during the sermon, and asks in a piercing whisper when it will be over.

Grace McDougall comes in to tea. She is our regimental bride, and really beautiful, with that matt white skin which makes everyone else look like a dairymaid. We are all having tea in the dining room, as Miss Hardcastle is away. Children become very wild. They are encouraged by Grace, who rags with Bryan until he behaves like a lunatic. (Query — Why do people with no children of their own seem to think the shocking behaviour of other people's offspring a fit subject for mirth?)

Bryan is sent to his room by his father.

Grace has the decency to apologise, and asks Tim not to be hard on Bryan, as it is all her fault. Grace being irresistible to the male sex, Tim agrees to let the young villain off this time, and accompanies Grace to the front door, where he stands talking to her for fifteen minutes.

I put the children to bed.

Fourth January

Grace appears shortly after breakfast to to ask if I can possibly lend her some meat plates, coffee cups, and finger bowls for her dinner party, as Fairlawn is deficient in crockery and glass. We adjourn hopefully to the pantry, where we discover eight meat plates to match, and five finger bowls — but coffee cups are odd patterns.

Grace says it does not matter whether they match or not — she will just take them. She has brought a large basket (being of an optimistic temperament), into which we pack the loot. I advise her to go to Nora Watt for more finger bowls, as I know Nora has some, having dined there on Boxing Night. (Unless, of course, they were borrowed.) Grace thanks me, and asks anxiously whether I think eight will be a squash in her dining room. Reassure her as convincingly as I can, although I am practically certain the eight *will* be a squash (who should know better than I, considering we had Fairlawn ourselves for nine months before we moved into Rokesby).

Grace then says, have I heard about the Carters? They are moving again. Their landlord is returning to Biddington in March. We agree that it is rotten luck, especially as Mamie Carter is going to add to her family in the near future.

"I am so sorry for Mamie," says Grace with a sigh.

Personally I am much more sorry for Herbert. (Mamie Carter is a person who sits still and smiles wistfully while everybody in the vicinity rushes around, wildly, doing *her* job.) Perhaps I am a trifle bitter about this, having assisted in the Carters' last move.

Grace — who is new to army life — says eagerly that of course everyone will help, and the first thing is to find a house, and that directly she has got this dinner off her chest she is going around to all the house agents in Biddington.

Feel that Grace is really rather a dear in spite of her enthusiasms.

Sixth January

Wet Day. Decide to write a lot of letters and clear off the remains of Christmas presents "thanks," which have got disgracefully hung up owing to holidays.

Tim comes in, just as I am starting, to ask if I have seen his pipe anywhere. We all join in the search. Betty and Bryan show great enthusiasm, as the winner of the treasure hunt has been promised a penny. Pipe is discovered in my work basket. Have no idea how it got there, and say so several times, adding that it is curious how a thing always turns up in the last place you think of looking for it. Bryan — who has won the penny — immediately replies that the reason is because you stop looking for it when you have found it.

I return to my letters.

Annie comes in to say there is a gentleman at the door who wants to see me "very partickler," and he will not keep me long. She asked was there a message, but he said he must see Mrs. Christie herself, and it was very important, and his name is Mr. John.

12

Am seized with a sudden and absolutely unfounded conviction that it is the great Augustus himself who has come to beseech me to sit for him — having seen me dashing about Biddington on my bicycle and taken an unaccountable fancy to the shape of my face. Or perhaps he wishes to paint Betty, whose colouring has been admired by various artistic friends.

Ask Annie rather shortly why she has not shown Mr. John into the drawing room. She replies that he "does not look that kind of gentleman," but adds that she will if I like. (Query — Is this Annie's reaction to the artistic note in sartorial fashion?)

Rush wildly to the front door, where I spend half an hour persuading Mr. John that I do not want a vacuum cleaner, and that I do not want a demonstration of a vacuum cleaner on my own stair carpet, even although — as he points out — I should thereby get them "beautifully cleaned for nothing."

I return to my letters.

Annie comes in to say will I telephone to the fishmonger, as they have sent bloaters instead of whiting for tonight's dinner, and Katie supposes it is a mistake? And will I do it now, as it is the half day?

I do it now.

Go upstairs to see what the children are doing, as they are ominously quiet. Find that they have taken my new bedcovers to make a tent, and that Bryan is wearing Tim's one and only silk hat, which he found in a box on the top of the wardrobe. He has also found Tim's sword and medals. Betty has contented herself with my Spanish shawl, and looks extraordinarily well in it. Remove Tim's belongings as tactfully as possible, but leave bedcovers, as I have not the heart to ruin tent, which is really quite ingenious. Offer to look for some other garments for dressing up, by which time it is one o'clock.

After lunch the children decide that they want to paint. Provide water and find paintboxes, hoping that I may get a few letters written during the afternoon.

Am disturbed by frightful screams from the nursery. Rush upstairs and find Betty in tears, and Bryan gazing out of the window, with his hands in his pockets. Demand an instant explanation of the uproar, but find it impossible to get to the root of the trouble, or to discover the true culprit, Betty saying that Bryan hit her, and Bryan saying, "Yes, because she pinched my arm," and Betty replying hotly, "That was only because you upset my painting water," and Bryan retorting, "Well, you spluttered green water all over my book."

Suggest hastily that they should put on their waterproofs and go for a walk.

Bryan says, "Yes, if Bollings can come — and may we go down to the lake and feed the swans?"

Agree to let Bollings go with them, thereby dooming my silver to languish as pewter for a whole week, this being his afternoon for cleaning the silver.

Seventh January

Leave the children playing happily with the admirable Bollings, and set forth to visit some of the married families. Inspect the new baby at the Frasers', and discourse learnedly with Mrs. F. *re* the infant's diet (nature not having provided sustenance with her usual foresight). Meet Major McGillveray, the M.O., on the stairs, and am greeted with the remark that he supposes there is no need for *him* to visit the latest recruit, as nobody listens to a word *he* says if they can get advice from *me*. Laugh brightly and reply that I have recommended orange juice, and I hope he approves. "Small matter whether I approve or not," he grumbles.

Visit several other families, and am regaled with tea and gossip about the regiment and whispered comments on the dark doings of the bad boys belonging to other families. It is a queer little world that inhabits these quarters — speaking every known dialect of the British Isles — but they get on together marvellously well considering their propinquity, and there is a warm welcome at every door.

"I put the kettle on when I heard you on the stair," says Mrs. Craven, the Scottish wife of a Lancashire corporal, and the proud mother of five naughty children. "Now, Miriam, leave yon cloth alone; are ye wanting a smack, ye wee hen? Erchie, come an' let Mistress Christie see yer finger that ye hurt in the snib of the door. I'm feared of it festering, Mistress Christie — John's getting on fine in D Company. He's that set on Captain Christie he blethers on aboot him the hale time."

I have left Mrs. Banks to the last because we are old cronies, and the doings of Stanley and Doris and Jimmy make good hearing. We sit down by the fire for a real good talk, which ranges from picture palaces to pigs — these last being the colonel's latest whim. They have been purchased with a view firstly to disposing of scraps culled from the married quarters, and secondly to providing bacon for the mess. Needless to say, their advent has given rise to something approaching a mutiny in the regiment. Scraps have miraculously vanished to a minimum and objections as to smell and noise are exaggerated to colossal proportions. Mrs. Banks pours out the grievances of herself and neighbours into my too sympathetic ears — "Missis Benson she came in the other diy, and there was Stanley with 'is fice as black as sin. 'Dear me, is this your son?' ses Missis Benson, 'aughty like. 'Yus, it is, Mum,' I ses! "'E's bin plying in the yard near them 'orrid hanimals," I ses. She didn't 'alf look sour." I try to look disapproving of this criticism of the colonel's lady, but feel I am not making a good job of it.

"Ye know, Mum," continues Mrs. Banks confidentially, "there's one good thing 'as come of this 'ere National Gov'ment. Stanley useter fight somethin' awful with that Ramsay Fraser. It reely was somethin' awful. 'Ardly a diy passed but 'e'd come 'ome with 'is nose all bloody or a black eye. But now the two of them's as thick as thieves. Sharin' an orange, suck about, they was yest'diy."

Tenth January

Meet Nora Watt on my way home from church. She has been lying in wait for me. We agree that the sermon was slightly dull, but that the singing has improved. I see Grace hovering about but there is no escape from

Nora. After some preliminary conversation Nora says that she particularly wanted to see me today, because I am so clever, and she wonders if I can help her with a crossword for which the *Sunday News* is offering a thousand-pound prize. Reply hastily that what cleverness I may possess runs in other directions. Nora takes no notice of my modest disclaimer — "A word of nine letters meaning 'Living in the abode of another,' " she says firmly.

Suggest "Officer's wife," but Nora says that is too many letters, and the third must be Q.

Am completely stumped by this, and feel that I have failed Nora in her hour of need.

Eleventh January

Great excitement at breakfast over a War Office letter appointing Tim to be adjutant of a territorial battalion at Westburgh. Joy somewhat qualified by the fact that we have just taken our house at Biddington for another six months. Betty is delighted at the prospect of going to Scotland, and demands whether there will be wolves at night, and shall we have haggis to eat, and wear kilts? Am horrified at the ignorance of my offspring.

Bryan, always practical, wants to know how he is to come home all the way from Nearhampton for the holidays; and will it take all day in the train? And if so can he have dinner in the dining car by himself instead of sandwiches?

Feel dazed at the speed with which children's minds seem to adjust themselves to new ideas.

Tim in an excellent humour at the prospect of more pay.

Self rather depressed at the prospect of hunting for servants in a strange town. (I have done this before, and know what it is.) Shall I or shall I not take Miss Hardcastle to Westburgh? No hope of taking Katie or Annie, as the former has a sick mother in Biddington, and the latter is "walking out" with Tim's batman. Reflect that I shall miss Bollings, who is always cheery and willing if a little heavy-handed with the crockery.

Twelfth January

Wake up with the conviction that something pleasant is going to happen today, and trace this to the fact that Miss Hardcastle is returning from her holiday this morning. Typical case of Absence making the Heart Grow Fonder, as I have never cared much for Miss H., and felt positively emancipated when she went away.

Bryan and Betty go to the station to meet Miss Hardcastle, and return hanging on each arm. Miss H. seems glad to be back, and is very cheerful and communicative about her holiday. Decide that Miss H. is really exceedingly nice, and capable, and that I must certainly try to persuade her to accompany us to Westburgh. Broach the subject with great tact, only to find that the children told her all about it on the way up from the station, and that the whole thing is settled. (Query — What would have happened if I had decided *not* to take Miss Hardcastle to Westburgh?)

Spend the afternoon with Miss H. looking over Bryan's school clothes, and compile a large list of what he requires, which will probably have to be ruthlessly revised on financial grounds. Present Miss H. with some outgrown shirts, shorts, and vests for her small brother, who is reported to be the same age as Bryan only (gratifyingly) not so big. (Query — Why should one be inordinately pleased at evidence of immense size of offspring compared to other children?)

Am so pleased to have Miss Hardcastle back again to put the children to bed that in the fullness of my heart I present her with a perfectly good overcoat — a generosity which I afterwards regret, as I shall now have to buy Bryan a new one, whereas the old one might have had hem and sleeves let down.

Tim returns from barracks in high spirits because he has been asked by Major Morley to ride his horse Fireguard in a point-to-point. Tim explains that it is essential for him to go carefully over the course before the event, and for this reason he has been asked to go to Midshire the day before the race, and spend two nights with Major Morley's family.

Tim says that Neil Watt is as sick as a dog because he thought Morley would ask *him*, and Fireguard is a topping beast and will probably win the race.

Betty comes in and asks what a "point-to-point" *is*. Tim explains patiently, while Betty listens with one ear. Bryan then appears, and is informed by Betty that "Daddy is going to ride in a point race." He also is anxious for further information about the impending event, but Tim's limited stock of patience has run out,

19

and he retires behind the *Daily Mail*, while I try to answer Bryan's questions in an intelligent manner.

Betty informs us that she must go to bed, as it is half past six. Am amazed at this sudden attack of punctuality (it usually takes wild horses to drag Betty to bed), and ask with some anxiety if she feels quite well. Betty replies that she feels perfectly well, but Miss Hardcastle has brought back a large box of chocolates, which was given to her by her sweetheart when they spent the day at Brighton, and she promised to give one to Betty if she goes to bed without any fuss. Reflect that this method of dealing with Betty certainly saves trouble, but is exceedingly bad for morals and also for teeth. Decide regretfully that it must cease.

Thirteenth January

Miss Hardcastle being on duty, I decide to spend the morning writing to house agents at Westburgh.

Am interrupted in this necessary task by Nora, who felt she Positively Must come and see me the Moment she heard of Tim's appointment. Nora is a native of Westburgh, and according to her it is a paradise full of angels. Cheerfulness, friendliness, hospitality, and humour are a few of the virtues to be found in Westburgh in greater profusion than anywhere else in the world. There are good cheap shops, excellent theatres and cinemas, and the scenery of the surrounding country beggars description.

Begin to wonder for the first time whether I shall really like Westburgh as much as I had thought.

Interrupt Nora's eulogies with tentative enquiries as to prospect of finding a mansion in Paradise to suit our modest requirements, and am told vaguely that "of course there are lots of houses," and that my servant difficulties are over, as I shall find excellent cooks in abundance with kind hearts and light hands for pastry. Would be more impressed if I could extract any definite information as to how these desirable possessions could be acquired.

"I only wish that Neil and I were in your shoes!" Nora says, as she rises to go. "But of course dear Neil is so frightfully keen on the battalion — it would break his heart to leave it for three years." (Tim having told me yesterday that dear Neil sent his name up for the job, but is so darn lazy the C.O. wouldn't recommend him, I reply with inarticulate noises of admiration for Neil's devotion to duty.)

"How I envy you," Nora continues, pulling on one glove and looking at it pensively. "When I think of the lovely time you are going to have. Dear Westburgh is so gay, so cheery, so friendly. Oh, dear, if only the battalion were stationed there what a wonderful time we would have! A Scottish regiment should *be* in Scotland — at least that's what I think."

Ask again, more urgently, if she can advise me about houses or servants, but Nora obviously can't. She says that she has been away from Westburgh for So Long — and of course before she was married she never troubled her head with such things. She was much too busy enjoying herself — men simply flocked round her, my dear, it was too *awful* sometimes. But if I like she will write to Doreen. Doreen is her sister. Doreen knows all there *is* to know about Westburgh. Doreen is married and lives just outside Westburgh at a place called Kiltwinkle. She has a perfectly wonderful house there, with six bathrooms; her chauffeur has a better house than Rokesby. So lucky for Doreen to be settled for life in a lovely place like that — isn't it? They have a marvellous Rolls and their glass extends over acres, positively. Ask tactfully whether Doreen's husband is of very old family, but am told that he is in business which is far better. (This sounds so like an epitaph on a tombstone that I am shaken with internal laughter.)

Drift gently towards the door hoping that Nora will now depart and allow me to get back to my house agents in whom I place more faith than in the problematical helpfulness of Doreen. But Nora has not finished with me yet, she says, "Oh by the way, Hester, the word is INQUILINE."

Am on the point of saying, "What word?" when I remember the thousand-pound crossword. Try to look as if I knew the word well and it had merely escaped my memory for the time being. (Query — Why do I always want to appear more clever than I really am when Nora is anywhere about? Am much distressed at this discovery, as I have just read an article in this morning's paper saying that intellectual snobbery is snobbery in its worst form.)

Nora, still on the subject of INQUILINE explains that the definition given in the dictionary says, "Living in the abode of another like a pea crab in an oyster shell," and what *is* a pea crab when it is at home. Evade

22

the issue by pointing out to Nora that the pea crab is obviously not inquiline when it is at home, but only when it is living in an oyster shell and register my conviction that the compilers of the dictionary were not conversant with the habits of military folk, or they would have drawn their example from an officer's wife rather than a pea crab.

Nora goes away at last, but I feel that she divines my complete ignorance as to the nature of the pea crab and despises my subterfuge.

Fourteenth January

Go down early to the barracks to arrange about the Christmas tree and spend the morning trying to reconcile Mrs. Harris and Mrs. McInnes — both of whom had been asked by Mrs. Benson to decorate the tree. As Mrs. McInnes is the wife of the R.S.M., and Mrs. Harris the wife of the quartermaster sergeant it appears that Mrs. Benson has shown even less tact than usual in her choice. Find that the only possible way of getting tree decorated is to take a firm stand myself and overrule all suggestions of both my assistants.

After everything has been arranged Major Morley appears with his moving-picture projector followed by his batman bearing a large white screen. Mrs. Benson has asked him to give a movie entertainment but has quite forgotten to tell anybody else that she has done so.

There is nothing for it but to move tree into a corner, during which process most of the decorations fall off.

The screen is nailed up on the wall, and we all go home to lunch.

The entertainment starts with tea at three thirty. Infants are fed unsuitably with cake dipped in stewed tea, while larger children cram themselves to bursting point with sugar cakes and meringues.

Mrs. Norrie has brought her five children but they all look after each other, the eldest girl (who is Betty's age) has the baby on her knee so that Mrs. Norrie is freed of all material cares and can enjoy herself and gossip amiably with her neighbours. Feel that this is an excellent plan, and might be introduced into other circles with advantage.

Go round making inane remarks to everyone and asking after babies and absentees, but am conscious all the time that I am being a bit of a bore and that the party would go much more cheerily if I were not there.

One of the Clarke children is violently sick, but nobody seems to mind, Mrs C. saying in a deprecating manner that "Clarer 'as always suffered something crule from 'er stummick." Am full of admiration for her sangfroid, as I should have been covered with confusion if Betty had chosen such a public occasion for being unwell.

The tables and chairs are now pushed aside and Sergeant Banks appears dressed as Father Christmas to present the gifts off the tree. He keeps up a running fire of quips and jokes which causes much merriment, but is not calculated to conceal his identity, and it is evident that the youngest child present is not deceived by his red gown and long white beard.

"Here's a popgun for you, Willie Norrie," he says jovially, "and don't you be shooting at baby sister with it, that's all I say. Keep it to shoot the Germans next time they comes to Biddington. Well, Maisie MacDonald, there's a doll for you somewhere, if I didn't drop it coming down the chimney — No, here it is and not a speck of soot on it, I declare — Wonderful how clean the chimneys are in this barracks. Paintbox for Sammy Smith — You better ask Dad for one of his forms to paint on, Sammy." (This suggestion brings down the house, as Sammy's father is the orderly-room clerk.)

"What you got for me, Dad?" shouts the youngest Banks. Father Christmas raises his head and gazes sternly round the hall. "I'll trouble you to speak respectfully to me, young Jimmy Banks," he says gravely. "It's Father Christmas is my name — or maybe Santa to my closest pals, but I never remember being called Dad before. Never except once — and d'you know what happened to that young boy who called me Dad, before?"

"Got a lickin'," suggests someone facetiously.

"Lickin'!" echoes Father Christmas scornfully — "Well you *couldn't* guess, so I'll just tell you. — A bear come out of the wood and eat him up."

Have a vague feeling that Sergeant Banks has mixed up Father Christmas's mantle with that of Elisha, but have no time to think it out at present. What does it matter anyway, the children are pleasantly thrilled and everyone is pleased.

Major Morley arrives to give his cinema show long before Banks has finished, and we stand in a corner together and watch the fun.

"Banks is enjoying himself," Major Morley says.

"Everybody is," I reply vaguely, but with truth; and, indeed, there is not a dull or sulky person to be seen. Every face is shining, not only with the outward shininess of heat, and a good tea, but also with the inward glow of unselfconscious enjoyment.

"Simple people," Major Morley says thoughtfully. "I used to get a laugh out of this show — tongue in my cheek, you know — but I've grown wiser now. Awfully clean chaps soldiers, in spite of smells and bad language — awfully clean. Kind too. Look at old McInnes with that lame child of the Norries' — and then think of him on the barrack square. He's quite unselfconscious, that's what it is. *We're too civilized* — too afraid of what the next door feller is going to say about us."

Banks is finished now and is helped down off the platform by willing hands. He is still talking, having got completely wound up — something about his reindeer, I think it is — but Banks's hour is over and nobody is listening to him now.

We clear away the wreck of the tree and everyone helps to put the chairs in rows for the movie performance. Major Morley sets up his apparatus and the lights are lowered. There are gasps of joy when Mickey Mouse appears on the screen, he is an old favourite. Then comes Charlie Chaplin in one of his old

26

knockabout comedies, then a film for the little ones of comic monkeys riding on a train.

After the monkeys Major Morley turns to me with a wicked grin — which looks positively saturnine as he leans over the light of the projector in the dark hall — and says, "Remember that day at Littlehampton?"

I do remember it and say, "No! No! Don't please!" But the dreadful man has already started his infernal machine and I see myself coming towards me on the screen, clad in a bathing suit. There are wild cries of "Mrs. Christie, Mrs. Christie," as I wave my hand, and do a few steps of a dance in a perfectly idiotic manner. Betty and Bryan now appear running headlong down the sands, we chase each other madly, and then run into the sea where there is a lot of splashing. I emerge from the waves gasping like a codfish — Tim now comes on the scene and we all take hands and dance a "jingo-ring" in the water.

Such torrents of applause greet this film and such shouts of delight and excitement that Major Morley shows it again, and once more I see myself as others see me — a strange and not altogether gratifying experience.

Major Morley looks at me and says gravely, "I wonder if Mary Pickford has ever had such an ovation."

Am still pondering this remark and trying to make up my mind whether he is laughing at me or not, when Sergeant Norrie stands up and calls for silence.

"I don't wonder we are all clapping our 'ands off at this film," he says beaming round at the assembled company, "it's because we all knows Mrs. Christie, isn't it? Look at all she does for us and the interest she takes in the kiddies. Now we been told as how Mrs. Christie is going away, and we knows we'll all miss her very badly — because why? Because she always has a smile for everyone. Well, all I can say is we'll look forward to seeing her and the captain back to the regiment some day, and we wishes them luck, and we shan't forget them, and we hopes they won't forget us. So now we'll give three cheers for Mrs. Christie — Hip, hip, hurrah —"

Am absolutely overcome at this unexpected turn in events and stand there shaking like a jelly while the hall echoes and re-echoes with cheers. Major Morley jogs my arm and tells me to "say something."

I reply that I can't.

He says that I must.

I am hoisted willy-nilly and by main force on to the platform, where I stand for a few moments absolutely struck dumb. Then I hear my own voice saying feebly that I thank them all for the splendid cheers and that I shall miss them all frightfully, but that, however far away we are, we all belong to the same regiment — and they may be sure I shall never forget my friends.

More cheers.

I am hauled down off the platform in a state bordering on collapse and am taken home in a taxi by Major Morley.

Fifteenth January

Take Bryan over to Nearhampton in the car. Feel as if Tim and I were a couple of jailers taking Bryan to prison. Talk feverishly all the time about seeing Bryan at half term and of the fun we shall have in Easter holidays.

Tim and Bryan monosyllabic. Bryan very pale. Ask anxiously several times if he feels quite well (Bryan having been known to be sick in the car without adequate warning).

Several other prisoners have already been deposited by parents and these hail Bryan lugubriously as we drive up to the door.

Tim and I are invited to stay to tea with Mr. and Mrs. Parker and are conducted upstairs to a large room full of photographs of boys in cricket flannels, boys in football jerseys, boys in Etons either singly or in groups. We sit and make conversation for about half an hour drinking scented China tea and eating very small sandwiches filled with mashed banana. The Parkers talk about their boys past and present, and point out photographs of those who have achieved fame in the field of sport or learning.

We depart as soon as tea is over to the obvious relief of the Parkers. Suggest we should find Bryan to say "Goodbye," but Tim says, "Better not," so we drive off without having done so. Tim spends the next two hours explaining to me why it is So Good for Boys to Go to School, which confirms me in my suspicion that he feels like a jailer too.

I agree with all he says, but secretly I wonder whether it is really so necessary, and why.

Sixteenth January

Am bidden by a mysterious telephone message to "call at the barracks at 5:30 and fetch Captain Christie home." Cassandra and I haste to the assignation through torrents of rain. Darkness has fallen when we reach the mess buildings. I shut off the engine and for some minutes we remain in solitude and silence — silence save for the rain which beats heavily on Cassandra's not altogether waterproof hood and courses down the windshield in huge drops like the abnormal tears of a movie actress.

Suddenly a voice announces "My Gosh if it isn't Cassandra — AND Mrs. Tim — you'd better come in, Tim will be ages. He's been stung with Uncle Frankie's lecture on rear-guard actions."

It is the Child — so called from his immense size and domineering manner. I remonstrate feebly but am assured that it is absolutely OK as all the Senior Swabs are well occupied, or out, and he is alone in the mess except for Jack McDougall and Tubby. "You'll drown or freeze if you sit here much longer — what you need is a cocktail," he asserts. I suddenly discover that the Child is right, my feet are wet and my nose is blue with cold.

The mess is warm and comfortable, I am parked on the fender stool with a cocktail and a cigarette, and feel extraordinarily daring.

"What about a spot of bridge?" says Tubby Baxter, "it's been a ghastly afternoon. Three-handed bridge with the Child is like a game out of Alice in Wonderland.

He goes five spades with nothing above the Knave in his hand and picks up Ace, King, Queen in dummy!"

I make tentative enquiries as to how long Tim is likely to be. "Hours," says Jack comfortably, "Uncle Frankie handed over all his notes — which he culls from the campaigns of Hannibal — and poor old Tim is too conscientious not to work through the lot. The N.C.O.'s hate these Saturday afternoon lectures like sin."

"One of our dear C.O.'s most popular ideas," adds the Child, "Never knew a man to have so many popular ideas."

"Uncle Frankie's gone to have a binge with Aunt Loo in the great metropolis," says Tubby confidentially, "Westminster Abbey tomorrow morning, and the Zoo in the afternoon. Hope they won't mistake him for a sea lion."

"Now, now!" remonstrates the Child wagging a huge finger with mock severity, "Don't you let me hear you speaking disrespectfully of our colonel and his lady, Algernon Reginald Baxter, or I shall be obliged to clear the mess."

During this nonsensical conversation I have been looking round the mess — that holy of holies into which no woman is ever supposed to penetrate. Huge deep chairs of shabby leather stand round the fire. The carpet is thick and grey with dust. Dust lodges in the deep old-fashioned carving of a tall cupboard and nestles comfortably in the thick red curtains which cover the windows. Dust hangs in the air mingling with the blue smoke of Virginia tobacco and settles on the stags' antlers and battle pictures which decorate the walls. On shelves, mantelpiece and side tables, silver trophies gleam and twinkle in the light. I feel it is too like the popular idea of an officers' mess to be really real.

"Well," says the Child with mischief in his brown eye, "What's the verdict, Mrs. Tim?"

"The verdict is a vacuum cleaner," I reply instantly.

"That's the sentence." The Child points out with a wave of his pipe. "Just like a woman to give the sentence before the verdict. Now if women ever become judges, we shall see —"

But what we should see if women became judges is destined to remain in oblivion, for at this moment loud voices — or rather one loud voice is heard in the hall.

"My God, it's the C.O.," says Jack in awestruck tones.

The Child proves himself a man of action by seizing me bodily and stowing me behind the curtains before I can say a word.

"Your deal, Jack," says Tubby's voice firmly, and I gather that they have taken up their positions round the card table.

The room is suddenly full of the colonel's voice — "Still at it," he booms, and I can almost see him rubbing his hands in his hearty way. "When I was young I never spent a whole Saturday afternoon playing cutthroat bridge — it was golf or girls in those days. Haw, haw, haw! My God what a froust! Why don't you open one of the windows?"

"Tubby's got dreadful toothache, Sir," explains the Child blandly. "Neuralgia, you know, Sir — awfully afraid of a draught."

32

"Umph — better see the dentist and have it out. Lost my train by one minute so I thought I'd look in here and see how things were. Lost my handkerchief too — most annoying — thought I might have dropped it here somewhere — How did he lecture go, Christie?"

Tim's voice is heard announcing that the lecture went well. He must have come in with the colonel.

The dust of ages emanating from the curtain makes me want to sneeze — this would be fatal so I rub my nose and swallow hard hoping for the best.

"Must see Morley before I go," the colonel is saying. "That return must be sent in on Monday — the one about the rifles."

"Major Morley is in Orderly Room now, Sir," says the Child in honeyed accents. "Shall I tell him you want him, Sir?"

"Yes — no, I'll go round and see him there. Your car's outside, Christie. Perhaps you would give me a lift to the station for the 6:55?"

Under cover of the colonel's noisy exit I hear Tim asking anxiously if "the wife has gone home."

"You will find her at home, Sir," the Child assures him. They seem to have moved out into the hall now and I am wondering whether it is safe to leave my hiding place when I hear them coming back.

"It's a brown silk one with white spots," says the colonel. "I may have dropped it here at lunch time, perhaps in the window when I was looking out —"

"Oh no, Sir," says Tubby's voice anxiously, "I'm sure I should have noticed it, Sir."

"More likely to be in one of the chairs — down the side," suggests Jack.

I hear the squeak of castors as they move the chairs, and, for the first time, I began to be rather anxious as to the result of this absurd prank. Will these boys suffer if I am found? It has all happened so naturally — I see now that it would have been better to have been found smoking a cigarette on the fender stool than lurking behind the curtain.

"Look out, Baxter, clumsy fool — my foot," growls the colonel.

"Oh sorry, Sir."

"Here's your handkerchief, Sir."

"Better be quick if you want to catch Major Morley, Sir."

They move off again, the colonel trumpeting cheerfully among the white spots. "Missed it at the station," I hear him say. "Wouldn't have lost it for anything — given to me by a lady — haw, haw, haw."

All laugh loudly at this sally on the art of the henpecked colonel, and the irrepressible Child suggests respectfully that the colonel is a "gay dog."

I hear Cassandra's roar of protest as Tim starts her up, and in a few moments more I am released from my dusty hiding place by my fellow conspirators. They are all giggling feebly.

"My hat!" says Tubby wiping his forehead. "That was a near thing, boys — *Did* you see Uncle Frankie making for the window?"

"You rolled the chair over his pet corn!" cries the Child hysterically.

"I feel like the Johnny whose hair turned white in a single night," Jack owns. "Wondered whether I should pretend to go potty and collar the old man —"

"Drinks all round, and then home in my Rolls," announces the Child.

"The lies you told!" Tubby cries laughing helplessly.

"Lies — I told no lies," replies the Child indignantly. "I told Captain Tim he'd find wifie at home, and so he will when he's pushed off Uncle Frankie by the 6:55. Where are the lies? Fetch the drinks, Tubby, we can't ring for Smithers."

"Fetch them yourself," says Tubby. He is busy with paper and pencil, and is obviously perpetrating one of his celebrated poems on the occasion.

"My God!" cries the Child. "Is there nobody in this ruddy regiment to do a spot of work but myself!"

"What rhymes with station?" asks Tubby unabashed. "Damnation, of course," replies Jack. "And it's just what Uncle Frankie would have said — though why you are wasting your time I don't know. You can't put it in the magazine — there was nearly a riot in the mess over the last muck you put in."

"It's my muse," Tubby explains, moistening his pencil with the tip of a very tongue. "The urge for self-expression is very strong in great poets like me." He holds up his glass and calls upon us to bear witness that the Child is a murderer, having drowned a perfectly good drink which never did him any harm.

"What about the poem, Tubs?" says Jack.

Tubby simpers shyly, but after a very little persuasion he reads out the following effusion:

"Uncle Frankie.
Lost his hankie
Going to the station,
He lost his train
And was profane,
Just like the Bull of Bashan."

("I put that in because ladies are present.")

"His journey spoiled,
His purpose foiled,
He then returned to pester.
Then Uncle Frankie
Found his hankie
And, very nearly, Hester."

"Dashed cheek," says Jack, giggling inanely.

The Child makes no comment — poetry is not his strong point — but turning to me he enquires if I will come again another wet afternoon as it has been "such fun."

I reply that it is not my idea of fun.

"Why not?" cry all three imbeciles. "Is our fire not warm? Have our cocktails no sting? Is our conversation not witty? Are our chairs not comfortable?"

I reply in the words of Le Rat des Champs — "*Adieu donc, fie du plaisir que le craint peut corrompre.*"

"That's French," says Jack triumphantly, but Tubby who is more erudite — as well as being the regimental poet — replies:

"Italian, me lad, from a poem called Don Juan by a poet called Don Byrono. The poor man was drowned in a storm while escaping from his wife in a cockleshell on Lake Como —"

I hear no more of this potpourri of literary history as I am hustled away by the Child. Tubby follows us into the hall shouting that the second verse of his poem will be ready tomorrow and will deal faithfully with Aunt Loo's horror at the non-appearance of her spouse, and with Hannibal crossing the Alps, and Christopher Robin's lecture on a rear-guard action with elephants.

We hasten to the old Gun Stables where the officers keep their cars, the Child protesting volubly that I must be home before Tim so that my alibi may be secure. I am to be sitting by the fire with my darning basket when Tim returns — a picture of domesticity. (This wretched darning basket of mine is a perennial joke in the regiment.) Thus the Child babbles on, the while he tries vainly to get a kick out of his aged and battle-scarred Trojan.

"It's no damn use," he says at last. "I think the brute must have died in the night — we must just borrow Rex Bolton's Alvis. Fortunately my key fits his door."

Rex Bolton's Alvis being more amenable to persuasion, we are soon careering gaily out of the barracks gate where two sentries at rigid attention, and one mud-bespattered figure in a service burberry waves its arms and shouts upon its gods.

"Rex Bolton," says the Child succinctly as he jams the Alvis into top with a grating sound.

Thanks to the admirable speed of the Alvis, I am changed and seated by the fire when Tim and Cassandra reach home.

"It's a mercy you didn't wait," Tim informs me. "Had a lecture pushed on to me at the last moment and then had to take the old man to the station — what a life! Thank Heaven we'll be out of all this soon."

I make sympathetic noises.

Tim expands confidentially. "You know, Hester, I'm certain those young devils in the mess were up to some mischief this afternoon. Shouldn't be surprised if they had a girl hidden behind the curtain."

"Whatever made you think that?" I wonder, in a voice trembling with suppressed mirth. Having decided to make a clean breast of the whole adventure to Tim, I find these suspicions of his somewhat amusing.

Tim laughs — "You should have been there — they were tumbling over each other to be nice to Uncle Frankie and to get him out of the place. Jack went white as a ghost when the old man made a move towards the window. Wonder what Grace would say if she knew — I'll get onto them tomorrow about it, see if I don't."

I thread my needle carefully before I reply: "I wouldn't say anything about it if I were you — you might discover that the girl behind the curtain was your own wife."

Tim roars with laughter. "My good soul, I know better than that. I bet the girl behind the curtain was a peach — one of the Child's "specials." I very nearly went back after parking the old man with Morley, to have a look at her — I bet she was worth looking at."

Tim is very tiresome sometimes.

Eighteenth January

Letter from Bryan asking why we "went off without saying goodbye" and informing us that he has got his "remove" and is in a different "dorm." The rest of the letter is taken up with calculations as to how many days it is until the Easter holidays and ends with the pious hope that the writer may develop ringworm or some such complaint "like Brunton did last term," in which case he will be sent home forthwith. Feel that this would be an undesirable occurrence especially as we have just sent him a cheque for a large sum to defray the term's expenses.

I also receive a letter from Lady Morley of Charters Towers, inviting me to accompany Tim on the 29th January and stay two nights at Charters Towers for the point-to-point races. Great argument between Tim and self regarding the invitation as I feel I have no clothes worthy of the occasion, and Tim says that my last year's tweeds and a fur coat is all that I shall require. Am bitterly aware that Tim is one of those men who do not understand clothes or women, but reflect afterwards that perhaps this is just as well in some ways. Men who understand women being sometimes too understanding of women other than their wives.

Major Morley comes in to tea and says that of course I must go, and that he will take us in his car.

Nineteenth January

Tim reminds me unnecessarily at breakfast that the Bensons and the McDougalls are coming to dinner tonight and asks me to tell Annie not to breathe heavily down the back of his neck when she is waiting at table. Spend half an hour wondering how I can possibly put this in a tactful manner and realise that I can't. Decide to say nothing about it and hope for the best.

Am still in the later stages of my toilet when Mrs. Benson arrives and is shown straight into my bedroom. This is not Annie's fault — she is merely carrying out instructions — Mrs. Benson has upset plans by arriving ten minutes early. I am aware that Tim is not ready either, having fished a stud up his back for him about three minutes ago.

"And how do you think you will like Westburgh," says Mrs. Benson as she dabs her nose with blue powder in front of my glass. "I hear it does not rain all the time, and the smoke is really quite healthy."

Tim enters in his shirt sleeves to ask me to tie his tie for him, but backs out hastily at the sight of Mrs. Benson, while I make signs to him behind her back to hurry downstairs to the colonel. Can see he does not know in the least what I mean.

The McDougalls arrive about twenty minutes late, by which time we have all come to the end of our conversation, and the colonel is pacing up and down the room like a wild beast. They are full of the most abject apologies, their car wouldn't start and they have only just now been able to get a taxi from the garage.

Smile brightly and say it does not matter at all, though I am nearly frantic at the thought of the mushroom soufflé, which I know will be like leather.

The colonel is by now in a towering rage, and dabs at his burnt fish in positive disgust. Fortunately the beef olives are quite eatable, and the pudding is a trifle, so I breathe a sigh of relief.

Grace McDougall gradually wins the colonel to a better mood by flirting with him outrageously; but this annoys both Mrs. Benson and Captain McDougall, so things are not much improved. The soufflé does not turn up at all, its place on the menu is taken by a few cheese straws which I know have been mouldering at the back of the kitchen cupboard for about three weeks, but which look nice, having been dusted thoroughly and reheated.

Colonel now laughing uproariously at something said by Grace which neither of them will divulge.

Grace is looking really beautiful tonight in red chiffon which clashes diabolically with my old dyed pink satin. Her hair is black with a blue sheen and has obviously just been trimmed and waved, her creamy matt complexion is touched with a faint pink — her eyes are sparkling with mischief.

Notice with horror that Annie is breathing heavily down Tim's back, and am certain by the expression on his face that he thinks I have forgotten to tell her not to. Whereas my whole day has been completely poisoned by remembering it.

Make a move as soon as I possibly can. Mrs. Benson rises with alacrity but everyone else obviously surprised. Grace drops her bag and she and the colonel bump heads trying to pick it up. (The C.O.'s figure is not suited to retrieving bags from beneath tables.) Both laugh. Mrs. Benson sweeps out of the door which Tim has opened.

Find that I have left the frying pan for the fire, as Mrs. Benson will not speak to Grace. Decide that six is a very awkward number for dinner as it makes three women in the drawing room. (But as our table will not hold more I am aware that the decision is barren.) Contrive to talk to Mrs. Benson about Regimental Women's Welfare Club and to Grace about hairdressers. Very wearing.

Am thankful to see the men, and suggest bridge. Grace and I sit out and she tells me that she has offered to have the Carter baby and nurse while the new baby is arriving. Warn her about the nurse who upset my whole household when I had them to stay while a move was taking place. Grace says her household is already in such a parlous condition that she does not think the Carter nurse can do much harm.

Jack had to turn three men out of the kitchen at 11:30p.m. last night and the cook gave notice this morning, and what do I do about followers. Reply that Annie is engaged to Bollings and that Katie has a squint and protruding teeth — Grace says I am lucky.

Twentieth January

Nora comes in to retrieve three finger bowls which I borrowed for my dinner party. I washed and dried them myself as I was afraid to trust them to the tender mercies of Bollings — Nora is the kind of person whose belongings one is terrified of destroying. The kind of person who says, "Oh, my dear, of course it doesn't matter at *all*. The next time I am in town I can *order* another one to make up the set." When all the time you know perfectly well she got them at Woolworth's for threepence each. Nora talks for a long time without saying anything. Frightful wails from the nursery call me urgently to the scene — I feel sure that Betty and Miss Hardcastle have come to blows or that Betty has injured herself mortally — but Nora talks on. The wails die away into silence (they are either dead or reconciled) and at last Nora goes.

She has no sooner gone than Grace bursts in, and says she has been waiting outside for hours, as she saw Nora's Baby Austin at the gate, and she can't *think* how I can be bothered with that woman.

Reply that I can't think how I can be, either, but it is no use quarreling with a woman who is likely to be your neighbour for the rest of your life — quarrels in regiments are the devil — Besides Nora will be our C.O.'s wife one of these days (Neil being senior to Tim and Jack) with the powers of life and death in her hands.

Grace replies, " 'stuff and Nonsense said the Duchess.' Jack says there's not a dog's hope of Neil ever getting command. He hasn't even got the O.B.E. and he was at Dover the whole war. Besides, his Father is simply rolling, so they will probably retire if they get sent somewhere they don't like. Jack's got Neil down in his army list as L.R.," she adds with a laugh.

Reply gloomily that Neil is not nearly so likely to retire as Jack imagines — and change the subject hurriedly. It's bad enough to hear the men talking about promotion without starting on the same apparently inexhaustible topic ourselves.

Grace then says she really came in to see if I were alive after last night — isn't Mrs. Benson the limit? — and to tell me that Jack wouldn't speak to her at breakfast. (I am not in the least surprised to hear it as they have only been married three months and Grace really did force the pace with the colonel.)

"Aren't men silly?" she says pathetically. "As if I cared a button for the old bear — I only did it to put him in a good humour."

I point out to Grace that it all comes of her being so disgracefully pretty, after which we both laugh and kiss each other, and she says she doesn't know what on earth she is going to do when I have gone, as there is not another creature in Biddington who can see a joke, and do I think Jack could get a job somewhere — preferably in Westburgh.

Twenty-first January

Make up my mind I must really tell the servants about our plans today. Go into the kitchen with my knees knocking together. Katie dissolves into tears and says she would go to the end of the world with me if it were not for her mother, and will I give her a good character as she has done her best for the family, and do I think she could get a place in London as she is tired of the country, anyway, and Biddington is not what it was with Scotch regiments and no Guards now, and don't I think that a girl ought to see life before she settles down — mother or no mother — and can she have a whole day off to go and see Drury Lane next week?

Answer all questions in the affirmative and offer to put an advertisement in *The Times* for her.

Return to the drawing room, feeling somewhat spent, and sit down to recover myself before speaking to Annie. Door opens and Annie bursts in demanding indignantly what she has done not to be told about our plans — and she's been with us longer than Katie anyway — and if I think she is coming with us to the North Pole I am much mistaken (or words to that effect) and will I please take a month's notice from that moment. Decide that the only thing to be done is to lose my temper, and do so — (at first with some little difficulty, but soon with a glad abandon that astonishes both Annie and myself in equal proportion).

Annie, completely cowed by this unprecedented exhibition, agrees to stay on as long as I want her, and do all she can to help with the packing. She even offers to come to Westburgh and "settle us in."

Am so exhausted that I have to lie down on my bed to recover. Ask myself whether it would not be a good thing to assume an ungovernable temper when dealing with the servants instead of being a kind of buffer absorbing all the jars of the house in my own person.

But decide that the reaction is too severe and the nervous energy expended hardly worth the result.

Twenty-second January

Meet Grace in the fishmonger's. There is a huge cod with a gaping mouth lying on the slab. Grace seizes my arm and says, "My dear, isn't it *exactly* like Neil — those glazed eyes, the complete absence of forehead and chin — Yes, three whiting skinned and turned to Fairlawn — my dear, I've thought of a splendid plan. Why not sublet Rokesby to the Carters?"

Reply evasively, as I know that Tim will not let Rokesby to the Carters, having suggested it to him myself some days ago. Tim has a poor opinion of the Carter ménage and says with a good deal of truth that "they would tear the place to bits and we should have to pay for it." He also reminded me of a previous occasion when we sublet our house to a brother officer and had a good deal of unpleasantness over damages to same.

Grace says she has been to all the house agents in Biddington and can't hear of anything suitable for the Carters. She is so determined that there is nothing for it but to tell her that I know Tim will not sublet the house on account of unfortunate experience in the past. Grace turns away — more in sorrow than in anger — and leaves me to order haddocks in peace. Am rather distressed as I am very fond of Grace, but feel that it is useless to raise false hopes — Tim quite adamant once he makes up his mind.

Decide to rush home and write to landlord at once, asking him if we may give up the house about the middle of March. Have not done so before owing to uncertainty of finding a suitable house at Westburgh, and having no wish to be left without a roof over our heads — (this has happened before and it is most unpleasant). Now, however, I feel that it is the only thing to do as I can then say — with perfect truth — that I have written to give up Rokesby. Reflect comfortingly that Alexander the Great was justified by events when he burnt his boats.

Coming out of the fishmonger's we meet Miss Slingsby — a sweet young thing of sixty summers who thinks that all "army people are so dashing," and is always hoping against hope to be shocked at our conversation. Grace dashes at this inoffensive woman crying, "Oh, Miss Slingsby, you are the very person I wanted to see. You *will* join the B.B.G., *won't* you?"

The poor lady twitters like a bird. "Oh, my dear Mrs. McDougall, I simply couldn't — I never could make a speech in public. Of course I know you don't see your audience and they could always shut it off if they did not like it, but I feel sure that I would not be of any use — not even to read out the list of birthdays in the Children's Hour."

Grace explains rather ruthlessly that she never thought of such a thing, it is the B.B.G. she wants Miss Slingsby to join, not the British Broadcasting Company — "Buy British Goods, you know." Miss Slingsby says, "Oh, but I always do," and is hustled away by her niece

— who lives with her and treats her like a half-wit — before anything more can be done about it.

On the way home Grace assures me that she finds the atmosphere and the society of Biddington "So Stultifying." Feel that I can't agree with her conscientiously until I have looked it up in the dictionary.

Twenty-third January

The Child and Tubby "drop in" to tea — they hunt in couples, these two. Betty appears rather before her usual time and demands a game of "Bears." Game somewhat dangerous to our good landlord's furniture. Have a feeling that the Child wishes to speak to me privately — probably about the episode in mess — but decide that the least said on the subject the better and manage to evade his manœuvres for a tête-à-tête.

After their departure Tim says he wonders why they came, subalterns nowadays are a tame lot compared to what they were in his time — no initiative. Tim wonders how they would behave in an emergency — probably lose their heads altogether.

Twenty-seventh January

Decide to spend a busy morning looking over my clothes for Charters Towers, and mending a large rent in second-best evening dress which I caught on a nail in Cassandra last time we went out to dinner.

Annie comes in to say have I telephoned to the shops as Katie wants the potatoes early? And do I give anything to the Recreation Fund for Biddington Orphans as the man has called twice? Reply that I am an orphan myself without available funds for recreation, so perhaps my name might be added to the list of beneficiaries. Annie retires smiling and I lean over banisters to hear what she says to the man, but am, unfortunately, too late.

Am horrified to discover I have mislaid list of commodities required by Katie, search for it feverishly, but unavailingly. Am reduced to making out a fresh list from memory. Feel certain that I have forgotten several items of importance, but have not the moral courage to return to kitchen for information. Ring up all the shops and wonder anew why these establishments always detail their least intelligent assistants to answer the phone. Greengrocer especially idiotic, cannot understand my name, has to go away to find out if there are any mushrooms today, and again to enquire what price they are. Feel convinced that a law should be made compelling shops to answer the telephone by giving their name, instead of with conventional and meaningless "Hello."

Am interrupted in an important conversation on the subject of mutton, and asked if I will take a trunk call. Wait for ten minutes at the end of which an unknown man's voice says, "Hullo, darling — is that you? Can you meet me tomorrow in town and do a theatre?"

Reply that nothing would please me more, but that I am afraid he has got the wrong number. Voice says,

"What rotten luck! Don't I know you then? Your voice sounds charming." Reply hastily that I am fat and deeply pitted with smallpox. Voice says he doesn't believe a word of it, and that he can tell exactly what I am like by my voice, and will I lunch with him at the Malmaison.

Ring off at once as I feel sure that Tim would not approve of this conversation.

Twenty-ninth January

Major Morley calls for us in his Bentley according to plan. Bollings carries out our suitcases — which look small and shabby beside the shining glory of the car (but alas they look smaller and shabbier when we arrive at Charters Towers). I sit in front beside Major M., Tim in the back seat. Car purrs like a contented pussycat, so different from Cassandra's rattle and roar.

Try tentatively to find out the nature of the Morley family, but Major M. is in a facetious mood, so I can only elicit the information that Sir Abraham is an ogre who eats young women, and Lady Morley practises the black arts. I discover, however, that Major Morley's married sister is to be there complete with husband, also "some of the county."

Grow more and more terrified and wish devoutly that Major M. would not drive so fast — we shall be there far too soon. Country looking very beautiful after last night's rain. Diamonds sparkling on the bare black trees and in the hedges. The pale winter sun sucking up the moisture from the bare fields creates a grey haze shot with blue and lavender.

We arrive just before lunch, and are welcomed with warm dignity by our host and hostess. Three footmen rush out to unload the car and seem disappointed at finding so little luggage to carry in. Am seized with an insane wish that I had brought another suitcase — if necessary filled with stones — but reflect that this might have caused surprise to the maid, who will presumably do my unpacking. Am introduced to about a dozen other guests who are chattering in the lounge, but fail to hear any of their names except that of a large dark woman all in white who is Lady Angela Carruthers.

My bedroom is large and comfortable, with a sofa and chairs drawn up to a huge log fire. It is more like a sitting room than a bedroom. Tim is evidently lodged in a different part of the house as I see no more of him until I descend for lunch. Am so overawed by the size of the dining room and the variety of food that I have difficulty in finding anything to say to my neighbours. Difficulty increased by not knowing their names, conditions or tastes. Fortunately I find that they have plenty to say to me on a variety of subjects, so lunch passes swiftly and pleasantly.

After lunch the whole party walks out to see The Course. I find Major Morley beside me, he is in his *soft voice mood* which always makes me feel uncomfortable, as I don't know whether he means what he says or is trying to be funny. In front of us is a bunch of smart young women chattering hard. Major M. asks whether I have ever been to the Zoo and visited the Parrot House. Reply that I have, and that I like parrots, they are so amusing. Major M. thinks I would soon tire of parrots if I lived with them constantly. Am involved in an argument of double entendre which Major M. wins easily as he is far too clever for me and is not hampered by proper feelings towards his father's guests.

We come upon Lady Angela, still clad in white and walking by herself. Major Morley says softly, "Why do you walk through the fields in gloves?"

Cannot forbear a chuckle at this, but feel that Major M. is really very naughty. Point out to him that everyone is wearing gloves today because it is cold, and that Lady A. may be fat and white, but he can't be sure that nobody loves her. Major M. replies that that is just the very thing that he *can* be sure of.

The conversation becomes slightly unsafe, I look round hastily for Tim, but he is having an animated conversation with a young woman in tweeds and a letter-box mouth, so is ungetatable.

The course is distinctly muddy, but everyone thinks that "this wind will dry it up before tomorrow." Major M. produces his cinema Kodak, and takes pictures of girls climbing over fences, etc. Some of them seem to like it. Tim examines the jumps very solemnly and takes advice from a horsey-looking man in gaiters who is said to be the most reckless rider in Midshire. Feel slightly worried about this.

We return to Charters Towers for tea.

After tea, "all the young people" (which includes Tim and me) repair to the billiard room where we play curling on the billiard table. Major Morley instructs me where to send my ball and seems much surprised when I send it there. So much talking and laughing goes on that I find it impossible to make out the object of the game, but am relieved to hear at the end that "our side has won."

Dinner is not long but everything very good, I could eat a lot more. White wine is excellent so I drink three glasses and begin to feel that I can keep my end up. We sail off to the drawing room and find there a lovely log fire which everyone says is "delightful on a cold night." Very brown woman called Melita (whose surname I failed to catch) starts telling us about her appendix which went wrong in middle of Africa. Fortunately her "head boy" had some sense and fetched a native doctor from a mud village. He had been a medical student but failed to get his degree. This dusky "Luke" operated on her at her own request and she made a wonderful recovery. Talk veers to the subject of bed — amazing candour on the idiosyncrasies of husbands. Am impelled to tell funny story which I extracted from Tim after last Mess Guest Night and emerge from obscurity into a blaze of limelight. Everyone still laughing when they appear and ask what is the joke, but joke not suitable for mixed company.

Melita is induced to sing and does so to her own accompaniment in a queer hoarse voice. She manages to sing the most ridiculous songs with a grave face — am quite weak with laughing. Lady Angela who is sitting beside me on a small sofa remarks that "Melita is very amusing — is she not? Especially when thoroughly ginned." Feel that Lady Angela does not care for Melita. Discover the reason later when Lady Angela is asked to sing. She does not require pressing, and renders several of Tosti's most moving compositions in an astonishingly loud contralto.

The party melts away soon after this and I find myself upstairs, and am thankful to remove a pair of silver shoes which I bought at a sale and which are really too small for me. The horrible things have been torturing me the whole evening. Put on my best pyjamas — green silk with yellow flowers — and a cheap but effective Happi-Coat, and curl up on the sofa near the fire to write my diary.

Tim appears shortly with Major Morley and a tray of drinks, they come in and sit round the fire smoking and talking about tomorrow's point-to-point. Major M. advises Tim to "go slow at the brook" as the ground there is somewhat sticky. He thinks that "Black Witch" is likely to be Tim's most dangerous opponent, but "Lightning" (a tall grey) is a fine jumper and may quite likely be in the running. They also talk of a big bay which is called "My Hat," but Major M. says it's being ridden by a "poor stiff" which militates against its chances. Tim listens eagerly and says quite unnecessarily that he will "do his damnedest."

Major M. asks what on earth I am writing, and is informed by Tim that it is my strange custom (since 1st January) to record my daily doings in the enormous tome which he now beholds. Tim also volunteers the information that the book is kept securely locked and that he doesn't "think it will last long." Realise that it is my perseverance he doubts (not the book's durability) and throw a sofa cushion at his head.

Major M. seems interested and asks if *he* comes into the book. Reply that, since it is the veracious chronicle of my life, he comes into it whenever he crosses my path. Feel that Major M. is disappointed with this answer, he pours out another drink and goes away.

As Tim's room is miles away down several draughty corridors and I am rather nervous about strange houses — (possibly haunted by ghosts of long-dead Morleys) — we decide to share large bed. This in defiance of the conventions of high life which decree that husbands and wives shall sleep solo — or at any rate not with each other.

Bed is exceedingly soft and comfortable.

Thirtieth January

Cannot think where I am when I awake. Maid comes to light fire and enquire about baths; also asks diffidently whether "the major" will breakfast here or in his own room. Reply boldly that he will have it here and waken Tim to tell him of his rise in rank. Tim not particularly amused at what I consider a good joke.

Footman enters with enormous tray containing hot dishes with lamps beneath them. Tim dissertates on the excellent idea of breakfasting comfortably in one's own room instead of facing the world with false smiles concealing emptiness, and says he could put in a couple of weeks at Charters Towers.

We dawdle about, dressing, and talking about our fellow guests — Tim says what do I think of Melita, and do I think Morley is going to marry her. Am amazed at the question as I am sure he has never thought of her. We then discuss our host and hostess and calculate "How Much Sir Abraham must have per annum." Calculations extremely vague as neither Tim nor I have had any experience of establishments run on lines of Charters Towers with butlers and footmen and hunting stables, etc. Tim says he doesn't suppose Morley will go on in the regiment — at any rate not after Sir Abraham's death. Whereupon I point out that Sir Abraham is most hale and hearty and not the least likely to die for years.

Tim says, "He doesn't overeat himself either."

We go downstairs at eleven o'clock, but find nobody about, so feel that we have made a faux sortie, and decide to retire upstairs again and wait till twelve.

Meet Mrs. Winthrop (Major Morley's married sister) just leaving her room. She says, "Good God, where *have* you been?" and seems horrified to think we are together without visible means of relief from each other's company. Suggests that Tim should "beat up Tony" and have a look at the stables with him, or better still that Tim should go to the stables with her and I should "beat up Tony." I vote unhesitatingly for the first course of action. Tim, however, refuses to "beat up" his superior officer so Mrs. Winthrop beats him up, and we find him giving the finishing touches to his toilet with a clothes brush.

We all go together to the stables accompanied by a large white bulldog called Joseph who has a chronic tendency to adenoids. The party grows like a snowball as it rolls along — am struck by the ability of these people to talk nonsense incessantly, and decide that I am a dull dog.

Major Morley has a pocket full of sugar and instructs me in the art of conveying same to a horse's mouth without getting bitten. Gain confidence rapidly and begin to feel quite at home with the beautiful velvet-nosed creatures. Major M.'s favourite mare is black with a white nose and is called Nora.

Coming back from the stables I find myself walking with Lady Angela; she evidently knows her way about and leads me into the vinery which is very warm and steamy. Lady Angela says she is an enemy of convention and an apostle of free love. Goes into embarrassing details. Feel extermely hot but cannot decide whether this is the effect of Lady Angela's confidences or the tropical temperature of the vinery. Try to maintain an aloof and non-committal attitude towards Lady Angela's revelations, but Lady A. will have none of it. She says I need not fear *her*, and that *she* knows all about it, and sympathises with my attitude with all her heart, etc., etc.

Am completely mystified by these hints and innuendoes. Finally in disgust at my pretended (?) ignorance of her meaning, Lady Angela says that she *saw Tony Morley coming out of my bedroom at 1a.m.*

57

Am so astounded at the implication that I can do nothing but laugh. Lady Angela seems surprised at my levity and obviously thinks I am old in sin.

At last I recover sufficiently to gasp out that Major Morley merely came to speak to Tim about the race, and that we all sat talking by the fire and forgot the time.

Lady Angela says that anyone with "half an eye" can see that Tony is in love with me. Reply hastily that she is entirely mistaken in all her surmises, but I can see that she neither believes me, nor wishes to believe me.

The booming of the gong for lunch puts an end to our interesting conversation. Am thankful to escape from the heat and embarrassment of the vinery and Lady Angela combined.

Have no opportunity to tell Tim of my lost reputation until he is dressing for the race. Tim is horrified and shocked. Keeps on saying that "This must be put right," and that he will "speak to Morley." Beseech him to refrain. Tim says, "But good heavens, Hester, that hag will tell everyone." Reply that she has probably done so already, and that if Tim fusses about it he will make us the laughing stock of the party. Frightful argument ensues and continues until Major M. bangs on the door and says it is past two o'clock and is Tim a nineteenth-century débutante dressing for her first ball?

We rush downstairs and pack ourselves into various cars which are waiting at the door. Manœuvre with great guile for a seat in one which does not contain Major M. as I feel I can't face him at present. Find myself next to Commander Grey who is sulky because he hoped to sit next to Mrs. Winthrop whose seat I have taken.

We arrive at the course and find a crowd of tweedy county people with loud voices and weather-beaten complexions. The horses are being walked up and down by grooms. Fireguard looks splendid with a ripple of muscles beneath his silky coat.

Major M. appears at my elbow and asks if I want to put something on. Reply "Yes, on Fireguard." He goes away to do it.

Seize a good-looking boy who goes by the name of Smuts — real name unknown — and ask eagerly if he will show me where to get a good view. He looks surprised but quite pleased, and we sneak off together through a small wood to one of the jumps. Here Smuts hoists me on to the branch of a tree and scrambles up beside me. He points out that we can see two of the jumps and have a good view of Start and Winning Post. I compliment him on his sagacity and congratulate myself on having escaped from Major Morley and hidden myself successfully. Smuts very entertaining, he reminds me of Bryan in some ways, but his superior age is in his favour.

The first race is very exciting and is won by a man with a long nose riding a horse with a long neck. Point out to Smuts the advantage of a horse with a long neck in a close race. Smuts sees my idea and agrees that race horses should be bred with that end in view — We laugh at the pun.

Smuts says he sees "the major" looking for me and adds cryptically that "he won't half be ratty, but it's worth it" — Make no comment.

The second race is Tim's. We see the start, twelve horses running. Fireguard easily distinguishable on account of red foxy colour and light tail. Smuts says he has ten quid on Fireguard, and invites me to lunch at Giorgoni's if he wins. If Fireguard loses, Smuts says, he will have to sell his false teeth. Reply facetiously that he won't get much for them, and then have a qualm as to whether his teeth can possibly *be* false — if so, have I been rude? Can't tell whether they are or not as he keeps his mouth shut.

Loud cries of "They're off," cut short my meditations, and the horses sweep off down a field. Cries of "Black Witch — Black Witch leading" — See a huge black mare in front. Horses disappear over a hedge.

Major Morley is standing by himself with field glasses glued to his eyes. I wonder how much *he* has on Fireguard. Smuts points out a field on our left and says we shall see them there in a few minutes.

Hours elapse. Then three horses appear but no Fireguard. Somebody calls out that "Fireguard is down" — Have scarcely time to grow cold with fear before Fireguard appears and seems to be gaining on the others. Smuts bounds up and down on the branch shouting "Fireguard" until I am nearly dislodged. They thunder up to the jump nearest to us. Black Witch is leading, but jumps short, and she and her rider roll over into the ditch. The next two clear the hedge, and

60

Tim goes over in fine style — the rest follow. We are so near that I can see the horses' rolling eyes and the riders' frantic expressions — some of the horses are steaming with heat.

Smuts rushes to rescue the rider of Black Witch who seems stunned by his fall — am so thrilled over the race that I can't take my eyes off the horses. Away they go over another jump. My Hat pecks and loses distance — there is only one in front of Tim now. Somebody yells, "Mr. Maloney — Mr. Maloney" — am doubtful whether this is the name of the horse or the rider — probably the former. They start on the second round of the course.

By the time they appear again Tim is in front with a big grey close behind. Smuts says it is Lightning — The grey seems to be gaining on Tim, and they are neck and neck as they go over our jump. Frightful excitement as they tear up the last field to the Winning Post. Everyone waving their hats and shouting "Lightning" or "Fireguard." Smuts and I scramble off our perch and run back to the winning post to see who has won — We arrive in time to hear everyone shouting "Fireguard," and to see Tim getting smacked on the back by all those sagacious people who backed him. Huge lump in my throat at Tim's victory — feel perfectly idiotic and can't speak.

We wait for another race which is rather an anticlimax after the last, as only three horses run, and it is practically a walkover for a squat black-haired man whom nobody seems to know. Then we pack into the cars and return to Charters Towers for tea. Major

Morley asks me in a hurt tone where I have been hiding as he looked everywhere for me — reply that Smuts and I were in a tree and had a splendid view of the whole thing. Major M. looks surprised and says he wanted to explain the race to me and he had brought an extra pair of field glasses for my benefit — Feel I have been rather a brute.

He then says — "By the way here are your winnings," and hands me twenty pounds in rather grubby notes. Am simply staggered at the amount and say so. Major M. says he got four to one for me, and I realise that if Fireguard had lost I should have had to pay five pounds, whereas five shillings was the most I should have risked on the race (the more so as I don't possess five pounds in the world). My breath is almost taken away by the variety and depth of my emotions, but I realise that I had better keep them to myself especially as Fireguard has won and I am twenty pounds to the good.

Rush upstairs to change my shoes which are so heavy with mud that I can hardly walk, and find Tim struggling out of his riding boots. He is flushed with triumph and asks me where I was and whether I saw him at the last fence. Reply ecstatically that I did, and that he is a clever old thing and the best rider in Midshire. Tim says he thinks he showed them a thing or two. Reply suitably. Tim says, "It *is* fun, isn't it, Hester?" Reply in the affirmative, but am inwardly feeling somewhat jaded — So wearing to have to be clever all the time.

Show Tim my winnings at which he says, "Good God, Hester! What on earth were you thinking of? Supposing I hadn't won?" Reply that *I knew he was going to win* which cuts the ground from under his feet.

All the people from the point-to-point seem to be having tea at Charters Towers. Fearful squash in the dining room. Smuts sees me from afar and brings me a cup of tea and a tomato sandwich. Major M. also making his way through the crowd with tea for me but arrives too late. Seems rather annoyed about it, but it is not my fault.

Am told that there is to be a dance after dinner and that Mrs. Winthrop has wired to York for two violins and a pianist. Everyone seems to think this quite commonplace behaviour. Major M. is sent off to the telephone with a list of people to ask. He looks rather sulky over it, but has no option as everyone does what Mrs. Winthrop says.

Sit down beside Sir Abraham who remarks, "You women are never satisfied. Why can't you be content to sit down with a paper in the evening? This world would be a nice quiet place to live in, if it were not for you women."

Reply defensively that it is no use to blame women for being women. We were born that way and can't help it any more than a mosquito can help being born a mosquito and addicted to its annoying habits of biting people and giving them malaria. It is merely doing what it was born to do.

Sir Abraham opines that mosquitoes enjoy biting people, just as women enjoy bustling round and upsetting everyone's comfort.

Feel it is time to carry the war into the enemy's territory and point out to Sir Abraham that men are always down on women and yet they expect women to do the most marvellous things such as invisible patches and darns. They also expect them to be able to make a chicken soufflé out of the remains of yesterday's rabbit, and to make short ends not only meet, but tie in a fashionable bow. Sir Abraham roars with laughter and says he would like to see Freda (his daughter) trying to make a chicken soufflé, as long as he had not got to eat it afterwards, but adds that she is pretty useful at tying her income into knots.

Conversation cut short by dressing gong.

I decide to wear my silver, which Tim doesn't like. Haven't I brought my black? he says — I know he always likes my black.

Reply that my black is four years old.

Tim says how old do I think his tail coat is?

Reply facetiously that I really can't be expected to know as I am only thirty-two years old myself.

Tim says this place is spoiling me, and it's a good thing we are going home tomorrow.

Dance is a great success. Tim and I cause quite a sensation by dancing together several times. Also dance with Major M. and with Smuts and Captain Winthrop. Sir Abraham asks me to sit out a dance with him, and takes me into his library where he insists on giving me a glass of port.

64

My next dance is with Commander Grey, but he is nowhere to be seen. Stand about at the door talking to Lady Morley and trying to look animated. Tim comes up to me and says (holding out his watch) — do I realise it is now Sunday morning, and am I going to bed as I look absolutely All In. Realise that I must look frightfully plain for Tim to notice it and agree hurriedly to go to bed.

We meet Commander Grey and Mrs. Winthrop coming downstairs and hide behind a curtain till they pass. Tim says if he were David Winthrop he would give his wife a good beating.

Our room looks very comfortable and bed most inviting — a glance in the mirror convinces me that Tim is right about my appearance.

Thirty-first January

Wake very late after last night's revels. The sun is shining and everything looks and feels very Sunday-ish. Point out to Tim the strange fact (which has just struck me) that even the trees look like Sunday. Tim says they look the same as they did yesterday to him.

Breakfast in our room as before — it feels like months since yesterday morning. Tim says if he lived here long he would become a Socialist. Luxury is enervating — and isn't it dreadful to think there are people in the world actually starving? Reply that I am — and ask him to pass the marmalade.

Tim says he doesn't know why I can never be serious for two minutes. Feel that late hours do not really agree

65

with Tim's constitution (have noticed the same thing before) whereas I am always particularly bright and chirpy after a dance.

Major Morley knocks on the door and asks if Tim would like to come for a ride this morning as we need not start for Biddington until after lunch. Tim agrees joyfully and says no more about turning Socialist.

I go downstairs to see them start and find Lady Morley is going to church. Offer to accompany her which pleases her immensely. No other guests have appeared as yet, probably due to their exertions of last night.

Very pretty walk across the fields, church bells in the distance play hymns slightly out of tune. Find that Lady M. was donor of bells (fortunately before I remarked upon their dissonance).

Lady Morley says that the reason for all the unrest and troubles of modern life is because people do not go to church regularly. She hopes I will like Mr. Bridge, he is a very earnest man, and thoroughly orthodox. The choir is really quite good — church music is so uplifting when suitably rendered.

Here we enter a field of very fierce-looking animals which I feel sure must be bulls, and I hear no more of my companion's remarks until we have negotiated it safely. By this time Lady M. seems to have arrived at the subject of her son. She asks how I think Tony is looking — The dear boy works so hard. She thinks it is a shame the way all the work of the battalion is pushed on to Tony's shoulders. (This idea is so entirely new to me that I find some difficulty in making a suitable reply.)

We climb over a style and Lady Morley says — rather breathlessly — that real friendship between a man and a woman is so ennobling — don't I agree? She actually waits for an answer to this totally irrelevant question so I gather my scattered wits and reply that "one meets it so seldom" — a cliché which I feel sure will appeal to Lady Morley.

"Of course it must be a married woman," Lady Morley says. I reply vaguely that I suppose it must, and hasten forward to open the lych gate for her.

A crowd of villagers in the churchyard reply respectfully to Lady Morley's greetings and questions concerning Little Harry's tonsils and Maud's influenza. Then I find myself sailing up the aisle in Lady Morley's wake to the front pew where we are fastened in securely by a carved door. Am conscious of eyes boring into my back and wonder what I shall do if I feel unwell, as door seems to be bolted on the outside — Decide that there is no reason why I *should* feel unwell and strive to forget about it and to fix my attention on the service.

Mr. Bridge delivers himself of a sermon based upon Noah, and draws comparisons between flood, and present-day conditions of Europe. Am interested to observe large tomb with lifesize figure of a crusading Morley reclining on the top.

After the service we meet a great many people to whom Lady Morley chats in a condescending manner. Cannot help feeling that she is great draw to Charters Church (but perhaps this thought is slightly irreverent).

67

Mr. Bridge appears from the vestry and is invited to lunch at Charters Towers. We all walk back across the fields together. Conversation chiefly concerned with the laxness of various farmers and their wives who have failed to put in an appearance this morning — Mr. Bridge assures me that the large animals in the field are cows and quite harmless; I feel bound to believe the word of a clergyman, but hurry across nevertheless.

Tim is waiting for me in my room looking exceedingly worried and harassed. He wonders what he should give the butler, and should the first footman also receive a recognition of his services? And if so how much? And have I any half crowns about me?

Having foreseen this dilemma I am prepared with a small bag of half-crowns, which I procured from the bank before leaving Biddington. (Tim actually has the grace to compliment me on my foresight.) We divide them into piles, not without *Sturm und Drang*. The gong booms for lunch before we have decided what proportion is to go to the butler — Tim says he has done nothing for us except strut about and look well-fed, and he is dashed if he is going to give him more than five bob. Whereas the first footman has brought up our breakfast — or was that the second footman? Reply that I have no idea as they all look alike to me, but that I think the butler is too grand to tip five bob, and Tim had better give him ten. Tim says if he doesn't want five bob he can jolly well give it back and he (Tim) will know what to do with it.

The butler, when approached, pockets the five bob with dignified gratitude and all is well. After lunch the

Bentley appears — we say goodbye to everyone, thank our hostess for our delightful visit, and are whirled off down the drive. Once clear of Charters Towers my thoughts fly homewards, and I begin to wonder what has happened there during our absence (which feels like one of months) and whether Betty is all right —

February

Second February

Grace arrives just as I am starting out to see Mrs. Parsons and say "goodbye" to her. Grace says I am not to go, as she wants to hear all about Charters Towers. Explain to Grace as tactfully as possible that I must go (Mrs. Parsons being bedridden) and suggest that she should walk part of the way with me. Grace refuses to walk with me and asks why bedridden people must always be considered FIRST (also demands why "bedridden" — does Mrs. Parsons ride upon her bed, or her bed upon Mrs. Parsons?). She then says darkly that there are worse troubles than bed.

Suggest that she should come and tell me all about them tomorrow; but Grace says now is the time and she may not be alive tomorrow for all I know. She goes on to say that if I go to see Mrs. Parsons she will be very disappointed as she was looking forward to a nice long chat with me. Reply that if I don't go Mrs. Parsons will be disappointed. Grace says I can't possibly be sure of this. How do I know — she asks — that Mrs. Parsons really enjoys my visits? How do I know that a long-lost friend has not just arrived from Australia or Timbuctoo to see Mrs. Parsons and that my presence at their tête-à-tête will not be *de trop*?

Reply mildly that I am sorry for Grace as I sometimes feel that way myself, and advise her to take a course of "Jane." Grace says what is that patent medicine that I am always prescribing — it is *her* belief that I have shares in it.

She pursues me to the corner producing new and increasingly fantastic arguments against my proposed visit to Mrs. Parsons, to all of which I turn a deaf ear. Grace then says will I wait a moment while she goes into the fruiterer's and buys a bunch of black grapes for me to take to Mrs. Parsons? I ought to know better at my age — Grace says — than to visit a bedridden person without taking them a bunch of black grapes.

Accept the reproof humbly and the grapes with gratitude and board a bus which will take me to Mrs. Parsons' door.

I like going to see Mrs. Parsons because she is so different from myself. Whereas I have too little time to think, Mrs. Parsons has too much. Sometimes I think she is like Meredith's Emma — "There is nothing the body suffers that the soul may not profit by — that is Emma's history."

Mrs. Parsons is propped up in bed and her bright eyes greet me at the door. We talk.

I wish I could remember all Mrs. Parsons' sayings. She says stimulating things that make you think, whether you want to or not. After a little while I tell Mrs. Parsons about our move to Westburgh. She says she will miss me — there are so few people who bring her sunshine. Reply that I always find sunshine here, and add that I don't think I am as nice as I used to be.

(You can say foolish things like this to Mrs. Parsons.) She smiles and says I only think so because my standard has gone up. Reply that she really does not know me, I am a rebel at heart. "The only people who are not rebels are vegetable marrows," says Mrs. Parsons. Reply that it would be rather nice to be a vegetable marrow — never to be discontented or miserable without any reason for being so. Mrs. Parsons laughs and says "Perhaps — but how dull never to be joyful and happy without any reason for being so!"

We talk about Westburgh and she asks me how I think I will like it. So many people have asked me this, but Mrs. Parsons really wants to know. I reply that I can't tell, but that I hate the idea of leaving Biddington. I get rooted to places and it hurts tearing up roots. Of course, Scotland is not very far away, not like India — but all the same it will be a foreign land to me and *everybody* will be strange — not like moving with the regiment.

Mrs. Parsons says, "I know exactly what you mean but I envy you all the same. I envy you going to new places every few years — meeting new people and making new friends. It is such an interesting thing to study people, to get inside their skins and see life from their point of view. And *you* can do it. Some people travel all over the world and see nothing. They go about clad in a thick fog of their own making through which no impressions can penetrate. I know a girl who went to Africa and all she could tell me when she came back was that the negroes have woolly hair. I learned more about Africa from reading a travel book than that girl learned from living there for three months. You're not like that. You can see things and laugh at them."

My sense of humour is so obstreperous that it is a mixed blessing, and I tell her so.

"Nonsense," she says. "Laughter is a splendid disinfectant, take it with you to Westburgh, my dear."

"You sound as if you think I shall need it there," I remark.

"You will need it wherever you go," she replies, "and just as much if you stay at home. Goodness me, I often wonder how I would get through life without a sense of humour. When things are as bad as they can be you can always find something to laugh at, even if it is only your own gloomy face in the mirror. Wait a moment," she adds, as I rise to go. "There is a passage here I want to find for you. Give me that book, child. R. L. S. has said what I mean better than I could think it." She turns over the pages as if she loved them and reads in her soft, husky voice:

" 'The strangest thing in all man's travelling is that he should carry about with him incongruous memories. There is no foreign land; it is the traveller only who is foreign, and now and then, by a flash of recollection, lights up the contrasts of the earth.' "

Her hand lies in mine a shade longer than usual as we say "Goodbye" and her eyes are very bright. I say huskily that I will write to her and she replies hastily: "Only if you want to, my dear. Don't make me more of a burden than I need be. That is the hardest thing of all for me to bear. Promise only to write when you feel you want to, Hester dear."

I promise and hurry away. In retrospect I am rather ashamed that we have talked so much about my small troubles and so little about her big ones.

Fourth February

Drive over to Nearhampton to take Bryan out to lunch, this being one of the days appointed by the Parkers for that tantalising performance. (Tantalising both to parents and offspring to meet for a few hours with the shadow of an imminent parting lurking grimly in the background.) As we near the school we see other cars with other parents bent on the same errand (mostly large and expensive cars beside which Cassandra looks like a battered sparrow).

Bryan is at first shy and constrained. Conversation consists of Tim and self asking questions to which Bryan replies in a minimum of words.

We drive to Holehogger's Hotel where we lunch expensively, Bryan choosing the most indigestible dishes offered on the menu. My son is such a stranger to me I am quite unable to suggest that he would be wise to content himself with plainer fare. After lunch Bryan becomes more like himself and volunteers scraps of information which are avidly swallowed by Tim and self. I ask after the eldest Carter boy, who has been sent to Nearhampton this term on our recommendation. Bryan replies with relish that "Carter gets kicked all right." Feel rather worried about this revelation, as I have assured Mamie that Bryan will "be kind to Edward."

Several other Nearhampton boys are lunching in the hotel with relatives and friends. Bryan takes no notice of them, nor they of Bryan, and, when asked whether he does not know these boys, Bryan replies, "Of course I know them — Paterson is in my dorm," but vouchsafes no reason as to why they should ignore each other.

It has now started to rain, and neither Tim nor self views with enthusiasm "A long drive," which is Bryan's idea of spending the afternoon. We repair to the large billiard room upstairs, where we find the Anstruthers in the same circumstances as ourselves, complete with Nearhampton schoolboy son. Major Anstruther is in the Gunners and is an old crony of Tim's. They are delighted to meet.

Major Anstruther suggests a game of cockfighting (which is played on Mess Guest Nights) to amuse the boys. Tim agrees, and he and Major A. proceed to play at cockfighting with great vigour. They squat on the floor with billiard cues beneath their knees and their arms hooked under the ends and try to knock each other over. The boys look on, Bryan with the mulish look upon his face peculiar to sons whose fathers are behaving in too juvenile a manner.

Sylvia Anstruther and I sit on a sofa near the fire and discuss clothes, servants, the enormities of landladies, and whether it is really worth while preserving eggs when you are liable to be moved before you can use them.

Afternoon seems extremely long and we decide to have tea at four o'clock. The boys eat enormously of bacon and eggs (an amazing feat so soon after lunch).

We then drive Bryan back to Nearhampton and deposit him there.

Sixth February

Tim having got leave, we start off to Westburgh to look for a house. Funds are low — as usual — so we have decided to go in the car as this is cheaper (*on paper*) than our combined railway fares.

It is a fine morning, frosty and bright.

Cassandra at first refuses to start (she evidently has got wind of the long road before her and does not like the idea at all) but at last, for no apparent reason, she thinks better of it and does start, and we are off, somewhat exhausted with long drawn-out farewells to Betty and Miss Hardcastle.

Cassandra races along nobly with only an occasional backfire as a reminder of her incomprehensible behaviour. At one o'clock we begin to look for a suitable spot to eat our picnic lunch. Pass several likely-looking spots because Cassandra is going too fast to stop and Tim says it is not worth while backing as we shall find something just as good farther on. We go on slowly and stop near a wood which proves to be ankle-deep in mud. Go on again and stop near a hillside which is cold and windy. A straggling town intervenes, and when we have run through it we see a gate leading into a field — this is obviously ideal were it not for a large manure heap close by.

We are now both hungry and cross. Tim says he does not know why on earth I can't pick out a decent place for lunch, as I have nothing else to do but keep my eyes open. Offer to take the wheel for a bit so as to enable Tim to pick out a decent place for lunch, but the offer is not accepted. Stop again near a wood which combines all the drawbacks possible and decide to eat our lunch in the car.

Tim much soothed by sandwiches and a cup of coffee out of a Thermos. Self rather annoyed because Thermos with hot milk has been leaking and there is none left. (Fortunately this catastrophe does not affect Tim, who likes his coffee black.) We fill Cassandra's water jacket — which leaks — from a horse-trough and push on.

Soon after this it begins to rain. Tim says the weather forecast was Some Showers Locally and this is one of them, so it is not worth while putting up the hood, as we shall be clear of it in a few minutes. But it is evidently not One of Them because it goes on and on and eventually proves itself to be a Wet Afternoon. Wait until we are quite sure of this and then put up the hood, by which time we are exceedingly cold and wet.

Rain comes down faster. Cassandra surges through the water like a miniature destroyer in a heavy sea. We stop at an inn for tea, by which time it is dark. Continue through wind and water with our lights streaming out before us and cutting through the gloom like steel. The whole thing becomes dreamlike; I feel as if we had been travelling for days with Cassandra's roar in our ears and the water splashing on the mudguards, and would go on for ever and ever.

Tim remarks that he is feeling sleepy, which brings me back to earth with a bump and I start talking of everything that I can think of in a feverish manner to keep him awake.

We run down a steep hill into a village where a small inn stands by the bridge on the banks of a stream. Lights in the window behind red curtains give the place a cosy appearance and we decide to stop here for the night. Fat, pleasant landlady provides a large meal of bacon and eggs and tea, after which I retire thankfully to a large room with a brass bedstead.

The rain has now lessened in violence, and Tim says he "must have some exercise after sitting still all day," so he departs to walk round the village with the landlady's son.

Landlady follows me upstairs with small jug of hot water and remains for sometime talking to me. I learn that she has been a widow for twenty years — through no fault of the gentlemen, as she could have her pick of the village. But she does not care for matrimony and likes her bed to herself.

At this point I start undressing, as I feel it is the only way to get rid of her. She goes at last, but not until she has seen and admired my most intimate celanese underwear.

Discover that the mattress of the brass bedstead is evidently stuffed with stones, but am too tired and sleepy to care.

Seventh February

Waken early to hear the river splashing outside my window. Tim still asleep. The sun is shining as if rain were unknown — church bell is ringing in the distance and the birds are twittering on the bare trees. All is very peaceful and Sundayish. It seems an age since last Sunday. Is it *really* only a week since we were living in the lap of luxury at Charters Towers, with footmen dancing attendance on us, fires lighted in our bedrooms, and baths full of scented water all ready and waiting for our convenience? Last but not least, the difference in the beds is beyond belief, for whereas the bed at Charters Towers seemed to be made of clouds, that on which I am now reposing is — as I suspected last night — stuffed with stones. Decide that this must be one of the incongruous memories Mrs. Parsons spoke of, which light up the contrasts of the earth.

We push off early and find the road smooth as glass. Cassandra is unrecognisable beneath her coating of mud, but going bravely. There is something very beautiful in the tracery of the bare black branches of the trees against the pale blue sky. As we go northward it becomes much colder; we see patches of snow on the fields, ugly, forsaken-looking patches, which look for all the world like heaps of dirty washing left out overnight.

We stop for lunch at a small town, after which the road becomes snowy and yet more snowy. Here and there it is frozen into ruts and we skid in and out of them in a manner which reminds me forcibly of the bygone cab when its wheels stuck in the tram lines.

Snow begins to fall in thick flakes and Cassandra's windshield wiper sticks. We stop to clear the glass, as Tim cannot see to drive. While we are doing so a car comes in opposite direction and slows down; voice asks cheerfully if we have chains, as otherwise we shall not get through. Tim replies that we have no chains, but we must get through somehow. Voice says facetiously, "Eh, well, if the worst comes to the worst I suppose you can put the thing in your pocket and walk." We are so tired of this kind of joke about Cassandra that it has ceased to enrage us.

We drive on through a deep cutting of snow, crawl up a hill with skidding wheels, slither into a small and deserted town, and breast a steep slope on the other side. Here the car hesitates for a moment (while the back wheels churn the snow impotently) and then slides backwards into a ditch. There is nothing to be done save to open the door and climb out. Cassandra looks small and rather pathetic, leaning drunkenly to one side. Darkness is falling.

Tim suggests that I shall walk back to the small town which we have just passed and send help from a garage. We agree to meet at an inn called the "Black Swan" which we noticed in passing. Discover a garage and send a rescue party to Tim and Cassandra and then make my way to the inn. It is an old-fashioned place brought up to date with electric light and other amenities of civilisation while yet retaining many of the old-time charms. After the cold and dreariness of the outside world, the large hall with its round table and comfortable chairs seems the acme of comfort. I cross over to the fire blazing in the huge old-fashioned hearth and try to warm my chilled fingers and frosted toes. Luckily I am wearing a pair of Russian boots which I always keep for motoring in winter, so my feet are dry; but the hem of my coat — although a good twelve inches from the ground — is crusted with snow. I am busy melting myself when a door opens and an old man in a black alpaca coat comes into the room. He starts when he sees me and then comes forward with old-fashioned courtesy to take my coat.

"You're not all alone," he says, with comical surprise, raising his eyebrows. I reply by telling him of our adventures in the snow. He holds up his hands in horror at the idea of a "lady" being treated in such a cavalier fashion by the weather (it is quite refreshing to meet someone to whom "ladies" are still sacrosanct).

I draw him out while I warm myself at the fire and wonder vaguely how Tim is getting on, and whether the "breakdown gang" has managed to rescue Cassandra from the ditch. Old Thomas is delighted to chat and tells me that this small town used to be the scene of border raids — a stronghold of the Percies. The inn itself flourished in the coaching days before the railways took the coaching traffic off the roads. Situated on the Great North Road and equipped with good stabling and cheer for man and beast, it boasted a well-deserved popularity. The hundred years of railway travel degraded it to the usual inn of a country town, asleep and dreaming, only awake on market days, when the jovial farmers filled its hospitable rooms to overflowing. But now once more the road has come into favour;

motorists stop to lunch or tea, or stay the night in capacious bedrooms on their way south or north, as the case may be. "Things is waking up now," Thomas adds, rubbing his hands together cheerfully.

The place is full of good old furniture — relics of former days — oak and mahogany, well-polished and seasoned. Pewter and copper, battered and shining with elbow grease, have their place on chests and sideboards. In the corner is an old blunderbuss with a ramrod. The very atmosphere is eighteenth century.

Over the mantelpiece is a picture of a post chaise with three horses, and poised on the step, a girl, swathed in what I suppose she would have called "wraps." Her poke bonnet frames a rosebud face. A young gentleman (perish the term) is handing her out of a conveyance in a gallant manner. After a bit Old Thomas seems to recede into the distance, the room swims before my eyes and I am glad to sink into a comfortable (modern) armchair which stands beside the fire.

Old Thomas goes away to prepare tea, and the big room is very quiet, only the ticking of the old clock which hangs on the wall is audible in the stillness. I realise that I am very tired. I take off my small felt hat and rumple my hair into comfortable disorder.

Suddenly there is a clatter of horses' hoofs outside in the street; it breaks the silence like a bubble. I hear men shouting and running — and then the door opens and a girl stands in the doorway. She is wrapped up to the eyes in scarves and shawls — a small poke bonnet frames her rosy face, her eyes are like stars. She comes forward to the fire with a little run and begins to divest herself of some of her shawls — holding out her slim hands to the warmth of the fire with little noises of pleasure and contentment.

She has not seen me as yet, for the room is dark save for the glow of the fire; I can therefore observe her at my leisure. Small feet in black sandals appear from beneath a dress of russet red, very full and frilled from waist to hem. The bodice is tight-fitting, rather becoming to the girl's rounded and graceful figure. I suppose I must have moved, for she looks round quickly and our eyes meet. "Lud, how you startled me!" she whispers, with one hand on her heart to still its beating. I reply quickly that I did not mean to do so. I was sitting here before she came in, very nearly asleep with the warmth and comfort.

She nods. "It is indeed comfortable — we were fortunate to reach this place before nightfall. I have heard that there are highwaymen about on the moor tonight."

"One could easily imagine that there might be," I reply, falling in with her mood.

"The postboy was frightened," she adds breathlessly. "And I too, for the chaise slipped this way and that — the drifts were so high. Oh, it was alarming, I assure you I nearly swooned with terror."

I laugh. The child is evidently on her way to a fancy-dress ball and is acting up to the character of her dress. "We are companions in misfortune," I tell her.

"Oh," she cries, clasping her hands, "are you, too, snowbound and unable to proceed? But it is not so disastrous for you as for me. You are with your father and a day spent here is of small account to you — but I —" She stops a moment and blushes a rosy red. And suddenly it all seems clear to me and quite natural somehow. I know that she is the girl in the picture and she is eloping to Gretna Green with the young gentleman in the highwayman's coat.

I am wondering what to say, when Old Thomas appears — he has changed out of his alpaca coat and is now attired exactly as if he has stepped out of a Dickens novel, with long, tight-fitting trousers to his ankle and a striped waistcoat. He carries in a silver sconce with candles and places it on a table with a low bow. I imagine that the snow must have affected the electric light, so make no remark about it. The poke-bonneted girl now perceives me more closely and holds up her hands with a little cry of horror. "You are wearing men's clothes — yet surely you are a young lady?"

It is years since I have been called a young lady — not since my schooldays has the term been applied to me and it sounds so funny that I cannot help laughing.

"You are merry," she says reproachfully. "You find amusement in this intolerable situation?"

It seems to me that her eyes glisten with tears and I feel sorry for her and unaccountably ashamed of laughing at her. She needs little encouragement to tell me her troubles and is soon deep in their recital. What a pretty picture she makes seated on the edge of a high-backed chair with her voluminous red frock spread out and her two little feet in their slim black slippers peeping coyly from beneath it! I watch her dreamily and it seems to me that what we moderns have gained in comfort we have lost in charm — her golden curls dangle in ringlets about her ears — her voice comes from a long way off. It seems a fairy tale that I am listening to; a young and handsome Prince Charming who has nothing more material than his looks, carries off an heiress from under her guardian's nose. "We intended to reach Berwick tonight," she says, dabbing her eyes with a tiny square of cambric. "My old nurse lives there and would do anything to help me. But we have been delayed by the inclemency of the weather — and now I am afraid — and I misdoubt Edward's affection — I would that I had never come with him — I told him so and he was so fierce that he alarmed me."

It seems small wonder that Edward was fierce — I feel sorry for him and decide to try a little guile on his behalf.

"This Edward of yours — I think I have seen him. He is rather stout, isn't he?"

"Stout!" cries Angelina (for so I have called her in my own mind). "He has the figure of a god — supple and graceful —"

"Oh, yes! But he has a slight squint in his right eye."

Angelina leaps to her feet and her eyes blaze. "It is obvious, Madame, that you have never seen my Edward."

"Has he got sandy hair?" I enquire blandly.

"He is the handsomest man in Yorkshire," she screams.

88

At this moment the curtain which screens the door is drawn back and a young man appears. He is dressed in a long fawn coat with capes and high boots, his dark hair is tied back with a black bow. Certainly he is handsome, and I feel glad that I have shot a bolt for him with his faint-hearted lady.

Angelina rushes across the room and flings herself into his arms with little cries and sobs. "How dare she say that you are stout and — and have a squint — my handsome Edward! How dearly I love you! How wicked to doubt your affection!"

He soothes her as best he can, completely puzzled by her words but well content to accept her changed attitude without question. "Come, my Angelina," he says tenderly. "If you are sufficiently rested we will pursue our way, for the landlord has had word that the road is now open to Berwick."

She runs back to the fire to collect her shawls and, without another glance in my direction, the pair go out together and the curtain falls behind them.

Suddenly there is a loud crash. I jump up in terror — to find that a coal has fallen out of the fire. I am still laughing at my own alarm when Old Thomas comes in.

"All in the dark!" he exclaims, and switches on the electric light, which makes me blink like an owl. "I comed in a few minutes ago and you was asleep, Miss," he continues. "The landlord 'as word that the road is open to Berwick."

"Yes, I know," I reply. "The gentleman said so."

"The gentleman? There 'asn't bin no gentleman 'ere as I know of," Thomas says, as he arranges the table for

89

tea and puts the muffins on a trivet near the fire. "What kind of a gentleman would he be, Miss?" He looks round at me with a curious expression on his smooth face. "It wasn't by any chance a lady now — was it? A young lady in a red dress."

"What do you know of a lady in a red dress?" I ask quickly.

"Nothing, Miss. Nothing."

"What a pity!" I reply, watching his face closely. "I am anxious to know what happened."

"How should I know what 'appened?" he says, looking down at his feet and shuffling them in an embarrassed way. "You was dreaming, Miss — just dreaming. I come in and found you fast asleep."

"It was a queer dream," I reply.

"Ah, folks often 'as queer dreams."

Once more the door opens, but this time it is the twentieth-century figure of Tim.

He stamps his feet and claps his hands and the wraiths of Edward and Angelina have vanished. "Tea," he says cheerfully. "*And* muffins — that's good."

I ask after Cassandra and am told that she is none the worse for her adventure and that she will be ready to start tomorrow morning. We doze and dream in the firelight and presently make our way up the shiny oak staircase to bed.

Eighth February

I sleep dreamlessly and waken early, and soon the events of yesterday come crowding into my mind. I

90

switch on the light beside my bed and the old, beautiful room takes shape — the four-poster with its carved oak pillars, the dark oak chest, the dressing table with its prude petticoat of spotted muslin, the low, uneven ceiling, the wavy oak floor. How many hundreds and thousands of people have awakened in this room; awakened to their sorrows and their joys, their hopes and their fears? Strange that I should have slept so well, untroubled by the haunting of their thoughts!

Soon the old house stirs, and I hear the usual domestic sounds of cleaning and cooking. A bright young chambermaid brings us hot water and morning tea, and asks if she shall turn on the bath which is next door. The "Black Swan" has evidently swum with the times.

Tim is shaving when I return from my bath; he is not impressed with the age of the place, but is delighted with the modern improvements. "All the same," he says as he screws his face into terrifying contortions to reach a difficult corner of his chin, "all the same, Hester, I don't care for these old houses — the drains are apt to be unhealthy. When we retire we'll have an absolutely modern house with all the latest improvements . . . Sickening, isn't it?" he adds grumblingly. "This trip is going to cost us a damn sight more than our railway fares would have been. An extra night on the road — and heaven knows how much this chap will rook us — and the garage charges for rescuing Cassandra, etc."

I reply with soothing noises. Personally I think it has been a lovely adventure and well worth the money.

We eat our breakfast, pay our bill, and take the road for Berwick which Edward and Angelina travelled last night or two hundred years ago — I really don't know which. As we fly along I can't help watching for a lumbering post chaise which may so easily have skidded off the road and overturned in a ditch.

We have engaged rooms in Westburgh at a certain "Brown's Hotel," and here we arrive without further adventure — cold and tired and very late. So late that I ask for a glass of hot milk and tumble sleepily into bed.

Ninth February

We visit Munroe and Horder — the house agents with whom we have been in correspondence — and are shown into a dark, musty office the like of which I had thought only to exist in the imagination of Charles Dickens. Mr. Horder has evidently never read any of our letters as he knows nothing about us or our requirements. He calls Tim "Mr. Johnstone" most of the time and ignores my presence completely. Tim explains patiently that we are looking for a small house with four or five bedrooms in the environs of Westburgh. Mr. Horder says there are plenty of houses of that description to be had for about £2000. Tim explains that we do not want to buy — only to rent furnished. Mr. Horder says we should be better advised to purchase a house; whereupon Tim explains that he is in the army and only here temporarily. After a great deal of irrelevant conversation we manage to extract a list of houses to visit and a packet of cards to view same.

"Depressing feller," Tim says as we leave the office, and I agree fervently. We repair to the garage where we have stabled Cassandra, and find that her radiator is leaking badly. Speak to mechanic who agrees with Tim that it is the water joint and promises to "have a look at her" when he has time. We then lunch frugally at a teashop and board a bus for a suburb called Kiltwinkle. It has started to rain gently but firmly, and I have no umbrella.

The bus is full of wet people with gloomy weather-beaten faces. Ask Tim if he thinks they can possibly be as disagreeable as they look, but receive no answer. Realise that Tim looks as gloomy as everyone else, and try to assume a brightly intelligent expression. We are whirled through a series of grey, wet streets. Tim rises and offers his seat to a stout woman with a baby who is swaying dangerously on a strap. She looks at him with surprise and disgust and accepts the seat without any expression of gratitude.

On arrival at Kiltwinkle, which seems an unexpectedly pleasant residential suburb, we have no difficulty in finding the first house on our list as it is exactly opposite the bus terminus. It has huge iron gates with heraldic animals on the gateposts. There is an avenue of rhododendron bushes, and the house (when it bursts upon our eyes) is about half the size of Buckingham Palace. I point out to Tim that it would take eight servants to run the place, and he agrees regretfully that it is too large. We are about to steal away silently when

93

an old lady comes out of the front door and shouts to us in a deep voice, "Come away in."

Tim raises his cap, and I explain that we are looking for a small furnished house, and that her mansion has been given to us in the house agent's list by mistake. In spite of our protestations we are dragged into the hall, which is paved with marble slabs and adorned with pillars of Stilton cheese. Explain again that "Rose Lodge" is much too large for our modest requirements, but the old lady insists upon conducting us all over the house — starting at the attics which would house Tim's company and ending with the cellars which would suit a wine merchant in a large way of business.

Tim admires everything he sees and waxes more and more enthusiastic as we proceed from room to room. I become more and more depressed at the prospect of trying to keep the place moderately clean with two maids. The drawing room is unfurnished and the old lady points out that the advantage of that is we can bring our own drawing-room furniture and so save storage. Am too proud to admit that we have none. Tim points out that the room would do splendidly for Bryan to play with his trains in the holidays as he could have the rails all over the floor and no need to clear them away at night. Begin to wonder if the old dame has bewitched Tim — she might easily be a sorceress with her long hooky nose and bright beady eyes.

We are then taken to see the garage in which the previous owner kept five cars — two of them Rolls Royces. Tim enchanted with the garage. Point out to Tim with heavy sarcasm that we could drive round and round the garage in Cassandra when too wet to go out. Tim does not reply.

Manage to drag Tim away before he has actually signed the lease of "Rose Lodge" and demand, as we trudge wearily down the drive (now ankle deep in mud) what he can be thinking of to consider the house for a moment. Tim replies that he could not be rude to the old thing and that I am always so ruthless with people. I point out that he has raised false hopes in the ancient lady's withered breast, and that it is sometimes kindest to be cruel.

We argue half-heartedly as we plod through the rain until we reach the next house on our list. This proves to be a miner's cottage in an incredibly sordid row with an unlimited view of a red mountain (rather the colour of underdone beef) which we learn later is called a "slag heap." Fat women with wizened babies appear at the doors of the other cottages and watch us silently. Dogs bark and half-clad children follow us and ask us for pennies. The rain comes down slowly but relentlessly. I can feel it trickling down my back.

We escape from this delectable neighbourhood by boarding a tramcar which sets us down at a row of villas of moderate size. Tim says this "looks more like us," and I agree gloomily.

"The Laurels" stands back from the road and has a pleasant garden. We are shown over it by a tall thin woman in black with blue nose. She does not seem very anxious to let it and enquires if there are any children and dogs. Assure her that we have no dogs and only two children, one of which is at boarding school. The house seems quite hopeful, and we are on the point of taking it for six months when it becomes known that Tim is an officer in His Majesty's Army. This immediately precludes any possibility of the house being let to us, and we are shown out of the door with all possible dispatch.

I am too cold and wet to be really angry, but Tim is boiling with rage. Conversation too lurid to record.

Return to Brown's Hotel and find a note from Richard who has come to Westburgh unexpectedly on business and proposes to dine with us; but not even the thought of seeing my only brother can raise my spirits. I retire upstairs and peel my wet stockings off my numbed legs.

Richard arrives in a dinner jacket which causes a mild sensation in Brown's Hotel. We drink our watery soup and proceed to order three whiskies and sodas — Richard assuring me that this is the correct thing in Scotland, and Tim adding that it may possibly save me from pneumonia. Discover that Brown's Hotel is Temperance, and that anyway it is After Hours for Drink.

So funny to sit and watch Richard and Tim drinking lemonade that I start to laugh and find that I can't stop. Horrible feeling — gasp out that I can't help it — that I am so awfully tired — that I shall be all right in a minute — and continue to laugh helplessly. Consternation in the dining room — the manager is fetched and brings a bottle of brandy which he proceeds to pour out for me with his own hands. Am told to drink it quickly — try to do so and choke — all the same it seems to have the desired effect and I manage to stop laughing. I drink my brandy with the disapproving eyes of the whole room and the envious eyes of Tim and Richard fixed upon me. This done I am ordered to bed by my husband, and am quite glad to obey him for once.

Tenth February

Am astonished to find that I have escaped pneumonia and rheumatic fever, but feel that the seeds of some more subtle complaint may be dormant in my frame.

Spend the whole day looking at houses each one more hopelessly unsuitable than the last. Tim admires and praises all he sees, and inspires the owners with the hope that we are on the point of settling with them. Impossible for me to tell what he really thinks of each house, which causes me untold anxiety. Can see myself being landed in totally uncongenial surroundings, not once but half a dozen times during the day. Speak of this fear to Tim en route from a baronial hall, whereupon he says mildly, "Don't be a fool, Hester, you don't suppose I would settle on a house without talking it over with you?"

Am somewhat comforted by this assurance.

At last we have exhausted Mr. Horder's list without finding anything remotely possible; we return once more to Brown's Hotel, where I spend the evening writing cheerful letters to Bryan and Betty.

Eleventh February

Tim having business connected with his prospective territorial battalion, I decide to visit a house which has been recommended to us by the waiter at Brown's Hotel. Tim says I may as well see what it is like as it can't be more unsuitable than those recommended to us by Munroe and Horder.

Accordingly I take a bus to a place incredibly called Pigspunkie, and descend a steep hill (locally known as the brae) at the bottom of which I find an ancient dwelling situated on a green islet between two streams, both in high flood (and no wonder).

The bell is hanging from its rightful place by a piece of rusty wire so I knock on the door with the handle of my umbrella, and am surprised in the act by a young man with red hair who asks me in a peremptory manner to "Mind the paint." Stifle an inclination to ask where the paint is, and substitute the question as to whether this is indeed the "Old Manse," although I am perfectly aware that it is, having been told so by the baker's van outside the gate.

"Ye'll be for the hoose," says the young man.

I look blank — but not (I hope) as blank as I feel.

"Ye're after the hoose," he reiterates, raising his voice evidently under the impression that I am hard of hearing.

Reply by showing card given to me by waiter at Brown's Hotel.

"Oh, mphm," he says as he reads it carefully. "Mister McGlasky tellt me he'd be sendin' oot a wumman tae see the hoose."

He invites me in with a grand gesture and we enter a hall and living room combined. I look about me with interest and try to visualise my own belongings in these unfamiliar surroundings. The furniture is of fumed oak which harmonises with the dark low-ceilinged room, the carpet is in rags — a death trap to unwary feet. A big cat, striped like a Bengal tiger, springs off the sideboard and vanishes under a chair.

I shudder involuntarily.

"Ye're no feart o' cats, are ye?" says the red-haired man incredulously.

Reply that I am not, but that I don't like them, and add (as I always do on similar occasions) that in this I resemble the late Lord Roberts who was said to have a strange antipathy to these supposedly harmless animals.

"She keeps doon the r-r-ats," says my guide shortly.

I pursue this line of argument and am informed casually that "the r-r-rats only come intae the hoose when the bur-rns are in spate."

Fortunately I am sufficiently acquainted with the language of our Kail-yard poets and novelists to understand this remark, and decide forthwith that the "Old Manse of Pigspunkie" is not for us.

It is, however, impossible for me to escape without having seen the entire house. The red-haired man has been told to show me over, and show me over he will. He is so conscientious that he will not allow me to miss a corner of the house. He ushers me into places which are usually glossed over in mixed company, descanting rapturously on the modern improvements which have recently been installed. He accompanies the tour with a running commentary of which two thirds is incomprehensible to me. I find myself gazing at him with a kind of awe for I have never believed (in my bones) that such a person with such a speech existed outside the pages of Scott, Stevenson, and Crockett.

Make several remarks to the red-haired man anent the extreme age of the "Old Manse," and suggest that it must possess interesting historical associations — possibly with the ill-fated Mary or with Bonnie Prince Charlie. (Mem. read up salient points of Scottish history as I find I am distinctly hazy on the subject.) Red-haired man does not understand a word of what I am saying. Conquer with difficulty an impulse to shout at him.

Having seen no trace of any living being in the house except young man and cat, I ask him — partly by signs — whether he lives by himself. He laughs in quite a human manner and replies that he "bides with his Anty," and, coming at last to the only room in the house which we have not yet examined, we find the red-haired man's "Anty" seated in front of a pleasant fire with her dress turned back over her knees. She is a small bird-like person with twinkling eyes. Find her more intelligible than her nephew. She informs me that she is pleased to meet any "freend" of Mr. McGlasky (the waiter at Brown's). (Query — is this form of greeting borrowed by America from the ancient Scots?)

Tea then appears — fetched by red-haired man on a large silver tray — and I partake of it gratefully, being cold and tired.

I discover that the red-haired man's Anty is blessed with the extraordinary name of McLoshary. We wax confidential on the subject of dogs — a subject of which I am peculiarly ignorant. Miss McLoshary breeds out of a West Heeland bitch, and goes into lurid details of her difficulties in protecting same from the attentions of an Irish terrier belonging to the "gentleman next door — a flesher by trade." Wonder vaguely what particular branch of trade this can be.

Miss McLoshary then offers me one of her own puppies, which, she avers, will grow up into a "fine wee dawg," and will be "just the thing" for the rats. She has known its father for years, and has known him kill six rats "without breath" — "I've known him sit twa hoors by yon hole in the wainscot," says Miss McLoshary proudly, "and tweak the r-r-rats as they r-r-ran oot."

I look at the hole and try to repress a shudder which I feel might seem rude to my hostess. The conversation has made me anxious to leave the "Old Manse" at the earliest possible moment, as I feel sure that if I see a rat I shall scream — I can hardly keep my eyes away from the hole. I drink my tea hastily, scalding as it is.

No mention has been made of my purpose in visiting the house, and I rise to take my leave hoping to escape before anything is said. It will be much easier to write to Miss McLoshary and explain that we are unable to take the Manse, than to tell her so face to face. Can think of no polite reason at present, but feel that I *could* do so from the comparative safety of Brown's Hotel.

This, however, is not to be, for as I rise Miss McLoshary says abruptly, "Ye can get into the hoose on Wednesday, and it's ten pound a month I'm asking."

Reply hastily that the house is charming but that I can settle nothing without consulting my husband, and that *I will Write*.

The red-haired man looks at me sadly and says he "doots it's the r-r-rats."

I pretend to be in a great hurry, examine my watch with every appearance of dismay, shake hands with my hostess, thanking her warmly for the excellent tea, and hasten away from the rat-ridden abode.

When I am halfway up the hill I hear the red-haired man calling to me, but decide to pretend that I don't hear him. Nothing will induce me to re-enter the "Old Manse" and face the rats. A bus is approaching, I wave to it wildly and jump on board. The red-haired man having run after me all the way up the hill arrives a few seconds later, follows me into the bus, and hands me my umbrella which I have left behind in my anxiety to escape. He looks at me pityingly and is obviously under the impression that I am idiotic as well as deaf. Then he bows to me gravely and leaps off the bus as it starts on its way to Westburgh.

Thirteenth February

Visit our Mr. Horder who receives us as complete strangers, and says to Tim, "Oh! Ah! Mr. McFarlane, I think."

Tim replies that his name is Christie.

"Quite, quite," says Mr. Horder, "and what can I do for you, Mr. — um — ar — Christie?"

Tim suggests mildly that he might find us a house. Mr. Horder calls for his book and after some search — during which a lot of papers and photographs fall onto the floor — offers us a shooting lodge in Argyllshire with twelve bedrooms. He seems hurt when we do not close with it immediately, and assures us that it is a real bargain at fifty pounds a month. Tim enumerates our modest requirements for the fourth time (not including letters) whereupon Mr. Horder offers us a flat over a butcher's shop with three rooms and kitchen, and adds that the owner is willing to instal a bath should the tenant so desire.

Tim gets up and says that it is no use wasting Mr. Horder's valuable time —

At this moment a young man comes in and says mysteriously to Mr. Horder, "What aboot the Mackenzies?"

"Oh! Ah! The Mackenzies," says Mr. Horder.

"The Mackenzies are wanting to let," says the young man persuasively.

"Oh! Ah! The Mackenzies are wanting to *let* right enough."

"They might try the Mackenzies."

103

"Aye — they might try the Mackenzies."

Ask for particulars concerning the Mackenzies, and find that their house seems to tally exactly with our requirements, and that it is to be found at Kiltwinkle which is the least obnoxious suburb which we have visited. All this has to be dragged from Mr. Horder, who seems most unwilling that we should visit the Mackenzies, and puts all the obstacles that he can possibly think of in the way of our doing so. "And, anyway, you can't see it till Saturday," he says at last. "Saturday's the day, and Mrs. Mackenzie is a most particular lady."

Tim points out that today *is* Saturday.

Finally, we wring from Mr. Horder an unwilling admission that the name of the house is "Loanhead," and make our escape into the street where the rain has started to come down again in the quiet, hopeless fashion peculiar to Westburgh.

Ask Tim if he can imagine why Mr. Horder does not want us to see the Mackenzies. Tim says that it is probably Just His Way. Reflect on the many mysterious ways of doing business, until a woman nearly spikes me in the eye with her umbrella and so diverts my thoughts.

In the afternoon we take a bus for Kiltwinkle, and after several abortive enquiries (made of complete strangers to the district and congenital idiots who fail to understand our English speech) we discover a boy who says we are to "Go west for twa hundred yairds, and then sooth up the brae, and it's the second on the left."

Tim says he has left his compass at home, whereupon the boy offers to lead us to Loanhead — he obviously thinks we are not all there, and is sorry for us.

Loanhead is a square, grey, stone house in a good-sized garden — a great many trees stand about it, and all are dripping wet. Am agreeably surprised to find that the house answers more or less to the agent's description.

Mr. Mackenzie is exceedingly thin with a drooping walrus moustache. Mrs. Mackenzie is fat and florid and inclined to be skittish. They show us over their house with great pride and assure us that they have never let it before, and are only doing so now because they want to travel — or, at any rate, Mrs. Mackenzie wants to travel.

Ask politely whether they are thinking of going abroad, to which Mr. Mackenzie replies that "England is far enough." There is, however, a gleam in Mrs. Mackenzie's small eyes which makes me think she is determined on a further flight.

I have made up my mind that Loanhead must do (chiefly because I feel that I cannot bear to look at another house), but I am horrified to find that Tim looks more and more gloomy as we follow the Mackenzies from room to room, and objects unreasonably to the size of the bathroom, the wallpaper in the dining room, the old-fashioned kitchen range, strange smell in the pantry, and various other details (so different from the extravagant praise lavished on the hovels which we have already inspected).

Mr. Mackenzie asks us to go and look at the garage, so we don our waterproofs and emerge from the house. Tim takes the opportunity, while Mr. Mackenzie is looking for the key, to seize my arm and whisper, "What about it, Hester?"

"Take it," I reply like the teeny tiny woman with the teeny tiny bone.

"Leave it all to me," Tim hisses.

I leave it to Tim, and after some beating round the bush we find ourselves possessed of Loanhead for a period of one year from the 12th March. Mrs. Mackenzie says coyly that she hopes we are not "supersteetious," and I realise today is the thirteenth.

Business over, we are regaled with tea and polite conversation. Mrs. MacKenzie offers to leave her "gurll" to help us out on arrival, an offer which I thankfully accept. The girl is summoned, and is seen to be young and pretty, except for her teeth, which are dreadful beyond words. She is evidently very anxious to be "taken on." "This is me. Will I do?" she seems to say behind the hopefully arranged curtain of her face.

The rain stops as we leave the house, and the street lamps twinkle merrily. Westburgh suddenly seems a friendlier, kindlier sort of place.

I ask Tim why he was so gloomy when the Mackenzies were showing us round the house, to which he replies, "Never crack up a horse you want to buy."

Am astounded at his duplicity.

Fourteenth February

Spend the day in bed writing letters and reading *Rob Roy* in the hopes that this will improve my historical knowledge. Get up for dinner and am informed during fish course that a lady has called to see me. She was told that I was at dinner, but can't wait.

Can it be Nora's sister, the great Doreen McTurk? Suggest this to Tim, who says it is a queer hour for anyone to call, but Westburgh is a queer place and I had better go and see.

Find a stern-looking woman of uncertain age sitting beneath a palm tree in the hall. She remarks that she has come in answer to my advertisement for "cook general," but that she Doesn't Wash. Reply hastily that that does not matter at all. Go into intimate details of health and experience with some trepidation, but have not the moral courage to enquire as to age. Cook says she has "been with Miss Clarke two years," and suggests that I should ring up Miss C. immediately as she has several ladies to interview if I don't suit her.

This suggestion seems strange to me, but I comply with it and learn that Jean McGinty is quite perfect in every way and an excellent cook. Make special enquiries with regard to her temper, and am still dubious about it in spite of Miss Clarke's assurances as to its sweetness and reliability. As I can find no reason to do otherwise, I engage cook to come on the 13th March and return to my fish, which is stone cold.

Tim asks what on earth I have been doing as everyone else has finished dinner. Reply triumphantly that I have engaged a cook. Tim says she probably drinks.

Fifteenth February

Receive letters from Betty and Miss Hardcastle.

The latter informs me that all goes well. That the weather has been inclement. That Betty's galoshes are worn out. That Mrs. Benson very kindly asked Betty to go to tea, but the dear child did not seem to want to go. That she hopes we have been successful in our quest. That she hopes I will be returning soon, as the servants are apt to get out of hand when I am away, and they seem to go out at all hours of the day. That several of the window cords have broken which makes it extremely unsafe (not to say dangerous) to open the windows — she has pointed this out to Annie without any result. That milk pudding is doubtless very nourishing and sustaining, but one is apt to tire of it if eaten every day. And that she remains mine, sincerely, Greta Hardcastle.

Betty writes — "Dear Mummie — Hardy ses I have been norty but she won't tell so I'm telling. Hardy had her sister to lunsh and it was milk pudding again. Mrs. Benson arst me to tea but I sed no and Hardy sed it was rood. I mite of been rooder if I had gorn. Hardy ses my sums is bad. We had dog in a blangit for pudding today. Hardy dussent like it either. Annie is cross with Bollings becos he is cross with her for going to Skottland but I think they'll make it up dont you. Good by and luve xxx Betty."

Sixteenth February

Return to Biddington by train as Tim is remaining to Learn the Ropes from previous adjutant before he goes. Tim comes to see me off and buys me a *Queen* newspaper in an access of tenderness induced by my departure. Just as the train is starting a young man gets into my compartment. Tim suggests in a whisper that I should move into a "Ladies Only," next door, which already contains two women and three children. Refuse unconditionally to change, after which I worry all day in case anything should happen to Tim while I am away (he might be run over, or poisoned, or die of pneumonia — knowing the traffic in the streets, the food at Brown's Hotel, and the peculiar climate of the neighbourhood, all three deaths seem possible) and I have refused his last request.

Apart from the groanings of conscience the journey is very pleasant. Young man also very pleasant. Discover that he knows Richard — they were in the same battalion in Kitchener's during the war. We lunch together and I find myself telling him about the children. I stop at once (because I hate women who talk about their offspring) and switch the subject to books. We discuss *Moby Dick* which we both adore. He gives me a tip for the Grand National. We exchange cards, and part at Euston with expressions of mutual esteem.

Arrive very late at Biddington — Miss Hardcastle is waiting up for me in a pink silk kimono with embroidered flowers. Feel slightly aggrieved because I can't afford such a nice one, but reflect that anyhow it does not become her — in fact it makes her look more like a disgruntled camel than ever. Miss H. says in a mysterious voice that "Betty is in bed." — The hour being 11:30p.m. I am not surprised and say so. Miss H. continues that she knows I must be Tired after my Long Journey, and that it is really nothing serious — at least she hopes it is not.

I realise that she is trying to tell me that Betty is ill, and demand all details immediately. Discover that Betty has been very sick. Rush upstairs to her room and find her hot and flushed and muttering in her sleep. Make up my mind never to leave Betty again as she invariably gets ill when I am away. Am furious with Miss H., but try to disguise this beneath a polite and calm exterior. Miss H. points out in a hurt voice that she could not help Betty overeating herself on cream buns presented to her in a clandestine manner by Bollings. Feel there is more to this than meets the eye, but am too tired to pursue the subject tonight.

Seventeenth February

Lie awake for hours worrying about Betty, but manage to drop off to sleep at five o'clock or thereabouts. Am awakened at seven by Betty bounding into my room full of vim and life, and apparently none the worse of her sick attack. Am delighted to see the dear child looking so well, but can't help wishing she did not waken quite so early.

Betty hugs me, and says, "Oh, Mummie, have you found a house? Is there a swing in the garden? — You do look old this morning!"

Reply that I feel at least a hundred years old, and that I have found a house, but there is no swing in the garden. Betty's face falls, so I rashly promise to see what can be done about a swing. She is overjoyed, and tells me that I do not look *nearly* so old as a hundred; only about sixty or so.

She then hugs me again and says it is lovely that I am home, and shall she tell me what Bollings said yesterday? Bollings said that the Old Girl had heard about the cheering at the Christmas Tree, and she wasn't half in a wax. I beseech Betty to speak respectfully of the Commanding Officer's wife, and she replies, "Oh, but I *do*. I was only telling you what Bollings said to Annie. And Bollings says she was in a wax because she likes all the cheering that's going *herself*. And Bollings says they won't half cheer next year when she does go."

I ask innocently if that was why Bollings gave her the cream buns, and Betty replies, "Oh, no — that was because I made Annie be nice to Bollings, and they kissed each other. So then Bollings bought me the cream buns in a paper bag and I was sick."

Miss Hardcastle very polite and quiet at breakfast; follows me into the morning room where I am wrestling with the Bills which have accumulated alarmingly while I have been away, and says that she does not feel that I trust her now in the way in which she is used to being trusted. Lady Hallingford with

111

whom she had the Honour of Residing for Six Months used to Trust her Implicitly. But she Feels that I don't Trust her — I give her that impression. She is very sensitive to anything of that kind and would prefer to Tender her Resignation unless I can assure her that she is Entirely Mistaken — Adds that Betty has been exceedingly troublesome while I was away, but that she is aware that it is no use saying anything about that, as I am never pleased when she has to complain of the children.

I ask how she could possibly expect me to be *pleased* to hear the children were troublesome. But that of course if Betty has been naughty she must be punished. Miss Hardcastle does not reply to this except to say tearfully that without perfect trust we can do nothing.

Problem whether to patch up Miss Hardcastle and take her to Westburgh or to make a clean break and ask her to leave before we go. Very awkward to have Betty on my hands during the move, but awkward also to have to nurse Miss Hardcastle's wounded feelings while I am so busy.

Fortunately the telephone rings, so decision can be put aside for the moment. It is Nora to ask how I like Westburgh.

Nineteenth February

Am summoned to the kitchen to comfort Katie who has been insulted by the butcher's boy. Find Katie in tears. After some persuasion Katie reveals the fact that the butcher's boy on being asked if he had a tongue immediately put his out at her. Decide to treat the incident lightly, and point out to Katie that this was merely boyish ebullition. Katie replies through the tears that I am right and he *is* a pollution — that's what he is. Take no notice of this, but continue to persuade Katie that boys will be boys and a joke is a joke, and that the butcher boy meant nothing disrespectful.

Katie is actually drying her tears when Betty dances into the kitchen, and seizes my hand, shouting, "Oh, mummie, you must come and see the picture of Katie that the butcher's boy has been drawing on the back gate. I know it's meant for Katie because the eyes are squinty."

I realise at once that the situation is beyond me and retire hastily, murmuring that I hear the telephone. By a strange coincidence the telephone bell rings at that moment — it is Grace to ask if I will come to lunch today as Jack is bringing three Antiquities. On being asked for further particulars Grace replies that the Antiquities have been digging for bones and things in the Roman meadow, my dear, and that I must come and help. I realise that my help is required to entertain the guests, not to dig for bones, and accept gratefully as I feel it will be a relief to get away from the house and domestic troubles for a few hours.

I find the Antiquities (as Grace persists in calling them) seated in the drawing room at Fairlawn. Two of them are aged, bearded, and spectacled, but the third is young and has twinkling eyes and broad shoulders, and I suspect that he is included in the party to do the digging. From the conversation, I gather that Jack

McDougall found a Roman vase when his company was practising trenching in the meadow, and that these gentlemen have come from London to examine the site and see what else they can find.

Grace produces cocktails which she assures us are "harmless," but mine as usual goes straight to my head and makes everything look misty. The door (which I have got to walk out of when lunch is announced) seems miles away. I manage to find it, however, and am so pleased with my success that I join boldly in the conversation which is erudite in the extreme. We discuss Roman remains (a subject of which I know little).

With the pudding course the talk veers from Roman remains to Neanderthal Man (a subject of which I know less). Grace (who has evidently been studying the encyclopedia so as to have something suitable to discuss with her guests) remarks with great gravity that she "wonders what can have happened to Neanderthal Man." Jack says, "What's that, darling? I didn't know you were expecting anyone else."

The oldest Antiquity whose beard is quite white (or was, previous to the tomato soup) pricks up his ears, and gives it as his opinion that N.M. died out on account of some infectious disease. The second oldest Antiquity thinks he was eliminated by climatic conditions. They wrangle acidly for a few minutes quoting various authorities to strengthen their opinions.

By this time my cocktail has settled down and I feel big and brave and beautiful. I suggest brightly that there was only one Neanderthal Man — that he was a freak, like Mr. S — , and that he probably died of old age.

Suggestion not well received.

After lunch the Antiquities go off to dig and I spend a pleasant afternoon with Grace. Return home with domestic worries in proper proportion.

Twentieth February

Having been invited to lunch with the Bensons on account of grass-widowhood, I put on my best hat, take my umbrella (a habit formed in Westburgh) and sally forth. On my way to the barracks I hear martial music, and stand on the edge of the pavement in company with about twenty errand boys with baskets, half a dozen nurses with prams, and a nondescript crowd of loafers to watch the battalion pass on its return from what has obviously been a route march. Can't help thinking how well the officers look in uniform compared to their usual appearance in mufti. Colonel Benson looks splendid on his white horse. The men are marching with a lovely swing of kilts. The pipes are playing "The Barren Rocks of Aden." The sun shines, the drums clatter, it is all splendid. Feel quite maudlin at the thought of leaving the regiment for three years. Pipes always make me cry, and today is no exception to the rule.

"Big drum's my fancy," says a young nurse beside me with twins in a pram.

"Ain't 'e got long arms?" replies her companion admiringly.

Feel inclined to dispel her illusions by telling her that Big Drum is a very much married man with four children, but resist the temptation.

Mrs. Benson is waiting for me in the drawing room, and we settle down to what I know she would describe as "a nice chat" before the colonel arrives.

Mrs. Benson starts by asking me what I think of "that young Mrs. McDougall," but fortunately does not wait for an answer. Mrs. B. is of the opinion that she is not quite the right type for the regiment. We have always been so fortunate with our wives, and it will be a great pity if our pleasant family party is to be spoiled.

Reply that I like Grace and find her very amusing.

Mrs. Benson says — Ah! Amusing no doubt. But don't I think that it would be better if she did not paint her mouth that very peculiar shade of red. And don't I think also that her manner with men is just a little —

Reply that I feel sure she means no harm, and that it is just because she is young and pretty.

Mrs. B. says she is sure she hopes I am right and that I shall never have cause to think otherwise.

The colonel comes in rubbing his hands and looking more like a turkey than ever, whereupon Mrs. B. begins to talk feverishly about other matters, and asks how Bryan is getting on at school and whether he is going into the regiment. Reply modestly as to Bryan's attainments and vaguely as to his future.

Mrs. Benson then says it is a pity that Betty is so shy. Am surprised at this remark as shyness is certainly not Betty's failing (in fact I have more often been informed by kind friends that Betty was too forward). Mrs. B.

116

goes on to say that she met Betty in the town one day while I was away and asked her to tea, as she thought the dear child might be feeling dull, but that Betty was too shy to come. And do I think that Miss Castlemain is quite the right type of woman to look after a nervous child. Reply at once and with the utmost conviction that Miss Hardcastle is a most estimable person, and has my entire confidence. (Such is the peculiar influence of my colonel's wife that this is true at the time though probably merely temporary.)

Twenty-first February

Betty and I go to church. On the way Betty informs me that the Carters' cat has had kittens. Leonard Carter took her into the shed to see them and they had no eyes; but Leonard says their eyes will grow. She then says — as an after thought — "Mummie, when we go to Westburgh will you bath me?" I reply that Miss Hardcastle will bath her as usual. "But Hardy's not coming," says Betty brightly. "She told Leonard's nurse yesterday that she isn't."

Suggest that Betty is mistaken, but her conviction is unalterable, and she confirms it with the interesting piece of information that "Hardy has got a sweetheart, and he has gone to London, so Hardy is going to London too."

Meditate during the sermon on Miss Hardcastle's duplicity, and decide that she has really behaved very badly not to tell me sooner of her change in plans. Several things which have happened lately now occur to my mind all tending to corroborate Betty's statement that Miss H. does not mean to come north with us. Of course she need not come if she does not want to, but how much better to have told me so in a straightforward manner instead of letting me find out in this roundabout way. I arrive at the conclusion that the woman is a perfect fool, and that her departure will be an unmixed blessing — but I am very angry all the same.

After church we meet Major Morley who walks home with us and stays to lunch — Major M. very pleasant and chatty, he is very nice with children and always at his best when Betty is present. Major M. says I made a great impression at Charters Towers (which I don't altogether believe) and that Sir Abraham, in particular, is always asking when we are going back there for another weekend. Reply that it is very kind of Sir Abraham — but reflect that I cannot return to Charters Towers for some time as I wore my only presentable frocks the two nights that we were there, and have no money to buy others, the twenty pounds that I won on Fireguard having disappeared in the astonishing manner that a windfall always does.

After lunch Betty follows us into the drawing room and accepts a spoonful of coffee sugar from Major Morley with every appearance of enjoyment. She informs us that "Hardy" is writing letters — Betty *thinks* it is to her sweetheart.

Major M. says "Lucky man" in his soft voice which always leaves me wondering whether or not he is being sarcastic. Betty, however, takes the remark at face value and says that *she* doesn't think he *is* lucky because "Hardy" isn't a bit pretty. And doesn't Major Morley think it would be much nicer to get letters from somebody really pretty — like Mummie, for instance.

Major Morley agrees fervently, and I change the subject by asking Betty if she has not got a book to read.

Betty replies that she has read all her books several times, and that they are very dull anyway, and will Major Morley tell her a story — preferably about the Sleeping Beauty.

Major Morley agrees to do this, but is very shaky about the history of the unfortunate princess, and is corrected indignantly by Betty at every slip. After she has at last been married off to live happily ever after we discuss in all gravity the gifts that *we* would have chosen from the good fairies. Betty after some deliberation says that she would have chosen wings, while Major Morley plumps for unlimited cash. Personally I am inclined to think that a third set of teeth would be a useful asset (my second set being in a parlous condition with no hope of replacement). Major M. points out that with unlimited cash he could buy an aeroplane and as many sets of teeth as he wanted so that his gift would include both ours besides others such as ponies, dolls' houses, and strawberry ices every day. Betty agrees rapturously and tells Major M. that he is a "clever man," which pleases him immensely.

At this point Miss Hardcastle appears and says it is time for Betty to go for a walk. Betty, anything but pleased at the idea, suggests that Miss H. should "write

119

some more letters." Feel great sympathy with Betty, but realise that it is my duty to side with Miss Hardcastle, and suggest with great guile that they should go and feed the swans in the lake at Biddington Park, which usually solves all difficulties. Am particularly anxious to have no scene with Betty as I can see that Major M. is amused at this glimpse of parental troubles. After some argument Betty departs with great reluctance, but mercifully without tears or lamentations. Feel sorry for Miss Hardcastle, but cannot help the reflection that, if she made herself interesting to the child, Betty would not show such an aversion to her company.

When Major Morley goes away he says that he will miss us very much when we leave Biddington, and obviously, for once, he really means what he says.

Later in the day Miss Hardcastle and I have a very difficult interview. I tax her with her intention of leaving us before we go to Westburgh. She admits that she has thought of tendering her resignation, but adds that it is because my manner towards her has completely altered. She reiterates her hankering for perfect trust and once more drags in Lady Hallingford's name, which I find unnecessary and exasperating. She goes on to say that Betty is becoming more troublesome, and that it is because I do not uphold her authority or support her in the way I should. This annoys me excessively as I feel I *do* support Miss H. — sometimes against my own inclinations (*vide* this afternoon). I put it to Miss H. that she wishes to leave for "private reasons," and that she should have informed me before of her change of plans. (All this very difficult as I must not betray Betty in case it should lead to trouble for the child.) We eventually terminate the argument without having convinced each other, but having agreed unanimously that Miss H. is to leave us the day we go to Westburgh.

I feel better after this is settled, and am surprised to find how much it has been weighing on my mind.

Decide to go to evensong, as I was too preoccupied in the morning to attend to the service as I should. Church is very full, but I manage to get a seat in our usual pew immediately behind the Bowaters of Nether Biddington.

Miss Bowater is known to Tim and me as The Foolish Virgin, for no other reason than that her appearance suggests a general incompetence. She is tall and thin and round-shouldered, with a pale face and a floppy mouth; and her eyes have a yearning expression which Tim thinks is due to her lack of oil. Her hands are loose and clammy, obviously quite incapable of the niceties of wick trimming. One of Miss Bowater's least endearing peculiarities is that she does not always wash behind her ears, and tonight I am reminded, *malgré moi*, of the first time that this dereliction of duty was observed by Bryan. The subject happened to be a sore one with him at the time, and he improved the occasion by remarking to me in a triumphant whisper, "Mummie, Miss Bowater does not wash behind her ears *either*."

In spite of these digressive thoughts I follow the service with assiduity, and listen with interest to the sermon which is all about St. Paul. Mr. Black makes

121

him quite human — even lovable — and I feel sorry to think that hitherto I have misjudged him, deeming him a misogynist of the deepest dye.

Twenty-second February

Am engaged in counting china in the pantry and making list of breakages to replace, when Annie appears at the door and asks in a mysterious manner if she can speak to me. My heart sinks into my shoes with dark foreboding, but I reply brightly that she can.

Annie says, "Is it true that Miss 'Ardcastle isn't going to Westburgh?" Reply that it is true. Annie then goes on to say that she would like to look after Miss Betty — "Do 'er 'air and bath 'er and all that" — unless of course I have someone in my eye.

Realise at once that this would be an excellent plan. I have known Annie for two years and found her trustworthy and pleasant, which are the essential virtues; she gets on well with Betty, and, last but not least, I shall have somebody that I know and who knows me and understands my ways in the strange land for which I am bound. Reply that I have nobody in my eye, and that I would be willing to accept her in the rôle of Betty's keeper, but does she really think she would like to settle down in Westburgh so far away from all her friends. Annie says she has thought about that and would like to come for six months anyway; she thinks a girl ought to go about a bit and see new places before getting married and settling down. Agree with her fervently.

Annie then says in a ruminative manner that Bollings has never been to Scotland — he has been to India, of course, and the tales he tells — well a girl has to take tales like that with a bit of salt — doesn't she?

Agree again with equal fervour. I now perceive that Annie hopes, after her visit to the Far North, to be able to cap Bollings' Indian stories with some of her own adventures, and can thoroughly sympathise with her in her endeavour to be upsides with her future husband, as I have been suffering all my married life from an inability to cope with Tim's Traveller's Tales and an inferiority complex resulting from same. I do not anticipate any hair-raising adventures in the law-abiding precincts of Westburgh, but must hope for Annie's sake that her imagination will be equal to the task of manufacturing some of a sufficiently plausible nature.

Having settled this important matter to our mutual satisfaction. Annie and I set to work once more on the glass and china, which (chiefly owing to Bollings' misguided vigour) we find to be lamentably depleted. So much so that even Annie is left with no illusions on the subject, and remarks (*sotto voce*) that when she is married she will do all the washing up herself.

Twenty-third February

Receive a postcard from Tim to say that he is returning today by train and will arrive at Biddington late tonight. He is leaving Cassandra at Westburgh to await our arrival, having been completely disillusioned as to the theoretical economy of doing the journey by car.

Am wildly excited all day at the prospect of Tim's return as I have not seen him for a whole week. Husbands are annoying at times, but they are a habit which grows on one, and life is extraordinarily dull without them. Spend the day tidying up and putting fresh flowers in the vases, though I do not suppose for a moment that Tim will notice them.

Tim looks well and seems quite pleased with his new job which he is to take over officially on 17th March. He has been twice to Kiltwinkle to arrange various matters with the Mackenzies. The inventory is to be taken the day we go in — he has ordered coal — and agreed to take on the telephone. He feels sure that we shall be extremely comfortable at Loanhead. It will be rather fun to be away from the regiment, absolutely on our own, and he (Tim) going in daily to his work like a civilian.

I agree with all he says, as a good wife should. And so to bed.

Twenty-ninth February

Receive a bulky epistle from unknown lady residing in Kent asking for information concerning a certain Alice Bowles who was with me as cook. Must be quite eighteen months since she left me as Katie has been here for a year, and I had various other horrors before that. Letter enquires whether Alice is sober, honest, and respectable, thoroughly trustworthy and conscientious about her duties, clean and tidy in work and person, willing and obliging, cheerful in the house and amiable in the kitchen. Will she do what she is told with a good grace? Has she good manners? Are her people of a nice respectable class? Do I consider her a *really* good cook, hygienic and economical? Does she take a *real* interest in keeping down expenses? Is she particularly good at nourishing soups? Can she bake well? Is she capable of sending up a good dinner for eight or ten people at short notice? Has she any men friends? As such are not allowed to enter Kent lady's establishment — women friends are allowed in strict moderation. Can she keep order in the kitchen without unpleasantness, etc., etc.?

Feel that the Kent lady really requires an angel straight from heaven to fulfil her requirements — recollections of Alice Bowles point to the conclusion that she falls far short of this; decide that I must try to write a reference which, while being mainly true, will yet not blight disastrously all chances of her getting the situation.

Find the task beyond my powers as my recollections of Alice are distinctly hazy, and include watery stews, and interminable rows in the kitchen. Ask Tim in desperation whether *he* remembers her, to which he replies, "By Jove yes — she tried to get off with Bollings, didn't she? Or was she the one who cleaned my new brown shoes with black boot polish?"

Leave the letter to be answered at leisure as I have an appointment with the dentist, made several days ago when my tooth was rather troublesome.

Today it is perfectly well and the moment I see the dentist's chair I know that I have been a fool to come. Is it too late to escape? Shall I feign a sudden indisposition?

Mr. Hood smiles at me encouragingly, and I climb into the chair only because I am too much of a coward to run away. The window in front of me looks out into a small garden where Mr. Hood's pyjamas and Mrs. Hood's stockings are tossing gaily in the breeze. There are also some small garments which obviously belong to several sizes of little Hoods. Beyond this cheerful scene is a street — an errand boy passes on his bicycle whistling gaily. Reflect on the cheerfulness of errand boys. What a happy life they lead! Am overwhelmed with self-pity.

Mr. Hood seizes an instrument like a deformed buttonhook, inserts it into a long metal holder to give him more purchase and plunges it unerringly into the heart of my hollowest tooth. I can feel the point sticking into my spine — my scalp rises — "This will have to come out," says Mr. Hood cheerfully.

An hour — or is it a year — later, I emerge into the street with tottering steps.

March

Third March

Tim announces at teatime that he quite forgot to tell me that Ledgard is coming to dinner, but he supposes it will be all right. Reply in the affirmative with more confidence than I feel, and rush to the kitchen to see what can be done about it. Katie says she will put some curry in the rabbit, but there's no soup and it is the half day. Annie says there is only one apple and a few nuts for dessert.

Send Miss Hardcastle and Betty round to Grace McDougall with SOS message asking if she can lend me a tin of soup and some fruit for dessert, also a bottle of soda water as I know that Captain Ledgard drinks whisky. Tell Katie to make an omelet and remind her about coffee (which Tim and I never take at night as it is supposed to keep us from sleeping). Look through table napkins with Annie and find one for our guest without too many thin places and darns. Revive the flowers (which are slightly jaded) by cutting the stalks and putting an aspirin tablet in the water. Send Bollings down to the station for two packets of cigarettes.

Tim follows me about saying that he doesn't know why on earth I always make a fuss when he asks a feller in to dinner. Ledgard is only a bachelor and can easily take potluck. He only asked the chap because he felt

129

sorry for him having to eat the food in mess. And do I think Ledgard is likely to notice the flowers? Reply that bachelors notice more than you think, and try to make it sound as mysterious as possible to keep Tim quiet.

Miss H. and Betty return from their foraging party with a tin of tomato soup, four apples, three bananas, and half a siphon of soda water. Feel that Grace is indeed a noble character.

It is now seven o'clock so I rush upstairs to change. Come down to find the drawing-room fire nearly dead. Revive it with sticks and paraffin because Annie is busy laying the table.

Annie comes in to say that Bollings was polishing the glasses and a tumbler "slipped out of his hand" so will I have a kitchen tumbler as there's only two dining room ones left. Reply that I will have *no* tumblers, only wine glasses. Rush up to the bathroom to wash my hands which is very necessary after my struggles with the fire. Am just washing my hands, and reflecting that the evening has started stickily when I hear Captain Ledgard arrive and Tim asking in hospitable tones if he would like a wash. Rokesby only boasts one lavatory so I am trapped and have to lie low while Tim rattles the door handle and says angrily that there is evidently someone there.

At dinner the conversation turns inevitably on to the Regiment; Tim saying that Hardford will never get command because he was Stellenbosched at Gallipoli. Captain Ledgard says Hardford *will* get command because his sister's husband has got a job at the War House, and anyway everybody has forgotten all about the war now. Look at Threadmorton of the 12th who commanded a brigade for eight months and they have brought in a feller from the Midshires to command his battalion. As if a chap who commanded a brigade in the war couldn't command his own battalion in peacetime!

Tim says he wonders if Morley will retire, as if so Lester will get the foreign battalion and Stoddart the home battalion, but if Morley doesn't retire —

Ledgard says it is just touch and go whether *he* ever gets command at all before being superannuated. Whereupon Tim says, "My dear chap don't be so pessimistic. Crighton's bound to go, and Watt will never get command and McPherson is frightfully bad with malaria at Julaparajapore." And Ledgard says gloomily, "Not so bad as you think, and he hasn't a bob to his name so he's bound to go on as long as he can stick it."

Then Tim says, "What about Carruthers?"

And Captain Ledgard says, "*What* about him?"

And Tim says hasn't Ledgard heard that Carruthers' rich uncle has gone west at last and left Carruthers all his money?

And Captain Ledgard says, "No, by Jove! Has he really? That's the best news I've heard for a long time. Perhaps he will get married now, he's a perfect nuisance in mess."

And Tim says, "Perhaps he will retire?"

I leave them hard at it and run upstairs to say "Good night" to Betty (who wants to know what we had for dinner) and to have a little chat with Miss Hardcastle (who is obviously gloating over a letter from her young man) and then down to the drawing room where I have

131

time to write a letter to Bryan before Tim and Captain Ledgard appear.

After that I sit and listen while Tim and Captain L. discuss the musketry returns and fulminate on the degeneracy of the last batch of recruits from the dépôt, and digress from that to comment bitterly on the incompetency of the new R.S.M.

Then Tim says that Benson is nothing but an old woman, and if it were not for Morley the battalion would go to pot. And Ledgard replies that Morley isn't much better and he's got far too much money anyway. And Carruthers is the worst P.M.C. they've ever had. He wonders that they have not all been poisoned long ago. And as for the new subalterns they are beyond words. They think of nothing but girls and cinemas.

Tim agrees wholeheartedly and says that in *his* time subalterns were kept in their place, but now they seem to think the mess Belongs to them.

At last Captain Ledgard says he really must go as he is captain of the week and has to go round the guards, and that's what comes of being a wretched bachelor and living in mess. And he does not know what on earth we ladies are thinking of not to have found him a wife before now.

Whereupon Tim pokes him in the ribs and says he doesn't know when he's well off "with his huntin' and shootin' and sprees in town — what what!" And if he were married and had to fork out to butchers and bakers and candlestick makers every week, all that would cease. So he had better think twice about it. And

132

they repair to the dining room to have a "wee deoch an doruis," and remain there talking for another hour.

After which Tim comes up to bed, yawning, and saying that he can't think what has come over Ledgard. He used to be quite amusing, but he is degenerating into an absolute bore. Tim supposes it is living in mess. He (Tim) would rather be dead than live in mess — and did I notice the feller hadn't even the common politeness to open the door for me.

Fifth March

Visit Miss Edgar's china shop to replace breakages at Rokesby. Miss Edgar is the largest woman I have ever seen, but full of good humour as fat people often are. (Query — Does fat beget amiability or amiability fat?)

"I wouldn't have no small spry people about my shop, it's them as does the breakages," Miss Edgar says, as she oozes in and out of the piled-up china like an immense boa constrictor. "It's them with their whiskings here and whiskings there — give me a fat person as moves slow. And which house is it to be now, if I may make so bold?" she asks, for we are old friends and she takes a motherly interest in the everlasting flittings of her army clientèle.

I tell her we are leaving Biddington altogether this time and going to Westburgh in Scotland, whereupon she raises her hands in consternation, and says, "Dear me, dear me! And you so bright!" As if I had informed her of my early demise.

Meet Mrs. Benson on the way home; she is coming to see me to lend me a "Little book" which is so wonderful — she knowa it will help me to bring up the dear children. I accept it with gratitude and spend the afternoon studying its pages.

According to this book I have been sowing the seeds of complexes and cultivating inhibitions in Bryan and Betty ever since they were a few months old. Feel much worried about this, but decide that it is too late now to do anything, and that Bryan and Betty must just take their chance.

Tenth March

Spend the morning writing to grocer, milkman, butcher, etc. at Kiltwinkle. (Having obtained their names from Mrs. Mackenzie.) Also write to new cook pointing out that as the 13th March appears to be a Sunday I shall expect her on Monday morning. Suggest to Tim that he should go North on Saturday and take over the house from the Mackenzies, and that Betty and I follow with luggage on the Monday. Tim overjoyed to find an excuse not to travel with baggage consents after half-hearted expostulations.

Annie and I pack several hampers to be sent in advance.

Memo. —
    Pay Smith.
    Engage seats in train and cart to station on Monday.
    Two wooden packing cases for books (ask Bollings).

134

Ask Grace to take Mothers' Meeting tomorrow.

Speak to Mrs. Benson about Clarke's thin baby.

Tim's boots to be fetched from Compton's.

Packing paper. Rope for boxes.

Katie's insurance card (stamps).

See Mr. Brown at Bank about drawing money at Westburgh.

Post office about forwarding letters.

Counter-order milk, bread, papers, and weekly order at   Maypole.

Close account at library.

Arrange laundry to post washing to Kiltwinkle.

Eleventh March

Start packing in real earnest. Bollings has procured two splendid packing cases for books — also hay. (Better not enquire where). Tim says when we retire we shall have Bollings as a butler and handyman. Useful to have someone good at packing. I point out that when we retire we shall settle down and shall not need anyone good at packing. This starts us off on the inexhaustible theme of when we retire and settle down. Am transported on rosy dreams to the day when the War Office will cease to trouble and the pea crab be at rest.

Annie rushes in to say that the inventory man has arrived and has started on the drawing room, and do I know where we have put an "accidental" table with brass flower pot and aspidistra which ought to stand in the window. My thoughts are immediately snatched

135

back to real life just as Aunt Ethel's pince-nez are snatched back to concealment under the folds of her real lace jabot by the hidden spring to which they are attached. Reply hastily that the occasional table is beside my bed and the brass flower pot on the hall table, but that the aspidistra has gone the way of all flesh. Tim says (with a strange flash of insight) that he supposes I forgot to water it, and that he can't think why I forget things like that when I have absolutely nothing to do all day long, and that we shall probably have to pay for the aspidistra now. He hurries out to see what can be done about it.

Bollings who is packing books in the hall approaches me in a mysterious manner, and says that he knows where he can get an aspidistra for a bob — and shall he? Reply by giving him the bob.

On entering the drawing room after lunch we find the occasional table in the window complete with brass flower pot and flourishing aspidistra. Tim asks why I made such a fuss about the thing when it was there all the time.

Twelfth March

Tim goes off to Westburgh with suitcase and hatbox — he points out that it is much better for him to "travel light" as *we* shall need a lorry *anyway*, and he can carry his suitcase and so save taxi in London, but he will take his hatbox with him as he knows that if he does not do so I will put my best hat in on the top of his silk hat. Feel that this is unjust as it did his silk hat no harm, and, anyway, I ironed it for him afterwards. Telegram arrives later from Crewe to say he has left his spectacles in the drawer of his writing table. Find spectacles down the back of drawing-room sofa and post them to Brown's Hotel. Send off prepaid wire to Brown's Hotel to ask if he has arrived safely.

Annie and I pack all possible luggage to be sent in advance which leaves me with an inconvenient minimum of spoons and forks and personal attire.

Grace comes in to ask if she can "do anything," and insists that Betty and I shall lunch at Fairlawn tomorrow. Am thankful to sit down and talk to Grace for half an hour as my legs ache so from running up and down stairs that I could weep. Grace says that Mrs. Benson was quite impossible at the Mothers' Welfare Meeting. She is narrow-minded and vindictive and has no soul. It is a great pity that a woman of that type should be in the position of C.O.'s wife as it creates bad feeling in the regiment, but anyway, she has no influence at all in the regiment because everyone sees through her. Grace has made up her mind not to think about the woman any more as she is not worth a moment's thought, and she has been worrying about it ever since Thursday.

Am irresistibly reminded of Mrs. Palmer's fulminations on the egregious Willoughby, but realise that Grace is too upset to see the humour of it so content myself with making soothing noises.

Annie appears and says breathlessly, "The Railway has come," and do I know where the rod and padlock of the linen hamper has gone to. Reply from bitter experience that it is probably at the bottom of the linen hamper which is now packed. Grace helps me to unpack and repack hamper while "The Railway" waits at the door, and is regaled with cigarettes and facetious conversation by the indispensable Annie.

Spend the rest of the day hanging up clean curtains in all the windows and patching up the wall in the night nursery where Betty has relieved the tedium of a sleepless hour by picking a hole in the wallpaper beside her bed.

Bollings comes, just as I am finishing the job by touching up the roses with Bryan's paintbox, and is kind enough to say that I have made "a real neat job of it and nobody would ever know unless they was to look close."

Telegram arrives from Tim to say "Survived frightful dangers safely." — I knew he would be annoyed with me for wiring, but am glad I did so all the same.

Go to bed early — tired out.

Fourteenth March

We leave Rokesby very early — it is quite dark. Am too busy to feel sad, but am conscious of the knowledge that if I were not so busy I *would* feel *very* sad, as I have been happy in the little house. Annie is full of importance at the prospect of her journey. Katie remains to "hand-over" — we leave her in tears. Miss Hardcastle is to accompany us to London and alternates between artificial gaiety and loud sniffs of woe. Betty is quite unconcerned at leaving, and much interested in all she sees. Reflect that Betty is a true soldier's daughter and quite different from myself when a child — I should have been frightened and miserable at leaving home and friends and venturing into the unknown, whereas Betty enjoys the excitement. (Query — Is army life with its constant uprooting and change of scene good or bad for the young?)

We arrive in London without mishap. Annie who has constituted herself custodian of luggage counts it over from a crumpled list which she holds in her black-gloved hand. I hear her murmuring to the perspiring porter, "Three black trunks, one 'amper, two 'at-boxes" — I leave her to it and run on to engage a couple of taxis, we cross London and catch the Royal Scot with half an hour to spare — half-hour an extremely long and difficult one. Miss Hardcastle stands on the platform sniffing miserably while Betty tears up and down the corridor and exclaims rapturously over all her discoveries. Feel that my child would show to better advantage if she were not so blatant in her rejoicing. Try to sympathise with sorrow and joy at the same time, but feel I am doing neither to advantage. Am thankful when the train starts.

Thankfulness does not last long as Betty is violently sick and continues to be so all day. Annie is kind and helpful. Am glad that Tim is not with us as he has no sympathy with the frailties of the human frame. Do what I can for poor Betty and reflect that everything passes — even a day in the train with a sick child. Probably there are people in England who are finding today so happy that they wish it would last for ever; but how fortunate for Betty and self that it will not last a moment longer than usual!

We are ready to disembark an hour before time of arrival at Westburgh, but even this hour passes, and we draw in to the station and see Tim anxiously scrutinising every window. He has chartered a large car and has brought Cassandra as well, but even this embryo fleet cannot deal with our mountain of luggage. Tim is very scathing about the mountain and remarks with injustice that it is no use ever thinking that I could go to India with all that stuff. Am too weary and miserable to point out that I never intended to take the stuff to India, and that at least a quarter of it is his own personal luggage — uniform being exceedingly bulky and heavy attire.

We pack into Cassandra covered with golf bags, tennis racquets and other small but awkward packages — Annie goes in the hired car with the rest of the luggage. Tim says he took over the house this morning and everything is all right. The Mackenzies' girl is there and cook has arrived with a large wooden box — it took two men to carry it in, and it must obviously be full of coal, or pig iron judging from the weight.

After a quarter of an hour's drive we arrive at Loanhead; the lights are all on and Maggie (the Mackenzies' girl) meets us at the door with a beaming smile which shows up her bad teeth to great disadvantage. Annie seems pleased to find all the usual conveniences in the benighted country to which she has come, and proceeds at once in her new rôle to bath Betty and put her to bed.

140

The gong sounds while I am washing — a most necessary performance as I seem to have gathered the grime and grit of a lifetime on my face and person — it sounds again two minutes later with terrific vigour. Fly downstairs to find cook in the hall beating gong with her own hands, and realise that Tim and I are expected to be in time for meals.

Dinner is exceedingly good.

Unpack as much as is necessary with Annie's help. Annie informs me confidentially that "Cook is a Tartar" — had my suspicions on this point before, but feel depressed at having them confirmed. The beds are comfortable.

Fifteenth March

Interview Cook after breakfast; she receives me with a smile which looks as if it hurt her face, and proceeds to show me the pots and pans, pronouncing them entirely inadequate for a family of our proportions. Agree to write to Mrs. Mackenzie and ask for more. She also asks for a girdle (which seems to be a cooking utensil and not an ornament for the waist as I had previously imagined). Promise to obtain same in Westburgh if obtainable. She suggests a gigot for tomorrow's dinner — agree hastily as I am much too frightened of her to do anything else, but secretly wonder what this can be, and whether Tim will eat it when it appears. Betty is to have "hough soup" as Cook says it is "fine for weans."

Having arranged about food, Cook volunteers the information that "Maggie is no' sae bad," which cheers me unduly, but I am plunged back in gloom when she follows this up by remarking that she "can't make oot the half of what yon Annie says with her fancy talk."

As I rise to go I am shown a scrubbing brush and broom, both in the last stages of dissolution, and asked indignantly "how a body is to keep her places clean with such-like trash."

Go upstairs convinced that there are possibilities of volcanic disturbances in my new ménage.

Seventeenth March

Note arrives from a certain Mrs. Porter asking me to excuse the formality of a call and come to luncheon with her on Wednesday 23rd March at 1:30p.m. My acceptance of her invitation will cause her untold pleasure. Can't imagine who she is nor how she knows my name. Tim says I had better go, as we must not get the name of being "stand-offish," and, anyway, they may be useful people to know. He asks where the Porters "hang out" and, on being informed, remarks that Lauderdale Square is the "oofiest part of Westburgh." I reply to the note, with an enthusiasm I am far from feeling, that I am *delighted* to accept and it is *so* kind of her to ask me.

Tim takes me to Westburgh in Cassandra and we buy brushes for cook, also a girdle (which appears to be a large iron plate with a handle over the top). The assistant in the shop says it is for bannocks — which leaves me as wise as I was before.

Nineteenth March

On returning from my daily pilgrimage to the village I am informed that a lady has called and is waiting to see me in the drawing room. Annie thinks she said her name was Mrs. Loudon, and, anyway, she is the lady from "Holmgarth" next door, because Annie was in the garden hanging up my stockings on the rope and saw the lady walk out of the next house and in at our gate.

Rush upstairs and find my visitor seated in a straight-backed chair. She is all in black and wears pince-nez and button boots, and has rather an alarming appearance until she smiles. Express great contrition for lack of fire. Mrs. Loudon says the room is warm enough and she has called for me because her son is in the navy. She evidently sees that her words have puzzled me because she explains that if her son went to a strange place she would like the neighbors to call for *him*. Am still somewhat at sea, but reply that I am very pleased to see her, which seems safe. We talk of various matters and discover to our mutual surprise and satisfaction that her son is in the same ship as my cousin, Harold Fotheringay. Am wondering all the time whether she wants me to go out with her as her words seem to imply, but finally decide that this is just an ordinary call. Mrs. Loudon says that neighbours should be neighbourly — but in Westburgh and its environs this is not always possible; for, unless people are the same sort of people as yourself, you can have little in common with them and they don't want you, what's more. It was very different in the country (she used to

143

live in Ayrshire) — it was a recognised thing to call for a newcomer, but things are changed now. "And here am I singing the Old Folk's Litany already," she adds with a twinkle in her eye, "and you'll be thinking Mrs. Loudon is like the other folks and a bit of a nuisance forbye. But it *does* seem to me that the people I used to know were more human and wise-like. There was surely less struggle for money and less running after the great ones — who aren't so very great after all's said and done. There was less vulgarity and we were content with simpler pleasures."

Mrs. Loudon interests me, I have never met anyone like her before. I like her downright manner and her trenchant Scots tongue. Even at this stage of affairs I feel she may be a friend worth having. I suggest (more to see what she will say than because I disagree with her criticisms of modern life) that even in Jane Austen's day there were those who ran after the so-called great.

Her eyes light up with humour — "My dear," she says, "you're laughing at me now, and it's not seemly to laugh at an old done woman, but I'll forgive you it all, if you know your Jane — Come and see me some day at teatime," she adds as she rises to go. "I've a cook who loves nothing better than to bake and it would be a kindness to come and eat some teabread. I've outgrown my sweet tooth now, much to Mary's sorrow. We'll have a crack about Jane, and whether the old days or the new days are better."

She takes my hand in a firm clasp and departs without further delay, and I count this an additional merit to Mrs. Loudon, for there is nothing so annoying to me as a long-drawn-out departure.

Twenty-first March

Visit Hillcrest School which I have been told is an excellent scholastic establishment for young children. The headmistress interviews me in a small, office-like apartment and puts me through a searching examination as to Betty's attainments. I answer as best I can and tell her that Miss Hardcastle found Betty very quick.

"Quickness is more often than not a sign of a superficial brain," says Miss McCarthy severely.

I relapse into a species of jelly, but still have sufficient strength to say that I think she will find Betty is a good child and very reasonable.

"They're all good here — they have to be," says Miss McCarthy. "The child seems backward, but what can you expect, living in England. We'll bring her up to the standard, but she'll have to work."

I murmur faintly that Betty is very young, but Miss McCarthy treats this excuse with contempt, and decrees that Betty is to start on Thursday, "and not waste any more precious time." She hands me a printed list of the school uniform, and bows me to the door — I emerge from the interview completely disillusioned as to my adequacy as a parent.

The more I reflect upon this interview, the more curious it seems to me that I should have sat there so meekly and allowed myself to be browbeaten by the woman. Her strong mental dominance has probably been engendered by years of teaching school (as the Americans say). I can't imagine any child having the moral strength to be naughty anywhere near Miss McCarthy, and I wonder whether this is altogether desirable. If her dread presence keeps them good, what chance is there for the development of their own self-control, and what happens when they emerge from her influence? Tim says I am mad, and if she can manage the little devils without a whip he takes off his hat to her.

Twenty-third March

I am late in arriving for the luncheon, having got hopelessly lost amongst a perfect jungle of terraces and crescents and squares of enormous and affluent-looking houses. Am shown into a large room full of large women, none of whom I have ever seen before — hostess identified by absence of hat. We proceed downstairs to lunch (I mean luncheon), all talking intimately and animatedly about Hilda and Carrie and Isabel and dear Guthrie, and other well-known people of whom I have never heard. Am so dazed and embarrassed by my late arrival and friendless condition that I sit down in the seat nearest me and have to be removed to make way for a lady with a beard and an ostrich feather in her hat. (Feel untold sympathy for the unfortunate person in the Bible who sat down in the wrong seat and was asked to make way for a more important guest.)

Try to make conversation with my right-hand neighbour without any result. Discover that my right-hand neighbour is stone deaf in her left ear.

Find myself partaking of grapefruit, which always gives me a violent headache, but feel that I cannot draw attention to myself by refusing it. Left-hand neighbour turns to me and remarks, "I am always so sorry for army people — so dreadful to be moved away from a place when you are fond of it." Reply that there is some consolation in the fact that you are also moved away from places you are not fond of.

L.H.N. evidently thinks she has performed her duty to me, and resumes an interesting conversation with *her* L.H.N. about Alistair's appendix.

Luncheon is long and rich — I cease to marvel at the size of everybody, but am considerably impressed by the fact that sixteen plates all to match can be produced for every course.

We return to the drawing room, where we partake of coffee. Several people ask me how I like Westburgh, and add that it must be such a delightful change for me — smile and nod. Hostess comes over to me and asks if I have been in Scotland before, and adds that it must be delightful to visit Scotland for the first time. Reply that I was born in Eastburgh, but find this is not to my credit.

I am introduced to a woman whose name sounds like "Miss Horse." She asks me if I hunt. Reply in a moment of idiocy, "Only for servants." Miss Horse — if that is really her name, which scarcely seems possible — takes no notice of my levity and says I really ought to hunt, as it's the only sport worth talking about and I should think seriously of taking it up while I am in Westburgh — adds that she can't think how I am going to fill in my time unless I hunt at least three days a week. Promise to think about it — which is perfectly safe.

Miss Horse then says can I guess what her shoeing bill is for six months. This seems an extraordinary question to me, and after a glance at her extremely expensive-looking lizard-shod feet I evade the issue by saying, "They *are* expensive nowadays, aren't they? Especially if you do much dancing."

A diversion is caused by entrance of host, who is greeted rapturously as "William" by fourteen female guests. He is quite unmoved by either joy or embarrassment. He is introduced to me, and says, in a deep voice without moving his lips, "You bin Ittly? We jus' got back Ittly. Beastly hawt!" Reply that I have been to Venice. (It was on the occasion of our honeymoon, but I hope that he will imagine it was quite recently.) He replies, "We bin Venice too. Beastly hawt. Smelly place, Venice."

Miss Horse murmurs to me that "William is so English."

Host is smoking an excellent cigarette — it smells like a Sobrani (which is my favourite brand). Realise that the smell of the Sobrani is all I am to get, and take my departure in the wake of Miss Horse. Host accompanies us downstairs, and I hear him saying to her (as I am searching for my umbrella amongst those of the other guests), "You bin Ittly? We jus' got back Ittly — beastly hawt."

Twenty-fourth March

After breakfast Betty appears, all ready to start for school. I have promised to take her and see her settled in, so I rush for my hat, waterproof, and faithful umbrella, and we set off together in torrents of rain. Tim accompanies us to the gate, giving jocular advice to Betty as to her behaviour in school towards teachers and fellow scholars. Try to point out to Betty as we walk up the hill that of course it is "Only Daddy's fun," and she must be very good and quiet and do all she is told; to which Betty replies gaily, "Oh yes, I never take any notice of what he says." Feel that this is not quite the lesson I intended to impart, but am powerless to put my meaning into words.

The moment we enter the school Betty rushes up to an unknown child with red hair and says, "What's your name? Mine's Betty," and is immediately absorbed into a group of children all about her own size and all dressed alike in regulation navy gym tunic and cream silk blouse.

I stand about in the passage for a few minutes, jostled by everybody who passes, until — as Betty takes no further notice of me — I decide to go home.

On the way home I reflect — not for the first time — on the strange difference between Betty and myself when a child. My first day at school was torture — I was so shy and miserable that I could scarcely answer rationally when spoken to. There was a huge lump in my throat, and I nearly fainted with sheer fright when any of the mistresses looked in my direction. No fond but misguided parent accompanied me to my doom — perhaps this was just as well, as I should probably have disgraced myself with tears. How fortunate is Betty, with her modern, unselfconscious attitude to life. The world is her oyster, and she goes forward eagerly to open it. Is this because her upbringing has been different — because she has not been kept in the dark, relegated to the nursery, and told that she should be seen and not heard? Will she continue to face the world full of confidence and security, or will her first serious snub shrivel up the untried plant of her self-assurance? What kind of men and women will result from this postwar generation of childhood?

Twenty-sixth March

Receive a letter from Bryan which says, "Dear Mum, Could you possibly send me half a crown? I got swished [caned] on Wednesday for cheeking Codfish. We went to the village on Tuesday, and I bought chocolate cigarets when the master wasn't looking, but I had to give Dennison some because he saw me. We had rugger on Saturday and Villiers kicked me on the shin; he said it was not on purposs but it looked like it. Love from Bryan."

Decide *not* to show letter to Tim as I know that Tim will merely say *he* never got more than five shillings per term when he was Bryan's age, and would have been

150

ashamed to ask his parents for more. This will lead to the usual argument as to the purchasing power of five bob then and now. Tim will not approve of the spelling, nor of cheeking Codfish (whoever he may be), nor of the clandestine purchase of chocolate cigarettes, and will end by forbidding me to send the money. This would be a pity, as I always feel uncomfortable when I do things forbidden by Tim. (A relic of Victorianism, I suppose.)

Grace has an extraordinary theory, which she has propounded to me more than once, that anyone born in Victoria's reign is bound to have the seeds of Victorian complexes dormant in their subconscious mind. The truth being, of course, that the atmosphere of hypocrisy lay like a miasma on the land, infecting the youngest children with its poisonous breath.

Must try this on Mrs. Loudon, and see how she reacts to it.

Twenty-eighth March

Decide to call on Mrs. Loudon this afternoon. Put on my best hat and sally forth. Am absurdly disappointed when informed by the neat maid that "Mrs. Loudon is out, and she'll be awful sorry to miss you, I'm sure." Leave cards, and return to Loanhead.

As I open my front gate a small boy rushes out, nearly knocking me over, and two other children vanish into the shrubbery. I call out to know what this invasion means, and Betty appears, looking very hot and dirty and dishevelled. "Oh, they're just Sandy and Ian and

151

Marion," she says rather breathlessly. "They've come to play in my garden because it's bigger than their garden, and you see you must have a big garden for hide-and-seek."

I point out to Betty that it is usual to have your parent's permission before asking children to tea.

"Oh, but I told them they couldn't stay to tea," replies Betty consolingly, "and they said it didn't matter. They don't have their tea till six o'clock, so they can sit and watch me have mine. I don't take long over it."

This arrangement seems to me the height of inhospitality — I find it impossible to enjoy my tea with three pairs of bright eyes watching every mouthful. At last, in desperation, I ask them if they would like some tea — they assent unanimously, and fall to as if they were starving. I discover that their manners are atrocious and their speech incomprehensible — the more so as they usually choose to take part in the conversation when their mouths are full of cake. Decide to speak seriously to Betty about her unfortunate choice of friends.

After tea they all go out in the garden and make as much noise as ten ordinary children. Betty comes in at six o'clock with a crimson face, and says she is boiling and it was lovely. She adds that she suggested to her guests that they should come in and say goodbye to me, but they said they "wouldn't fash." Point out to Betty that they are not very nice-mannered children, to which she replies, "No, but Sandy can run awfully fast — faster than Bryan, I should think."

I then ask what their names are, and Betty says, "Oh, just Sandy and Ian and Marion — I don't know their other names. They're all in my class except Marion, and she's awfully stupid." Try to find out from Betty if there are any other children in her class who might be more orderly in their behavior, but Betty says they are all the same — only Sandy and Ian are the most fun, and they won't come without Marion, so Betty had to have her too.

Am obliged to leave it at that, although I feel somewhat worried about the matter. It seems strange not to know the children's parents. Tim — when approached — is very unhelpful, and says, "When in Rome do as the Romans do," adding that the Romans of Westburgh do queer things sometimes, and I need not think I am the only one to have to put up with their vagaries.

Thirtieth March

Find a telegram on the hall table — it is from Grace, and says tersely, "Can you have me weekend?" Immediately feel ten years younger, and send a joyful affirmative.

Rush upstairs to spare room (which is to be Bryan's in the holidays). This room has been used as a dump for unwanted furniture from all over the house and contains rickety tables, a plant stand made of painted pottery, china vases of all shapes and sizes, several very uneasy chairs, and two life-sized photographs of Mr.

153

and Mrs. Mackenzie in which a hairy mole upon the latter's chin is realistically portrayed.

Annie finds me gazing hopelessly upon the collection. She grasps the situation at once, and says comfortingly that we will easily find somewhere to put them. Suggest that we should restore them to their original places all over the house (as I feel they will not look so dreadful if they are distributed evenly over a large surface), but Annie says she doesn't think the captain would stand it, he *did* say as how the pore lady's photygraph gave him the shudders. Don't I think it would be better to wrap them in newspaper and put them on the top of the wardrobe? I do think so, and Annie goes away to find paper and the steps.

We spend the morning hiding the atrocities. Find it necessary to explain to Maggie (who probably admires them) that I am *so* afraid of them getting knocked over and broken by Betty. But realise that this scarcely accounts for the removal of the photographs from the dining room walls or for the segregation of the uneasy chairs.

April

First April

Morning slightly disorganised owing to Betty's fertile imagination given free rein in the matter of practical jokes. Find the toes of my shoes stuffed with paper, and while I am removing same, I can hear Tim anathematising his daughter in the bathroom.

The key of the garage is missing from its usual hook, and Tim accuses Betty of hiding it, an imputation which she hotly denies. Tim says he would not be surprised if she *had* taken it, as it is just about on a par with putting salt in his shaving water. He could not think why the damned stuff wouldn't lather. Betty points out that that was just the joke — and Annie thought it was awfully funny. Tim says his idea of a joke and Annie's are entirely different.

At this psychological moment Annie appears with the garage key, which she found in the pocket of Tim's other suit.

Tim then changes the subject by saying why don't I go for a walk this morning — I don't take nearly enough exercise. Reply that I *would* go for a walk if I had anyone to go for a walk *with*; but it is dull going for a walk by yourself without an object. Time says we had better get a dog — and drives off to his work.

After he has gone and Betty has departed cheerfully to school, I decide that I might do worse than go for a walk, so I perambulate Kiltwinkle, solemnly, for about an hour, and do not feel much the better for it.

Look forward all day to Grace's arrival, which takes place before dinner. She looks tired after her journey, but seems unnaturally gay and talkative. (Query — Is this because I have been leading such a quiet life and have heard nobody talk for so long?)

Tim and I both hang on her words and drink in all the news of Biddington with avidity. Feel as if it were years since we left. Grace says that Mamie Carter's baby has arrived and is exceedingly large and fat and pink — (more like a pig than a human being, Grace thinks). The Nurse and ex-baby stayed with Grace for three days, and the nurse is an absolute fiend. Tim asks tenderly after the regiment, and is told comfortingly that it is going to pot. Mrs. Benson has the old man under her thumb, and everybody hates her, down to the last joined recruit, and Alec Watt is the worst adjutant we've ever had — everybody says so. Of course if Major Morley sends in his papers, as there is some talk of his doing owing to Sir Abraham being afflicted with that new and mysterious complaint known as blood pressure, Alec Watt will get his majority.

Tim says, "By Jove, is he really going? Poor Old Sir Abraham — and I'm next on the list of promotion. What a lark!"

During this talk I notice that Jack's name has scarcely been mentioned, whereas usually it is never off Grace's lips, and I wonder whether anything has happened. Has Grace been flirting with the colonel again — or perhaps somebody more dangerous? Or has Jack — but it is no use wondering, I shall probably hear all about it sooner or later.

Tim goes off to drill his territorials after dinner, and Grace and I settle down by the fire for a "good talk" — (self accompanied by a bulging basket of socks and stockings full of holes and ladders to be renovated — how I hate the job!). Grace remains silent for quite two minutes which confirms me in my suspicion that something is wrong.

Presently Grace says — as if propounding some new and intensely original idea — have I ever noticed how awfully selfish men are? I stifle an impulse to ask what Jack has been up to, and reply that I *have* noticed it once or twice. Grace says it is simply incredible to her and she absolutely can't believe it — she never would have thought it possible Jack could be like that. Feel the time has now arrived to ask what Jack has been up to, and do so in appropriate words. Grace says I can have no conception of the selfishness of Jack, and even if she were to tell me I would not believe her. She elaborates the theme for several minutes which brings her to the verge of tears.

At length I gather from Grace's fulminations that she has not been feeling at all well, and Jack suggested that it was biliousness and advised exercise and Kruschen Salts. Then he went off to play golf taking the car, although he knew perfectly well that Grace had promised to go to tea at Mamie Carter's and inspect the new baby. When taxed with this Jack said the walk would do Grace good. Grace was so tired when she returned from Mamie's that she went straight to bed — but this was not all by any means. When Jack returned from golf he brought a man — a strange man that Grace had never seen in her life — and Jack came upstairs and tried to persuade Grace to come down to dinner and entertain the man. Grace refused — and don't I think she had a perfect right to refuse when her head was splitting, all through Jack's selfishness? So then Jack and the man had dinner together and talked and laughed the whole evening in the drawing room, which, as I know, is just underneath Grace's bedroom — and I know also how thin the floors are at Fairlawn — How would I like to be in bed with a frightful headache and hear all that noise going on for hours?

Reply truthfully that I would not like it at all.

Grace then says don't I think she was perfectly justified in giving Jack a good fright?

Have an absurd vision of Grace bouncing out on Jack from behind a curtain, but realise immediately that of course it can't be that kind of fright — sometimes I wish my sense of humour did not run away with me in this ridiculous fashion. Grace continues (fortunately without noticing my internal struggles) that it will serve Jack right to be anxious about her for a few days, and she wonders whether he has rung up her mother yet, and discovered she is not there, and she wonders also what he is doing now, and whether he is wondering where she is.

From this I gather that Jack has not been told of Grace's visit to Westburgh, and I become alarmed. I visualise myself and Tim in a similar situation and my alarm increases. All desire to laugh has left me. I am appalled. It seems to me, as I try to consider the whole matter from a strictly impartial viewpoint, that Jack has not been guilty of more than ordinary male density and perversity. He had asked the wretched man home to dinner and could hardly turn him out in the street unfed. He was also bound by the laws of hospitality (which mean considerably more to men than they do to women) to entertain the man as best he could in the absence of his wife. But it is no use putting this sane view of the matter before Grace in her present condition — Grace has only been married for a few months, whereas I have been married for twelve years. In twelve years one becomes inured to suggestions of exercise and Kruschen Salts, and even to laughter and talk in the presence of a headache. But what on earth am I to do with Grace? What on earth am I to say to her? I am so fond of them both that I must make things right somehow or other.

I look at Grace as she sits huddled in her chair, miserable and dejected. She certainly looks far from well — there is a pinched look about her — of course she has had a long journey, but that would scarcely account for it — she was always so strong and full of vitality. A sudden idea strikes me, and I look at Grace again — can it be that? I remember how I felt before Bryan arrived upon the scene — ill and wretched and ready to take offence at the slightest provocation — and my suspicion grows into a certainty. How will this affect the situation?

161

Grace is at first incredulous of my suggestion, but after a few searching questions I convince her that I am right.

"Oh!" she says with eyes like saucers. "Oh, Hester, how wonderful! Oh Hester, is it too late to wire to Jack tonight? Can I get a train home tomorrow? Oh, Hester!"

It is much too late to wire to Jack, and I absolutely refuse to allow her to travel home tomorrow after the long and tiring journey today; but we can wire to Jack tomorrow, and Grace can travel on Monday if she likes. So overwhelmed is she with her new responsibility that she agrees like a lamb to all my suggestions, merely saying, with a sigh, that she does not know how on earth she will manage to exist until Monday without seeing Jack. Feel this is somewhat ungrateful on Grace's part, but am thankful she seems to have forgotten all about Jack's delinquencies.

Second April

Two wires are sent off to Jack. That from Grace is long and intimate and obscure, mine merely says, "*Grace well. Will expect you first possible train.*"

Tim wants to know what on earth it is all about and why on earth Grace has come all the way to Westburgh to tell me she is going to have a baby, when a letter would have done equally well. Fortunately, Grace is staying in bed for breakfast, so Tim's indignation can be worked off thoroughly before he meets his guest. Tim goes on to say Grace is neurotic — that's what it is, and it will be a good thing for her to have children. Women with children have no time to be neurotic — Tim hopes that Grace will have twins.

Telegraph boys besiege Loanhead all the morning, Grace's wire having completely mystified her adoring husband. Am thankful Tim has gone to his headquarters, as he abhors telegrams, considering them an invention of the Evil One for wasting money. Make three separate pilgrimages to the post office to send off telegrams for Grace, as the contents are such I am ashamed to let the servants see them nor have I the face to read them over the telephone to unsympathetic operator. On the third occasion an unworthy wish invades my being — namely, that I had allowed Grace to return to Biddington today.

Mrs. Loudon is raking her path when I return from my third journey. She is attired for gardening in an exceedingly ancient naval burberry (which probably in the dim ages belonged to her son), and a black straw hat, with a large hole in the crown; but in spite of her peculiar turn-out she still manages to look a perfect lady (this is a much abused term, but I can think of no other to describe her natural dignity).

"Mrs. Christie," she says, coming to the gate rake in hand, "pardon an old woman for being inquisitive, but I've been wondering all the morning if there's anything wrong. Yon telegraph laddies always give me the shudders — I've not been able to stand the sight of them since the war, and there have been three on your doorstep already — and gracious me, here's another!"

163

she exclaims, as a red bicycle comes flying up the road to stop at Loanhead gate.

The whole thing is so ridiculous that I start to laugh weakly, and find to my horror that I can't stop. I am seized by the arm in a firm grip, and dragged into the dining room at Holmgarth, where I am planted in a chair with a glass of cherry brandy before me.

"Drink it up like a good lassie," says Mrs. Loudon, patting my shoulder as if I were a child. "There now, you're feeling better, but don't tell me a word about it unless you want."

Of course, I tell her the whole thing — it is such a relief to get it off my chest, and Mrs. Loudon is a good listener.

"Well, well!" she says comfortingly, "We were all young once — and when the baby's safely here she'll have no time for such like cantrips. Well, well! And me thinking there had been a death in the family at least!"

Third April

Holiday today — which means that I have not got to see Cook. I rise joyfully and bathe with song. Tim says I seem in good fettle this morning — Curious how seldom Tim and I are in good fettle at the same moment. Tim says we ought to go to the Parish Church, which is Presbyterian, of course, and repeats his favourite maxim about doing what the Romans do. Grace is in bed for breakfast, but says she will get up and come too, as she is anxious to see what it is like. I point out that we have no books, but Tim says they don't have prayer books, but just make it up as they go along — Grace says she thinks it is very clever of them.

We impress Grace with the necessity of taking her umbrella (although the sky is cloudless), and join the throng of fashionably attired churchgoers, all of whom seem to be making their way to the Parish Church. I reflect that neither of my companions is attending church with orthodox motives, but perhaps it is better to attend with unorthodox motives than not at all.

The verger (or whatever he is called) informs us in a loud voice that the "place is thrang today because Mister McPhoy is retiring," but finds us three seats in the gallery, from which we can look down upon the Sunday hats of the assembled multitude.

Am surprised at the amount of talking that goes on before the service starts, also at the odour of peppermint and cinnamon that emanates from the congregation, but what astonishes me most is the fact that nobody makes any attempt to kneel down during the prayers. Grace has noticed this peculiarity also, and mentions it to Tim on the way home. He replies that these people are descendants of the Covenanters, who held services on the hillside where it was often too damp to kneel down, and the custom has survived.

After lunch Grace and I break the Sabbath by painting a seat in a secluded corner of the garden. We have nearly finished the job when Annie approaches and says breathlessly that she has been looking everywhere for us as Colonel and Mrs. Walker have called. I realise that this is the colonel of Tim's territorial battalion and his wife upon whom Tim

165

wished me to make a good impression. Grace offers to entertain the Walkers while I remove the ravages of the green paint from my person, she points out that it is not so important for *her* to make a good impression, which of course is true. I advise her, however, to remove green paint from her nose before entering the drawing room. Grace says — Why? The Walkers will merely think a green nose is the latest fashion from London. Have no time to argue with Grace — seize the turpentine bottle and fly upstairs to the bathroom.

When I am at last in a presentable condition, I go into the drawing room and find that Grace's nose is the usual colour — or perhaps slightly more pink — and am glad to think she has taken my advice. Colonel Walker seems quite pleased with my deputy, but Mrs. Walker looks slightly peevish. I confine my attentions to the latter, and talk feverishly about the first thing that comes into my head, which happens to be Epstein's method of sculpture — an article upon the subject having appeared in the morning's papers. The choice is unfortunate, as Mrs. Walker never reads the Sunday papers, and has a confused idea that the sculptor and the inventor of relativity are one and the same man. Feel that the best thing to do is to drop the subject.

At this moment a diversion is created by Betty, who appears at the door with a crimson face and says that the Man Who Lives Next Door has stolen her ball — the new one that I got her at Woolworth's. Suggest that she should say "How do you do?" in the approved manner before explaining herself further. Betty shakes hands rapidly with the visitors and says that she was playing with her ball in the garden, and it went over the fence, and the Man Who Lives Next Door said he wouldn't give it to her because it was Sunday, and will I come at once and tell him he is to. The situation is delicate as I have no idea whether the Walkers share the views of the Man Who Lives Next Door as to the wickedness of playing ball on Sunday, or whether their observance of the Sabbath merely consists of banning newspapers printed on this day of rest. I hedge feebly by suggesting that she should find some more fitting occupation for Sunday afternoon and assure her that she will get her ball tomorrow. "But you never said I wasn't to play with it," she points out, "and I've got to go to school tomorrow. Annie says the man is a thief to keep my ball, and I think so too."

Mrs. Walker's face remains sphinx-like during this exhibition of parental weakness, and I feel sure that any impression she may be receiving is not so good as Tim would wish. Fortunately Betty realises that I will do nothing about her ball, and goes away without any further remarks upon the subject. Soon after, the Walkers depart in a large Armstrong-Siddeley, and Grace and I relapse into chairs thoroughly exhausted by our efforts to be entertaining.

"Hester," says Grace suddenly, "Don't you think Hamish is a nice name? Hamish McDougall sounds well; please remember to tell Jack that I wanted the baby called Hamish."

I suggest mildly that the information would come better from Grace herself, whereupon she replies that she will not be here — she is quite sure she will die —

and will I remember her words when she is gone and be the baby's godmother and help poor Jack to bring it up. "And oh Hester!" she continues, "how lovely it will be when Hamish is grown up and we can go about together — I do hope he will be fair like Jack and awfully good at cricket, and we shall go to Lords and see him play for Eton — I think I shall be sick with fright when he goes in to bat."

Feel it would be tactless to point out that if Grace is dead she won't be able to go to Lords (or at any rate will not be sick, not having a body) — so I merely reply that it is sure to be an anxious moment for her when Hamish goes in to bat, and that I hope his godmother will be asked to join the party on that auspicious occasion.

Jack arrives by the late train. I take him up to Grace's room and shut the door upon their transports of affection and delight at their reunion.

Tim says he is going to bed, and does so. I remain in the dining room to feed the traveller when his ardour shall have abated sufficiently to allow him to partake of sustenance. After about an hour Jack appears with a dazed but rapturous expression, and says Grace is simply wonderful. She has forgiven him and everything is all right. He thinks it shows a most wonderful character to be able to forgive like that — Grace's character is wonderful. I can have no conception — not having lived with Grace — what a wonderful girl she is. So brave, and good, and altogether wonderful.

By this time I am so sleepy I can hardly keep my eyes open. Fortunately Jack is too intent on extolling his wife to notice my smothered yawns. It is one o'clock before I manage to get rid of the man and crawl into bed more dead than alive.

My last thought is one of inhospitable thankfulness that our guests are going away tomorrow.

Fourth April

Our guests announce their intention of going south by the midday train, and of spending tomorrow in London, as Jack wants to buy a hat for Grace. Try to remember whether Tim ever felt he wanted to buy anything for me in London, but cannot recollect any occasion of the sort. Grace breakfasts in bed, waited on hand and foot by her adoring mate.

After Tim has departed Jack attaches himself to me. He is still full of admiration for his wife, and the only way I can shake him off is by visiting the kitchen, whereupon Jack takes the local paper and vanishes into the garden with it. I find him half an hour later reclining upon the garden seat Grace and I painted yesterday. The paint is not yet dry upon the seat, and Jack has the greatest difficulty in tearing himself from its hospitable embrace. "Good Heavens, Hester!" he says, trying to look at his back and failing in the attempt, "how was I to know? Why didn't you put Wet Paint on the beastly thing?" Reply hysterically that I did put wet paint on the beastly thing — Grace and I spent most of Sunday afternoon putting wet paint on the beastly thing.

Jack is too annoyed about his new summer suiting to see the joke. We retire to the bathroom, and Jack removes his trousers (the only ones he has brought with him), while I do my best to clean them with turpentine. The paint comes off remarkably well, but the smell of the turpentine remains. Grace says it is horrible, and requests Jack to sit as far away from her as possible; upon which Jack says she is very unreasonable, and that it is not his fault, and that he does not know what people in the train will think, and Grace replies that anybody with any sense would have seen that the paint was wet.

Fortunately the arrival of the taxi puts a stop to this unprofitable discussion. Grace hugs me and says, "Hester, you really are a brick — don't forget about Hamish and being his godmother, will you?" And our guests depart in an odour of turpentine.

Tim and I go out and try to obliterate the outline of Jack's form from the garden seat, which we find is difficult if not impossible. Tim says it is a tiring thing having visitors in the house unless, of course, your establishment is run on the lines of Charters Towers, in which case you need not see more of them than you want, and he wonders if it is true about Morley sending in his papers.

Fifth April

Am late for breakfast owing to lassitude engendered by the emotional crisis which has taken place in our house. Find Tim in an irritable mood — he has opened by

170

mistake an account of mine from Madame Harcourt at Biddington for a New Evening Dress, which I got at her sale before leaving Biddington on the strength of the myriads of dinners and balls predicted for me at Westburgh by Nora Watt. I have not had the moral courage to confess this extravagance to Tim, and my cowardliness has found me out. Tim says what on earth do I want a new dress for, when my cupboard upstairs is full of perfectly good ones? Couldn't I have got an old one done up if I really need it? Explain hastily that it was a sale and I got the dress very cheap. Tim says there is probably a crab in it somewhere if it *was* cheap. He becomes exceedingly gloomy about financial affairs in general. There are rumours of a drop in pay which is said to be due to the decrease in cost of living. Have not noticed the latter myself, and say so with some force. Tim has not noticed it either. He waxes eloquent on the subject of tariffs.

Tim then opens another letter and finds that it is from Mrs. Strutts, the proprietor of Rokesby, containing a demand for the sum of £6. 4s. $2\frac{1}{2}$d. for damages and breakages during our tenancy. (Feel that this has arrived at an unfortunate moment.) Tim says what on earth does this mean, he thought I had replaced all the breakages. Reply that I did so to the best of my ability, and that this must be for damages. Tim says "Damages be blowed!" If Mrs. Strutts thinks she has only got to send in a bill like this for him to sit down and send off a cheque by return she will find herself mistaken. He won't pay a halfpenny without a fully detailed statement. The whole thing is just a try on

— and after we had that beastly drawing-room chair repaired at our own expense! Tim hopes that Mrs. Strutts will get someone like the Carters in her house next time, and then she'll see the difference between damages, and fair wear and tear. Do I realise — Tim says — that we paid for fair wear and tear in the rent (which was high enough in all conscience for a poky little den like Rokesby), and that therefore she has no right whatsoever to charge extra for it?

Reply that I do realise it, and that I agree with him but point out that she may have discovered for one thing that the leg of the small table in the morning room was broken.

"You glued it on, didn't you?" Tim says indignantly. "Well then, what more can she want?"

There are one or two other small items which I have been slightly uneasy about. I review them hurriedly in my mind, but decide not to trouble Tim with them at present.

Tim now takes up the paper and reads aloud a long article about the financial situation of Britain and the possibility of the country being reduced to beggary in three years. Feel so depressed about everything that I refuse marmalade. Tim is astonished at this, as my fondness for marmalade is a family joke. He wants to know if I am ill, or only trying to save the country from bankruptcy. Reply haughtily that if everyone in the country gave up something, the saving would be considerable. Tim laughs, and says that is so like a woman — to throw away seven guineas on a perfectly useless dress and save a halfpenny-worth of marmalade at breakfast.

Silence alone can express my injured feelings.

Tim then turns to the Financial News, and reads that the Mo Sin Orange Grove — in which we hold a hundred shares — proposes to pass its dividend.

A gloomy silence ensues, and is only broken when Maggie appears to clear away the breakfast. "Cook's waiting on you, Mistress Christie," she whispers. I gather my scattered wits and sail into the kitchen with a fixed smile, where I am greeted by the remark that, "It is bad enough to get through the work without being *kept back*."

Am conscious that my hour for visiting the kitchen has been getting later and later owing to the increased terror and hatred which I feel for its denizen, but I merely smile more brightly and say, "Captain Christie and I were rather late for breakfast this morning, I'm afraid."

We start work on the day's menu forthwith.

Sixth April

Mrs. Loudon rings me to ask me to go to tea this afternoon, an invitation which I accept with pleasurable anticipations. Unfortunately Tim arrives home just as I am starting, and says "Why is it when I have the whole day to do what I like I must go out just as he gets home from his work?" Reply mildly that I have been asked to *tea* with Mrs Loudon, and that the usual hour for same is 4:30p.m. Tim says it does not matter, he will spend the time greasing Cassandra. I know from this that Tim is really hurt at my desertion, as Cassandra only receives grease when Tim feels thoroughly neglected. Offer to forgo tea with Mrs. Loudon, but Tim says no, I had better go. No use to offend people to start off with, *he* will be all right, *he* ought to be used to being alone by this time, etc., etc.

Mrs. Loudon is really pleased to see me, and asks what I have been doing. Tell her about my luncheon party, which I feel sure will amuse her. Mrs. Loudon laughs and says that Mrs. Porter always was a "crouse cat." I realise at once that she must know Mrs. Porter, and feel that my account of the good lady's hospitality has been rather too humorous to be altogether kind. Try to retract some of my more flagrant statements, but Mrs. Loudon will have none of it — "Never heed, Mrs. Christie," she says with a twinkle in her eye, "I can't be bothered with people who never say an ill word about their neighbours. They're as savourless as porridge without salt. Now as to that other woman you met — would that be Jean Horsburgh? I used to know her mother well, a homely body she was, with no airs and graces to her. The girls are of a different ilk, for the money came when they were young, and they were sent to boarding schools, where they got little enough in the way of learning but grand ideas galore. I mind the day that Miriam told me Addie was sharing a bedroom with a princess. It was only a German princess, of course, and they're as thick as flies in August, but it was enough to turn the Horsburgh girls' heads. I told Miriam I hoped the princess was clean, and she was

174

black affronted." Mrs. Loudon laughs merrily at the recollection. "Jean's not so bad as the others. There's a substratum of sense in her, beneath yon silly talk of horses. I admit I have a kind of liking for the woman, especially if I haven't seen her for a while, but the other two are foolish to the core. I wonder what Miriam would have made of it, poor body. It's an ill thing to bear fools — but why am I raging about the Horsburghs and letting you sit there with an empty plate before you? Have another scone, Mrs. Christie, or a piece of this cake — it was only fired this morning, and it will be a real kindness to Mary to take a piece."

Thus adjured, I take a piece of chocolate cake, which tastes as good as it looks; Mrs. Loudon pours out another cup of tea, and continues, "That's a dear wee lassie you've got, Mrs. Christie. I've seen her in the garden with her doll. You're a lucky woman to have the two. My laddie is the light of my eyes, but I would have liked a girl as well — boys go away from you so early, and you never really get them back. It's a queer thing to me that women are always craiking for sons — it's the daughters who stay with you and remain your own, even if they marry. It's the daughters who lighten the darkness when you're left alone to sit by the fire, and the days draw in, and the night gets longer and sneller, and the light has gone out of your life . . . Aye, that's a dowie business, Mrs. Christie, but please God it will be many a long year before you'll understand the meaning of it."

There is a little silence which I dare not break, and then my hostess continues, more as if she were speaking to herself than to me, "It's a queer thing how your life can fall to pieces about your head in a few minutes. It happened to me like that — at one moment I was a happy wife, loved and cosseted, without a care in the world, and five minutes later I was — alone —"

A coal falls off the fire, and Mrs. Loudon jumps up and puts it back with a great clatter of fire-irons. "Gracious me," she says, smiling at me with dewy eyes, "I don't know what you will be thinking about me, Mrs. Christie — it's not a habit of mine to be havering about my sorrows to every chance-met body. I'm thinking you must be a wee witch with your bright eyes and your racy tongue."

I can't help smiling at the reference to my tongue, which has been singularly idle — except for its work on Mrs. Loudon's homemade scones — ever since I entered the house. "Oh! you wicked lassie!" cries my hostess, who seems in some mysterious way to guess my unuttered thoughts. "You're sitting there thinking you've not had a chance to get a word in edgeways with all my blether, but I've done now and it's your turn for speiring — let's hope you'll be a bit more joco than the old woman."

We chat for a little while and I manage to get in a few words (edgeways as my hostess has it) until I suddenly realise it is nearly seven o'clock, and fly home to my deserted husband in a repentant mood.

Seventh April

Great excitement. Bryan is to arrive tonight by the late train. Have anxious moments all day wondering what he is doing and whether he will arrive safely. Tim says it will do him good to travel by himself and that no harm can possibly befall him. After Tim has said the same thing half a dozen times in different words with varying emphasis, I realise he is just as anxious about Bryan as I am.

Betty's holidays have started, and the garden is full of children playing and shouting at one another, and running across the vegetable garden where the gardener has been planting his seed. Reflect sadly that the local accent is unmusical, and send up silent prayer that Betty may not acquire it. Am about to sally forth and request my turbulent guests to refrain from utterly destroying the cabbage patch when Maggie appears with a feather brush which I bought the other day in Westburgh to dust the banisters — She holds it out for me to see without any remark. I ask faintly whether she thinks there are any mice in the housemaid's pantry to which Maggie replies, "Maybe there are, but I never mind seein' a moose that would eat feathers."

Just at this moment Betty is seen to run across the lawn pursued by two unknown children in Red Indian costume. I have time to notice, before all three disappear into the shrubbery, that Betty has made a valiant attempt to conform to the prevailing fashion. She is wearing a red tablecloth with a long fringe, and a

177

headdress of feathers — I look at Maggie who nods gravely.

"You'll not be hard on Betty," she says with her customary lack of formality. "She's a great wee kid, is Betty. A' the ithers had their feather hats, but that wouldna' pit Betty up nor down. Ye'll not have *her* beat in a hurry. I'm telling ye, Mistress Christie, she's a great wee kid."

This is all very well and I appreciate the encomium on my child, but the feather brush cost five and sixpence, and is now quite unfit for further service. Betty and I have an interview later in which I try to point out the enormity of her offence.

"But Maggie doesn't mind about the brush," says Betty brightly. Explain patiently that Maggie did not pay for the brush.

Bryan's train arrives at 11p.m. Tim and I both go in to Westburgh to meet him and arrive at the station for too early. Pass the time by weighing ourselves and having our fortunes told by penny-in-the-slot machines. Tim's fortune is to "Beware of a dark woman," which he is sure must be Grace, and mine is "A long journey and a change of abode." Tim says I am evidently going to leave him as he is dug in at Westburgh for the next three years.

Bryan arrives looking small, and tired, and very sleepy. He assures us that he got on splendidly, and is scornful when Tim asks if he was sick. "Only kids like Betty are sick in the train," says Bryan grandly.

As we drive out to Kiltwinkle I feel his warm little hand steal into mine and I wonder how I have been able to do without him all these weeks and how I shall bear parting with him at the end of the holidays.

Ninth April

Find Bryan wandering about disconsolately. He says Betty has gone off with "those awful kids," and he doesn't know how she can stand them. To begin with he can't understand a word they say.

This is a new difficulty, unforeseen by me, but now extremely obvious and threatening. If Bryan sets his standard by Nearhampton and Betty by Kiltwinkle (as is not only natural but inevitable), there is bound to be an ever-widening gap between the two children which time will merely increase. The reflection that both are young does not comfort me, for standards set in youth are solidly set. Can we possibly afford to send Betty away to a decent boarding school? I know we cannot. I know also that this is one of the difficulties which Tim will not appreciate, he will merely say that Bryan is a snob and that it will do Betty no harm to mix with Kiltwinklians for a few years.

All this passes through my mind while Bryan is standing twisting the button of his coat (an annoying habit of his), and gazing dejectedly out of the window. I suggest that we should mow the lawn together.

We are mowing the lawn when Mrs. Loudon looks over the fence and says, without any sort of formal greeting, "How did you get your house?" Bryan stares at the apparition in amazement but I have become used to Mrs. Loudon's abrupt manner and reply to her

179

question with an account of our dealings with Munroe and Horder, and the peculiar business methods of that well-known firm. From this I drift naturally into a description of my adventures in the Old Manse of Pigspunkie with the red-haired man and his "Anty," and their crying need for the Pied Piper.

By this time Bryan has tired of the conversation and is mowing the lawn himself. Like all males he becomes easily bored with a conversation in which he cannot take part. Mrs. Loudon waits until he has got to the other end of the lawn and then says forcibly — "Aunt my foot! — She's no more his aunt than I am. You red laddie is her own child. Let's see, now, he'll be about nineteen years old by this time. I mind Mary McLoshary when she was a girl — a wise-like lassie. She was betrothed to a young man of good family, but his father was against the match, and his mother had no say in the matter though she liked Mary well enough. Mrs. McFarlane always put me in mind of Mrs. Weir — 'A dwaibly body.' Well, the man went away out to Australia or some such place to make a home for Mary, by his way of it, and was never heard of again. The boy was born after he had gone — nine months to a day. I was sorry for Mary, there was no harm in the lassie. Men cause a weary lot of sorrow in this old world, Mrs. Christie. But here we are, havering about 'Old unhappy, far-off things,' and I was minded to get some information out of you about house agents and such-like for a friend of mine who is coming to Westburgh for a while."

180

I give Mrs. Loudon all particulars that I think may be useful to her, but cannot help feeling sorry for anybody who has to tackle Munroe and Horder and go through all the troubles and trials that we did before we found Loanhead.

Tenth April

I prevail on Tim — Romans or no Romans — to accompany his family to the English church. The service is very pleasant and familiar, and the church prettily decorated with daffodils, but the sermon is dull beyond belief. Can see Tim becoming more and more restive, and wish I had not persuaded him to come. Am not surprised when he remarks, on the way home, that that will last him until Christmas — but feel glad that the children have run on ahead.

Annie is out this afternoon, so *I* take the children for a walk. We explore various roads, and discover a park with a small pond, which Bryan says will be great for sailing his yacht. At the far end of the park (which is filled with fathers, mothers, and offspring of all sizes, in Sunday clothes, and uncomfortable shoes) we discover some German guns, relics of the war, lying about in a decrepit condition, Betty clutches my arm excitedly and cries, "Oh, Mummie, is this where they had the war?"

I am trying to find an answer to this amazing question when Bryan saves me the trouble by replying scornfully, "Silly! Don't you know the war was in France? What do they teach you at your rotten school?"

181

This leads to an argument in which Betty hotly defends Miss McCarthy's establishment and says it is much better than an English school anyway — and much more fun. Bryan says, "Fun? What sort of fun?" and Betty replies, "Ragging Miss McCarthy is fun — you should just see her when she's ratty. Her face gets purple."

Realise from this passage at arms that my fears of Miss McCarthy's personal magnetism being too strong for the children's good were unfounded, and decide that the modern child must be fashioned in a courageous mould since I can imagine nothing more terrifying on earth than the head mistress of Hillcrest School with a rage-empurpled countenance.

Several aeroplanes are now seen which inspires Bryan to announce that he is going to be an ace in the next war. Reflect on the futility of all this talk anent disarmament in the face of the warlike spirit of the rising generation.

Return home to tea, after which we play Ludo until bedtime. This game always reminds me of croquet on account of its irritating character. No sooner have you got your men in sight of home than they are taken by somebody and sent back to their base. When this happens to Betty for the third time she dissolves into tears at which Bryan remarks scornfully, "It's no use to try to play a decent game with a girl, they are absolutely rotten."

Discover to my horror, on undressing Betty that her back is covered with spots, rush downstairs and tell Tim that Betty has got measles and he must telephone to the doctor to come at once. Tim, quite unmoved by this catastrophic intelligence, says, well, what did I expect when I sent her to school? She will probably get whooping cough next and chickenpox after that. Am too worried and distressed to argue with Tim, but reiterate my request that he shall telephone to the doctor immediately. Tim says "What doctor?" Reply that I don't know, whereupon Tim says we had better wait until the morning as nothing can be done tonight. If a doctor did come, Tim says he would only tell us to put the child to bed and keep her warm and would probably charge at least half a guinea for the advice.

Spend a miserable evening.

Eleventh April

Betty's spots still in evidence, but no other symptoms apparent. Annie suggests we should ask Mrs. Loudon about a doctor, which we do, and are advised to have Doctor Ewing.

Doctor Ewing is old, but has a twinkle in his eye. He pronounces Betty's spots to be a "spring rash," and orders magnesia and a low diet. Am tremendously relieved.

Bryan and I revisit the park discovered yesterday and spend the entire afternoon sailing his yacht — a fascinating sport. Return home to tea damp but undefeated. Betty much better already.

Twelfth April

Sit down after dinner feeling very tired. Tim points out that I have done nothing all day to make me tired (which is true in a way). He continues that I have no business to be tired. *I* have not got a crowd of half-boiled soldiers to plague my life out from morning to night. Am surprised at this statement (as Tim has been very keen on his territorials up to now), but conclude that something must have occurred to upset him, and resign myself to listen and sympathise instead of starting Sheila Kaye Smith's latest novel, which I have just procured with vast trouble from the library.

Tim then asks if I have ever seen *him* sitting at a table with three men, playing poker, with his tunic unbuttoned, and a glass of whisky at his elbow. Reply hastily that I never have. Tim does not seem the least bit soothed at my reply, but goes on to ask gloomily how I suppose any officer can possibly keep his position with the men if he indulges in such behaviour, and whether I think it likely to be good for discipline. Begin to feel that the whole thing is my fault, but can only murmur weakly, "Something ought to be done about it." Tim says bitterly that he dares say something ought, but will I tell him what one man can do against a thousand — especially if the colonel refuses to say a word to the fellow simply because he happens to be his nephew by marriage? Say at once, "In that case, of course, nothing can be done about it." At which Tim replies — Oh — I think that, do I? Perhaps I think *he* ought to hobnob with the men too — stand drinks all

184

round and get thoroughly tight with them. Perhaps I would like to ask them out to Kiltwinkle and hobnob with them myself. This may be a democratic country — says Tim with intense bitterness — but there *are* limits.

Feel that I have done so badly up to now that perhaps silence would be best, but apparently silence is equally wrong — Tim says I am not much help, am I? Reply that I am afraid I am not — think feverishly for a few moments and then suggest tentatively that we might ask the democratic officer to dinner, and Tim make a few tactful suggestions to him over a glass of port.

Tim very scornful of my solitary idea. Thinks it is condoning what is really a serious breach of discipline, and making a mock of the whole thing.

Thirteenth April

Tim comes down to breakfast whistling cheerfully and announces that he has been considering the affair of the democratic officer from every point of view, and that, in his opinion, there is only one thing to be done. Tim's idea is to ask young Weir out to dinner some night (just quietly by ourselves, I know the sort of thing), and Tim will have a talk with him over a glass of port and put it to him in a tactful way — the feller is a bit of a bounder, but perhaps I won't mind for once. Reply that I don't mind at all, and I am glad that he has thought of such a good way out of his troubles.

While we are on the subject I broach an idea which I have been turning over in my mind for some time — I feel I ought to get in touch with the wives of Tim's territorials; it seems strange not to have any wives to visit or babies to admire. I could go and visit them — as I did in the married quarters of the battalion, where I was always sure of a warm welcome — and perhaps have some of them out to tea. I feel it shows a lack of interest on my part not to make any attempt to get to know them. Tim says it is quite a good idea, but, of course, these people are quite different from the regulars, and how do I propose to get in touch with them. I have thought of this and suggest that Tim should pin up a notice at headquarters asking any of the men whose wives would like me to call on them to append their names and addresses below. Tim promises to have this done "forthwith."

Fourteenth April

Announce at breakfast that I intend to go to Westburgh this morning. Tim in an unguarded moment says that I can have Cassandra if I like, whereupon the children ask if they can come too. Thus it is that I am embarked upon a family expedition when I merely intended a solitary prowl round the shops to buy Tim's birthday present — his birthday being on Saturday.

Unfortunately, we are ready to start before Tim has left the house, and he makes me so nervous by his directions and injunctions that I scrape a piece off the gate. Tim then says I had better not take the car into the Westburgh traffic. What will happen when I have cars moving all round me, if I can't avoid a stationary object? Bryan — who is very keen to go in the car — replies at once — "It's all right, Daddy, nobody ever has two accidents in one day," and we speed off, leaving Tim gesticulating wildly on the pavement.

All goes well until we reach Westburgh Cross where cars seem to be coming in six directions at once. Cassandra is almost squashed between a dray full of beer barrels and a corporation bus, compared with which a Juggernaut would look like a child's toy.

We escape this danger only to be pursued by a policeman who asks grimly, "Did ye no' see me holding oot ma hand?" I answer humbly that I didn't, I was so terrified of being trampled on by the bus. "Och, well!" he says with a twinkle in his eye, "ma hand is no' that big," and he holds out a fist as big as a coconut. The children gasp with hysterical joy and we crawl on behind an iron girder drawn by three horses which I am too nervous to pass.

At last we reach Parker and Simpson's, and park Cassandra in the care of a ragged urchin who offers to "watch the car." We discover, with some trouble, the Men's Department, and spend a long time there examining dressing gowns for Tim's birthday present. His old one is falling to pieces and this seems a good opportunity to replace it without the usual struggle. A young man serves us and is agreeable and amazingly patient. Bryan and Betty offer candid advice upon the subject, but I feel confident that their choice of a loud tartan piped with red would not synchronise with Tim's mature taste.

The young man tries on the dressing gowns and walks up and down to let me see how Tim would look in them. After a serious discussion we decide on a brown woolly one with lighter coloured revers. Young man says if my husband would prefer a different colour he is at liberty to change it, which confirms me in my belief that he has had long experience in the Men's Department in spite of his youthful appearance.

The children, who have been slightly restive since my rejection of their advice, demand ices, so we make our way to the restaurant where they indulge in large pink ones, the mere sight of which gives me cold shivers up my back.

Ask Betty whether she is really enjoying her ice, or whether she would like to leave the rest of it. She replies ecstatically, "I *love* it, my inside is *perfectly numb*." Upon which I realise that Betty's idea of bliss is different from mine.

The way to the Haberdashery Department — where I wish to purchase buttons, tapes, elastic, and needles — lies through the Toy Department, which is unfortunate, as Betty falls madly in love with a small black china doll. After some persuasion I agree to give it to her. This entails a present for Bryan also, otherwise it would not be fair, and Bryan spends half an hour trying to make up his mind between a small model aeroplane and a magic lantern with coloured slides. He eventually decides on the aeroplane, and regrets his choice before we are halfway home.

Tim is waiting for us at the gate and remarks that he is thankful to see us safely home, and did I do much crashing of the gears? Pretend that I have not heard this insulting question.

Fifteenth April

A glorious day — we decide to call on an old cousin of my father's who lives at Pennyburn. Tim says now we have come to live in Scotland we must look up our kin. Cousin Ellen is the only "kin" I can think of offhand, hence our decision to visit her. We start off in Cassandra immediately after lunch, taking with us road maps, in which I have elucidated our course.

The country is looking very beautiful in its pale green garments. It is as if a green cloud has fallen from heaven upon the fields and hedges, resting there so lightly that one feels a stiff breeze might blow it away. Cassandra careers along happily. We pass through small whitewashed villages, where ancient men sun themselves in the doorways, and small children disport themselves dangerously in the road. We climb a long incline and find ourselves on a deserted moor amongst rolling hills clad in green tufted grass, and small valleys with little streams trickling melodiously between their rocks. It is here that Cassandra chooses to misbehave herself — there are a few spluttering noises, a couple of misfires, and the engine peters out. We run down a short hill and stop helplessly at the bottom.

I get out and climb a little knoll while Tim tinkers with the engine. I know from experience that it is of no use to offer *help* on these occasions, much better to absent myself while running repairs are in progress.

MRS TIM OF THE REGIMENT

Tim can then relieve his feelings by language unfit for female ears.

From my point of vantage I can look across the valley where the black-faced sheep browse quietly upon the slopes, their paths cut deeply in the resilient turf. A small farm on the far side of the valley stands alone amongst its patched garments of fields — it belongs to the hills, as do the clouds, whose swift race across the sky paints grey shadows on the sunlit slopes. The house is not beautiful in itself, but it is fitting as the dwellings of men so seldom are. It looks utterly fearless of the winter wind and snow, for, like them, it belongs to the weather. Behind the hills the mountains reach up strongly, one behind another, in a mist that is like the suspended breath of sheep.

I feel that Cassandra has chosen a good place to rest in for once in her life. She usually selects a crowded street or a slum.

In a little while Tim approaches, lighting his pipe. I conclude that all is not well, and call to him to come to admire the view which is simply glorious in the afternoon sunlight. Tim says he is glad I like the view in sunlight. I shall probably have an opportunity of judging the effect of moonlight on the same view. From this I realise Cassandra's indisposition is of a serious nature, and the view ceases to allure me.

Tim says *he* doesn't know what's the matter with the beastly car. He has cleaned the carburettor and tested the plugs, and there is not a kick in her. We return to Cassandra and try the self-starter again with no result. Tim says he will walk back to the last village and try to

190

get help; can I remember how far it is to the last village? Try vainly to remember. Tim says, anyhow, that is the only thing to do unless we want to camp here for the night. He takes off his leather coat and starts to walk back. Watch him become gradually smaller and smaller. He stops at the top of the hill to wave to me, then he disappears.

I climb into Cassandra and sit for a long time thinking of various things, but chiefly about Tim — How good he is, and how exactly he suits me, how easily he is managed once you understand his little peculiarities! I have been reading a book lately about a man called Julian Stanley Williams who was spoilt by an adoring mother, and grew up into a most impossible creature, vain and unreliable. I realise what a treasure I possess in Tim, who never looks at another woman, who doesn't know how to tell me a lie, and whose appearance is his last concern. Of course, this virtue has its attendant drawbacks, as his clothes are unfit to be seen before he can be induced to part with them and buy others — we have periodical arguments of great intensity upon the subject — still, how much better than the selfish vanity of a Julian Stanley Williams!

My chief complaint about Tim is that he does not appreciate me for my best qualities. He loves me — so he says — for my dimple, and because my mouth has a funny crooked curve when I smile, and because my hair goes wavy behind my ears. I would rather he loved me for certain qualities of mind and heart, which, despite my many faults, I am conscious that I possess — but at any rate he loves me, which is the main thing after all. I look back with horror on the time preceding Betty's birth, when Tim was ordered to India and had to leave me behind — How horribly I suffered! It seemed nothing mattered to me because Tim was not there to share it. I could not be bothered to order meals for my solitary consumption, and became as thin as a rake and as miserable as a sick jackdaw. If he has to go out there again I am determined to go too (even although it means leaving the children) because life without Tim is quite unbearable. However dull and dreary Westburgh may be (and I have a shrewd suspicion it is going to be both, in spite of Nora Watt's prognostications), I make up my mind that I shall never complain, not even to myself, for what does anything matter so long as we can all be together?

So occupied am I with my thoughts that I do not perceive the approach of a dirty man on a bicycle until he dismounts, and asks in a soft up-and-down sort of voice (quite different from the Westburgh whine), whether I am waiting for somebody or whether anything is the matter. I tell him about Cassandra's attack of paralysis, and he offers to see if he can put her right. In a few minutes he discovers trouble in the magneto, takes it to bits and puts it together again in a miraculous manner, and the engine springs to life at a touch.

"Can you be driving her at all?" he asks thoughtfully. I reply that I can be, and offer him a shilling. "Och, it was nothing — nothing at all," he says, with the gesture of a king refusing tribute, and is away on his bicycle before I have half thanked him for his help.

I spend some minutes turning Cassandra in the narrow road and then speed off after Tim. It seems miles before I catch sight of him; he is just entering a small garage in the outskirts of the first village to be seen. He is hot and dusty, and is not as pleased to see me as I could wish.

We agree that it is too late to think of visiting Cousin Ellen today — in fact if we do not hurry home we shall be late for dinner (an eventuality which cannot be contemplated with equanimity). As we near home and the hour advances, I beseech Tim to hurry. He replies indignantly that he will do nothing of the kind; why should we race home, jeopardising our very lives, for the sake of a cantankerous old woman (only he does not say "woman")? Do I realise — he says bitterly — that I am becoming absolutely under the creature's thumb? Reply that I do realise it. He then says why on earth don't I get rid of the brute? Reply that I am too frightened of her. Tim says the thing is absolutely preposterous, Cook must go.

Fortunately, we arrive just in time for dinner, and it is such an excellent meal that Tim's heart is softened, and he says we had better give her another chance, but I must take a strong line with her and stand no nonsense. Make no reply to this command as I feel in my bones I shall not be able to comply with it.

Sixteenth April

Tim's birthday today. Present him with the dressing gown for which he thanks me so effusively that I realise it is a complete failure, and suggest that he should change it at Parker and Simpson's. Tim at first scouts the idea, but afterwards owns that he would prefer one exactly like his old one. Have great difficulty in convincing Tim that I am not in the least bit offended, disappointed or hurt.

Betty gives Tim a bright green handkerchief bought at Woolworth's when she was in Westburgh with Annie. She explains that Annie got one just like it to send to Bollings which she evidently thinks will enhance its value in Tim's eyes. Bryan's present is a pencil — also procured at Woolworth's.

There is a large parcel with a French postmark — decidedly Aunt Ethel. We open this and find three dozen wizened tangerine oranges and a letter from Aunt E. saying that she is sending Tim a "Breath of the Riviera." She wishes she could be at Westburgh in person to wish her dear nephew All Possible Happiness on his Natal Day. She also refers to her recollections of his birth at which she appears to have assisted, and goes into intimate obstetrical details of same.

Tim does not care for tangerine oranges and discourses at length upon the stinginess of people with money — and leaves no doubt in our minds that he is referring to his paternal aunt.

Twenty-second April

Have great difficulty in finding material for my diary in this part of the world — one day is very like another and is varied only by Cook's temper, of which the less said the better, and by household differences on the subject of milk.

Is there any commodity on earth more conducive to bad feeling than milk? (Query — Why do we speak of the milk of human kindness? Why not water or barley or something less controversial?) At Loanhead we have either too little milk or too much, and I am forever ringing up the dairy to regulate the quantity. If there is too much milk, we are condemned to milk puddings for days on end; if too little, Cook forages in the nursery and robs Betty's private bottle of "Certified," which necessitates Betty having some patent food for her supper, and invariably leads to tears on Betty's part, and angry rumblings on Annie's.

Having written the above I pause for inspiration, and Tim comes up to bed. He asks unnecessarily if I am still writing my diary, and says he thought I had chucked it long ago. If I must write — Tim says — why not write something which might be published and bring in a little ready cash. Reply that I am aware that a historical romance illustrative of the August House of Coburg might be more to the purpose of profit or popularity than such pictures of domestic life as I deal in, but I could not sit seriously down to write a serious romance under any other motive than to save my life — and if it were indispensable to me to keep it up and never relax into laughing at myself or at other people, I am sure I should be hung before I had finished the first chapter.

Quotation entirely lost on Tim as I knew it would be — but so apt as to be irresistible. Tim says he never suggested a historical romance. If I *did* write one nobody would read it. But why not try my hand at a detective story — a thriller with a murder and buried treasure, etc. — he will help me with it if I like.

Twenty-fifth April

Mrs. Loudon rings up to ask if I will go and have tea with her and meet Mrs. Walker Young. We shall have tea in the dining room — she says — but I won't mind that.

Reply that I don't mind at all, but cannot help wondering why tea in the dining room should be necessary. Wondering also what Mrs. Walker Young is like; have mental picture of her evoked by her name — Tall, strong, and fresh complexioned; perhaps we may go for walks together, she probably has a police dog that requires a great deal of exercise.

When teatime arrives I discover that Mrs. Walker Young is exceedingly old and has to be wheeled about in a Bath chair (hence tea in the dining room, the drawing room at Holmgarth being upstairs). Am absurdly disappointed in Mrs. Walker Young, and can't help wondering as I return home early whether there are any young people at all in Kiltwinkle.

Tim is polishing the car; he looks up and says, "There you are, Hester — always gadding about, aren't you? Another tea party, I suppose. Look here, I'm afraid that notice about you calling on the wives hasn't met with much success. It has been on the board for about ten days and there are no names down yet."

Reply that Tim had better remove the notice before it becomes indecipherable, and retire to the drawing room feeling depressed.

Twenty-ninth April

Am informed that Mrs. McTurk wants to speak to me on the telephone, and realise that this is Nora Watt's affluent sister at last. I have been expecting her to call ever since we arrived in Westburgh, but have lately given her up as a bad job. Her name recalls to me the almost legendary figure evoked by Nora's description of her cars, her fabulous wealth, and her "positively acres" of glass.

Voice (rather like Nora's only more so), asks how Nora was looking when I last saw her, and how we are liking Westburgh. Make suitable replies. Voice then says do we play tennis — oh splendid! — well, will I excuse a formal call — such a waste of time, isn't it — and come and play tennis this afternoon after tea? Voice makes it quite clear that we are to expect no sustenance either before or after our exertions.

Tim, furious at the news of the invitation, remarks that it seems a cheap way of entertaining your friends, and he supposes this is the far-famed Westburgh hospitality. Suggest soothingly that they may want to see what we are like before asking us to dinner. Chase Tim upstairs immediately after tea to put on his whites, which he does with manifest reluctance.

Pinelands — called so without arboreal justification — is a large square house surrounded by parks containing fat cows, and an enormous garden surrounded by laurels and rhododendrons. Two Rolls Royces stand at the door and several other cars of an affluent and shiny appearance. Cassandra seems to shrink in their company, and Tim parks her as far away from them as circumstances will allow. We are conducted to the tennis courts by a footman, and here we find about a dozen people, all of whom have obviously just partaken of an enormous tea. Our hostess greets us in a *dégagé* manner; she is easily distinguishable on account of her likeness to Nora, only the likeness is embedded in rolls of fat. Her legs fascinate me, they are the same thickness all the way down and are encased in silk stockings of a peculiarly bright pink. The rest of her is white save for a green eyeshade which casts an unbecoming shadow upon her dough-like face.

I sit out the first set near a thin woman in black silk who says — after the usual conversational opening *re* weather — "I would have called for you, Mrs. Christie, but I make a point of never calling for army people — it's really not worth while when they're only here three years." My breath is taken by this entirely new point of view, and I am "dumb with silence."

Another woman now chips in and remarks that she has just got a new car costing eighteen hundred pounds, and she has had to raise her head chauffeur's wages in consequence. She gives him five pounds a week, and she has got five gardeners who cost her fifteen hundred a year, and they have grapes from their own vineries practically all the year round. I can see that this puts the other woman on her mettle; her eyes blaze and she remarks that her son has just gone to Eton, and her daughter, who has just left the most expensive finishing school in Paris, is very anxious to buy a Moth out of her pocket money, but her father thinks it too dangerous, and has offered her four hunters instead. This conversation amazes me so that I feel like Cinderella at an Arabian Nights Entertainment. I have always been used to people who protested they were on the verge of bankruptcy, and the richer they were the more fervently did they protest. Am quite disappointed when a set finishes, and I am asked to play as I feel sure that the thin lady in black silk will wipe the floor with her opponent, Moth and all.

Am put to play with a left-handed man in glasses who warns me that he has "just star-r-rted to play after thir-r-rteen years," against my corpulent, black-haired host, and a sporty-looking female of uncertain age. Find that they are all exceedingly bad, but I am even worse. Hit every ball into the net and develop an inferiority complex which completely demoralises me. Am rescued at the end of the set by a short stout elderly person in coffee-coloured lace with a large black shiny hat trimmed with roses. She introduces herself as Miss Paul and suggests that she and I shall take on two very athletic-looking girls (with bare brawny arms and eyeshades), in a ladies' four. Am filled with despair at the prospect of abject defeat, but endeavour to smile bravely and follow my partner on to the court. Discover that my partner is a brick, and plays — or seems to me to play — like Helen Wills and Betty Nuthall rolled into one.

It is an awe-inspiring sight to me to see the coffee-coloured lace whirling hither and thither, and to watch the roses on the shiny hat nodding and dancing as she hits the ball down the side lines with strong and accurate forehand drives. Am so cheered by the exhibition that I begin to hit the ball myself, and we win a love set. Make some feeble remark anent my improved play to which my partner replies tersely, "R-r-rabits beget r-r-rabits."

Tim has been absorbed into a men's four. I realise by his careless and erratic play that he is *not* enjoying himself, and decide it is time to go. We make our "adieux" just as the rest of the party is trooping in to dinner. Unfortunately, Cassandra is sulky and refuses to start; we are surrounded by people offering advice as to carburettor, plugs, magneto, etc. The woman with the eighteen hundred pound car offers to send for her chauffeur who is down at the garage as she is sure that he would know at once what to do. Finally we are pushed off down the drive by the united efforts of the men. Mrs. McTurk waves her tennis racquet and screams shrilly as we career out of sight.

"And that's the last time I ever go there," says Tim bitterly.

I marvel at his moderation.

May

First May

Tim says will I go with him to the parish church, otherwise he will spend the morning cleaning Cassandra's body, as cleanliness is next to godliness. Agree hastily before he has time to mention Romans. Church is full of very smart people in satin coats and new spring hats. The new minister takes for his text the controversial passage about the rich man whose entry into heaven is as impossible as the passing of a camel through the eye of a needle. He is exceedingly bitter on the subject, and I feel sure that the congregation cannot have come up to the scratch at the recent church bazaar, and marvel afresh at the meekness of people in church. After assuring his affluent audience that their hopes of heaven are negligible he goes on to speak with grisly gusto of the other place, whose doors are apparently wide and lofty enough for the entire congregation to pass, feathers and all. It is so long since I heard the nether regions referred to in the pulpit as a definite place, that I listen with horror. My backbone positively freezes at the lurid description of the torments in store for the unelect — a description which loses nothing by the rolling R's and broad vowels with which it is bedewed. The congregation appears unmoved by the new minister's eloquence and joins with force and fervour in singing the last hymn — unknown to me — evidently chosen on account of its gloomy and terrifying nature.

Meet the McTurks walking home. Mrs. McTurk is in beige silk and sables. They seem quite cheerful in the face of their terrible fate, and greet us with condescension. Mrs. McTurk asks me what I think of the new minister; a question which I find embarrassing under the circumstances. She goes on to say comfortably that of course riches are comparative, and implies that Rolls Royces and steam yachts are as necessary to some people as bread and butter is to others. Feel there is a flaw somewhere in her argument, but am too dazed by the awful sermon to detect it at the moment.

We encounter Mrs. Loudon who bows to me with a stiffness which I attribute to my company. Mrs. McTurk says with obvious suprise — Do I know Mrs. Loudon? Reply that she lives next door to us. Mrs. McTurk says *that* does not always mean that you *know* a person. Admit the truth of this statement but reply that Mrs. Loudon called upon me before I had been in Loanhead a week. (Feel that this dig is rather beneath me, but cannot resist it all the same). Mrs. McTurk seems even more surprised, and says Mrs. Loudon is "county" and very "stuck up," and that she never calls on anybody in Kiltwinkle as she thinks they are "not good enough for her." Realise that I have gone up in Mrs. McTurk's estimation, and that the social circles of Kiltwinkle are more complicated than I had imagined.

Mrs. McTurk then asks in an engaging manner if Tim and I will dine at Pinelands on Wednesday night — or would Friday suit us better? Am about to accept this invitation when Tim, who has overheard the conversation (owing to Mr. McTurk's absence of small talk), says he is sorry we are engaged every night this week, and are probably going away the week after. Realise that Tim is not of a forgiving nature, and give up with regret all idea of wearing my new frock.

Mrs. McTurk says she is sorry about that because "Mew reel" is coming to stay with her, and she would like me to meet "Mew reel." Discover that "Mew reel" is another sister who is married to a stockbroker in London.

Second May

Go in to see Mrs. Loudon to ask for the loan of her steps, those belonging to Loanhead being in a crippled condition and tied together with string. So ancient are they that I really cannot blame Cook for refusing to trust her not altogether fairy-like person on their fragile support. Cook points out to me in her usual trenchant manner that the spring sunshine shows up the dirt on the windows, and she can't thole it any more, adding sourly, that if she breaks her leg, couping off the steps, there will be nobody to cook the dinner. Can't quite make out whether Cook is more annoyed with the spring sunshine for showing up the condition of the kitchen windows or with me for incarcerating her in such an ill-found house, but offer hastily to procure steps from next door, which pacifies her temporarily.

Find that Mrs. Loudon's attitude towards the sunshine is entirely different from Cook's. She says this is the kind of day that makes her weary for Avielochan. She always goes to the Highlands for June — it is the best month to her thinking, everything is so fresh, and there are no Americans. She takes the same wee house, every year, set on the hillside amongst the pines, and a burn tumbling down beside her door. She has been wondering if there is any chance of being able to get me for a week or ten days — it would not be worth while coming for less as the journey is long and troublesome.

It is very kind of her to think of it, but I am sure I could not leave Tim alone at Loanhead. He has no friends and would be frightfully dull and lonely without me. Have awful visions of Cassandra being greased daily for a week.

Mrs. Loudon then says how did I get to know Those Terrible McTurks? She was amazed to see me in that galley. Reply that Mrs. McTurk's sister is in the regiment, and go on to give her an account of the tennis party on Saturday, at which she laughs so heartily that she cries.

The upshot of all this is that I return to Loanhead without the steps, and have to go back for them.

Third May

Find Annie in tears and demand an explanation of same. After some persuasion Annie admits that

Scotland is not what she thought it would be. She was willing to face discomfort and privations (which do not exist), and was even prepared to take her chance of wolves prowling about at night, and wild Highlanders in kilts — but fiends in cooks' clothing is more than any girl can bear.

As my experience has been much the same as Annie's, I feel intense sympathy for her, and declare indignantly that this is the last straw and that Cook must go, and I will tell her so immediately. Annie is aghast at my temerity and beseeches me to wait until the captain comes home; but I know if I wait five minutes my courage will evaporate, and I march downstairs and into the kitchen with a firm step.

Cook is very much taken aback at receiving her congé, and says quite mildly she hopes we are not dissatisfied with her cooking. I reply with truth that she is the best cook I ever had, but she is so disagreeable that the whole house is upset and uncomfortable. She stares at me in amazement and remarks that in that case she had better go. I reply that there is nothing else for it.

Annie is waiting for me when I emerge from the kitchen, and seems relieved to see me with a whole skin. She admits that she was afraid Cook would "go for" me, and adds that she throws things about something awful when she's in a rage. This confirms me in the opinion that I have done the right thing, and I reflect that Cook's temper is too high a price to pay for the fluffiest soufflé on earth — I can even contemplate

207

with equanimity the search for someone to take her place.

Fifth May

Decide to go into Westburgh and buy myself a spring hat as the sunshine is showing up the defects of my old one in a most distressing manner. The bus is unpleasantly full — men sitting and girls standing, which seems the usual thing in this part of the world.

Discover to my surprise that Mrs. McTurk is also an inmate of the bus. She explains in a loud voice — as we hang grimly to our straps and are bumped together like straw stuffed bolsters at every jolt — that the Rolls is really too big for shopping, and the Armstrong is being decarbonised, and Mew reel and Mr. McTurk have gone to golf at Westerberry in the Alvis, so she has had to make use of this exceedingly plebeian method of transport much against her will. I make sounds of commiseration for her plight, but am secretly delighted that she should be enduring discomforts like other people.

Mrs. McTurk asks where I am going, and I confess to my intention of purchasing a new hat. "Oh, you must go to my woman," she says — rather breathlessly, for we have just swung round a corner and the bolsters have bumped with more than usual force — "My woman is *reelly* clever, she understands fitting the hat to the facial contours. Nothing under four guineas, of course, which makes her place *so* select — you really *must* go to her." I memorise the address of Mrs.

McTurk's woman with the express intention of avoiding her establishment.

The conductress coming for our fares discloses the fact that Mrs. McTurk has nothing under a pound. A heated discussion takes place which only ends when I offer to pay her fare. Mrs. McTurk accepts somewhat ungraciously adding that thrippence is too much to pay for the privilege of hanging onto a strap and being bumped about for a quarter of an hour. Notice during the discussion that the bus conductress is pretty, but decide that diamond earrings look peculiar with a uniform and peaked cap. Point this out to Mrs. McTurk, who replies, "Oh, but they're not reel, Mrs. Christie — she probably got them at Woolworth's." Feel unequal to the effort of explaining my point.

Mrs. McTurk then informs me that Mr. McTurk has just presented her with a pair of "reel diamond earrings from Piffanie's, and they cost him a hundred and twenty pounds." I congratulate her on her husband, to which she replies complacently, "Yes, Mr. McTurk is very wealthy."

Once more the good lady has missed my point. I begin to feel as if I were conversing in a foreign language or with somebody very deaf. There was an old gentleman at Hythe who prided himself upon his hearing. A conversation with him was always fraught with surprises. I remember asking him whether he had been for a long walk today, to which he replied smilingly, "Yes, May is my favourite month too." Decide that Mrs. McTurk suffers from mental deafness. She has ears but hears not — at least I suppose she must have ears concealed under her rolls of mud-coloured hair or Mr. McTurk would not have paid a hundred and twenty pounds for diamond earrings for her.

Thus occupied with foolish thoughts I am whirled through the long grey streets of Westburgh, and find myself disgorged on to the crowded pavement at Westburgh Cross in company with Mrs. McTurk, slightly dizzy with the smoky atmosphere of the bus and the jolting to which I have been subjected.

"This way," says my companion, seizing my arm in a firm grip and dragging me across the street under the noses of buses and cars. "They'll not hurt you, Mrs. Christie — they've no more desire to run over you than you have to be run over."

I realise that this may be true, but feel that I would rather be on the safe side. "It would hurt me more," I gasp.

"Nonsense! Take a firm line — they would have their licence endorsed," is the amazing reply.

I manage to shake off Mrs. McTurk by losing her in the crowd at Woolworth's where she is laying in a store of kitchen china, and hasten to Parker and Simpson's whose window is full of hats at fourteen and eleven. Here an amiable girl produces hats of all shapes, colours and sizes for my selection. She takes a great and friendly interest in my choice, and is anxious for me to decide on a bright green bowler, assuring me that I suit it awful well. Feel that I cannot altogether agree with her and say so with some diffidence. "Righto, you know best," she says brightly, "but I must say I liked you fine in yon solid green."

After long discussion I decide on a dark-red straw which really seems rather nice, and is surprisingly cheap. So cheap that I feel I am entitled to a scarf to match, which is a pleasing thought. My new friend suggests that I should "wear it away," and she will send my old hat home for me. This is an excellent idea and I am frightfully pleased with my appearance until I catch a glimpse of a strange-looking female in a mirror in the Children's Department (where I am looking at summer dresses for Betty), and realise that the strange-looking female is myself in my new hat — the mirror here being less flattering than the one in the Millinery Department. This rather damps my spirits, and I reflect that perhaps I have been somewhat hasty in my choice. Too late for vain regrets, but fortunately the hat was cheap.

Spend the morning looking at dresses for Betty (who has outgrown every garment she possesses), and buying shirts and shorts and handkerchiefs for Bryan to take back to school.

The streets are filled with pale-yellow sunshine which gives them a curious shallow appearance; the shop windows sparkle in the sun. The people seem to move about with a jaunty air very unusual to behold in Westburgh, where they are generally blown crooked by gales, sweeping up the side streets, or cowering beneath umbrellas.

There is a fearful crush in Boots, everyone seems to have a companion except myself, and to be talking to that companion at the top of her voice. Drifts of conversation assail my ears: "It's not for me to tell him," says a woman behind me trenchantly.

"You must keep stirring till it boils," announces a thin, careworn sort of voice, "and then add the vinegar, dr-rop by dr-rop."

"She asked me six and eleven for it, and I said what did she take me for."

"Well, Minnie, if I hadn't hear-rd you with my own ear-rs —"

And then the thin voice again: "Three quarters of an hour late he was, and then told me it was bur-rnt, so I said —"

But I never heard what she said, for a loud familiar voice on the other side of a mountain of bath salts rivets my attention. "The Rolls is really too big for shopping," says the loud familiar voice, "and the Armstrong is being decarbonised."

I do not wait to hear about Mew reel and Mr. McTurk having gone to golf at Westerberry in the Alvis, but fly from the spot without having procured any powder for my nose (which was the object of my quest), for if Mrs. McTurk sees me in my new hat she will know that I have not been near her woman. In my present humble mood I feel sure that she will recognise it for Parker and Simpson's fourteen and elevenpenny model as easily as if it bore the price marked upon the crown in plain figures, like that of the immortal maniac in *Alice in Wonderland*.

Return home in a bus which is even more crowded and uncomfortable than the last. Tim does not like my hat.

Seventh May

Mrs. Walker Young calls upon me. She is wheeled up to the front door by a tall woman in black with iron-grey hair. Suggest that we should sit in the garden which would obviate the necessity of lifting her chair up the steps. I lead the way to the garden seat which is now quite dry, but which still retains evidence of Jack's disastrous tenancy. We discuss prohibition — Mrs. Walker Young thinks it ought to be brought in, only not for invalids of course — her daily glass of champagne is all that keeps her alive. Can't help wondering whether it is really worth while, but keep this uncharitable thought to myself.

At this moment Betty appears, looking very hot and dishevelled. She greets Mrs. Walker Young politely, and then stands on one leg like a stork, taking in the peculiarities of my guest. Mrs. W. Y. becomes slightly restive under her scrutiny, and proceeds to talk down to Betty in the manner of people who are not used to children.

"Your name is Betty?" she asks sweetly. Betty admits that she is correct in her surmise. "And what do you think my name is?" says Mrs. Walker Young.

"I couldn't say," replies Betty. She has picked up this strange expression from the Kiltwinklians and uses it in season and out of season with relish.

"My name is Mrs. Walker Young," says that lady, still in the sugary tones specially adapted to Betty's youth. "What do you think of that?"

"I think it's a pity you're not," says Betty candidly.

There is an awful pause while I rack my brain for something to say, and finally suggest wildly that we should go in and have tea. Mrs. W. Y. says that she never takes tea so early in the afternoon, and that anyway it is time for her to go home or she will be late for her Bengers. Betty is sent to summon the attendant who has been walking round the garden during our conversation, and we all move slowly towards the gate.

Here we stand talking — or rather listening — for at least ten minutes while Mrs. Walker Young tells me exactly what she thinks of the new minister's wife (whose chief fault seems to lie in the fact that her hats are too smart, and her tablemaid wears silk stockings to open the door), until she suddenly remembers her Bengers and allows herself to be wheeled away.

Although I have had no speech with Mrs. Walker Young's attendant I feel a strange interest in her, and wonder, off and on during the evening, what her history can be (she looks as if she had a history), and whether she is happy in her present post, which seems unlikely. I remind myself that it has nothing to do with me, but in spite of this her face rises hauntingly before my eyes. It possesses that austere beauty which is sometimes found in Scots faces — a beauty which does not strike one immediately, but which grows more apparent at every glance, and which embodies high cheekbones, shadowy eyes, and a large and mobile mouth.

214

Feel sure that Mrs. Walker Young is fortunate in her attendant, but doubtful whether she appreciates the fact.

Ninth May

Telephone bell rings while I am in the kitchen, rush into the dining room (where the telephone is situated) primed with orders for the butcher who usually rings up at this hour, and am astonished to hear Tim's voice. Tim having left the house about twenty minutes ago, I wonder what he can possibly want to speak to me about, as I know he has not forgotten his pipe, having seen him put it in his pocket just before his departure.

"I say, Hester," says Tim's voice. "Hullo — I say — is that you? Well I've just found a letter here from Command. I've got my majority."

Make sounds of delight and congratulation.

"Yes, Morley's sent in his papers, and poor old McPherson has gone west — You didn't know him, did you? — what? — Yes, 2nd Battalion, always has been — Yes, frightfully sad, isn't it? — What? — Oh yes, he's been frightfully bad with malaria for ages, at Julaparajapore — Yes, frightfully sad — Yes, married but no kids — No, no details as yet, they must have cabled War Office and the 1st Battalion — I say, Hester, you know what this means, don't you? — What? — Well, when will you learn to take an interest, an intelligent interest in army affairs? — I can't hear what you say — Well, according to King's Regs, it means return to regimental duty forthwith. Nice, isn't it, when I've just

215

begun to get into the way of this blinking job? — What? Oh, just because the Finance Department won't sanction a major holding the job, a captain's cheaper, you see — Yes, it is rather, isn't it — Oh, yes, we'll have to sublet it, I suppose — Good thing I insisted on that clause in the lease — Yes — I say, Hester, you're not awfully sick about it, are you?"

The telephone goes dumb, and I lay it down with a click — my head is whirling with the unexpectedness of the news. Am I sorry, Tim wonders? Sorry to go back to the regiment; to see all my old friends; to take part once more in the amusing dinner parties which necessitate so much borrowing and lending of plates, glasses, and finger bowls; to have Grace popping in at odd moments and asking foolish questions about her coming baby; to see the N.C.O.'s and their nice natural wives; to attend the welfare meetings and teas, and to visit the married quarters with their large complement of babies and small children, where one is always a welcome guest. Even Nora Watt appears a friendly and amiable figure by comparison with her impossible sister — even Mrs. Benson can be borne with equanimity.

Of course, it will be a bother letting the house, and moving and finding another house and cook at Biddington, but these are mere details, and the shadow of them fails to dim my joy. Tim is evidently quite pleased in spite of having to give up his new job — Bryan will be delighted for us to be near him again, and last but not least I shall be able to take Betty away from "those awful kids" as Bryan calls them. I seize my best hat feeling that it — and it only — can express my mood, and dash out to the shops.

Mrs. Loudon is in the butcher's choosing a gigot with a great deal of discussion and argument. (I have discovered to my surprise that a gigot is merely Scots for a leg of mutton.) She looks up from her task and says, "Hullo, Mrs. Christie! you look for all the world as if you had lost a penny and found a threepenny bit."

Feel rather ashamed of looking so blatantly pleased at leaving Westburgh, and reply that Tim has got his majority. Mrs. Loudon is delighted, and congratulates me heartily. She waves her hand to the butcher and tells him if he has got a head to send it along with the gigot, and follows me out of the shop. "It will mean more pay, too," she says, hitting the nail on the head in her usual forcible manner. Reply that it will, but it will also mean our leaving Westburgh as the adjutancy is a captain's appointment — endeavour to look suitably gloomy as I announce this.

"Get away with you, Mrs. Christie," says Mrs. Loudon with a twinkle in her eye behind her glasses. "I may be an old done woman, but I'm not so easily taken in as that — you need never try to pull a poor mouth to me over leaving Westburgh. Do you think I can't see that you're like a fish out of water? You never complain — I grant you that much — but I can see through a brick wall as far as my neighbour, and it's no life this, for a lassie like you. Away back to your regiment and your friends, and be thankful. Westburgh's no place for you."

Since Mrs. Loudon has read my thoughts I admit that I am rather disappointed in my impressions of Scotland. "Scotland," she cries, stopping in the middle of the street and gazing at me in horror, "my dear soul, Westburgh's never Scotland! Don't you go away with the idea that you've been living in Scotland. What would you think of a person who spent two months in Manchester and said they didn't like England?"

I realise the enormity of my offence and shake my head in a suitably disgusted manner. "Gracious me!" cries Mrs. Loudon, scarcely soothed by my amends, "I thought you would have had more sense in your head. I just wish you could have a peep of the real Scotland and makes friends with a few decent Scottish bodies before going away back to your benighted England."

Remain blissfully happy until lunchtime when Tim returns from his headquarters and destroys my airy castles with his first words. "Don't you see, Hester," he says impatiently, "I'm just as likely to be sent to the 2nd Battalion as I am to the 1st?"

"India!" I gasp.

"Yes, India. There are two vacancies for majors, aren't there? One in each battalion and Neil Watt and I are available to fill them. Neil Watt has a brother-in-law in S.D. 3 and he's pretty sure to get Neil posted to the home battalion if he can possibly wangle it. You don't suppose the War Office takes into consideration the fact that I have children and Neil hasn't, do you? Now that we are comfortably settled here with a decent house you had better just remain here with Betty — and it will be somewhere for Bryan to come to in the holidays."

218

"But, Tim," I cry, aghast at the frightful prospect, "Tim, I couldn't remain here. If you go to India we must send Betty to a boarding school so that I can come with you — I can't be left behind."

"My dear girl," says Tim firmly, "you can't possibly come to Julaparajapore — the place is in a confounded mess — it's no use you looking at me like that, I won't take the responsibility of having you there. Supposing there was trouble there — shooting and rioting? No, no, it won't do. Besides Betty is too young to go to school, and we can't afford it either. Make up your mind to remain here in this comfortable house — that's the best plan."

It is a horrible plan and I tell Tim so, and suggest — a sudden bright idea — that he should get an exchange. "My dear lamb," Tim says patiently. "Nobody wants to go to India now. One wouldn't mind a war, that's all in the day's work, but nobody likes being plugged in the back from behind a bush with no hope of redress — and where do you propose we should find the money to pay for an exchange, unless we rob the McTurks' house?"

Reply that I would willingly rob the McTurks' house — or any other house — rather than let Tim go to India without me.

The discussion persists all day and far into the night without any decision being arrived at, and at last we both fall asleep from sheer exhaustion.

Tenth May

On my return from the village I am surprised to see a large Bentley standing at the gate — it looks familiar — I hurry in and find Major Morley waiting for me in the drawing room. So delighted am I to see an old friend that I make no objection when he takes both my hands and shakes them warmly. "Mrs. Tim!" he says. "This is nice — I hope you are half as glad to see me as I am to see you."

We sit down and chat, and he tells me that he is on his way north for some fishing, and looked in at Kiltwinkle on the way to give us all the news. "I feel rather guilty about this upheaval in your plans," he says gravely. "You see I had no idea that old McPherson was dying when I sent in my papers. The poor old feller had been seedy for so long that one thought he would carry on indefinitely. If I had known he was as bad as all that I would have hung on a bit longer and let Tim know what I proposed doing. It's frightfully bad luck on old Tim to have to give up this job when he was getting on so well — and you just settled here and everything — I feel awful about it."

I reply that we don't really mind leaving Westburgh, but are hoping it won't mean India.

"Don't worry about that," he says quickly. "Of course, Watt's been pulling wires at the War House — you know his brother-in-law is there — but he's not the only one who can pull wires. Benson has turned up trumps and applied for Tim — naturally he would rather have old Tim than that slacker Watt — and I went up and saw Jack Darley who is in A.G.20 — I think you'll find Tim is posted to the 1st Battalion all right."

It is frightfully kind of Major Morley to have taken all that trouble, and I tell him so. "Nonsense," he replies, smiling, "I only did it in self-preservation. My life would not have been worth a moment's purchase at Biddington if I had been the cause of sending Mary Pickford to the foreign battalion."

I try to smile at this ancient joke, but find that my eyes are full of tears. It is such a tremendous relief to find that Tim and I are not to be parted after all that I can't help behaving in an idiotic manner. Major Morley is frightfully kind, he pats me on the back and tells me to "Buck up, everything is all right now," and adds that it is all his fault for not wiring yesterday, but he wanted to come and tell me about it himself. He is so nice and big-brotherly that I like him better than ever, and wonder how I could possibly have felt afraid of him as I did once or twice at Biddington and Charters Towers. I feel that I owe him an explanation of my extraordinary lapse, and point out that it was only because I was so afraid that Tim would go to India without me, and that I simply can't do without Tim. At which he sighs and says, "I know, I know — Tim's a lucky devil, and he knows it too, which makes it worse."

After delivering himself of this cryptic utterance, Major M. says he must be off as he is going to Ross-shire and wants to arrive before dark. I press him to stay to lunch and see Tim, but he says he can't possibly stay a moment. Point out hospitably that he must have lunch somewhere, and therefore may just as well lunch here and be done with it. To which he replies that I am mistaken, there is no need for him to lunch anywhere, and hastens out to the car. Hurry after him offering biscuits and whisky, and demanding why he is suddenly in such a hurry.

Major M. takes no notice of my suggestions, but, once in the driving seat, his desire to be gone seems to evaporate, he lights a cigarette.

"What would you say if I told you I was going to be married?" he asks. "No, it's not a subject for congratulations, it's just a — just a question."

It seems an unfair question when I am entirely ignorant of the details — the nature of the lady in the case and the state of Major Morley's feelings. He laughs when I tell him this, and says that isn't the point. If he marries it will be because Sir Abraham is keen on it — wants a grandson for Charters Towers and all that. He knows it seems an unusual reason for plunging into matrimony, but there might be worse. The old Governor is pretty rotten — Major Morley says — this blood pressure seems rather a horrible sort of thing — and after all what does it matter whether he marries or not — everything is absolutely foul anyway.

Reply if that is how he feels it would be a great mistake to marry, and he had better wait until he sees someone he cares for, and that I feel sure if Sir Abraham knew how he was feeling he would be the last man to want his son to marry. It all sounds rather muddled, but Major Morley evidently understands what I mean. "Oh, well!" he says, "if that's what you say it's all off — I'll wait a bit — not that there's any hope of anything being different, but just because" — he puts his foot on the accelerator, lets in the clutch and glides off before I have gathered my scattered wits sufficiently to say goodbye.

I realise after he has gone that I have not half thanked him for what he has done — what a narrow escape we have had!

Tim returns at teatime and is amazed to hear of Major Morley's visit and the news brought by him, and agrees with me that it is frightfully decent of him to take so much trouble. Tim seems even more surprised than I was, and says several times over that he never thought Morley would have bothered himself about a thing like that, and he must write and thank the old josser. We agree that there is no need to waste any sympathy on the Watts; Nora will probably enjoy India, and, having no children, they can go abroad without tearing their hearts to bits and leaving large pieces behind.

The subject is still under discussion when Mrs. Loudon is announced. She refuses to partake of tea and says she just came in to tell us about an idea which has occurred to her. Why not sublet Loanhead to her friends? They are careful bodies and will do the house no harm being free from young children and dogs, those perennial sources of anxiety to the owners of houses. Can see that Tim is impressed with her forceful and businesslike manner, and will probably allow her friends to have the house, in spite of his prejudice against subletting. She assumes the whole thing is

223

settled — which is much the best way with Tim — and goes on to say that Betty and I are to come and stay with her at Avielochan for the first fortnight in June while Tim goes south and arranges about a house at Biddington. Tim is not quite so cheerful about this suggestion, and asks pathetically what Mrs. Loudon thinks will happen to *him*, alone at Biddington. Mrs. Loudon replies that she has heard there are places called barracks where single men may dwell in comfort and security. Tim says there are also places called prisons where an equal degree of comfort and security may be found. "Hoots man!" retorts Mrs. Loudon, "Can you not see the lassie needs a wee rest from housekeeping? Away south with you and find a house."

Tim takes this ordering of his affairs with surprising meekness. I think he is slightly dazed at the swift movement of events and the rapid change of outlook when he imagined himself securely settled in his job. But, whatever the cause, the whole affair is cut and dried before we have time to find any more objections.

I decide in my own mind that if there is any talk of greasing Cassandra I will give up my visit to Mrs. Loudon, although the idea is vastly attractive — not only because I am longing to see the Highlands so vividly described by my prospective hostess, but also on account of Mrs. Loudon herself, whose sincerity and outspokenness are after my own heart — I discover, however, that Tim is not nearly so dejected as he pretends at the prospect of a fortnight in mess. There will be threads to gather up after two months' absence from the battalion, and he can gather them more easily

224

if he is on the spot, and it will be rather jolly to see all the old faces again, to command a company, and to lord it over the captains.

The evening passes swiftly with discussions about our plans. We shall have to borrow money from the bank as the recent move has swallowed up our tiny nest egg, but this is less worrying than it might be owing to Tim's rise in pay. Tim will go south in Cassandra, and deposit Bryan at school. Cook is leaving anyway, and Maggie can stay on with the new tenants, while Annie comes with us to Avielochan to look after Betty. Everything seems to fit like a well-made jigsaw puzzle. How lovely it will be to have a rest from all the small household worries which afflict the just and to wander through the pine forests on the hillsides which Mrs. Loudon has made so real to me — and, after that, Biddington to look forward to.

Am just writing up my diary by the window — it is still quite light though after ten o'clock. Tim is standing on the garden path with his hands in his pockets, smoking his bedtime pipe — the smoke hangs in the air in a blue cloud, and drifts up to my nostrils with the mellow tang which seems so much a part of Tim. He is so deep in thought that I cannot resist having a shot at him with my bedroom slipper, and by great good luck manage to hit him on the head. He picks it up and throws it back at me in an instant. I make a grab for it but the wretched thing falls into the balcony outside my window, and I have to lean halfway out of the window to get it — "Don't fall out, you ass!" says Tim, chuckling.

At this moment I look up and see the Man Who Lives Next Door standing on his doorstep watching my antics, and disapproving (I feel sure) of my flowered-silk dressing gown. Probably his own wife wears one of red flannel, and most certainly has never been seen leaning out of the window in it — The Awful Carrying On of Those Army People — he is thinking.

I dive backwards into my room and pull the curtains, and Tim comes galloping up the stairs to see what on earth is the matter. Of course, I throw a pillow at him, which catches him fair and square and nearly takes his breath away. After that he seizes me round the waist and we waltz madly round the room.

Feel ten years younger after this absurd performance, and decide that I don't care a button what the Man Who Lives Next Door thinks of me — these little idiocies are the salt of life.

June

First June

The morning dawns bright and warm, sunshine falls in golden swathes on the faded carpets of Loanhead. The house is filled with the bustle of departure. Gloom descends upon me as I dress, and I follow Tim to the bathroom — where he is shaving — to tell him that I wish I were going south with him.

"Well, you can't get out of it *now*," he replies, scraping fiercely at his chin. "Besides, you need a spot of leave and you're sure to enjoy it when you get there. I only wish *I* had a chance of spending a fortnight in the Highlands. You can think of me grilling in the heat at Biddington and toiling and moiling to get my company into trim — I bet that ass Neil Watt has made a complete hash of it while I've been away."

I am in no whit comforted by the conversation. Of course I have been looking forward to my visit to the Highlands, but the scattering of my family fills me with sadness and a strange fear. Soon we shall be hundreds of miles apart — Tim at Biddington with the regiment, Bryan at school, and Betty and I with Mrs. Loudon at Avielochan.

A letter in Mrs. Loudon's firm hand is waiting for me on the breakfast table — perhaps it is to say she cannot have us after all. This would have been a disaster yesterday, but today it would be a reprieve. I scan it eagerly, and find that it is no reprieve, but merely confirmation of exile. In other words an itinerary of our journey, and a list of various places where we shall have to "change." It also contains the news that Mrs. Loudon's son — a Lieutenant-Commander in His Majesty's Navy — has arrived unexpectedly on leave, and that the house party is further augmented by a cousin (about whom no information is given). The letter adds to my gloom. I feel convinced that I shall be *de trop* in this family party, and that Mrs. Loudon is now regretting her impulsive invitation to Betty and me. (I am frequently beset with the uncomfortable conviction that people don't really want me and have only asked me from a stern sense of duty. I am told this is really a complex, and probably has its origin in some forgotten episode of my childhood. Complex or no, it seizes upon me at inopportune moments, and makes my life a misery. Often, when bidden to lunch or tea with hospitable friends, it descends upon me suddenly when I am standing upon the doorstep, and wages a battle royal with my common sense, so that I can hardly force myself to ring the bell and enquire if Mrs. So-and-so is at home. This subconscious self of mine insists with devilish plausibility that Mrs. So-and-so did not really want me to come, has now quite forgotten that she asked me, and will be disagreeably surprised when she sees me walk in.)

I point out to Tim (who is now busy stoking up for his journey, with bacon and eggs) that I could send a wire to Mrs. Loudon and tell her I can't come after all.

"Don't be silly, Hester," he says. "You'll enjoy it, and it will do you good. Besides, where would you go? You know how expensive hotels are. We ought to start soon if Bryan is ready."

It is all quite true and sensible. How I wish I were not tortured by vague fears! I retrieve Bryan from the garden, where he has been taking tender farewell of his hedgehog, and pack him into the car.

"There you are!" exclaims Tim, with a cheerfulness which I feel is slightly artificial, "all ready, Bryan? Got the maps?"

Bryan has got the maps safely, and is very proud of having them in his possession. He has also got a compass, and explains to me that this will come in very handy if they should lose their way. As long as they keep due south they can't go wrong, Bryan says. I have a sudden vision of the car rushing due south, over fields and through hedges like a miniature tank, which makes me feel quite hysterical.

There is a slight lull in the activities after their departure, and I become conscious of an empty feeling in my interior — have I or have I not had any breakfast? I decide that I have not, and repair to the dining room, to remedy the omission, only to find that breakfast has been cleared away. Perhaps I did have breakfast after all, the empty feeling may be due to Tim's departure and not — as I had supposed — to lack of nourishment.

I pay Cook and Maggie and present them with their insurance cards, duly stamped. Maggie says she hopes the new lady will be as nice (this is a typically Scottish compliment and I drink it down with smiles of gratitude, and shake her warmly by the hand). Cook says her hands are wet, and we had better be away if we're thinking of getting the train.

A few minutes later Betty and I, accompanied by the faithful Annie, are on our way to the station in the taxi.

Annie has arrayed herself in a thick black coat with a fur collar, and is obviously prepared for the climatic rigours of the north.

"Your face is very red, Annie," says Betty suddenly. Fortunately Annie is not in the least disturbed by the personal nature of the remark. She replies, amiably, that it's the heat, and I realise afresh that Annie is an ideal custodian for a child.

Our station wears an air of leisure quite unknown to those bustling termini where the trains run southward. The porter greets us with a smile and asks if we are "away for our holidays." He discusses at length the merits of different carriages and, eventually, deposits Betty and me in an empty compartment, with Annie next door.

"You call me if — you know what, ma'am," says Annie mysteriously, as she disappears, and I remember — with a shudder of horror — my last journey with Betty, and send up a silent prayer that Annie's kind ministrations may not be needed.

The train is late in starting, having been delayed by the arrival of a large family with mountains of luggage. Nobody minds the delay, there is a happy-go-lucky feeling about the whole affair; the very barrows seem to grumble along in a placid way, quite different from the querulous creak of the ordinary station barrow. I can imagine the engine looking round like a fatherly old horse: "You all ready, people?" it enquires kindly. "Quite sure you haven't left anything behind? Well then, off we go."

And off we do go.

Quite soon we are out of the environs of the town; cruising along amongst rolling hills. Whitewashed cottages nestle in green hollows. Cattle standing knee-deep in reeds lift their slow heads and gaze at us with surprise.

Betty eats an orange and discourses in her usual practical manner — scenery has no charms for her.

After about an hour she asks if we are nearly there, and I reply firmly that we shall not be there for hours and hours.

"But we've been hours and hours already," she says, "and we were *in* Scotland when we started so we *must* be nearly there. Scotland's quite small on the map." I decide that it is now time to produce some picture papers, which I have hidden in my bag to beguile the monotony of the journey for Betty and ensure a little peace for myself. Betty seizes upon them eagerly, and forgets all about the dimensions of Scotland in her enjoyment of the antics of Mr. Rhino's scholars.

We cross a deep river with a rumble of wheels, and immediately the scenery changes and becomes wild. The rolling hills give place to mountains, which stand back in sullen splendour and allow us to pass. The cattle become sheep, snowy lambs with black wobbly legs and cheeky little black faces interrupt their

233

breakfast to stare at the train. Streams leap down the hillsides amongst the rocks, and dive beneath our wheels to emerge on the other side in beds of gravel and yellow stones. The gorse is like a shower of minted sovereigns, flung down with a careless hand as far as eye can reach.

Now the land falls away, we creep along the shoulder of a hill, and a vista of green valley is disclosed. Farmhouses, with their patchwork of fields, are scattered hither and thither, and on the farther slopes of the mountains, a few wind-swept cottages stand amongst sparse trees.

Suddenly the spell is broken, the door of our compartment is pushed ajar, and through the aperture appears the fat white face of Mrs. McTurk. Of all the people in the world Mrs. McTurk is, perhaps, the one I least want to see. I can't help wondering what she is doing in the train, and how she has found me. She must be — I suppose — one of those peculiar people who *walk about* in trains. Why couldn't she have remained peacefully where she was put by the porter amidst her own belongings in (I have no doubt) a comfortable first-class compartment?

"Is this really you?" she says.

I reply that it is. The woman has the knack of saying things which invite a fatuous answer.

"Well I never!" she says.

I fix a false smile upon my countenance, whereupon she insinuates her cumbrous body through the door, and sits down beside Betty.

"So you are going north for a holiday," she says.

234

Betty bounces up and down on the seat. "Do you know Mummie?" she cries excitedly. "Fancy you knowing Mummie! I thought Mummie didn't know anybody in Kiltwinkle. Of course I knew lots of children at school, but it was awfully dull for Mummie. Mrs. Watt said there would be lots of parties, and Mummie bought a new dress, and then nobody asked her."

I plunge wildly into the conversation, wishing, not for the first time, that Betty were shy with strangers.

"How wonderful the gorse is!" I exclaim rapturously.

It is unfortunate that at this moment we happen to be creeping through a narrow ravine strewn with boulders. Mrs. McTurk looks out of the window and then at me in surprise.

"This gorge," I scream, above the roar of the train. "So wild and rocky."

"Oh, I thought you said *gorse*," says Mrs. McTurk.

Her voice is admirably suited for conversation in a railway train, its strident note can be heard with ease. Bridges leap at us with a roar, mountains peer in at the windows and vanish, but above all these ear-splitting noises comes the strident voice in futile discourse.

"And where are you bound for?" she asks with a toothy smile.

I am about to reply truthfully to her question when I suddenly remember that Mrs. Loudon "can't abide the woman," and remember also the diplomatic attempts of Mrs. McTurk to procure an introduction to my prospective hostess. How awkward it will be if Mrs. Turk's destination is within motoring distance of

Avielochan. It is unlikely, of course, but unlikely things sometimes happen, especially if you don't want them to. On the whole I feel that it will be wiser to conceal the fact of our visit to Mrs. Loudon.

"How is Mr. McTurk?" I shout.

My red herring is successful, and for some minutes Mrs. McTurk is to be heard describing the tortures of her husband's rheumatism.

"And Nora," I scream, when Mr. McTurk's symptoms show signs of waning. "Have you heard from her lately?"

"Poor souls!" says Mrs. McTurk. "They are away to India in the autumn."

"Nora will enjoy India," I bellow.

"That's to be seen," replies Mrs. McTurk. "It's very unsettling for the poor girl and bound to ruin her complexion. Mr. McTurk and I were just saying it's a fortunate thing they're not burdened with children, or we should feel obliged to offer them a home at Pinelands. I'm sure I don't know what I should do if I had to move about from one place to another like you soldiers' wives. We've been at Pinelands ten years now — ever since our marriage — and I'm sure I don't know what I would do if we had to leave. There were only three greenhouses when we went, and the garage was most inconvenient for the Rolls, but Mr. McTurk soon altered all that — and he put in three bathrooms, and built a billiard room — Mr. McTurk has spent thousands of pounds on the place."

I now ask with well-feigned interest how the Rolls is rolling — and feel annoyed with myself the next moment. "What a hypocrite you are!" says that other Hester who dwells with me in the same skin, and causes me endless trouble. "You know perfectly well you would be delighted to hear the Rolls had come to a bad end. Why do you try to please people, even when you dislike them as you dislike Mrs. McTurk?" I have no excuse to give for my conduct but am fitly punished for my falseness by having to listen to the detailed history of the Rolls, the Alvis, and the Armstrong-Siddeley, and to the various reasons why none of them is at liberty to convey Mrs. McTurk to Avielochan, where she is to join her gilded spouse for three weeks' fishing.

"Oh, how funny!" cries Betty, jumping up and down in the manner usual to her when moved by excitement. "Are *you* going to stay with Mrs. Loudon *too*?"

Alas for all my efforts! The cat is now out of the bag beyond recall. Mrs. McTurk's small eyes gleam as she replies that she is going to stay at the hotel, but it is not far from the house which Mrs. Loudon always occupies, and it will be very nice to see us there.

"You must come and dine with us at the hotel some evening," she adds hospitably. "When will you come?"

I reply with haste that there is a large house party at Burnside, and I do not know my hostess's plans, so it would be useless for me to make any engagements.

"Oh well, you can send me a note when you get there and see what's on," says Mrs. McTurk. "It doesn't matter a bit how many people there are, Mr. McTurk will be quite glad to see them all — any day will suit Mr. McTurk and I," she adds blandly.

The worst has now happened, and there is no further need for me to keep up the conversation, nor to try and make my voice audible above the roar of the train. I murmur that I have a headache — which I discover afterwards is absolutely true — and relapse into my corner. Mrs. McTurk finds me dull and goes away.

We change at various small stations with unpronounceable names, and arrive at Inverquill about teatime. This is the station for Avielochan, and I am relieved and delighted to see Mrs. Loudon's tall spare figure, clad in its usual shabby fashion, waiting on the platform. For the last hour I have been torturing myself with conjectures as to what I shall do if she is not there. But there she is, the same strange, shabby, dignified creature who was so kind to me at Kiltwinkle. She is accompanied by a tall dark man, easily recognisable as her son. His resemblance to his mother is striking, and he has the unmistakable brand of NAVY stamped upon his clean-shaven countenance. Betty takes instantaneous possession of him (she has a habit of appropriating men, which, looking to the future, is somewhat disquieting) and announces to him confidentially, but with great pride, that she was not sick at all. He congratulates her gravely upon her achievement.

"I think it was because the train went along nice and quietly," Betty says. "I like a nice quiet train that stops a lot — don't you?"

"That depends on whether I want to get there quickly or not," replies Mr. Loudon patiently.

Fortunately for me Mrs. McTurk is too busy marshalling her stupendous array of luggage to be troublesome to anybody except her porter. Our modest suitcases are disentangled from the pile, and we pack into Mrs. Loudon's roomy Austin for the last stage of our journey.

The road is glaring white in the afternoon sunshine, golden gorse gleams on the hills. Pine woods, carpeted with brown needles and full of dark shadows and golden lights, creep up to the road's edge, and then retreat in soldierly order, leaving the curling white ribbon bare and sunlit as before. The ribbon unwinds over the moor, where a few black-faced sheep with bouncing lambs crop the scanty herbage between patches of brown heather, raising their heads timidly to watch us roll by. The hills divide, showing glimpses of small lochs, delphinium blue in colour, fed with sparkling burns. Far away against the skyline, a ring of purple hills, with small white patches of snow in their crevices, keeps guard over the peaceful land.

The conversation is desultory, and confined to questions regarding our journey. Whether the train was up to time at Dalmawhagger or some name like that, and did we see Ben something or other. Unfortunately none of us is able to answer intelligently. I can't help feeling that Mrs. Loudon is depressed, or has something on her mind — her remarks seem to lack the trenchant note which I remember so well — but perhaps this is merely my imagination, or perhaps the presence of Annie, sitting up very straight on the folding seat in front of us, is embarrassing her.

We are now passing through a small grey-stone village which seems deserted in the bright white

239

sunshine. A few draggled-looking hens scutter out of our way, and a white cur dog snarls at us from an open doorway.

"This is Avielochan," says Mr. Loudon, turning round from his seat beside the chauffeur, and pointing to the houses. "Mother, you are not doing the honours properly. Look at the shop, Mrs. Christie! It is the pride of the countryside — you can buy everything there, except the one thing you happen to want."

We all look at the shop, and Betty, who seems by no means damped by her long journey, says it looks a very small place to have everything, and do they keep pianos?

"I said they had everything except what you want," says Mr. Loudon gravely. "So, of course, if you want a piano they haven't got one, and if you don't want one you don't ask for it."

"It's like Alice in Wonderland," says Betty after a moment's thought. "Jam every other day, but never today."

"You've got it exactly," replies Mr. Loudon.

By this time we had left the village far behind; we pass through two gates which have to be opened and shut, run along a pebbly road by the side of a biggish loch, and slow down to take a sharp bend round a huge bush of rhododendrons.

"Here we are! This is Burnside!" cries Mr. Loudon.

The house bursts into view — it is a long, low, whitewashed building with a slate roof which sags a little, as if the hand of Time had pressed it very gently in the middle. It is surrounded on two sides by pines and firs; on the third side a moory hill stretches skywards, and on the fourth, a green lawn covered with buttercups and daisies leads to an orchard in full bloom. A burn splashes gaily past the door and runs down towards the loch. Clumps of rhododendrons and masses of daffodils are the only flowers; it is a wild garden fitted to its surroundings of mountain and moor. A small path leads to some stepping-stones over the burn, the pine woods creep down to a wooden fence; there is a gate in the fence, and the path disappears into the gloom of the woods.

I stand at the door for a few moments drinking in the strange sweetness of the place.

"Is it like you thought it would be?" asks Mrs. Loudon, with her hand on my arm.

"How could I think — this," I reply vaguely.

"You must be starving," she says. "Come away up to your rooms, and we'll have tea whenever you're ready."

The room allotted to me is large and sunny; it has a plain wooden floor, and plain wooden furniture. Somehow it reminds me — though not unpleasantly — of a hospital ward. Betty and Annie are next door.

It is lovely to take off my hat, my headache has quite gone — nobody could have a headache in this sweet piercing air. I note, as I wash my hands, that the water is slightly brown and smells of peat; there is a faint peaty smell about the whole house, mixed with the resinous smell of sun-kissed pines. There are no carpets on the landing or on the stairs, everything has the same bare look as my bedroom — a pleasant change after the crowded carpeted rooms of Loanhead.

How far away I am from Loanhead in body and spirit! Where are Tim and Bryan? Are they still travelling southward, getting farther and farther away from me every moment? This is an unpleasant thought, and I decide to drown it in tea.

In the drawing room I find a bright fire, and a burdened tea table, and seated near the fire, a small wispy lady of what is usually called an uncertain age, knitting a large shapeless garment in cherry-coloured wool. She looks up at my approach and narrows a pair of short-sighted eyes.

"Oh!" she says vaguely. "Elspeth told me about you — you got here all right, did you? I can't remember your name for the moment, but I know it has something to do with music — now who do you think I am?"

She cocks her head on one side and looks at me coyly.

"Dr. Livingstone, I presume?" I reply inanely. I can't think what makes me say it, unless it was the picture of the historic meeting in darkest Africa which caught my eye coming down the stairs. Obviously the greeting is entirely unsuitable to the occasion, and to the lady — no more like the bearded Livingstone than a sheep is like a walrus — I have not even the faint hope that she will understand the allusion, and she doesn't.

"Oh, how funny you should think I was a doctor!" she says, tittering in a lady-like fashion. "That really is *very* funny — I must tell Elspeth about it when she comes down. Of course ladies *are* sometimes doctors nowadays, but I never went in for it. I once had a

242

course of first aid — that was during the war, of course — but I found the bandaging rather tiring, so I joined a society for providing the soldiers with pocket handkerchiefs instead. It seemed to me such an excellent idea to provide the poor fellows with pocket handkerchiefs. In a battle, for instance," says the good lady, waving her hands vaguely, "so easy to *lose* your pocket handkerchief in a battle, wouldn't it be? We made thousands of them, and sent them to the front packed in soap boxes — such charming letters we got from the poor fellows."

By this time I have pulled myself together, and decided that this must be the cousin, mentioned casually in Mrs. Loudon's letter. I had forgotten the cousin, or, to be more exact, I had imagined the cousin to be of the male sex — a strong silent individual, possibly an Anglo-Indian, and therefore, to be packed off with Mrs. Loudon's son on fishing expeditions, leaving my hostess and myself to chat comfortably together in the garden. (Is there any other woman on earth who would be so foolish as to build up such a detailed picture from a chance allusion to a cousin?)

My airy dreams fall with a crash, and I realise that my visit to Burnside will be absolutely ruined — I feel extremely annoyed with the cousin for being a woman, and with the woman for being here. Why couldn't she have stayed at home for this one short fortnight — or gone to a spa? (She looks like a woman addicted to spas.) I realise, of course, that my feeling is unreasonable, as, being a cousin, she has far more right to be here than I have.

These thoughts pass swiftly through my head, and the lady is still staring at me with unseeing eyes. "Perhaps I should tell you that my name is Mrs. Falconer," she says at last. "I've been hearing about you, of course. You live at Kiltwinkle, don't you? I can't say I ever cared very much for Kiltwinkle, but Elspeth *would* settle there. Oh, I remember your name now — *Christie*, isn't it? I knew it had something to do with music — we used often to go and see the Christie Minstrels when we were children; they had black faces and played banjos — *most* amusing. Of course they had nothing to do with *you*, but it is so strange having the same name — such a coincidence."

I am now beginning to feel positively light-headed, but whether this is due to the good lady's volubility, or the effects of the long day in the train with insufficient food I cannot determine.

"I wonder if you are related to some charming people I met at Bournemouth," Mrs. Falconer continues, still with that unseeing stare which seems to have some strange hypnotic power over its victim. "It must have been in 1911 or perhaps 1912 — anyhow, it was a very warm summer and long before the war — they were staying at my hotel — I wish I could remember the name of it. 'Parkfield' or 'Chatterton' or something like that. Such a comfortable hotel it was, with central heating in all the bedrooms. Of course we did not require it, because it was eighty in the shade at the time, but I remember thinking how pleasant it would be in chilly weather."

"Were your friends called Christie?" asks Mr. Loudon, who has come into the drawing room during Mrs. Falconer's dissertation.

"I think so," she replies. "It was either Christie or Christison, or it might have been Gilchrist — at any rate they were very charming; there was a mother, very aristocratic-looking with white hair, but the story got about that she was on the stage when he married her. Not that I have anything against the stage myself — and, of course, if they were related to Mrs. Christie it couldn't have been true — I'm only telling you what was said in the hotel —"

Mrs. Loudon now appears and interrupts the story to enquire about milk and sugar. "Hand Mrs. Christie the hot scones, Guthrie," she says. "Here's a letter from the MacQuills asking us all over to tennis on Monday. Hester, you ought to see Castle Quill while you're here. Millie, take one of these biscuits — I know you like them, and Mary made them specially. She'll be black affronted if none of them are eaten."

We all eat largely of the good things pressed upon us by our hostess, and the conversation paces along very pleasantly, but somehow I can't get rid of the feeling that Mrs. Loudon is not herself; there is something wanting in her manner. I miss those trenchant comments, those dashing pounces which enchanted me at Kiltwinkle.

It was not until we are dressing for dinner that the cause of Mrs. Loudon's depression is made manifest. She calls me into her bedroom in a mysterious manner, and asks me to admire the view. It is indeed admirable,

245

for the trees have been cleared to give a peep of the loch, behind which a thickly wooded hill sweeps upward to meet the sky in a bold curve. To the left the country slopes gently and is covered with pale green bracken, interspersed by feathery birch trees, their barks like silver in the afternoon sun.

"But you didn't call me in here to admire the view," I point out to her, when I have exhausted my scanty stock of adjectives, and marvelled afresh at the paucity of the English language.

Mrs. Loudon nods. "I've been wearying for you, Hester," she says, taking up a comb from her dressing table and scraping fiercely at her thick grey hair. "The truth is Guthrie's being chased by a cat, and I've no more idea what to do about it than fly. Millie's no use to talk to — she likes doing the talking herself — and if I can't talk to somebody about it I'll burst. You know the kind of a girl, with a cat face — all soft and furry — and red lips from the chemist's shop. Of course, the man has been starved of girls for eighteen months — I'm not blaming him, though how any son of mine can be such a fool — sitting and yearning at her like a codfish."

"I can't imagine him yearning at anyone."

"Wait till you see him," says Mrs. Loudon, threateningly, "I couldn't have imagined it either — Guthrie of all men! Guthrie who's never looked at a girl in his life! I've often wished he'd give me a daughter-in-law — God forgive me for not knowing I was lucky!"

"Where did she meet him?"

246

"At a dance in Portsmouth — one of the ships gave a dance — and now she's followed him here, and she's staying at the hotel in Avielochan — 'fishing with Dad,' that's the excuse. 'Fishing with Dad,' " repeats Mrs. Loudon scornfully. "The girl's never fished for anything except men! Oh yes, I'm being nice to her — I hope I know better than to let him see what a scunner I've taken at her — but it's not easy for me to hide my feelings, Hester. Surely at my age a woman should be past the need to wear a false face."

I don't see what help I can be in the matter, and say so as sympathetically as possible.

"Oh well — I was just hoping he'd see the difference," said Mrs. Loudon cryptically. "I was just hoping — perhaps — you would be nice to Guthrie and that —" here the scheming woman actually has the grace to blush — "and anyway, I'll have someone to talk to."

I can't help laughing at the idea of a staid married woman like myself being cast for the rôle of vamp.

Second June

Spend the morning lying in a deck chair in the garden pretending to knit. How glorious to have nothing to do! Mrs. Loudon comes out and consults me about Betty's food. The conversation strays (by some path not retraceable) to Guthrie's infatuation. We are to see the young woman this afternoon, as she has been invited to tea and to fish on the loch afterwards. I realise, after a few moments' conversation, that I am being asked to go out in the boat with them and "prevent anything from happening." The abandonment of her usual direct method of speech shows how much Mrs. Loudon is *bouleversée* by Guthrie's attachment, and I feel so sorry for her that I consent against my better judgment.

Mrs. Falconer strolls down about midday, and remarks that the sun is very hot and the loch very calm. "I can see it from the right-hand corner of my window if I lean out a little," she informs us. "Now where is Guthrie? He should not be wasting his time, you know, Elspeth. Why doesn't he go and fish? He would have no trouble with the boat today, the water is as calm as a mill pond, and there is not a suspicion of wind to blow his flies about."

Poor Mrs. Loudon is too upset to battle with Mrs. Falconer; she departs hastily for the house, saying that she forgot to tell Mary about the curds.

"So unrestful," Mrs. Falconer says with a sigh. "Dear Elspeth, we are all so fond of her, but she is *too much* of a Martha. Just to sit here quietly in the golden sunshine, with the pine trees standing on the hill, is not enough. Some people are incapable of admiring the beauties of Nature in silence — don't you agree, Mrs. Christie?" I agree fervently.

Mrs. Falconer continues: "It was in the autumn of 1905 that I first really saw Nature at its best. Before then I was like the man in the poem, who saw a violet by a mossy stone, and it was nothing more. I dare say you may not know the poem, but it is very beautiful, I can assure you. I heard it recited at a concert by a tall man with a glass eye, and it made an indelible impression on my memory. It may have been something to do with the glass eye, which was a slightly different colour from the other one. Very strange, isn't it, how a glass eye remains fixed, while the other one rolls about, but I dare say it would be stranger if they both rolled in different directions."

At this moment a tall form is seen hurrying across the garden. "Guthrie! Guthrie dear!" cries Mrs. Falconer. "Come here and tell us where you have been. You can hold my wool for me — there — like that, dear. No, not over the thumb — move your hands slowly from side to side as I wind. Now we are all comfortable. Did you catch a lot of fish this morning?"

"I didn't try," replies Guthrie, waving his hands in the air like a praying mantis.

"Now Guthrie, that's too bad of you. Fancy wasting a glorious day like this! Tomorrow may be wet for all we know — not so quickly, dear, and keep your hands lower — you know your mother paid pounds and pounds for the fishing, and there you go mouching round as if there were nothing to do."

Guthrie replies, with admirable restraint, that he had to go to the village to fetch meat.

"But if you had caught some nice fish it would have done just as well," says Mrs. Falconer kindly. "However, I dare say you never thought of that, or you would not have gone that long hot walk in the sun. I never was a great one for meat, myself. Dear Papa used to say *that* was the reason I had such a nice complexion. I don't know whether you remember my father, Guthrie; he was a very fine man. His beard was

249

considered one of the finest in the Conservative Club in London."

Guthrie says he never saw Mrs. Falconer's father. I can see that his patience is wearing thin, and welcome the appearance of my daughter. She and Annie have spent the morning down near the loch. Betty approaches, hopping first on one leg and then on the other.

"Oh, Mummie," she says breathlessly, "is it dinner yet? The water is frightfully cold, and I've found seventeen tadpoles. Annie is carrying them in my pail. They've got wiggly tails."

The gong rings for lunch.

Guthrie's young woman, who rejoices in the name of Elsie Baker, arrives at teatime in a Daimler from the hotel. She is welcomed by Guthrie with servile adoration. Mrs. Loudon smiles grimly, and says she hopes Miss Baker is well; then she turns to the chauffeur and asks him fiercely if he will take tea in the servants' hall. The poor man is so alarmed by her manner that he says it doesn't matter at all, and he often does without tea, anyway.

"Nonsense," says Mrs. Loudon. "Away with you to the kitchen, and mind and take a good tea while you're about it."

The man disappears hastily, and we all troop into the dining room.

Miss Baker is attired in a gown of printed voile which looks more suitable for a garden party than for a fishing expedition. She is certainly pretty, and has quite a nice dimple when she smiles. I can see her resemblance to a pussycat, something about the short, pointed chin and the way her eyes go up at the corners — green eyes.

Guthrie secures a seat next to his divinity, and admires her, mostly in silence. The rest of us make futile conversation. Mrs. Falconer, from whom I expected a useful flow, seems to have dried up at the source. She reminds me of the rivers of Australia, which, I have been told, are either rushing along in full flood, or else mere stagnant ditches with no refreshment for man or beast.

Mrs. Loudon, behind two large tea cosies, whispers to me, "Did you ever see the like?" To which I reply, "Yes, I've seen dozens exactly the same."

Mrs. Falconer pricks up her ears at this, and says "Dozens of what?" which completely stumps me.

Luckily Mrs. Falconer does not wait long for a reply. She is one of those blessed people who would rather give than receive information. "Aren't people queer?" she says, looking round the table to see if we are all listening. "I once knew a man called Charles Wood, and one day when he was going to Filey by train — or perhaps it was Bristol, I can't be quite certain — he saw a train starting off with Charleswood written on it. And what do you think he did? Well, he jumped into the train and went there, although he had a ticket in his pocket for Filey — or it may have been Bristol — and when he got there, he bought a house and insisted on going there to live, although it was most inconvenient for his work and didn't suit his wife. She was an invalid, of course, having broken her leg out hunting — or it may have been falling off a bus — no, that was

251

somebody else I am thinking of; it was falling off a horse she broke it, but I can't remember, just for the moment, whether that happened before they went to live at Charleswood or after they got there. She disliked the place intensely, it was so awkward ordering things on the telephone — Mrs. Charles Wood, Charleswood — such a muddle it was, for the poor thing."

Guthrie, who has been waiting with ill-concealed impatience for the end of the story, now jumps up and says we had better be getting under way. Whereupon Mrs. Falconer exclaims that these nautical expressions are so intriguing, and how do you spell it? Is it *weigh*? And has it anything to do with weighing the anchor?

"Yes, rather," says Guthrie. "We weight the anchor every morning to see how much it has lost during the night. You've heard the expression that a ship is losing way, haven't you, Cousin Milly?" And goes out hurriedly, before anything more can be said.

Mrs. Falconer smiles vaguely and repeats her conviction that it is all most intriguing, adding, that if she had a son, she would insist on his going into the navy just like dear Elspeth. Whereupon "dear Elspeth" replies, uncompromisingly, that she did everything she could to prevent Guthrie from going into the navy, short of locking him in the tool shed.

We start off for the loch, Guthrie laden with mackintoshes, rollocks, fish bags, rods, etc. He refuses to let Miss Baker carry anything, but I am allowed to carry the landing net and a fly book without any argument. It is still very warm and I am nearly boiled in my tweeds, but have been too well drilled by Tim to think of donning any other garb for a sporting expedition. Miss Baker glides along in her light frock, collecting wild flowers, and looking very charming indeed. Guthrie can't keep his eyes off her, nor reply rationally to my attempts at conversation.

Guthrie sits down in the thwarts, and assembles his rod with the loving care of an experienced fisherman. His hands look big and clumsy, but they are strangely neat as he threads the reel line from ring to ring. I have made up my mind to assume the role of boatman, in which I have had considerable experience when fishing with Tim. So far from any objection being raised at this altruism on my part, I find that both my companions accept it as the obvious solution to the problem. In fact, so far as they are concerned, it is not a problem at all. Feel slightly aggrieved at this, as I should have liked the chance of refusing to throw a cast.

"What are you putting on, Elsie?" says Guthrie, frowning over his flies. His face changes as he looks up and sees her open a large flybook full of made-up casts.

"These are the ones for Scotch lochs," says Elsie brightly.

"I'll show you how to make up your own," he offers with a shy smile.

"But these are the right thing," Elsie replies. "I mean to say they're specially made for Scotch lochs; the man in the shop said so."

Nothing more is said about casts, but the next two hours provide an interesting object lesson in the counter-attractions of love and sport. I feel quite sorry for the wretched girl, she puts her foot in it so often, and so unconsciously. Guthrie starts, like a perfect gentleman, by giving his young woman the best drifts, but begins to tire of the game when she has lost two good trout, dropped her rod into the water, and caught him on the ear with her tail fly.

"I'll take the right-hand cast this time," he says as we approach a black rock, which, even to my inexperienced eye, looks a likely spot for a big one.

Suddenly Guthrie's reel screams, and his rod is bent like a hoop: "It's a whopper!" he says excitedly. "Back the boat, Mrs. Christie."

The boat is already backed for Guthrie to play his fish. Twice he brings it up to the boat, and twice it rushes away and lurks beneath the shadow of the rock. Miss Baker has laid down her rod in the boat so as to land Guthrie's fish for him; two of her flies are deeply embedded in my skirt, but the moment is too thrilling for trifles to matter.

"Here we are," Guthrie says, winding in his reel. "The fight's out of him now — well under him, Elsie."

Miss Baker seizes the net, and dashes at the fish excitedly, and the next moment the fish has gone, and Guthrie's line lies limply on the water.

"Good heavens! Have you never landed a fish before?" he cries.

"Of course I have," replies Elsie hotly. "I always land them for Dad — that one wasn't hooked properly —"

"Hooked? Of course it was hooked — you knocked the hook right out of its mouth."

Elsie looks at him with dewy eyes.

"Never mind," he says hastily. "I expect it was my fault — better luck next time."

Peace is restored. We try another drift — a good one near some weeds. This time Miss Baker catches herself.

I am about to back away from the weeds to rescue the damsel in distress when Guthrie says: "Never mind just now, Mrs. Christie, we'll just *drift gently on to the weeds* — keep the boat round a little for me. That's great!"

There is a light in his eye that I have seen before in Tim's — I know the meaning of it well. I edge the boat gently along, hardly daring to breathe. Meanwhile, Miss Baker struggles wildly to disentangle the Greenwell's Glory from the lace of her hat — I can see she is anxious not to tear the lace.

Suddenly a trout rises and turns over Guthrie's tail fly, eyeing it with suspicion. He casts again over the same place, and the next moment his reel is running out.

"You've got him!" I cry breathlessly.

We back out of the drift, and I land a beautiful fat trout for him with great success.

"I've torn the lace," says Elsie, with a singular lack of discernment. She ought — of course — to have admired Guthrie's trout.

"I say, what a pity!" Guthrie says sympathetically. "And it's such a pretty hat, too — must be a pound and a half at least," he adds, gazing with admiring eyes at the still wriggling trout with its spotted sides and silver scales. Elsie replies that it was three guineas, but

255

Guthrie is not listening; he is planning a fresh campaign.

"We might try the bay on the north side," he says. "I've often got a good fish over there."

It has suddenly become colder, and a nice breeze has got up. The bitter-sweet smell of sun-warmed gorse comes in an occasional hot whiff of scent over the cooling water. Miss Baker shivers, and remarks that she thinks we had better go in now.

"Good Lord!" cries Guthrie. "We've only just started. *You* don't want to go in, do you, Mrs. Christie?"

"Oh, no! This is the best time of day," I reply. I feel rather a traitor to my sex, but comfort myself by the reflection that it is for Mrs. Loudon's sake. I hope the girl will not get pneumonia or I shall feel like a murderer. Miss Baker evidently realises that she has not shown to advantage as a fisherwoman; she offers to take the oars for a bit, so we change places and try the north bay. Guthrie is torn between his fondness for the new boatwoman and annoyance at her inefficiency.

"That's right, Elsie!" he says. "You're doing splendidly — keep her out a bit more, can't you see you're drifting over the best bit of water? You're an excellent boatman. Good Lord, don't splash like that, you're frightening every fish in the loch! Keep out, keep out — splendid — we're sure to get one in a minute — don't let the boat turn round like that —"

By this time the wretched girl is blue with cold. Even Guthrie sees it. He looks at her appraisingly, and says she ought to have *put more on*. "Perhaps we had better land you," he adds kindly. Miss Baker jumps at the suggestion, and we row back to the boathouse.

"You'll come, too, won't you, Guthrie?" she says, as she watches him land her rod and fishing tackle.

Guthrie hesitates; he looks at the loch, which is covered with small ripples from shore to shore. "Well," he says, "I think, if you don't mind, we'll go on for a bit — we've only got one so far — and you can easily find the way up to the house — it's no distance — just follow the path, you can't go wrong."

Miss Baker looks surprised and disappointed, but has the sense not to make a scene. Their "goodbye" can be no more than friendly, with me sitting in boat. Guthrie does not think of leading her behind the boathouse, his mind is too full of ripples; he does not even follow her with his eyes as she trips gracefully up the path, carrying her rod and fly book.

We fish until nine o'clock, and return tired and cold, but at peace with the world. Our bag consists of nine good trout, of which two are mine.

Third June

Mrs. Loudon having disappeared into the kitchen, I find my way to the flower room with the laudable intention of helping my hostess by doing the flowers for her. (I rather pride myself on my skill in this branch of domestic economy.) I am discovered in the act by Mrs. Loudon, who has polished off her housekeeping in record time.

257

"You'll take your hands off those flowers at once," she says fiercely. "What do you think you're here for? You're here for a holiday, my girl, and don't you let me catch you doing a hand's turn in this house or I'll pack you into the next south train, bag and baggage."

Fortunately I am sufficiently acquainted with my hostess not to be alarmed by her ferocity, so I merely put my arm round her waist, and give her a little squeeze.

"You and your blandishments!" she says scornfully, but is quite pleased all the same.

Mrs. Loudon's idea of doing the flowers is to cram every receptacle as full as she possibly can. I remain and offer a few words of advice on the subject, although I am not allowed to touch them. Suddenly she throws the flowers into the sink, and seizing me by the arm, demands in a hoarse whisper, "Hester, how did you do it? I've been wondering the whole night long. How on earth did you get rid of her?"

I reply that I made a cold breeze spring up, and covered the loch with the most fascinating ripples.

"Well, I wouldn't put it past you," she says, with a twinkle in her eye. "I may tell you the lassie was starved with cold when she got here — frozen to the marrow. I couldn't help feeling a bit sorry for her."

I reply that I was sorry for her, too, and that I trust she will not die of pneumonia.

"Not she. I gave her a good dose of cherry brandy —" this is Mrs. Loudon's panacea for every ill, and not a bad one either. "And now away with you," she adds in her normal voice. "I'll never get those flowers dressed with you standing there trying to cram your newfangled notions down my throat —" here she forces three more wretched tulips into an already bursting vase. "Away with you into the garden. Take a book with you, and give an old woman some peace."

So I depart into the garden with a book; but I have no intention of reading it. Instead, I lie in a long chair, and look at the mountains. Small clouds are trailing grey shadows over their calm bosoms. There is a single pine tree on the lower slopes, so near, it looks, that I could almost reach upward and pick it. The things pertaining to Martha fall away from me, and a blessed feeling of idleness encompasses my soul. I have not got to remember anything — neither to order fish, nor to count the washing. I need not write an order for the grocer, nor hunt after Maggie to see if she has cleaned the silver and brushed the stairs. The condition of Cook's temper is of no consequence to me, there are no domestic jars to be smoothed over. No sudden appeals to my authority, requiring the wisdom of Solomon and the diplomacy of Richelieu, can disturb my peace.

My thoughts drift across the garden and hang upon the trees like fairy lights, or curl upwards and vanish like the smoke of Burnside chimney. I can take a thought from the cupboard of my memory — just as I take a dress from my wardrobe — give it a little shake and put it on, or fold it away.

A bird singing in a pear tree brings back my childhood, and an orchard knee-deep in grass. Richard stands before me with the sun shining in his fair hair. "Have a bite, Hessy," he says — and the strange sour

259

tang of that pear makes my mouth water at this very moment.

How nice it is to lie here in blameless idleness, and let these vagrant memories flow through my body like a cool stream!

Somewhere in the world there must be a formula (am I trembling upon the edge of it now?) which, could I but grasp it, would reveal to me the Secret of the Universe. For there must be a secret, of course; the world would never roll over and over on its way through Time and Space if everyone's thoughts were as vagrant and purposeless as mine. This secret, once known, would string my thoughts together like a necklace of pearls.

But where to look for the secret — where to find it? Those mountains, dreaming so peacefully in the sunshine — do they possess it? Could I wrest it from their eternal silence? Shall I find it in the swallow's jagged flight, as it darts across the garden in pursuit of flies? Shall I find it in the call of the cuckoo, echoing sadly from the pine-clad hills? Or is it hidden deep in the hearts of human beings — a piece here and a piece there — so that if you could find all the pieces and fit them together, the puzzle would be complete? But the hearts of human beings are so difficult to find — people are so sealed up in themselves, withdrawn behind impenetrable barriers.

A bee drones past seeking honey in the golden bells of the daffodils — from one to another he quests with intermittent buzz. Are the flowers secret to him as people are to me? Or does he, tasting their sweetness, taste the very essence of their being, and know their souls? . . .

"Oh, to be in England now that May has come!" exclaims a rapturous voice from behind my chair. (I have been so deep in thought that I have not heard Mrs. Falconer's approach.) "Only, of course, we are in Scotland really — and it's June. Perhaps you don't know the poem I was quoting, Mrs. Christie. It is by a man called Byron — or was it Rupert Brooke? No," she continues, sitting down beside me and producing her knitting. "No, it couldn't have been Rupert Brooke, because he only wrote things about the war (although he did write something about 'England being here,' I know), but I remember learning *this* poem in 1892 when I was quite a child. I really was *quite* young at the time, but I have never forgotten it. Us girls did not go to school. Papa did not approve of school for girls. We were taught at home by a Miss Posten — such a very ladylike woman, she was, and most accomplished."

I murmur feebly that I feel sure she must have been.

"Yes, indeed, *most* accomplished," says Mrs. Falconer complacently. "I always think us girls owe a lot to Miss Posten, and I make a point of saying so whenever possible. I think it is only right to give people their due. I never saw anybody who could make a ribbon-work rose so beautifully as Miss Posten. It was so like a real rose that I used to tell her the birds would come and peck at it if she left it out of doors. Just like that artist who painted a picture of fruit, and the birds pecked at it because they thought it was real. I can't remember the name of the man, but Miss Posten always enjoyed the little joke."

Mrs. Falconer flows on until the gong sounds for lunch. We take our usual places round the table, and I proceed to enjoy the excellent food, which tastes all the better because I have not ordered it.

"Well, Guthrie, dear!" says Mrs. Falconer as she unfolds her table napkin, "I haven't seen a hair of you all the morning. You remember, Elspeth, what a favourite expression that was with dear Papa — I have not seen a hair of you, he used to say."

Mrs. Loudon replies, rather shortly, that she has no recollection of hearing Mrs. Falconer's father make use of the expression.

"Oh, but you *must* remember, Elspeth. Hardly a day passed but he would come out with it. How we used to laugh! — 'I haven't seen a hair of you all day' — Papa had the *drollest* way of saying things. And have you seen Miss Baker, Guthrie? Aha, you naughty boy! — I'm sure that's where *you*'ve been."

Guthrie admits sulkily that he met Miss Baker in the village.

Mrs. Falconer laughs. "I can't help laughing," she says. "Such a funny name — BAKER — isn't it? I always expect to see her hands all covered with flour, don't you?"

Guthrie replies with asperity: "No more than I expect to see you with a hawk on your wrist."

"A hawk!" cries Mrs. Falconer. "My dear Guthrie, you need never expect to find *me* having anything to do with a *hawk*. Horrible creatures, pouncing down out of the sky and picking out your eyeballs. I once read a book about India which said that there was a hawk waiting in the sky every three miles. It made me feel quite creepy, and took away all my desire to go to India. Snakes I *could* bear, but hawks every three miles — no, no!"

"Those were kites," Guthrie says, handing in his plate for a second helping of meringue. (I notice that, like most men, he has a very sweet tooth.)

"Kites? Oh no, Guthrie dear! It was I who read the book, and you must really allow me to know best. A kite isn't a bird at all; it is a sort of box made of paper. One of the boys had one the year we went to Littlehampton. (You remember me telling you about the year we went to Littlehampton, Elspeth?) He sailed it on a long piece of string. It always puzzled *me* how it stayed up in the air. Well, one day there was a high wind, and Edward's kite went sailing over the housetops. We had a great hunt for it, and eventually we found it hanging on a rope in somebody's garden, all amongst the clean clothes, and the clothes were so beautifully white that Mama decided, then and there, to send our linen to the woman to wash. The laundry we had before used to send the things home a sort of grey colour, and we found afterwards that they were hung out to dry next to the station yard. Well, that was all very well, and the linen was beautifully done, but things went amissing — first one of Papa's collars, and then a very beautiful embroidered tablecloth which my grandmother had brought home from India. It was embroidered with elephants with hurdles on their backs

263

— so quaint! There was an ivory fan as well, all made out of elephant's tusks, but Mama broke it when she was out at dinner one night. Dear me, what *was* the name of those people? I'm sure it began with a W. Elspeth, you must surely remember the people I mean. Papa and Mama used often to dine with them, they lived in Holland Park, and kept a pug. I believe it was Abernethy or Golding, or something like that. Anyway, he was a Jew and very rich. So strange, isn't it, that Jews never eat pork. I'm very fond of roast pork myself, but I must say I find it very indigestible."

"Shall we have coffee on the veranda?" says Mrs. Loudon suddenly.

Fourth June

> "Up the airy mountain,
> Down the rushy glen,
> We daren't go a-hunting
> For fear of little men."

Guthrie Loudon and I are on our way to the laundry to make enquiries about a garment belonging to Mrs. Falconer, which has failed to return from the wash. Guthrie is acting as guide (for the washer woman lives in a remote spot, and pursues her useful calling in the wilds). I am to be spokesman, since the missing garment cannot be enquired for by the opposite sex.

I am aware that the garment in question is handmade, in pink crêpe de chine, trimmed with

264

Valenciennes lace — these salient facts having been communicated to me in mysterious whispers by the owner. Mrs. Falconer has spent the morning bewailing her loss, so that our expedition has been undertaken for the sake of peace. I can't make myself believe that it really matters very much whether the expedition is successful or not; the Highland air has this strange effect upon me, that I care for nothing but the enjoyment of the moment — and the moment is exceedingly enjoyable.

Guthrie takes up the song where I left off.

> "Wee folk, good folk
> Trooping all together,
> Green jacket, red cap,
> And white owl's feather."

He has a nice deep bass voice, which rolls up the narrow path between the trees, and echoes amongst the rocks.

"It's a good thing we're not superstitious," he says, when the last echo has died away. "The Little People don't like being spoken of, you know. Wouldn't you be frightened if they came crowding down on us out of their hiding places in the glen, and led us astray?"

"What would they do to us, I wonder."

"They would bind us with silken cords, and keep us prisoners for a hundred years," he replies with relish.

"Then in a hundred years, you and I would return to the world," I tell him. "I wonder whether we should be

265

old and white-haired, or eternally young, like Mary Rose."

"We shall be young," Guthrie decides, "and we shall make lots of money by going about giving lectures, and telling people what a strange place the world was a hundred years ago."

This is the right sort of nonsense for a Highland afternoon, and we elaborate the theme with a wealth of fantastic detail.

"We'll start by telling them about meals," Guthrie continues. "People will be horrified and disgusted when we tell them that we used to sit down round a table four times every day and feed in company. A hundred years hence nobody will dream of eating in public. Each person will retire to his room once a day and swallow enough tablets of protein and carbohydrates to last him for twenty-four hours."

"It sounds a little dull," I protest.

"That may be, but eating in public is a relic of barbarism, and it is better to be dull than disgusting. A pretty woman looks her worst at mealtimes, and a greedy man is the foulest sight on earth. I knew a fellow who applied to be transferred to another ship, simply because he couldn't stand the sight of the owner eating soup."

While we are thus talking the path curves upward, and there are hundreds of little flowers in the grass — blue and yellow and white and mauve. A few gay butterflies flutter across from side to side, and the sunshine falls like golden largesse between the shadows of the leaves. We emerge from the woods on to the shoulder of a hill — and pause for a moment to admire the view. The air is so clear that the pine trees seem conscious of the lochs, and the lochs seem conscious of the pine trees, as if they were whispering to each other some secret message of their own. A scroll of smoke, from a small farmhouse, hangs in the still air like a smudge of dirt on the blue gauze of the sky. Everything is crystal clear, bright, bright like spring water, like diamonds, like the wide tear-washed eyes of a young child. Brightness seems to me the most astonishing quality of this new world. The brightness of it washes through my body and brain, until I feel clear all through, until I feel utterly transparent, and the sweet hill wind blows through my very soul — cool, lovely clean wind. Every branch of every tree has a song of its own, and the note of the cuckoo echoes from the hills.

"What would you say if I told you we were lost?" says Guthrie suddenly, in a conversational tone. I reply instantly that I should be extremely angry, and cancel his pilot's certificate.

"Well, I told you the Little People would be angry," he says deprecatingly.

We sit down upon the brown carpet beneath an enormous fir tree and light cigarettes. "You see," he exclaims, "I thought we might take a short cut. The woods are lovely, aren't they? Are you enjoying yourself?"

"That's neither here nor there," I reply sternly. "We were sent out upon a definite mission — to recover Mrs. Falconer's — er — property at all costs. I am surprised and pained to find that a naval officer, of your service, has so little sense of responsibility."

"Oh damn!" exclaims Guthrie, without rancour. "What does it matter about Cousin Millie's pants, as long as you are enjoying yourself? Can't you see how much more important the one thing is than the other? Try to cultivate a sense of proportion — Hester."

"Certainly, Guthrie," I reply meekly.

He rolls over and looks at me. "You don't mind, do you?"

"Why should I? Everyone calls everyone else by their Christian names nowadays."

"Oh, but this is different!" he says, wrinkling his forehead with the effort to explain. "You're not like everyone, or I would have done it without thinking — and I've been trying to do it all the afternoon — so you see it's different, and I'm doing it differently."

"Well, in that case perhaps I had better say 'no,'" I reply primly.

He looks at me quickly, to see if I really mean it.

"Guthrie, do you smell a lovely smell of peat smoke?" I ask, trying to look very innocent.

"Hester, I believe I do," he replies gravely.

We walk on about fifty yards through a little wood, and come upon a clearing amongst the trees. The sunshine fills it with a golden haze — it is like a bowl of gold. In the middle is a thatched cottage, and all about are lines of rope, with dozens of cheerful garments hung upon them to dry.

"Why, here we are after all!" exclaims Guthrie, and, as I follow him down the path, bending my head beneath a snowy sheet, and dodging the dancing legs of some pale pink pyjamas — are they Guthrie's, I wonder — I can't help suspecting that we were never lost at all.

Miss Campbell receives us with a natural dignity. She is a woman of about forty, tall and straight, with blue-black hair drawn into a knot at the back of her shapely head. "Come away in and have a drink of milk," she says hospitably, as she squeezes the soapsuds off her hands, and wipes them on her checked apron. "Did you walk all the way from Burnside, then?"

"We did," replies Guthrie. "It was a lovely walk. I don't know when I've enjoyed a walk so much. Mrs. Christie has a message for you."

"Is that so?" says Miss Campbell. "I hope it's not to complain of anything, then."

I disclose my errand while Guthrie, with great delicacy of feeling, interests himself in the pictures which adorn the walls. A highly coloured oleograph of a young man offering his heart to a beautiful lady in a Grecian garden seems to claim his particular attention. I can't help wondering whether he sees any resemblance to Elsie in the classic profile of the lady, or is taking hints from the picture as to the exact position it would be correct to assume when he pops the question himself.

"If Mrs. Christie would just come into the laundry a minute," suggests Miss Campbell, in mysterious whispers.

We repair at once to the laundry, a long wooden shed, redolent with the warm smell of freshly ironed clothes. A young girl — tall and dark like Miss

269

Campbell, and with the same graceful and dignified manner — is busily engaged in ironing a pile of fine garments.

"Morag, would you be after seeing Mrs. Falconer's camiknickers?" asks Miss Campbell bluntly.

"I would not," replies the girl, raising her head and looking at us with a pair of night-blue eyes.

"Where would they be, then?"

"You might be after finding them upon the lines," suggests Morag, after a moment's thought.

I follow Miss Campbell into the garden. "I suppose that is your niece," I remark conversationally. "She is very like you."

"She might be," is the cryptic reply, but whether this refers to the likeness or the relationship remains in doubt.

The lines run in all directions like a gigantic spider's web. Miss Campbell looks about her with some pride. "It's a pleasure to be washing some people's clothes," she says, "and to wash for some people is no pleasure at all. You would be surprised, Mrs. Christie, if you could be seeing the things some people wear. It's whited sepulchres, they remind me of, and others, that you might not give the credit to, are all glorious within. It gives you a sight into human nature to wash. See what a pretty line this is! These things belong to Miss MacArbin, now. They are fine and pretty, but quite plain. I like things to be plain, for they come up so nice in the ironing."

I agree with Miss Campbell, and admire Miss MacArbin's taste.

"Miss MacArbin has a lot of new things lately," she continues. "I'm wondering if she will be thinking of marrying. Would you be hearing anything of that nature about Miss MacArbin?"

I reply that I have not the pleasure of her acquaintance.

"That's a pity now. I think you would like Miss MacArbin — she is a very pretty young lady, and clever with her hands. She makes all her own clothes, for they are not well off now, though they own a great deal of property. I would not be surprised to be hearing of her marriage. It's a pity you do not know her. There will be a baby coming to The Hall," continues Miss Campbell, passing down another line full of tiny garments, white as snow. "I like to wash baby clothes best of all."

I perceive that Miss Campbell — like most people who are buried in the wilds — takes a keen interest in the affairs of her neighbours, and this is her strange manner of keeping a hand on the pulse of life. It must be an amusing game, on long winter evenings, to guess at the meaning of a christening robe amongst the washing from Mrs. A, and to deduce the possibility of an early marriage for Miss B from the fact that she has invested in half a dozen crêpe de chine nightdresses.

"Of course I was aware that Mr. Guthrie was home from sea," continues Miss Campbell, confidentially, as she runs her eyes down a line hung with gentleman's underwear, and moves on. "But I could not be placing *you* at all. You are not so plain as Mrs. Loudon herself, nor yet so frilly as Mrs. Falconer. I was wondering could you be Mr. Guthrie's betrothed — but then there

271

was the little girl to account for. Is it your little girl that has the wee pyjamas with the pink collars then?"

We have been all round the garden by this time without any success. Miss Campbell says we'll take one more look down Miss MacArbin's line —

"Ah!" she says suddenly. "This will be the thing we are looking for. The idea of Morag putting it on Miss MacArbin's line — foolish lassie — it is not like Miss MacArbin at all, at all. Miss MacArbin has a different style altogether."

We retrieve Mrs. Falconer's despised garment from the line, and Morag irons it, and makes it up into a neat parcel.

Guthrie has made an exhaustive survey of the pictures in Miss Campbell's sitting room, and is now pawing the ground like a restive horse. "You might have *made* the things, the time you took," he says crossly. "You don't mean to tell *me* they're in that parcel! There can't be much *warmth* in them."

He stuffs the parcel into his pocket, and, after taking a polite farewell of Miss Campbell, we set off home.

Fifth June

I accompany my hostess to the parish church. We take our seats near the back, and Mrs. Loudon points out some of the notabilities of the neighbourhood as they arrive. Chief among these are Sir Peter and Lady MacQuill, to whose ancestral halls we have been bidden. Sir Peter is a square man with reddish hair and a pink face, his kilt swings in an authoritative manner as he strides up the aisle in the wake of his lady to the front pew.

"She was a MacMarrow of Auchwallachan," says Mrs. Loudon in an awed whisper, and I conclude that this must be a great distinction. I feel glad that Mrs. Loudon has told me about Lady MacQuill, for she looks as if she might easily have descended from that well-known family the Smiths of Peckham. It is her spouse who carries all the dignity of the MacQuills, and his broad shoulders look capable of bearing it.

We speak to them afterwards at the church gate, and they profess themselves charmed to have my company at the tennis party tomorrow.

"Guthrie asked Hector if he could bring a friend of his, who is staying at the hotel," adds Lady MacQuill, "a Miss Baker, I think it was. Please tell him we shall be delighted to see her."

Mrs. Loudon tries to look pleased at this information, but makes a poor job of it.

"I hope you are making a long stay this year, Mrs. Loudon," says Sir Peter, somewhat in the manner of a king inviting a foreign duchess to settle in his kingdom.

"I'm staying six weeks," replies Mrs. Loudon bluntly.

"Are you enjoying your visit here, Mrs. Christie?" he enquires.

"It is an enchanting spot," I reply gravely.

After this exchange of courtesies, the MacQuills step into the car — an exceedingly ancient and battered Rolls — and are whirled away.

"They're pleasant folk when you get to know them," says Mrs. Loudon, as we return home. "If *he* could forget for a moment that he was Sir Peter MacQuill he'd be easier to speak to — there's no nonsense about *her*. You'll enjoy seeing Castle Quill. Parts of it date from the twelfth century."

Later in the day I find myself strolling with my hostess in the walled garden. This lies upon the hillside some distance from the house. It is a delightful spot with a southern aspect, where vegetables and flowers riot together in happy confusion. I remark on the strangeness of the proximity of onions and sweet peas, and point out a single damask rose amongst the potatoes.

"That's Donald," says Mrs. Loudon. "It's a little puzzling till you get used to it. But I could never complain to the MacRaes about Donald. The man's a poet, and you have always to make allowances for poets in practical matters. Why, there's the man himself pottering about in his Sunday suit! He can't keep away from his flowers — sometimes I think they're more to him than his children. Donald, here's Mrs. Christie wanting to know why you've got your sweet peas planted amongst the onions."

The man rises slowly from his knees, and takes off his hat with a natural grace. He is very tall and broad-shouldered, and his rugged face is full of the grandeur of his native hills. These people seem to have more bone in their faces than their southern neighbours — I can't describe it better than by comparing them to their mountains, whose rocks show boldly through the thin covering of earth. A slow smile spreads over Donald's face at Mrs. Loudon's words,

274

and he replies in a soft low voice, "Perhaps I was thinking it would be pleasant to be smelling the sweet peas when I would be picking up the onions for Mrs. Loudon's dinner."

"There," says Mrs. Loudon triumphantly. "I knew Donald would have some poetical reason for it."

We move on slowly in the warm air, and Mrs. Loudon begins to talk about Mrs. Falconer. "Sometimes I get deaved with the woman," she admits, "and then I'm sorry. There was a tragedy in her life. You'll have noticed that in all her havering she never mentions her husband. Harry Falconer was a gem. Some of us never understood what he saw in Millie, but that's neither here nor there. They were married, and away they went to Paris for their honeymoon. Three weeks of it they had, and then, one day, they ran after a tram — they were going out to Versailles, or some such place. I don't know the rights of it, for the poor soul never mentions a word about it, but, apparently, Harry suddenly collapsed — the man must have had a weak heart, and nobody knew, not even himself. He died before they could get him back to the hotel. So that was the end of Millie's happiness, poor soul, and that's why I have her here when I can, and bear with her as patiently as I am able — which isn't very patiently, I'm afraid, when all's said and done, because I'm an impatient old woman by nature. Millie was always a talker," continues Mrs. Loudon, after a little pause. "But it wasn't until after she lost Harry that she became so — so trying to her friends. I sometimes think the shock must have affected

275

her brain. They say we're all a wee thing mad on some subject or other."

"Well, what are *we* mad about?" I ask, giving her arm a little squeeze.

"I'm mad about yon girl of Guthrie's," says Mrs. Loudon in a strained voice. "I declare I can think of nothing else, and, if I do think of other things, the girl is nagging away at the back of my mind, for all the world like an aching tooth. Sometimes I think if I could just get him out of her clutches I'd die happy."

"He's not married yet," I point out optimistically.

"No, but he's on his way to it," she replies. "You don't think I'm wrong to try to influence Guthrie's life, do you, Hester?"

"She's not the right person for him."

"She's all wrong in every way. I'm not that despicable creature, a jealous mother. I'd welcome any girl I thought would make the man a good wife. Someone like you," she continues, looking at me, almost with surprise. "Yes, somebody exactly like you. And I'd steal you from that Tim of yours if I could, but I know there's little hope of that — that's the sort of woman I am. People must marry, and have children — and yet I don't know why I should think so, for there's a deal of sorrow comes to most married folks that single ones escape."

"There are two to bear it," I tell her.

"Yes," she says. "That's the secret, and perhaps sad things don't happen to everybody."

"If we don't have troubles sent us we can generally make them for ourselves," I reply. "It's easy to make yourself miserable over trifles; I've done that sometimes, and then, quite suddenly, you get sent something to be sorry about, and you think — looking back — how happy I was yesterday, and I never knew it."

"Well, well!" she says. "It's all true, but these are sad croakings for a June day. I'll tell you what *you're* mad about now, just to show there's no ill-feeling. You're mad about that good-for-nothing husband of yours. You needn't waste your breath denying it, for I could see it in your face when there was all that talk of his going off to India without you. Oh yes! You're doing without him fine at the moment, but I'm not sure that your heart's really here. Part of you is away south, at Biddington, and you're wishing every now and then that Tim were here."

I am somewhat surprised that Mrs. Loudon should have guessed the state of my feelings so shrewdly, for I have not owned — even to myself — that I am missing Tim. "Perhaps I am missing him," I reply thoughtfully. "But it is really only because it is so lovely here."

"'Never the time, and the place, and the loved one all together,' " says Mrs. Loudon. "But what about suggesting to the man when you write him — if you ever do find time to write him, of course — that he might come up for a few days at the end of your visit, and take you away south with him?"

This sounds a delightful plan, and I say so with suitable expressions of gratitude — at the same time pointing out that Tim may not be able to get leave, and that the journey is expensive.

"Hoots!" she says, twinkling at me in her comical manner. "The man will get leave if he asks for it. I never knew a soldier that couldn't. And as for the journey, he has only to cook up a railway pass — or whatever they call it — and he'll get here and back for nothing."

Mrs. Loudon's ideas of the army seem slightly out of date. I point out to her that the Golden Age has passed away, but she pays no heed to my expostulations.

"Tell him to come, and he'll come," she says.

By this time we have reached the house. Betty's face appears at the bathroom window. "Come and see me in my bath, Mrs. Loudon," she calls out. "Come *now*. I'm all bare and ready."

Mrs. Loudon waves her hand. "I'll come and skelp you, then," she cries, and away she goes, running like a girl.

Sixth June

Castle Quill is approached by a drawbridge over a narrow ravine, at the bottom of which a swift river runs amidst rocks and ferns. The castle is of grey stone, with small dark windows which frown threateningly at the approaching guest.

We drive up to a nail-studded door, and are presently ushered through a large hall, paved with stone and hung with antlers, into an old-fashioned drawing room, full of furniture of the uncomfortable Early Victorian time. The castle is a strange blend of periods; it is lighted with electric light, and warmed by central heating, yet these concessions to modern comfort seem to fit into the ancient place, and the whole conglomeration of the ages is blended into an harmonious whole. Perhaps this is due to the atmosphere of the MacQuills, which fills the place. They have lived here ever since the castle was built, and the very stones are impregnated with their spirit.

The windows of the Victorian drawing room open on to fine lawns, flanked by herbaceous borders. Here the garden party is in full swing. We are greeted by the laird and his lady with hospitable warmth.

"Hector is somewhere about," says Lady MacQuill vaguely. "He is managing the tennis, I think."

Mrs. Loudon says we will find him, and we walk slowly towards the courts, stopping on the way to speak to various friends of Mrs. Loudon's, to all of whom I am introduced with pleasant old-world formality. Guthrie has now disappeared — probably to look for Miss Baker — so we find two chairs, and sit down to watch the people, and enjoy their peculiarities.

Mrs. Loudon points out "the Duchess," a small fat woman who — at first glance — might easily be mistaken for somebody's cook, but on closer examination is seen to be endued with a strange mantle of dignity befitting her rank.

"Who's that man?" says Mrs. Loudon suddenly. "He seems to know you, Hester, or is he trying to give you the glad eye?"

I look up and am amazed to see Major Morley — of all people — making his way towards us over the grass.

"It's Major Morley!" I gasp.

279

"What?" says Mrs. Loudon. "Not the man who came to see you at Kiltwinkle? Fancy him following you here!"

I reply hastily that he can't have "followed me here," for the simple reason that he did not know I was coming, and that he only came to see me at Kiltwinkle to relieve my mind about Tim being posted to India.

Mrs. Loudon says "The man's evidently an altruist."

By this time he has reached our retreat. "I've been looking everywhere for you," he says warmly.

"But how did you know I was here?" I enquire.

"Hector MacQuill told me. I'm staying at the hotel, you know. It's quite a comfortable place, and the fishing's fairly good."

It is very nice to find a friend amongst all these strangers, and Major Morley is usually amusing. He and Mrs. Loudon take an instant liking for each other — an occurrence which pleases and surprises me in equal proportions. They are both outspoken and definite in their ideas, and they both possess a dry sense of humour. I feel they might just as easily have hated each other at first sight — and this would not have been nearly so pleasant.

We sit and talk about our fellow guests — Major Morley seems to be acquainted with many of their foibles. The conversation is not easy to follow for one who does not know the district.

"Have you seen the MacDollachur girl?" asks Major Morley.

"Yon limmer!" exclaims Mrs. Loudon scornfully. "How can she show her face in any civilised place?"

"There's not much of her face to be seen. I doubt whether her best friend would know her if she washed the paint off."

"There's the bride!" exclaims Mrs. Loudon.

"But no groom in sight," replies Major Morley. "Now that she's got him safely married there's no need for any further effort, I suppose."

I find this kind of duet somewhat boring, and am not sorry when Major Morley and I are discovered by a tennis enthusiast, and invited to make up a four. We find ourselves partnered against Guthrie and Elsie Baker, and proceed to beat them without much difficulty, thanks to Major Morley's slashing service and brilliant returns. Guthrie is a sound player, and puts up a good fight, but his partner is too busy showing off her stylish strokes (most of which go out) to be of much help to him.

It is all very pleasant. The sun shines brightly, and the dresses, though slightly out-of-date according to London standards, look very pretty and gay on the green lawns amongst the flowers.

After the set we are joined by the son of the house, Hector MacQuill. He is very tall, with aquiline features and beautiful hands. Major Morley seems to know him well, and enquires with his usual lack of ceremony how on earth that awful Baker girl got here.

"She *is* rather awful," says young MacQuill. "I've never seen her before. Guthrie Loudon wanted her asked."

"Good God!" says Major Morley. "I spend my whole time avoiding her — she's staying at the hotel, and she makes eyes at everything in trousers."

"You should wear a kilt," suggests Hector, smiling.

It is now decreed that Mrs. Christie must really see the chapel and, Mrs. Christie professing herself enchanted to see anything she is shown, arrangements are instantly made for the expedition. Major Morley says Mrs. Loudon should see it too, and, this being agreed upon unanimously, he proposes to fetch the lady in question, and follow us with all speed.

Hector MacQuill and I start off down a mossy path by the side of the river and, after a few minutes' walk, we come upon a ruined chapel overgrown with ivy and surrounded by the gravestones of the MacQuills. I find my guide very interesting, and well-informed regarding the history and habits of his ancestors. He makes them real to me. Their strange barbaric form of life, and the mixture of simplicity and ferocity in their natures are easily understood in the wild setting of frowning crags and dashing river where the tale is told.

"I was named after the wildest of the lot," he says, with a friendly smile which lights up his austere contenance in a remarkable way. "Hector MacQuill was famous for his audacity in an age when audacity was the natural order of things. He was the hero of a hundred fights, and his raids were the most daring in the whole countryside. One day when Hector was out hunting he happened to see MacArbin's daughter, and fell in love with her at first sight. The MacArbins are our hereditary enemies, Mrs. Christie. We are still at

282

daggers drawn with them for no reason but the old feud. You will hardly believe such a thing can *be* in the twentieth century, but my father holds fast to the old traditions. He would as soon pull down the old chapel as give up his ancient enmity with the clan MacArbin. I'm hoping to alter all that, but it won't be easy."

"Well, to return to Hector — it was a sort of Montague and Capulet affair, but Hector was less civilised than Romeo and — shall we say? — more virile. One dark night he called the clan together, and made a raid on Castle Darroch (the stronghold of the MacArbins), carrying off his lady-love from under her father's nose. He kept her a prisoner at Castle Quill until she consented to marry him, and then he married her with splendour and feasting such as had never been seen in the memory of man. It was a strange wooing, but the strangest thing was that they were very happy together, and Seónaid MacArbin became a staunch MacQuill. Here are their graves, close together beside this holly bush."

We look at the two little mounds in silence. For my part I am enthralled with the story, caught back to those strange wild days where love and war went hand in hand.

"Hector was a wild devil," continues his namesake. "He was the terror of the countryside — always up to some mischief or other. Perhaps you think it strange that we should be proud of him?"

"He was a man," I reply.

"The MacArbins got him at last. They laid many traps for him, but Hector seemed to lead a charmed life. Perhaps he got careless in the end."

"What happened?"

He laughs. "I don't want to bore you, Mrs. Christie."

"It's thrilling," I tell him.

"Well, Hector was out hunting with some of the clan. Suddenly they heard a woman screaming for help. Hector called a halt. You can imagine the little band in the depths of the forest, looking at each other and wondering what was afoot. The screams came again, and without more ado, Hector led the way in the direction from whence they came. They were getting near to the MacArbin stronghold, and some of them must have felt a qualm of fear, for the feud was very fierce, and they could expect no mercy were their enemies to find them on MacArbin territory. But Hector did not know what fear was, he pressed on, and soon they came to a small clearing in the forest, and saw a girl bound to a tree with ropes. She called out that she had been robbed and ill-treated and besought them to loose her. The band were filled with fury at the outrage; they dismounted, and Hector cut her bonds. Scarcely had he done so when the MacArbin battle cry rang out, and a hundred of the MacArbin clan burst through the undergrowth, and fell upon the MacQuills tooth and nail. It was an ambush; Hector had walked into it blindfold."

"The MacQuills, totally unprepared for the onslaught, were soon defeated. Hector was taken, and only two of the band escaped to bring the news to Castle Quill.

Next morning Hector's body, full of wounds, and mutilated almost beyond recognition, was found on the road near the Castle gate. They had a grisly sense of humour in those days."

"Seónaid MacQuill was not the woman to take such an insult lying down. She determined to revenge his death. Calling the clan together, she delivered an impassioned address, reminding them of the prowess of their late chief in battle, and his kindness to them in troublous times, and asking for volunteers for certain death. The clan volunteered as one man. Seónaid chose a dozen of the stoutest, and laid before them her plan. That very night, when the MacArbins were celebrating the death of their enemy with wine and feasting, Seónaid led her chosen band into Castle Darroch by a secret passage from the loch. She was a MacArbin, of course — that was how she knew of its existence. When the feast was at its height, Seónaid, with a dozen fierce warriors armed to the teeth, sprang into the banqueting hall and laid about them with their claymores. They were overpowered in the end, and every man of them slain, but not before they had done a good deal of damage amongst their unarmed and unsuspecting hosts. Seónaid herself was killed in the mêlée. I think she intended that this should happen, for she was devoted to Hector, and life without him must have seemed impossible."

"The MacArbins had a custom of throwing the bodies of their dead into the loch upon which their Castle stands. It saved burial, and, truth to tell, there is very little ground round the place where you could dig for three feet without coming upon solid rock. For some unknown reason Loch-an-Darroch never gives up its dead. Nothing thrown into the loch is ever seen again. I suppose it is something to do with the currents or else because it is very deep."

"Seónaid's marriage with a hated MacQuill had rankled for years in the hearts of the MacArbins. They considered her a traitor to her clan, but she still belonged to them, so they decided to give her a MacArbin funeral. The night was dark; they pushed their boats out from the shore; torches made of pine resin threw a red glow upon the waters. The priest read the burial service and Seónaid's body was committed to the loch. Thus the MacArbins vindicated their honour, and reclaimed their own."

"Next morning some women, going down to the loch to wash clothes, found the body of Seónaid washed up in a little bay where the sand was white and the willows drooped over the water. They rushed up to the castle, screaming out the news, and in a few moments the whole clan was roused and had trooped down to the water's edge to see for itself whether the impossible and unheard-of had really happened. Yes, there was Seónaid lying on the sand, half in and half out of the water, and the little waves were lapping round her and moving the long strands of her hair — Loch-an-Darroch had given up its prey. A terrified silence fell upon the clan; they looked at each other in horror — what terrible thing did this portend?"

"'Throw her back again!' cried some of the hotheads, but the wiseacres would not hear of such a thing. This

286

was a sign and a portent; to throw her back would be to invite disaster.

"It was obvious that the loch would have none of her — or else she would have none of the loch. To throw her back was madness, for her spirit would not rest; it would haunt the castle and cause endless trouble to the clan. It was therefore decided to carry her back to the MacQuills, so that her spirit, if it felt restless in its narrow bed, might haunt clan MacQuill rather than clan MacArbin."

"So it was that Seónaid had another funeral — slightly more orthodox than her first — and was buried beside Hector in MacQuill ground."

"And does she haunt them?" I ask, for the story has seized upon my imagination, and a ghost would be a fitting and pleasantly creepy sequel.

The modern Hector laughs. "I'm afraid I don't believe in ghosts, Mrs. Christie, but some people are under the impression that they have seen the spirit of Seónaid walking upon Loch-an-Darroch or haunting the ruined castle of the MacArbins."

"What, have we a Highlander here who doesn't believe in ghosts?" says Mrs. Loudon. She and Major Morley have approached us while we were talking, and have overheard the last words of the story.

"Have you told Mrs. Christie about the bard?" enquires Major Morley.

"I think I've told her enough for one day," replies Hector MacQuill with a laugh; but I am determined to hear all I can, and after a little persuasion he continues. "In those days there was no written record of events, but every clan had a bard (or poet) who composed verses, commemorating the brave doings of his chief, and set them to music. These songs were handed down from father to son, and, in this way, some record was kept. The bard belonging to clan MacQuill composed an ode to Seónaid, and it is through this ode that the story I have told you has travelled down the centuries to the present day. Of course the poem was in Gaelic, but the last part might be translated something like this:

"In dark Loch-an-Darroch, beneath the stark crags,
Our Seónaid found no rest.
How should MacQuill sleep in MacArbin water?
How should a lioness find peace in the lair of a
    badger?
Would the proud eagle who nests on Ben Seoch
Seek shelter in the pigeon house?
Seónaid was ours from the day when we took her,
Our courage and cunning won her from our foes.
Brave Hector bore her home upon his black steed,
And the skies flashed and thundered.
Lovely as the night was Seónaid —
Her hair floated upon the waters of Darroch,
Like a black cloud it floated round her,
And like a water lily was her face.
She came back from the grave,
And brought fear to the black hearts of MacArbin.
They looked upon her and trembled.
Take her up and bring her safely home,
To her true home by the dashing river Quill,

Which comes down from Ben Seoch like a lion seeking
   its prey,
And all who drink of it are filled with courage.
Bring her home to her own people who loved her well.
Lay her down gently in the kindly warm earth.
Hector the brave, and Seónaid the beautiful —
Together they sleep in the shade of the holly."

None of us speaks for a moment or two, and perhaps this is the right tribute to pay.

"Do you think she really was very beautiful?" Major Morley asks at last.

"I think she was," replies Hector. "The MacArbin women have all been noted for their beauty, and Seónaid was the same type — pale as a lily, with dark hair — oh yes, she was certainly beautiful."

"How quiet it is here!" says Mrs. Loudon. "Even the river seems to run softly past this place, as if it were afraid of disturbing their rest."

"They had a wild time while it lasted," Major Morley says. "They've earned a peaceful sleep. I think I should have liked to live in those days —"

"What! — with no hot baths, Tony?" asks Hector MacQuill, smiling.

"That would be a drawback, of course," replies Major Morley, gravely. "But think how pleasant to be able to kill off your enemies whenever you felt inclined — unless, of course, they got you first — and if you fancied anybody as a wife you just carried her off and married her. On the whole we have lost more than we have gained by the march of civilisation."

"Isn't there a salmon loup near here?" asks Mrs. Loudon, looking round her as if she expects to see salmon leaping amongst the trees.

"Yes, there is," replies Hector MacQuill. "Why not walk down the river and have a look at it? Of course, there will be no salmon going up — October is the best month to see the salmon — but the falls are very pretty, and, anyway, it is a better occupation on a hot day than hitting a ball about in the sun. I shall have to go back to my duties as host. I'm afraid I have been away from them too long already — but Tony knows the way."

I have never seen a "salmon loup," and am delighted at the prospect of adding to my experiences — even if there are no salmon on view. At the back of my mind there lingers a faint hope that we might see one, foolish enough to have made a mistake in the date.

The three of us, therefore, bid a temporary farewell to our host, and stroll down the little path amongst feathery grasses, shaded from the sun by a canopy of tall trees.

The sound of falling water comes to our ears, at first faintly like the sound of the distant sea, but with every step it grows louder and louder, until our ears are filled with the thunder of it, and we see the river, which has hitherto kept us company, disappear over a rocky precipice, and fall in several green billows, broken by rocks and fringed with foam, into a dark pool some twenty feet below.

Major Morley seizes my arm, and we climb over the rocks and watch the falling water for a long time without speaking. Indeed the sound of the falls is too loud for conversation to be possible. I am dazed and mesmerised with the noise, and quite glad to cling to my companion's arm.

How beautiful it is! How wild and primeval! There is something almost terrifying in the relentless way the river flings itself over its barrier of rock and plunges down amongst flying spray and creamy foam. The spray is full of rainbows, and drops of rainbow hue sparkle upon the feathery fronds of the ferns which overhang the pool.

"A lot of water today," shouts Major Morley. "Melting snow — Ben Seoch —"

I wish he would be quiet and not try to talk. It is enough for me to watch the curling billows, and the rainbow spray — I don't want to know where it comes from — I could stand here all day just looking at it —

But Major Morley is tugging at my arm, and I realise that we have been here long enough, and it is time for tea.

We are bound with chains of iron to this strange custom of eating and drinking at set hours, whether we want to eat and drink or not. With unwilling feet I follow my companions up the path. Their conversation — which I can now overhear in snatches — is evidently a continuation of one started before, and appears to be on the subject of Elsie Baker.

Mrs. Loudon has found, not only a sympathetic ear in Major Morley, but a fellow sufferer who is prepared to go even farther than herself in the vilification of the wretched girl. I have purposely refrained from criticising Elsie Baker to Mrs. Loudon, because I feel in my bones that Guthrie intends to marry her, and probably will, unless something unforeseen occurs. Major Morley has no such scruples — he lays bare her manifold delinquencies before Mrs. Loudon's horrified eyes. According to Major Morley she is a cocktail drinker, a cigarette fiend, and a man hunter. He says that she lies in wait for him in the corridor, bumps into him on purpose, and then screams with pretended fear. He says that her plucked eyebrows give him shivers all down his back, and her golden hair sets his teeth on edge. He says that her lips and the tips of her fingers remind him of a cannibal after a meal of raw flesh —

Mrs. Loudon's eyes nearly fall out of their sockets. "What a like creature for a daughter-in-law!" she exclaims.

"Oh, come now, it's not as bad as all that," says Major Morley. "Sailors often fall for impossible women."

"And marry them," adds Mrs. Loudon with impenetrable gloom.

"I can't believe that *your son* —" Major Morley hints with flattering emphasis.

Even this compliment fails to raise the lady's spirits. "The man's bereft of his senses," she replies trenchantly.

"Something must be done about it," says Major Morley gravely. "It simply can't be allowed. Surely between us we can think of a plan to rescue this poor deluded man."

Mrs. Loudon brightens a little. "Major Morley! The creature is staying at your hotel. Couldn't you —"

292

"Nothing doing, I assure you," says Major Morley, laughing. "Not even for your son would I allow myself to fall into her clutches. Besides, it would be a fatal mistake. It would only make him all the keener if he saw another victim in her toils. No, there's a much better way than that — but I should need Mrs. Christie's help."

"Why, of course Hester will help you!" cries Mrs. Loudon, full of excitement at the prospect of something to be done.

I look at him doubtfully; he is so difficult to understand, such a queer mixture of kindness and wickedness. What mood is he in at the present moment? I rather think he is enjoying himself, in spite of his grave countenance and sympathetic manner.

"It's quite simple," says Major Morley, leading us to a garden seat which stands conveniently near. "Let's sit down for a few minutes and discuss the matter fully. You need not be alarmed, Mrs. Christie. All you have to do is to look charming and allow me to adore you from afar. The first is natural to you already, the second will come quite naturally in time."

"But I don't see what good that will do," I protest; for, to tell the truth, I don't like the plan at all.

"Surely, you see," says Major Morley, persuasively. "Our friend Guthrie sees me adoring, and takes one glance at Mrs. Christie — he has not seen her before, because he is blinded by his infatuation for his cannibal — one glance at Mrs. Christie is enough, he will never look at Miss Baker again."

293

The plan seems to me the height of foolishness, and I say so firmly. But Mrs. Loudon — who seems bewitched out of her usual sanity — is attracted by the idea, and beseeches me to "try it," pointing out that at any rate it can do no harm. It is really Mrs. Loudon's own original plan, only carried to insane lengths.

"I'm not so sure about its harmlessness," I reply.

"Why?" asks Mrs. Loudon. "What harm can it do?"

Major Morley seconds her by pointing out that I need do nothing. *He* will do all that is necessary. And adds, that surely I can bear to be adored from afar to save a poor young man from the clutches of a cannibal.

I feel certain that Tim would object to the plan, but all my arguments are overruled or swept aside by my companions. They settle everything to their entire satisfaction — though not to mine — and we return to the garden, where we find the sacred rites of afternoon tea are being celebrated with suitable solemnity.

"I'm afraid you will have to call me 'Tony,'" Major Morley says gravely, as he appears at my side with a cup of tea and a plate of cream buns. "It's rather a nuisance for you, of course, but we want to make the thing as real as possible, and there is no time to lose — poor 'Froggy' is fast hooked, I'm afraid."

"Froggy?" I enquire.

"He would a-wooing go, whether his mother would let him or no," explains Major Morley. "There is the poor wight, holding a lace parasol for the Cannibal Queen — and very silly he looks."

I glance in the direction indicated, and see that it is only too true. Guthrie is making a fool of himself.

294

"He's hardly worth rescuing, is he?" remarks my companion, guessing my thoughts in an uncanny way he has.

Mrs. Loudon has been claimed by an old crony, so we find a seat in the shade, and Major Morley (or Tony, as I suppose I must call him) sits down at my feet, and gazes at me with a yearning expression which is so realistic that it makes me feel quite uncomfortable.

Presently Guthrie appears, and asks if I will make up a four.

"Don't tire yourself, Hester," says Tony anxiously. "I really think you are more comfortable sitting here in the shade with me." But I have had quite enough of sitting in the shade with Tony, and profess myself quite ready for a game. Tony jumps up with alacrity, and says in that case he will play too, and we can have a return of our previous set. This does not appeal to Guthrie at all (he is not very fond of being beaten and he is quite aware that he and Elsie are not strong enough for us). He suggests that we should "split up," but Tony insists on playing with me. All Guthrie's feeble objections are countered — he is no match for Tony in diplomacy — and, a court falling vacant at the critical moment, we take them on again and beat them worse than before.

Guthrie's patience wears somewhat thin during the set, and he points out to his partner that her spectacular strokes are losing them every game. To which Elsie replies that her forehand drive has been much admired by Mr. Jones, the professional at her club in Portsmouth. At this exchange of pleasantries Tony winks at me, and serves an easy lob to Elsie,

295

which she promptly drives, with all her force, into the back net. This gives us the set.

It is now time to go. Tony rushes off to find our car, and packs us into it with anxious care — he is extraordinarily good at these small attentions. "I may call?" he enquires of Mrs. Loudon, as he tucks the rug round her feet.

"Of course — any friend of Hester's. Come over tomorrow afternoon," she murmurs hospitably.

Guthrie, who has elected to drive, starts the car with a jerk that nearly upsets Tony — the latter still having one foot on the step — and we career madly over the drawbridge, and down the drive, which is now crowded with departing guests.

"For any sake take care!" exclaims Mrs. Loudon in a surprised voice. "You nearly had the kilt off that man, Guthrie."

"The damned fool should keep off the road," replies Guthrie murderously. From all of which I deduce that the good Guthrie is slightly put out about something.

Seventh June

Annie has gone into the village on some mysterious errand that only she herself can do, so Betty and I take our favourite book of fairytales into the garden.

"Read about Snow-White and the Seven Dwarfs," says Betty. "You read much nicer than Annie. I like when you make them talk with different voices, Mummie."

We spread a rug under a fir tree and settle down.

At this moment there is a glimpse of a blue frock at the gate in the fence leading to the woods, and Guthrie hurries down the garden and leaps the burn. He has gone to meet her, of course. They must have arranged to meet, and go for a walk together — now we know why Guthrie was so distrait at lunchtime, and why he threw cold water on all his mother's suggestions for spending the afternoon.

Meanwhile the book has opened conveniently at the picture of Snow-White in her glass coffin, which must always be thoroughly examined before the story begins. "Don't the dwarfs look sad?" Betty says in sympathetic tones. "Of course they don't know she'll come to life again when the coffin gets banged against a tree. How hard could you bang a glass coffin against a tree without it breaking, Mummie?" she enquires interestedly.

Like most of Betty's questions this is difficult to answer, so I suggest we should begin the story.

"Yes, begin," says Betty, with a luxurious sigh.

"'Once upon a time there was a beautiful queen . . .'"

So we set off together on the well-known journey with the little princess whose skin was as white as snow, and whose cheeks were as red as the rose. Betty listens, enthralled, while the wicked queen tries to poison her beautiful stepdaughter with a poisoned comb, and to choke her with a magic apple. Custom cannot stale the thrill of the story for Betty, she knows it by heart, yet her eyes gleam with excitement and her small body is gathered into a tense ball.

"And what are they doing now?" I wonder to myself, for long practice has made it possible for me to think my own thoughts and read quite easily at the same time. The two threads mingle and commingle in a single strand. Snow-White strays through the dark woods with Guthrie and Elsie Baker, their fates seem bound together, and flow along in one melodious stream. The little dwarfs peer at them from behind the trees, and consult together in their strange gruff voices as to what had better be done about it all. And how I wish these same little dwarfs would cease their useless labour of making a glass coffin for Snow-White, and would rush after Guthrie and Elsie, and tear them apart! They are fitted for each other in no way that I can see, and, instead of growing together, they will grow apart. Guthrie is grave, with a taste for fantastic humour which Elsie will never appreciate; Elsie is frivolous and enjoys the society of frivolous people. They will hate each other's friends, and misunderstand each other's wit. What hope is there for them?

I sit on by myself long after the story is finished, and Betty has flown off to the garden to find Donald and pester him for gooseberries. The tale of Snow-White is finished, but the tale of Guthrie is still to be told. How sad it is to see a tale marred in the making! Why must we stand aside and see those we care for heading straight for shipwreck on the rocks of life?

I have become very fond of Guthrie in the last few days — there is something lovable in his very simplicity. I can see his faults, of course, but they are offset by his virtues. How strange are the differences in people!

Guthrie is boyish, almost childlike in nature; his sulkiness is short-lived, his selfishness is the selfishness of a child. The sun shines through him, and his every thought is mirrored on his open countenance. And Tony Morley is like a deep pool whose bottom you cannot see for the darkness of the water — not muddy water, not that kind of opaqueness, but clear dark water that reflects here a rock, there a patch of blue sky with a passing cloud — and the ripples play over the surface with every breath of wind.

I gaze up at the fir tree above my head, and admire its light green frills, which are sewn on to its dark green frock with invisible stitches — light green frills moving up and down gently in the faintly stirring air — while, with another part of my mind, I dissect the differences in these two men. Guthrie is this, Tony is that, I like Guthrie for this, I like Tony for that. Thoughts flicker about me quickly, vaguely, so that my brain, lulled to drowsiness by the afternoon peace, cannot follow them. They dance up and down before my eyes like a cloud of midges — up and down — up and down.

Take Tony first. How considerate he is! How quick to respond to an idea! How sensitive to other people's feelings! Yes, but sometimes he tramples on them on purpose (which Guthrie never does), and isn't it worse to trample purposely than to trample unconsciously, like Guthrie? — like a huge elephant in the jungle, leaving a track of broken flowers in its wake . . .

"Are you asleep, Hester?" Mrs. Loudon says, and I think I must have been, for Guthrie had turned into an elephant, and was standing trumpeting fiercely at his reflection in a dark pool — and the dark pool was rippling softly as if it were smiling to itself.

"Major Morley's come," continues my hostess. "He's talking to Millie in the drawing room — or perhaps it would be more like the thing to say that Millie's talking to him. I thought we'd have tea early, and you can take him fishing. Where's Guthrie?"

I rub my eyes and try to banish the mists which are still clouding my brain —

"Poor lassie — you're half asleep yet. I'd not have wakened you, but I can't leave the Major in Millie's clutches — the man will be deaved to death."

"You needn't worry about *him*," I reply, trying to smooth my hair, which seems to be standing straight on end. "Major Morley is quite capable of looking after himself."

"Come away," she adjures me impatiently. "The man's come to see *you*, not to listen to Millie's haverings."

I follow my hostess meekly towards the drawing-room windows which open on to the veranda. We pause outside and look at each other in bewilderment, for it is Major Morley's voice, and not Mrs. Falconer's, which comes clearly to our ears.

"Father always insisted that us boys should come home for the Christmas holidays," he says in confidential tones. "Sometimes we begged him to allow us to stay at school and continue our studies, but father wouldn't hear of it. 'You *must* have two helpings of plum pudding on Christmas Day,' he used to say. 'And how can I be sure that you eat it unless I have you under my own eye?' Well, one Christmas holidays a very strange thing happened — it may have been in the year 1900 or 1901, or possibly 1902. I remember distinctly that it was a Monday, because we had had cold beef for lunch (but you must not think it was anything to do with the cold beef; cold beef may be indigestible, but it does not predispose a person to hallucinations). It must have been about half past three in the afternoon, because I was just beginning to feel hungry for tea, and it was probably a few days after Christmas, because my young cousin had been given a new pair of football boots and was busy rubbing them with castor oil — castor oil has such a filthy smell," adds Tony thoughtfully.

"Yes, but what —"

"Suddenly," says Tony, interrupting the poor lady unmercifully. "Suddenly there were footsteps on the gravel outside the open window — it was an old man coming up the drive with a sack over his back, or it may have been a woman selling bootlaces, or an Italian boy selling onions, or a Punch-and-Judy man — the fact is, it was really too dark to see who it was, which shows it must have been a very dark afternoon, shouldn't you say so, Mrs. Falconer?"

Mrs. Falconer says, "But if you couldn't see who it was —"

"Ah, but I could smell the onions," replies Tony triumphantly. "And that proves conclusively that it must have been an Italian onion boy, because if it had been a Punch-and-Judy man he would have smelt of whisky — there was a Punch-and-Judy man who used to come round quite often during the holidays; he had a very red nose, poor fellow, and his breath always smelt of whisky — and bootlaces have a peculiar smell of their own, so it couldn't possibly have been the bootlace woman."

"Papa always used to say —" Mrs. Falconer begins, seizing her opportunity while her opponent pauses for breath.

"And he was perfectly right," agrees Tony earnestly. "Bootlaces are not what they were. I've never met a modern bootlace that could stand a good tug. And studs — the way they leap into corners and hide under mats! It's my belief, Mrs. Falconer, that all studs are possessed of an evil spirit, and I simply don't believe these fellows who write to the papers saying that they have used the same stud for thirty years. The thing's impossible. I once knew a man who was completely ruined by a stud —"

"Ruined by a stud!" gasps Mrs. Falconer.

"Don't ask me to tell you about it," Tony says, with a slight tremble in his voice. "The man was my friend — you will be the first to admit that silence is golden. Let us talk of shoes, or ships, or sealing wax — I know a fellow who uses pink sealing wax — a most disgusting habit! This man actually had the impertinence to write a proposal of marriage to a lady he had known for nine days — or it may have been nine years, I really can't remember which, and it doesn't matter, for both are equally insulting, you will agree. In nine days he couldn't possibly have known her well enough to propose, and in nine years he should have known her too well. But the point is he sealed the letter with pink sealing wax, which warned the poor girl in the nick of time. She was good enough to ask my advice on the subject. 'Shall I accept him, Tony?' she said to me with tears in her eyes. 'Shall I accept him, and spend my life trying to wean him from his vicious habits?' But, alas, I could give her no hope! I knew, only too well, that a man can never be broken of pink sealing wax, once it has a hold on him."

"But surely you don't mean —"

"No, no!" says Tony gravely. "You must not think I meant *that*. Let us leave the subject and go on to cabbages. Personally I would rather eat hay or thistles, but I am told that quite a number of people consider the cabbage fit for human consumption. The hard-hearted ones are best — they are tougher, and have more white stalk to the cubic inch."

"Dear Papa did not care for cabbage," Mrs. Falconer announces breathlessly.

"Of course not!" exclaims Tony with rapture. "Nobody did. It is only recently that the cabbage has come to the fore. In your father's time a gentleman ate to please his palate; nowadays he eats to pamper his stomach. Do not blush, Mrs. Falconer. I assure you that this important organ may now be spoken of with impunity in the drawing rooms of Mayfair. However, if you would rather go on to kings, you have only to say the word. It is the last subject on our list, but by no means the least worthy of exploration. Which is *your* favourite king? Mine has always been Charles the Second. I feel that he and I would have hit it off splendidly. For many years I found myself in the minority on this point, but I am glad to notice a distinct revulsion in his favour amongst thinking men and women. Why, only the other day the Y.W.C.A. had an exhibition of his relics! It is not a body in which one would expect to find appreciation of the Merry Monarch — but, after all, why not? Doubtless he gave pleasure to a great many young women who would otherwise have led somewhat drab lives —"

At this moment Mrs. Loudon sneezes violently, and discovers our presence. The monologue ceases abruptly.

"There you are," says Tony. "Mrs. Falconer and I have had a most interesting conversation — the time has simply flown."

Mrs. Falconer says nothing; there is a dazed look in her eyes.

"We must really continue our conversation some time," Tony says brazenly, as we take our places round the tea table. "We have not exhausted the subject of kings."

"Perhaps you have exhausted Mrs. Falconer," I suggest maliciously.

"Cruel!" he sighs, helping himself to a scone.

Guthrie's chair looks very empty — there are several other unoccupied chairs in the room, but only Guthrie's looks empty. I remark on the phenomenon, but nobody seems to get my point.

"Where *is* Guthrie?" enquires his mother, a trifle anxiously. "Have any of you seen him this afternoon?"

Tony says that he saw Guthrie and Miss Thingummy starting off for a walk, but he doesn't suppose they've gone far. When asked the reason for his supposition, he replies that people *don't* as a rule. They generally sit down on the first thing handy.

Mrs. Loudon sighs heavily, and Mrs. Falconer, somewhat revived by a cup of strong tea, whispers to me, "Do you think he's offered for her yet?" but I pretend not to hear.

After tea Tony and I go out on the loch together. Tony insists on acting as boatman, and gives me some valuable advice on the art of throwing a fly. I catch several fine trout, and enjoy myself thoroughly.

Tony is really much more unselfish than most men — or else he is not such a keen fisherman, or else — But there is no other explanation; he can't be such a keen fisherman.

About seven o'clock the breeze freshens, and Tony says we had better pack up now, it's too cold for me. I point out that he need not keep up the pretence of solicitude for my welfare when Guthrie is not here to see it, whereupon Tony replies that it is excellent practice for him, and rows firmly homewards.

We find Guthrie waiting for us at the boathouse. He seems slightly out of temper, and says he has been waiting for nearly an hour, and didn't we hear him shouting to us. (Now that I think of it I believe I did hear somebody shouting.)

Tony replies that the wind is in the other direction, and anyhow it is too cold to fish any more tonight.

"Cold!" snorts Guthrie. "I don't call it cold. Some people seem to be made of cotton wool."

Tony takes no notice of this strange remark; he busies himself collecting the fishing tackle, and making fast the boat.

"What about another hour's fishing?" Guthrie says, ignoring Tony, and addressing himself to me in a wheedling manner. "Dinner isn't till eight, you know, Hester."

I am about to reply when Tony says innocently, "I suppose there is a ghillie belonging to the place, isn't there, Loudon? Or do you depend entirely on your guests to work the boat for you?"

Guthrie opens his mouth to reply, but no sound comes. He watches in silence while Tony helps me out of the boat as if I were made of spun glass (this is for his especial benefit, of course) and we all walk up to the house together.

Mrs. Loudon comes into my room when I am going to bed and says THE PLAN is working admirably. Guthrie has just been advising her not to ask that fellow Morley to the house any more "as he seems rather gone on Hester." Whereupon I tell her flatly that I hate the plan and everything to do with it, and that I don't know what on earth Tim would say if he knew.

Mrs. Loudon replies, incoherently, that it would do Tim a lot of good, and that he will never know anything about it, and that anyway I'm not doing anything wrong. "And anyway I've asked the man to come over tomorrow afternoon," she adds firmly, "and I'll not put him off for all Guthrie's blethering."

She stays a few moments longer, talking about various matters, and then goes away.

I suppose I must have gone to sleep at once, for I seem to have been asleep for hours — but quite suddenly, I am wide awake. It is raining hard and quite dark. Perhaps it is the heavy rain that has wakened me. I lie very still and listen.

Somebody is on the veranda beneath my window. I can hear the sound of hushed voices, and the pad of stealthy feet on the tiles. The sounds are the more alarming because there have been several small burglaries lately in the neighbourhood, and I decide at once that the correct thing for me to do is to waken Guthrie. I slip on my dressing-gown in the dark, and grope my way along the passage to his room. How dark it is! It must be about midnight, for dawn comes early in these latitudes.

Guthrie is fast asleep, but he wakes quickly, and takes in the situation without loss of time.

"Gosh!" he exclaims excitedly. "They've come to the wrong house this time. I must put on my boots — you can't go after burglars without boots."

I point out that Guthrie's boots will make the most frightful noise on the uncarpeted stairs, and that by the time he has reached the bottom the burglars will have gone. After arguing obstinately for a few moments we compromise on tennis shoes. He dons a cardigan, and an overcoat — I never knew a man who could start to do anything without dressing for the part — and, opening the drawer of his dressing table, produces a small revolver, examines the chamber carefully, and slips it into his pocket. I begin to feel quite sorry for the burglars. A pocket torch completes our outfit. This is given into my charge with instructions to "flash it into their eyes." Guthrie will then wing them, tie them up with rope, and gag them with old socks — here the socks are produced and tucked into my dressing-gown pocket.

"By the way, Hester," he says anxiously, "I suppose there is some washing rope or something in the house — if not we shall have to make do with window-shade cord."

It all sounds quite easy.

Guthrie continues that, after having bound them securely, we shall lock them up in the coal cellar, and rouse Dobbie, and send him off to Inverquill for the police. It's most important to have all your plans cut and dried beforehand, Guthrie says, and then you know exactly where you are. If Jellicoe had been able to do this at Jutland we should have bagged the whole German fleet. I am suitably impressed by this statement, and follow Guthrie downstairs. It is very cold, and the rain is still coming down hard. I hear it swishing on the cupola with an eerie sound. My teeth show an impulse to chatter — I rather wish I had put on some warm stockings, and a jumper, but it is too late now.

We look in the pantry first, Guthrie explaining, in a hoarse whisper, that of course the burglars know where the silver is kept. They never undertake a job of this kind without obtaining a plan of the house. He thinks

308

the garden boy may have given it to them — he's a shifty-looking individual — or that man who came to look at the kitchen range.

There are no signs of burglars in the pantry — everything is in apple-pie order, and as quiet as the grave — the dining room is also innocent of their presence. We look carefully under the table and into various cupboards. Guthrie says they might have heard us coming and hidden themselves.

I point out to Guthrie that it was on the veranda outside the drawing-room window I heard them, so the inference is that they are in the drawing room, making a clean sweep of Mrs. Loudon's cherished snuffboxes and silver photograph frames. Guthrie replies that it is better to look elsewhere first, but can give no good reason for his statement, and I begin to wonder whether he is really very keen to meet them now that the time has come. I do not like to question the courage of an officer in His Majesty's Navy, but this is my impression.

We have now looked everywhere except in the drawing room, and there is no further excuse for delay. We listen outside the door and hear the sound of whispering — or else it may be the rain.

Suddenly Guthrie throws open the door and enters, revolver in hand. I flash the torch in their faces, and the tableau is revealed.

The burglars consist of a tall man in a check overcoat, and a girl in a burberry, with a green tammy on the back of her head. They have lighted one candle, but its fitful flame throws scarcely any light upon the scene.

"Hello, Loudon!" the man says. "Cleared for action, I see."

"Good God!" Guthrie exclaims. "What on earth are you doing here, Bones?"

I realise at once that this tall, thin, lanky individual must be a friend of Guthrie's — or perhaps it would be exaggerating to say a *friend*, for Guthrie does not seem enchanted to see him.

"What on earth brought you here at this time of night?" he asks again, in the irritable tone of one who has been thoroughly frightened and finds his bogy innocuous.

"An Austin Seven brought us here," replies the man addressed as Bones, with a nonchalant air. "Found you'd all cleared off to bed, so we thought we'd warm ourselves a bit — damned cold outside, and wet too."

"See here, I guess you'd better introduce us, Bones," says the girl suddenly, "and then we can get what we want and hook it. Your pal doesn't seem overjoyed to see us — I guess we must have woke him out of his beauty sleep. Say," she adds, turning to me, "you don't happen to have a baby's bottle, do you?"

I reply in a dazed manner that I have not. It flashes through my mind that they must have escaped from a lunatic asylum; perhaps the ropes may still be required.

Bones now perceives me in the gloom. "Good Lord!" he exclaims. "Didn't know you were married, Loudon. Won't you introduce me to your wife? Wouldn't have come, I assure you, if I'd known about it. When did it

310

happen, old man? Congratulations and all that — hope we didn't pop in at an inopportune moment?"

"I'm *not* married," Guthrie says indignantly.

"Even sorrier, then," says Bones, eyeing me with increased interest.

"Look here, I wish you'd say what you want and go," Guthrie says inhospitably. "This is Mrs. Christie — she's staying here with my mother —"

Bones takes this as a formal introduction, and bows gracefully.

"I don't know what on earth you want," Guthrie continues. "But I want to get back to bed."

"Don't wonder," murmurs Bones. "Don't wonder at all, old chap. I'd feel the same myself. By the way, you couldn't produce a spot, I suppose. Dry work, this treasure hunting."

"You've had quite enough," says the girl firmly. "You've got to drive that car back to Inverquill tonight."

"Lord! I've not begun," replies Bones. "You should see what I can take without rocking — I can still say Irish Constabulary without a hitch."

"Did you come here for a drink?" enquires Guthrie.

"Well, not exactly — still a spot never comes amiss —" suggests Bones hopefully.

"I guess you'd better explain — or let me," says the girl. "See here, Mr. — er — (Bones didn't say what your name was). This is the way of it — Bones and I are in a treasure hunt — we've staying over at Inverquill, with the MacKenzies. Well, Bones and I are in the last lap, and we're just mad to win, so —"

"Had a gin and bitters at Avielochan Hotel," says the lanky man, taking up the tale. "Suddenly remembered you were here — wonderful how a gin and bitters stimulates a fellow — took us hours to find you — but here we are."

"So I see," says Guthrie unpleasantly.

"You'll help us, won't you!" says the girl, producing a printed list, somewhat damp and crumpled, from her waterproof pocket. "I guess we've got nearly everything now, except a baby's bottle, and a warming pan, and a poker —"

"Here's a poker," Bones says, seizing the one out of the grate.

"You're not going to take that poker," says Guthrie suddenly.

"Bring it back tomorrow, old man," Bones replies, trying to stuff it into his pocket.

The girl continues to consult the list anxiously, holding it near the solitary candle. I perceive that it is she who is the moving spirit in the treasure hunt. Bones is but lukewarm.

"Look here, Bones," says Guthrie, with a sudden access of rage. "You put that poker back in its place, and clear out of here — I'm just about fed up with this nonsense."

"Make it a deoch an doruis and I'm your man," replies Bones quickly. "One small one, and out we go. You couldn't turn a dog out without a drink on a night like this."

Perhaps Guthrie thinks that this is the quickest way to get rid of the man. At any rate he relents.

"All right," he says ungraciously. "You'll get a small one and you'll clear out. Hester, you had better go back to bed, you'll get your death of cold. I'll see these lunatics off the premises."

I realise that I am almost frozen, and am quite glad to take Guthrie's advice — besides, the fun is over. I grope my way upstairs, and creep into bed with my dressing gown on — thank goodness there is still a little warmth in my hot-water bottle. My room is turning a soft grey colour, dawn is not far off. I reflect what strange ways people have of enjoying themselves, rushing round the country on a wet dark night collecting baby's bottles and warming pans.

It is some little while before I hear our burglars departing. Guthrie seems to have some trouble with the lock of the door on to the veranda, then I hear his tennis shoes come padding up the stairs and along the passage. He stops at my door and knocks gently.

"What happened?" I enquire.

The door half opens, and Guthrie's head appears. "Are you all right, Hester?" he asks softly. "They've gone at last — I had to give them the poker, and a warming pan which was hanging in the hall — they wouldn't go away without them."

"You looked as if you wanted to throw them out," I giggled feebly.

"Oh, I'd have thrown Bones out — but I couldn't throw out a girl. Wait till we get back to the *Polyphon*," he adds ferociously. "I'll set the whole wardroom onto him. They hate him as it is, and they'll be too pleased to make his life a burden — he'll wish he'd never been

313

born when I've done with him — the blinkety, blankety fool!"

In his excitement Guthrie has come into my room, and stands beside my bed, a huge dark-looming figure in the half light.

"I can't help laughing when I think of us and our 'cut and dried' plans," I tell him.

Guthrie says he doesn't see anything funny about it — naturally we thought it was burglars and prepared accordingly.

"Yes, but it wasn't burglars."

"No, it was lunatics."

I can see that Guthrie feels he has been made to look a fool, and does not like it — few men do.

"Look here," he continues, "let's keep the whole thing dark — it's no use worrying Mother by telling *her* about it — she might be nervous if she knew it was so easy to get into the house. Those two just walked in by the veranda door. There's something funny about the lock. Sometimes it locks all right, and sometimes it doesn't."

"Anyone might get in!" I exclaim, sitting up in bed.

"There's just where you're wrong. Nobody would except an ass like Bones. No burglar would ever think of trying the handle of a door. Besides I know now, and I'll make it my business to lock it every night, so you see there's no need to tell Mother."

"She'll miss the poker and the warming pan."

"Oh, well, we must trust to luck," he says. "You'd better go to sleep; it's nearly dawn."

"I can't go to sleep with you standing there looking like a giant," I announce pettishly.

"Oh no, of course not," he says. "Well, good night, Hester. You won't say anything to Mother, will you?"

I make no reply, except to snuggle down in bed, and he goes away, shutting the door carefully. As a matter of fact I have made up my mind to tell Mrs. Loudon the whole story at the earliest opportunity — she is the last woman to be alarmed at the idea of burglars, and she would thoroughly enjoy the joke.

Eighth June

Guthrie is late in appearing for breakfast, and admits that he did not sleep well. Mrs. Loudon commiserates him on his insomnia, and says the rain was awful, but she supposes the country needed it, and anyway it was better to rain at night if it had to rain at all.

I wait until I see Guthrie going off with his gun to shoot rabbits, and then track my hostess to her desk.

"Well!" she says, looking up at me. "What happened last night?"

"How did you know that anything happened?" I ask in amazement.

"Circumstantial evidence," she replies, smiling rather strangely. "The warming pan has vanished from the hall, Guthrie owns to a sleepless night, and a pair of his socks have been discovered in the pocket of your dressing gown."

I can do nothing but laugh.

315

"You may laugh," she says. "The whole thing's a mystery to me. I've been trying to unravel it for the last hour."

"You never will."

"No, I dare say not, but there's no need for me to worry my head any more about it since you followed me in here to tell me the whole thing. I could see you were like a cat on hot bricks till you got Guthrie out of the house."

"He said I wasn't to tell you," I reply. "But I made up my mind I would — you will enjoy the joke."

"I'm glad of that," she says, with her twinkle.

Without further ado I embark upon my tale.

Mrs. Loudon follows with interest, and laughs at the right moment; she is an admirable listener. "Well," she says. "I never heard the like of that — the idea of a girl racketing about all night with a man in a car collecting baby's bottles. Mercy me! You're quite right, Hester. I never would have guessed *that*, if I'd spent the rest of my life at it."

"Wait and see what I'll say to Guthrie," she adds, chuckling to herself. "I'll get on to him about this."

"You are not to say a word about it to Guthrie," I tell her firmly. "If you do I'll have nothing more to do with that ridiculous plan of yours and Tony's."

This threat is enough, and she reluctantly consents to spare Guthrie this time. We are still discussing things when a large car drives up to the door, and a wooden-faced chauffeur hands in the warming pan and the poker. Mrs. Loudon says she is glad to see them, for she would not know how to account for their absence to Mrs. MacRae. We restore them to their rightful places without further comment.

The afternoon being fine and warm, with no suspicion of the all-essential breeze, it is decided to give the fish a holiday, and that the whole party shall take car for Loch-an-Darroch and picnic there. Everyone assures me that I really must see this loch, and the castle upon its brink, as it is one of the wildest and most beautiful spots in Scotland. Feel suitably excited and impressed.

Tony Morley arrives soon after lunch in his Bentley. Betty greets him rapturously, for they are old friends, and asks if she can sit beside him on the front seat. There is no false pride about my daughter. If she wants a thing she asks for it, and usually attains her desire, very few people having the moral courage to urge their own preferences in the face of her demands. Guthrie and Miss Baker — who is also of the party — elect to travel in the Bentley, which leaves Mrs. Loudon, Mrs. Falconer and myself for the Austin. We squeeze into the back seat, and the picnic baskets are piled up beside Dobbie.

Tony calls out that he will wait for us at the loch, and away goes the Bentley with a scrunch of gravel. Dobbie remarks enviously that they could be there and back before we have started, which is an obvious libel on his mistress's comfortable car. We follow the others at a reasonable pace, cruising along very peacefully over the white roads, and admiring the scenery. Mrs. Loudon is subdued, owing, I feel sure, to the knowledge that Guthrie and Miss Baker are ensconced in the back seat of Tony's car, and therefore at liberty to hold each other's hands without fear of intrusion upon their privacy.

"I suppose Dobbie knows the way," Mrs. Falconer suggests, in a dubious tone.

Mrs. Loudon replies that he does.

"Well, it's really extraordinary to me how he knows which road to take. All these roads look just the same to me — mountains on one side or the other, or in front or behind, and forests scattered about! If *I* had to drive we should probably go round in circles, and end up at Burnside in time for tea. Imagine Mary's feelings if we walked in at teatime after all the trouble she's had cutting the sandwiches and filling the thermoses. By the way, I often wonder if it is correct to say thermoses for the plural. Dear Papa was very particular about grammar. There were no thermoses in those days, of course, but I remember how he jumped on me for talking about crocuses — or it may have been irises. I can't remember what the right way is, which shows it did not do me much good, doesn't it?"

"Dear me, what a dangerous place!" she continues, as we skirt a precipice at the bottom of which a small blue loch lies dreaming in the afternoon sunshine. "If Dobbie were to take his hands off the wheel for an instant we should shoot over the edge, and nobody any the wiser. You may smile, Elspeth, but look at the dreadful accidents you read of in the papers. Who knows but Dobbie might take it into his head to put an end to us all, and nobody to know it wasn't an accident? People *do* get queer ideas like that

318

sometimes. It was only this morning I read in the papers about a man who shot his wife and three children, because they could not agree where to go for their holidays — only it turned out afterwards that the woman was not *really* his *wife*, which, of course, makes a difference."

Mrs. Loudon usually bears Mrs. Falconer's wanderings with remarkable patience, but she has evidently reached the end of her tether. Quite suddenly she rouses herself, and remarks irritably, "Do you mean that Dobbie is likely to murder us all because he is not married to me?"

"*Married to you?* Dobbie? — my dear Elspeth, I am sure the man has never *thought* of it," says Mrs. Falconer, aghast.

"I could suggest it to him, of course," replies Mrs. Loudon reflectively.

"Elspeth, you can't be serious! *What* put such an extraordinary idea into your head?"

"You did, Millie."

"I?" gasps poor Mrs. Falconer.

"You seemed to think we should all be safer if I were married to Dobbie."

"Elspeth, you misunderstood me *entirely* —"

At this moment we fortunately arrive at our destination, and the subject is dropped. Tony Morley is waiting for us. "The others have gone on," he says. "Young Betty decided to go with them — she is one of those fortunate people who never know when they are de trop. Young Betty is in great form today. Give me that basket and the rug, Hester."

319

Through the trees I can see glimpses of green water. We follow Tony down a narrow path, and presently find ourselves standing in the shadow of a towering mass of rock. A toy castle is perched securely on the top, its windows gape with sightless eyes, and, here and there, a piece of crumbled wall or a roofless tower shows that it is no longer habitable. The whole thing is so battered by the weather, and so welded with the natural rock, that it is impossible to tell where the one ends and the other begins. Down the dark smooth sides of the cliff there trickles a constant film of water, and in every crevice grow moss and feathery ferns.

"What an impregnable fortress!" I whisper to Tony — there is an eerie silence in the place which one fears to break.

"Shall we climb the rock?" he suggests. "It is fairly steep, but there is a wonderful view from the top."

I agree, and we set off up a steep stony path which leads us — after a breathtaking climb — into the courtyard of the castle. This is paved with solid rock and is open to the sky. There is a well in the centre. Only one of the towers remains in reasonable repair. It contains a stone stairway worn by countless feet, and a small round room which actually boasts a roof.

The view from the window of the tower is indeed marvellous. The loch stretches in both directions. It is a peculiar shade of green, and is surrounded on all sides by tall trees which, in some places, lean over the water. There is something rather uncanny about the place; perhaps this feeling of something uncanny and awesome exists only in my own imagination — which

320

was so stirred by the tale of Hector and Seónaid — perhaps not. I can well believe that this loch is not like other lochs.

Tony points out Seónaid's Bay — a little cove of white sand about two hundred yards from the castle. It was here that her body was discovered by the women going down to wash their clothes.

We visit the dungeon — a damp, dark cave in the solid rock — and peer through the rusting bars into the green water below us, as many a poor creature must have done long ago. "I don't suppose the MacArbins kept their prisoners here very long," says Tony comfortably. "It was so easy to get rid of them on account of the peculiarity of the loch. Just one little push, and away they went, never to be seen again —"

I ask Tony if he thinks the castle is very old.

"It was built sometime in the thirteenth century by one Dermid MacArbin," Tony replies. "The clan was here before that, of course, but just living in hovels or caves in the mountains. This Dermid was the second son, and therefore of little importance in the scheme of things, but, being of an ambitious turn of mind, he killed his elder brother, and threw his body into the loch, thereby becoming head of the clan. Dermid's first act as chief was to set about the building of a stronghold — Castle Darroch. Some say he imported an Italian architect, others that he designed the place himself; in any case it is a very creditable piece of work, considering the primitive tools at his command. Every stone had to be hewn out of the solid rock, and carried up the cliff by human labour — of course, the whole

321

clan toiled at it, and, I expect, they cursed old Dermid properly when his back was turned. Dermid must have been very proud of the castle — it must have been exciting watching it grow, day by day, and seeing his dream take shape — but he never lived to enjoy it, for the very day that it was finished his brother's ghost rose up out of the loch and carried him off."

The scene is so awe-inspiring that the story is easily believed — those dark green waters look as though they could hold many a fearsome secret.

"But Dermid's dream fortress remained," I suggest thoughtfully.

"Yes, it was the MacArbin stronghold for many centuries, until civilisation taught them to value comfort higher than safety," replies Tony, who seems to have the history of the place by heart. "The present MacArbin's grandfather built a hideous square house farther down the loch and allowed the castle to fall into ruins. Perhaps he felt slightly unsafe in the new house after his fortress, for he surrounded it with a palisade of high iron railings, so that it looks for all the world like a lion in a cage at the Zoo. There are no ghosts there, but their absence is made up for by three bathrooms, complete with hot and cold. My informant was the waiter at the hotel; he is keeping company with Miss MacArbin's housemaid, so, of course, he knows all there is to know about them."

"What a pity!" I exclaim.

"Good heavens, would you rather have ghosts than bathrooms, Hester?" cries Tony in amazement. "You are incurably romantic! Or do you mean that you would

322

like to see the MacArbins living in their stronghold with their ghosts, but not to live here yourself? If so, I agree with you, people should not think of their own comfort; they should continue to live in their ancestral halls to add to the interest of the countryside."

"Let us people these ruins with long-dead MacArbins. There was the one who threw herself into the loch because her lover was killed at Culloden Moor, and another who was drowned in the loch in a sudden storm beneath the very walls of his home and in full view of his wife and children. His wife pined away and was dead in a month, so they threw her body into the loch to keep him company. I will show you the stone commemorating their fate as we go back — and then there was Seónaid, of course —"

"Were there no happy ones?" I ask sadly.

"Look at the surroundings," he replies. "Nobody could be *happy* here. The stage is set for tragedy. One could imagine wild scenes of excitement, and orgies of feasting and banqueting, but there could never be peace and happiness amongst scenery like this."

We climb the slimy stair and emerge once more into the courtyard. It is very still, and the sun shines down, painting strong shadows across the stones.

"Who's that?" says Tony suddenly in a queer voice.

I look up in time to see a tall woman, all in white, disappear into the doorway of the little tower.

"I suppose it was Elsie Baker," he adds in a not very convincing tone of voice.

323

"It was much too tall," I reply breathlessly. "And Elsie has a bright green frock on — who could it have been?"

"Somebody playing jokes, I suppose," says Tony. "I'll go and see who it is. Wait here for me, Hester."

I sit down on a corner of the ruined rampart to wait for him. Far down below, like toy figures on the green grass, I can see Mrs. Loudon and Mrs. Falconer laying the cloth for tea. It is strange to see everything so quiet and to remember the wild scenes this place has witnessed. How many times have these old walls echoed and re-echoed with the wild cries of battle when the MacQuills attacked their hereditary foes! From this eyrie the fierce Hector stole his bride, and here, within this very building, she revenged his death and met her own. These walls have sheltered joys, and sorrows, and hopes and fears innumerable; they have rung with the noise of revelry and the sound of grief; children have been born, and grown to manhood and died within their shelter — and now they are crumbling to ruin, fit only for the owl and the jackdaw to live in and build their nests.

It would not be strange if the place were haunted, visited by some of the fierce creatures who have dwelt here, and suffered, and known it as their home.

Thus musing I pass the time until I see Tony returning from his quest.

"There's nobody," he says with a laugh. "It must have been the effect of light on the wall."

324

"Nonsense, Tony," I reply sharply. "It was a woman dressed in white; she must have gone out some other way."

"She must have had wings, then," says Tony. "I've looked everywhere, and there's no other way out of the tower."

"But I *saw* her."

"Well, I suppose she flew out of the window, then," he replies rather crossly.

"*You* saw her first," I point out.

"I thought I did, but now I know I didn't," he retorts.

We wrangle half-heartedly about the disappearing lady as we climb down the steep path to tea.

By this time the rugs have been spread out and the tea laid beneath the spreading branches of a great oak. I am relieved to hear my daughter's voice, and to see her appear with Guthrie and Elsie from among the trees. This place has a disquieting effect upon my nerves; it is the sort of place where anything horrible might happen.

Betty comes running up to us, calling out that Guthrie found an owl's nest in a big tree and there was a little owl in it all soft and furry. The others say nothing about their adventures, but take their places in silence, Guthrie sitting down between me and Tony, and leaving Miss Baker to find a place for herself.

"I say, Loudon, you're sitting on a thistle," says Tony with solicitude. "Wouldn't you be more comfortable on the rug?"

"I am quite comfortable where I am," Guthrie replies ungraciously.

"I wouldn't like to sit on a thistle," gurgles Betty, between two mouthfuls of egg sandwich.

Apart from this slightly acrimonious exchange, tea is a silent meal. Mrs. Falconer is in one of her silent moods, and confines her remarks to requests for more tea or another scone. Elsie and Guthrie are obviously out of tune, and my thoughts are busy with the phenomenon of the lady in white.

The place itself is sufficient to depress the spirits of most people. There is a damp chill feeling in the air, for the sunshine never falls on this side of the rock. The trees are covered with moss and lichen and a few bright red toadstools cluster round their roots. A huge black bird flies past slowly, the flap of its wings echoing strangely from the overhanging cliff.

"Raven," says Tony quietly.

Just at this moment there is a loud peal of thunder, and a gust of wind steals through the trees, shaking their heavy branches and stirring the green water on the loch.

"We had better get back to the cars," Mrs. Loudon says, looking anxiously at the sky, which has clouded over with remarkable suddenness. "It's going to rain, and when it rains here it comes down in buckets."

"Oh no, don't let's go!" cries Betty. "It's lovely — just like the pantomime before the wizard appears. It gives me the same shuddery feeling in my spine."

"There's MacQuill," says Guthrie suddenly, looking up from his task of packing the basket of crockery.

326

"Shall I shout to him to come with us? He'll get drenched."

We all look up, and I am just in time to see a man running up the little path between the trees. He is wearing a grey flannel suit and has no hat.

"It can't be Hector MacQuill," Tony points out. "This is the last place *he* would come."

"It *was* Hector. I saw him distinctly," replies Guthrie, white with rage.

Tony merely smiles incredulously.

I realise there are the makings of a first-class row — it seems strange that these two men can never speak to each other without getting hot.

"Whoever it was, he will get frightfully wet," I remark pacifically, as a few large splashes of rain fall on my bare arms, and another peal of thunder echoes rumblingly amongst the mountains.

"It was Hector MacQuill," says Guthrie obstinately. He picks up two large baskets and several rugs, and, thus laden, marches off.

The rest of us collect the remainder of the feast, and follow him as fast as we are able. Dobbie is struggling with the hood of the Bentley. Tony rushes to help him. We all scramble into our seats, and the coats and rugs are thrown in on the top of us. Then the heavens seem to open, and the rain comes down in a blinding white sheet of water. The very trees bend under its weight.

"It's not been a very nice afternoon," Dobbie remarks, understating the facts with typical Lowland phlegm, as he climbs into his seat and shuts the door. I notice that, in these few moments, his uniform is soaked through, and the water is trickling down the back of his neck.

Mrs. Loudon agrees with him; she is too used to Dobbie's imperturbability to be surprised at his words.

"Will we start home, Mrs. Loudon?" he enquires, mopping his face with a blue handkerchief, "or will we wait a wee while till the shower's past?"

The "shower" is drumming on the roof like the rattle of musketry, and Mrs. Loudon has to raise her voice to make herself heard.

"We'll get home as quickly as we can," she says. "I'll not have your death at my door, sitting there dripping as if you'd just been taken out of the loch. Away home, and mind you get changed as soon as possible."

Dobbie murmurs something about "a wee thing damp," but he knows Mrs. Loudon too well to argue about it, and soon we are squelching through the mud like a buffalo in a wallow, with the rain beating on the windows and the thunder growling overhead.

"Who would have thought it would turn out like this?" enquires Mrs. Falconer blandly. "It reminds me of a picnic I went to when I was a child —"

The thunder has made my head ache, so I lie back in my corner and try not to hear; but it is impossible not to hear. Why are we not provided with earlids to work in the same way as eyelids, so that if we want to be quiet we may shut our ears and drift away upon our own thoughts? As it is I am forced to listen to a lengthy account of the picnic which Mrs. Falconer attended at the age of eight, clad in a muslin frock and a blue sash. Today being what it is, and Mrs. Falconer being reminded of the occasion by the storm, it is only logical to suppose that these frail garments were completely ruined by the elements; but I can't be certain of this, for I never heard the story finished. Mrs. Loudon, who for some time has been wrapped in her own thoughts — perhaps *she* has invisible earlids — suddenly leans forward and says:

"Dobbie — was that young Mr. MacQuill who passed up the path just before the storm broke?"

"There wasn't anybody passed *me*," Dobbie replies. "I never saw anybody all the time I was there. It's a lonely sort of spot — a bit eerie to my mind."

"Yes, it is," replies Mrs. Loudon thoughtfully.

I can see she is puzzled by the mystery of the disappearing man (and it certainly seems very queer, for the path he took was narrow and led only to the place where we left the cars) but the disappearing lady was an even more perplexing phenomenon, and I can't help wondering what Mrs. Loudon would have made of that. For myself I can make nothing of it at all, and, in spite of an inner voice which assures me that there are no such things as ghosts, I am forced to the somewhat awesome conclusion that there must be, and that I have seen one with my own eyes in broad daylight. If Tony had not seen it too — but then he did. It is all very puzzling.

Ninth June

Guthrie says, "But people *do* take the wrong turning sometimes, Hester, and then they can't go back."

329

We have been talking trivialities until now — I can't remember what — but there is suddenly a strained note in Guthrie's voice which catches my attention and holds it fast. I roll over on the soft turf and look at him in surprise. He is raised on one elbow, and is very busy digging little holes in the grass with his fingers.

High up in the blue sky a lark is singing a perfect paean of praise to its Creator, the loch dreams in the sunshine, devoid of the slightest ripple, a faint haze hovers over the low marshy ground, and shimmers in the noonday heat.

"But people can always go back to the crossroads, Guthrie."

"Not in life," he says gravely.

Suddenly my heart hammers in my throat, and I search wildly for words. "Guthrie, if people have only gone a little way down the wrong road, they can still turn back — the crossroads are in sight —"

"No," he replies, digging his little holes with frightful industry. "No, Hester. A man's got to go forward all the time. Besides, people are sometimes farther down the road than you think — distance is deceptive sometimes."

"Guthrie!"

"Let's go home," he says. "It's hopeless for fishing today. I think I shall take my gun, and get a few rabbits for Mother."

As we stroll over the hill I search wildly for words to influence Guthrie. Quite obviously his strange talk refers to his relations with Elsie. He has come to see her in her true light, but intends — like the obstinate

330

chivalrous creature he is — to marry her all the same. It would have been bad enough for him to marry Elsie thinking her a paragon amongst women, but to marry her with no such delusion is infinitely worse. Sailors don't see very much of their wives, and Guthrie might have gone on for years thinking her perfect in every way. The awful thing about it is that it is all my fault. I have laid myself out to be nice to him. I have tried to show him that a woman can be a friend, and it seems that he has learnt his lesson only too well. I have rushed in where angels might well have feared to tread, and destroyed his illusions to no purpose. Far better if I had left Guthrie alone, and returned to Biddington by the first train. Far better if I had stood aside, or made myself deliberately disagreeable to the man. This is what comes of trying to meddle with people's lives; you achieve your object and find it is a disaster.

At last I can bear it no longer, and I seize my companion by the arm.

"Guthrie!" I cry, "it's not fair to tell me a little and then not let me speak to you. You've simply got to listen to me."

He smiles down at me a little wearily. "My dear, I didn't mean to tell you anything. I'm kicking myself now — if that's any consolation to you."

"None whatever," I reply firmly. "Sit down there and let me speak to you."

We sit down upon a fallen tree, whereupon speech deserts me. I have so much to say that nothing will come.

"Well, go on," he says quite gently.

"Guthrie, you really mustn't do it," I say at last. "You've no idea what you're doing, or you would not *think* of it. You've no idea what marriage is. I've been married for twelve years, and I can tell you this — happiness is only possible when two people have the same ideas."

"Everybody says marriage is a lottery, so what does it matter?" says Guthrie.

"It may be a lottery, but why draw the wrong number on purpose?" I reply quickly.

"I've drawn my number."

"Oh, Guthrie, do listen to me! Don't make a mess of your whole life because you are too proud to say you have made a mistake."

"There is no question of making a mess of my life. Elsie is a dear little girl, and I'm very fond of her; it is only —"

"It is only that you have nothing in common," I interrupt him breathlessly. "Guthrie, do listen to me, and believe that I know what I'm talking about — it wouldn't be quite so bad if you could marry and settle down in a home with friends round you, and each have your own interests and amusements, but Service people can't do that. They've *got* to be pals, making each other do for everything, finding their home, and their friends, and their interests all in each other."

He looks at me with a face gone suddenly white under its tan. "My dear, I know. But I can't go back — she trusts me — she has promised to marry me."

332

I cry to him angrily, "And do you suppose that *she* will be happy? Be sensible for *her* sake if you won't be sensible for your own."

"I think I can make her happy," he replies stiffly.

We walk on in silence.

Tenth June

Mrs. Loudon announces at breakfast that she is going to have a dinner party. The announcement is received by Guthrie with unmitigated scorn. He says that dinner parties are a winter sport, only just bearable in towns where people are herded together in any case — and that it will spoil an evening's fishing, and, anyway, nobody will come.

Mrs. Loudon replies with spirit that *he* need not come unless he wants to, there are plenty of people to ask. That nice Major Morley, for instance.

Guthrie says *he* won't come.

Mrs. Loudon retorts that we shall see whether he will or not, but, for her part, she has no doubt about it — and we can ask Miss Baker and her father, if Guthrie likes.

Guthrie says *he* won't come, *anyway* — he never goes out anywhere.

Mrs. Loudon says if he doesn't want to come he can refuse the invitation, and she intends to ask the MacArbins, because they never have any fun, and Hester ought to see them.

Guthrie says why not ask the MacQuills too.

Mrs. Loudon says it's a pity we can't, but it might be a little *too* exciting if they went for each other in the drawing room.

Guthrie says, "My God, what a party!" and opens the newspaper ostentatiously.

Mrs. Loudon repairs to her desk, writes three notes in record time, and summons Dobbie to deliver them — she is not in the habit of letting the grass grow under her feet.

"— and we can just go ahead with the preparations," she says, looking at me over the top of her spectacles as she sits at her desk. "For they'll all jump at it."

"When is it to be?" I ask her.

"Tonight, of course," replies the indomitable woman. "Where's the sense of putting things off? If I'm feeling like having a dinner party, I have it. And you can dress the flowers for the table," she adds trenchantly, "for I know perfectly well that you'll not let *me* do it in peace."

I am about to leave the room when Mrs. Loudon recalls me — "Salmon, and lamb, and peas, and trifle," she says, frowning anxiously. "Would you give them soup as well, Hester, or yon newfangled grapefruit?"

I vote for soup, whereupon Mrs. Loudon's brow clears.

"It's cold fare for an empty stomach, grapefruit," she says. "I'll admit they always give me the gooseflesh. Whereas a nice spoonful of Julienne is a comforting sort of start."

Guthrie now appears, looking quite pleasant again — his ill humours are always short-lived — and remarks

334

that there is a fine breeze on the loch, and can Hester come, or does his mother intend to work her all day long like a galley slave over this forsaken dinner?

Mrs. Loudon replies that *she* does not work Hester like a galley slave, and perhaps Guthrie has forgotten that galley slaves were used to row ships when he chose that particular metaphor.

Guthrie actually has the grace to blush, though protesting, not altogether truthfully, that we always take it in turns to row.

We collect the fishing tackle and make our way down to the loch, where we find Betty and a boy of about her own age — or slightly older — digging in the gravel. Annie is sitting close by, knitting a multicoloured jumper, which, I feel sure, must be intended for Bollings — Tim's batman — to whom she is engaged.

Guthrie says he has no idea who the boy can be unless he is one of Donald's offspring, which are numbered as the sands of the sea. I reply that Betty would find another child to play with her if she were marooned upon a desert island.

At this moment Betty sees us, and calls out that Ian is showing her how to dam the burn with stones. Guthrie says *he* knowns how to damn the burn without stones.

"Oh, do you? *How?*" says Betty with interest.

I feel slightly worried at the probable development of this conversation, as it looks as though it might turn out to have a damaging effect upon my child's morals (no pun intended).

Ian now remarks, in a soft Highland voice, that he is aware the burn *could* be dammed with sods, but he doots the laird would like us to be cutting them.

I can see that Guthrie is about to say that he can damn it without sods, so I make a face at him and he remains silent.

Betty now says that she is tired of damming burns, so can she and Ian come fishing with us if they promise to be very quiet? (She knows from experience that this promise usually appeals to the adult mind.) Guthrie says they may, and we all embark without further ado.

It is a grey, cloudy day with small ripples and a whitish glare upon the water. The top of Ben Seoch is swathed in mist. Guthrie takes out his rod and says solemnly he is doubtful about the fish today. They don't as a rule take well with mist on the mountains. I reply facetiously that the fish can't possibly know about the mist unless somebody has told them.

"But the kelpies tell them, of course," replies Guthrie gravely. "I thought you knew that much, Hester. How ignorant you are, to be sure!"

Ian gazes at Guthrie with large brown eyes, and asks if Mr. Loudon has ever seen a kelpie talking to the fishes. This puts the good man in rather a hole, and he spends some time fabricating a long and somewhat complicated answer to the question.

After a couple of drifts during which no rise is seen, Betty begins to get slightly restive, and asks why Guthrie doesn't catch a fish — don't the fish *want* to get caught? *She* thinks that fish like worms best, and, if

Guthrie likes, she and Ian will go and dig some up for him. Bryan always uses worms when he goes fishing.

Ian suddenly says, "Whisht!" and points to a ring in the water about twenty yards from the boat. He is obviously no tyro at the sport. We approach our prey, and Guthrie casts over the place with great skill. A large fish rises and looks at the flies disdainfully, but utterly refuses to be caught. Betty reiterates her conviction that fish prefer worms.

The morning passes without success. We learn from Ian that he is indeed the son of Donald, and that he intends to become a ghillie. Guthrie suggests the navy as a more suitable profession, but Ian is not attracted by the idea and says he would not like to be spending his whole time climbing masts; it would be an easier thing to be tracking the deer upon the mountains — so it would.

After some time spent in flogging the water without any result, even Guthrie has to admit that it seems pretty useless, and we return home with an empty bag. We are walking back to the house somewhat disconsolately, when Betty suddenly turns to me and asks with her usual directness, "What is the *use* of fishing, Mummie?"

I am slightly taken aback, but reply, after a moment's thought, that it is to catch fish, of course.

"I'm sure I could invent a better way," she says. "I would make a little trap for them with flies inside — if they really *like* flies, though *I* think they like worms better — and then, when they were all inside eating the flies — or worms — the trapdoor would shut, and there they'd be."

Guthrie says bitterly that after this morning's so-called sport he is inclined to agree with Betty.

Betty says, after reflection, that she likes damming burns much better than fishing.

The afternoon is spent doing the flowers — a task which is made more difficult for me by Mrs. Loudon, whose ideas on floral decorations have already been chronicled. We also write out the menu cards, and arrange how everyone is to sit at table.

"I wonder what like that Baker man will be?" says Mrs. Loudon. "I'll have to have him on my left, and I'll put you next to him, so mind and talk to the creature, Hester, and you can have Major Morley on the other side to make up."

"What good will that be if I can't talk to him?" I enquire innocently.

"You know what I mean well enough," she replies. "You're getting too uppish altogether, and if there's any more of it I'll pack you off home. Now where will we put Miss MacArbin?"

Our deliberations are interrupted by the arrival of the post, and I am overjoyed to receive a letter from Tim. He has written before, of course, but only miserable, scrappy communications to convey the news that he is well and very busy getting his company into trim. This letter looks more promising, and I have hopes that it may contain information about houses. Perhaps Tim has had time to visit some of the

338

"desirable residences to let," whose names I obtained from the agent at Biddington.

"Away with you and read it in peace," says Mrs. Loudon suddenly, so I fly upstairs with it to digest it at my leisure.

The letter begins with the announcement that Tim has been very busy with his company, but that he has found time to examine some of the pigsties on the agent's list, and most of them are absolutely foul. There is only one he likes the look of — it is called "Heathery Hill," on account of one small piece of heather which is dragging out an exiled existence in the rockery. I perceive at once that the charm of "Heathery Hill" consists in the fact that there is a stable at the back which Tim can use for his charger, and I have grave doubts whether Tim has looked at any of its other amenities. The beds, the furniture, the kitchen range, and water supply, the condition of the roof, and the drains are completely ignored in Tim's description. He touches lightly on the fact that the drawing room has a southern aspect, and the existence of a cupboard under the stairs, and asks me to wire at once whether or not he is to take it, as there are several other people after it. This threat does not disturb me, as agents invariably try to hustle prospective tenants in this manner, but I hastily scan the remainder of Tim's letter in the hope that I may gather a few more crumbs of information anent my future home. Alas, there are no crumbs! The rest of the letter deals exclusively with a description of his charger, whom he has named Boanerges on account of his dark colour and rolling eye. Tim hopes that I approve of the name. Boanerges is absolutely the pick of the officers' mounts, but not up to the colonel's weight, of course, and old MacPherson likes something quieter. He is very comfortable to ride, and has excellent paces. Boanerges seems such an admirable steed that I can't help wondering why he has been relegated to the junior major of the battalion — perhaps the postscript explains in some part the anomaly; it is added in pencil and is ominously brief — "Have just discovered, rather unexpectedly, that Boanerges does not like his father."

I dress early for the dinner party, and don my new frock with great satisfaction. It is beige lace with orange flowers, and I note in the mirror that it is really very becoming.

Betty calls to me to come and say "Goodnight" to her, and, when I comply with her request, I find her having her supper in bed, with the faithful Annie in attendance.

"Oh, you *do* look nice, m'm!" exclaims the latter ecstatically.

Betty looks at me appraisingly, and says that *she* likes me much better in my Fair Isle jumper.

"But your mother could never wear it for dinner," says the scandalised Annie.

"Why not?" asks Betty truculently. "When I'm grown up I shall wear what I like best all the time — I shall wear my pyjamas all day if I want to."

I kiss my daughter, and suggest to Annie in an undertone that perhaps a little fig syrup might be a good thing, and, having fulfilled my maternal duties, wend my way downstairs.

Although I am early on the scene my hostess is before me. She is seated by the fire, looking very dignified in black lace, and engaged in reading *The Times*, which only reaches this remote spot at dinner time.

She looks up and says, "I hoped you'd be early. What a pretty thing you are! Come and warm yourself, child."

I sit down beside her chair on a footstool, and we both gaze at the fire for a little while without speaking. A fire of birch logs is a lovely sight. The under part glows redly, like a miniature forge, and little blue tongues of flame come licking round the bark as if it tastes nice.

At last Mrs. Loudon breaks the spell of silence. "Hester, I'm beginning to think Guthrie sees through that girl," she says thoughtfully. "What do you think about it?"

I don't know what to reply — I would tell her about our conversation if I thought she could persuade Guthrie where I have failed, but she couldn't, I know. If she were to speak to him they would both lose their tempers, and there would be a row, and Guthrie would rush off and marry the girl offhand. Besides, if he *is* going to marry the girl it will be better for Mrs. Loudon to think that he is still infatuated with her. All these thoughts have boiled in my head for two days, until I am quite muddled with them. I see no loophole of escape. Guthrie has all his mother's obstinacy in him —

he is determined to marry Elsie — and the more opposition he finds to his foolish course, the more determined he will be.

"Well?" she says. "You haven't answered — what a girl you are for dreaming!" She turns my face up to hers and looks at me earnestly. "He has spoken to you," she says, in a breathless voice.

"He is quite determined to marry her," I reply in the same low tone. "My dear, you will have to make the best of it. I've done all I can. I'm sorry."

Mrs. Loudon clings to my hand. "He's all I've got left," she says, "and I can't be friends with that girl. She's got nothing in her that I can get hold of — nothing that I can understand. She's not a bad girl, I know, but she's just different. She'll take Guthrie right away from me — she hates me."

"She's rather frightened of you, I think."

"Yes, I suppose I *am* rather a fearsome old woman to people — to people who don't understand my way," she says pathetically. "It's the way I'm made, and I'm too old to change now."

I hold her tightly. I can hear her heart beating very quickly under my ear, and feel the rise and fall of her hurried breathing.

"It will ruin him," she says, still in that low breathless voice. "They will both be miserable. He needs a woman to understand him — for the creature's a fool in some ways, though I say it. The right woman could have made Guthrie, the wrong woman will ruin him."

Of course she is right. I can only hold her thin body close and pat her shoulder.

342

"Gracious me!" she exclaims at last, pushing me away and blowing her nose loudly on a large linen handkerchief. "What a fool I am! It's no wonder Guthrie's one, with a mother like me. Here are we, croaking like sybils, and guests expected any minute! Me with a red nose, too! No, Hester, you can keep your powder — I'm too old now to start powdering my nose. If it's red, it's red, and there's an end to it."

"It's not very red," I reassure her.

"That's a mercy," she replies. "For they'll be here directly. Dobbie's gone to fetch the MacArbins. They're very poor, and their car is a ramshackle affair to go out at night. By the way, Guthrie said I was to warn you that you've to call the man MacArbin — they're a brother and sister, you know — 'last scions of a noble race.' "

"Mr. MacArbin," I suggest, wondering what else I would be likely to call him.

"No, just MacArbin — here they are, I declare — he's *the* MacArbin, you see."

I don't see, and decide not to address the man under any circumstances whatever, and then I shall not betray my ignorance.

His appearance completely overwhelms me. I have seen lots of kilts, but never one worn with such an air of confidence and pride.

"Mrs. Christie, may I introduce MacArbin," says my hostess, in her dignified manner.

We both bow, he with a strangely foreign grace, which seems to spread upwards from the chased silver buckles on his shoes to the crown of his iron-grey hair.

343

I take in at a glance the perfection of his attire: his green kilt, his snowy falls of lace at neck and wrist, the silver buttons on his black cloth doublet, the jewelled dagger in his stocking. From this I go on to take stock of himself: flashing brown eyes, long thin nose, long thin fingers and sensitive hands — and decide that here, indeed, is the portrait of a Highland gentleman come to life.

I try to think of some remark — not too utterly inane — to address him with, but can think of nothing more original than the weather. We decide that it was fine this morning, but somewhat showery in the afternoon, and then look at each other blankly.

Fortunately Tony Morley arrives to rescue me, and the two men are soon deep in the technicalities of stalking. I am thus able to observe them at my leisure. They are typical examples of their race. Tony's tail coat makes him look taller, while the Highlander's kilt gives him breadth with grace. It suits me well that they should talk to each other, for I want to be at hand to help Mrs. Loudon if required.

Mrs. Falconer has captured Miss MacArbin, a tall slim girl in a night-blue frock, and is telling her a long and complicated story in confidential tones. I look with interest at Miss MacArbin and wonder whether Miss Campbell was correct in her surmise. I can easily understand any man falling madly in love with her, for there is something fatally attractive about her pale beauty and her rather languid grace.

Mrs. Loudon seizes my arm, and says: "Hester, I should never have asked the Bakers."

I realise the truth of this, but it is much too late now; in fact the Bakers' wheels are crunching over the gravel at this very moment. Guthrie goes into the hall to meet them, and returns escorting a small red-faced man with silver hair and amazingly bushy silver eyebrows. He shakes hands all round, and says, with a beaming smile, that he is pleased to meet us — he is really rather a lovable little man.

"I'm so glad you could come," Mrs. Loudon says. "Your daughter told us you don't go out much."

"Oh well, it's not everybody wants the old man," replies Mr. Baker with engaging simplicity. "But I just said to Elsie — I *must* go to Mrs. Loudon's party, seeing she's been good enough to ask me. Elsie wasn't too keen on me coming, but you must be firm sometimes, and, after all, you've *got* to see me sooner or later. Of course it's quite natural Elsie shouldn't want to have me tagged on to her — my little girl can take her place in any society — I tell you I'm proud of my little Elsie, she's all I've got, ma'am. I've spared no expense to give her a good education, and I tell you I've got my money's worth."

There is an awkward pause in the general conversation. I, for one, am speechless, and the others seem to be in a like condition. Mrs. Falconer finds her tongue first, and dashes into the breach — is it sheer good luck, or is she not really quite so vague and foolish as she seems?

"That is just what dear Papa always said," she announces ecstatically. "'A good education is the best foundation,' he used to say. I've always remembered it

345

because it rhymes — and it's so *true*, isn't it? I always think it is easier to remember things when they rhyme. We used to learn history like that:

> " 'Ten sixty-six on Hastings' strand
> Harold the Norman comes to land.' "

Guthrie has now started to hand round sherry. I have just taken a glass from the tray when I look up and see Elsie Baker standing at the door, her eyes fixed upon MacArbin with an incredulous stare. She is obviously on the brink of hysterical laughter. This would be fatal, so I edge nearer to her and whisper:

"Isn't he magnificent, Miss Baker? *The* MacArbin, you know. Descended from the great chief —"

"My!" she exclaims with a gasp. "He's just like Duggie Fairweather in *Scotland's Bath of Blood*."

I realise at once, with relief, that she has no higher meed of praise, and drink my sherry in peace.

Everyone is now talking at the top of his voice — an excellent sign at this stage of the proceedings. We finish our sherry, and are herded into the dining room, and distributed round the table by our hostess.

MacArbin sits upon his hostess's right, then comes Mrs. Falconer and Elsie Baker. Guthrie and Miss MacArbin are next, and then Tony and myself, with Mr. Baker on Mrs. Loudon's left.

Tony starts his nonsense before we have finished the excellent Julienne, and I realise that he is in one of his most irresponsible moods.

"Is this a betrothal feast?" he whispers. "The gloom upon the brow of our good hostess is more fitting to the baked meats of a funeral collation."

"You will probably get an excellent dinner," I replied shortly.

"I don't doubt it," says Tony, "but it is most essential for me to know whether I am to be my usual gay and witty self — the life and soul of the party — or to put on the gloomy gravity which I invariably reserve for sad and solemn occasions."

I reply that he can do as he pleases, and turn my left shoulder towards him — he really deserves a snub. Unfortunately Mr. Baker is too deep in conversation with Mrs. Loudon to notice my movement, and I have the choice of listening to the said conversation — which I realise is of a distinctly private nature — or withdrawing my left shoulder from Tony and making it up with him.

"It's a good little business," Mr. Baker is saying earnestly. "Two thousand a year it brings in, regular as clockwork — too much for a man with simple tastes like me. Elsie likes her comforts, you know, and I shall settle a thousand a year on her if she marries the right chap — or I'd be willing to take him into the business and expand a bit."

Mrs. Loudon says she is delighted to hear he is comfortably off, but implies delicately that she is not interested in his financial affairs.

"Oh, I dare say I'm a bit premature, as the chicken said when it cracked the shell," replies Mr. Baker, winking at her slyly. "But I do like to have things cut and dried and aboveboard. You're quite right to pull me up a bit, ma'am. Elsie said herself I was to go easy, and I'll go as easy as you please. You'll drive me on a snaffle before we've gone far, see if you don't."

Mrs. Loudon's face is a study; she gazes at Mr. Baker as if he were some strange and rather dangerous reptile, but she is too rigid in her ideas of hospitality to attempt a snub. Besides, the little man is so devoid of all desire to offend, his friendliness and simplicity are disarming. Her eyes meet mine with a pleading, anguished look. "Hester, I don't know if I introduced Mr. Baker," she murmurs weakly.

"Indeed you did, ma'am; you know your job as hostess, as anyone can see with half an eye," replies Mr. Baker gallantly. "You introduced Mrs. Christie and me right off, and very pleased I was. I've heard a lot about Mrs. Christie from some friends of hers staying at the hotel — Mr. and Mrs. McTurk."

I try to explain that I don't know them very well, but Mr. Baker does not listen. "Very nice friends to have, Mrs. Christie, especially the lady. She's always saying how sorry she is at you leaving Kiltwinkle. It must be a bit trying for a lady like you not to have a settled home of your own, isn't it now?"

This statement is often made to me, and it always annoys me, chiefly, I think, because it is true. But some time ago I found a quotation which seemed to meet the case, and I always make use of it on these occasions.

" 'To a resolved mind his home is everywhere,' " I reply sententiously.

Mr. Baker looks suitably impressed, but Tony, who has now recovered from my snub, and has evidently been able to make very little of Miss MacArbin, turns round and says, "Since when have you had a resolved mind, O Dame of the Burning Pestle? The quotation is apt, I admit, and the provocation considerable, but I should advise you to keep your erudite literary quotations for an erudite literary audience. To cast pearls before swine is not a sign of superiority, but the sign of a narrow mind. Swine have their own standard of values, and a really clever and adaptable person should be able to adapt himself to his company."

"Grunt at them, I suppose," I suggest, for I am slightly hurt at being called narrow-minded.

Mr. Baker looks thoroughly puzzled at Tony's dissertation, but brightens up at the word "swine." "D'you know much about the value of swine, sir?" he asks interestedly. "I deal in 'ides, you know. Quite a paying business it is."

Mrs. Loudon has turned thankfully to the MacArbin, and is listening to his ideas on the subject of grouse moors with an appearance of intense interest.

Elsie now leans forward across the table and asks Tony if he was talking about *The Burning Thistle* — she thought she heard him mention it. She went to Inverness yesterday with a boy from the hotel, and they saw it at the picture house, and isn't Molly Greateyes just wonderful?

Tony replies, "Simply divine! That close up where the lovers are united after passing through fire and flood —"

349

Elsie knits her brows and says, "But that's not till they meet in the burning house."

"Oh, of course," agrees Tony. "And he seizes her in his arms and staggers out of the blazing pile, just when everyone thinks they are burned to death."

Elsie says she doesn't remember that bit, and I am not surprised to hear it, for of course, Tony has never seen the film and is just being naughty.

Dinner flows on with admirable smoothness, for Mrs. Loudon's maids are well-trained; but the conversation is interrupted by a good many crossquestions and crooked answers owing to the strange conglomeration of people which Mrs. Loudon has seen fit to invite. I find it difficult to converse with Tony and Mr. Baker at the same time. Their tastes are different and their outlook upon life irreconcilable, and can't help wishing that Mrs. Loudon would take part in entertaining my right-hand neighbour, or else that Miss MacArbin would produce some small talk for Tony.

Mrs. Falconer, who has been somewhat subdued, suddenly wakes up and starts telling the MacArbin about her old nurse who suffered greatly from chilblains. She even had one on her nose. Mrs. Falconer, who was then about seven years old, or possibly eight, made a little nose bag and presented it to Old Nannie for a Christmas present. "The nose bag was made of red flannel, and had two little pieces of elastic which went round the ears," continues Mrs. Falconer reminiscently. "I can see her now, going about her work with that little red bag on her nose. It really did her a lot of good — that, or the cod liver oil which was ordered for her by the doctor. But one day she went to the back door in it by mistake, and the greengrocer's boy, who was handing in a bag of potatoes, nearly had a fit when he saw her, and poor Nannie was so offended at the way he laughed that she never wore the nose bag again."

"— so there it is," Mr. Baker is saying with his beaming smile. "What do *you* think about it, Mrs. Christie?"

I gaze at him in despair, for I have not been listening to a word, and have no idea what I think about it. I have been caught out in the reprehensible act of listening to other people's conversation, and neglecting my own.

"It took me some time to get used to it," he admits with a chuckle. "But there, I'm only an old-fashioned buffer and girls have to be in the mode — and if Elsie's pleased, well, so am I!"

I smile at him vaguely.

"I see you haven't been done, Mrs. Christie," he whispers confidentially. "Elsie'd tell you where she went, in a minute she would. Very satisfied she was —"

What *is* the man talking about? Some sort of inoculation, perhaps.

"Are you going to be done?" I ask, hoping that his reply may elucidate the problem.

He looks at me and suddenly shouts with laughter. "Ha, ha! That's rich, that is. You're a wit, Mrs. Christie, and no mistake — ha, ha, ha. Fancy the old Dad having his eyebrows plucked! Ha, ha! Ha, ha, ha!"

The attention of the entire table is centred upon us. Mr. Baker mops his eyes with his table napkin and then tries to stuff it into his pocket. "Ha, ha!" he shouts. "Ha, ha, ha! Thought it was my serviette — I mean my 'andkerchief — ha, ha, ha!"

The MacArbin places an eyeglass in his eye, and looks across the table at Mr. Baker as if he were a strange animal which has never been seen before. Guthrie asks what is the joke.

At this moment Mrs. Loudon gives the signal for departure — she evidently thinks it unsafe to wait until Mr. Baker recovers his breath. Mrs. Falconer, who has got behind-hand in dessert, owing to her story about old Nannie's nose bag, is still eating an apple.

"Elspeth!" she exclaims piteously.

But Elspeth is already at the door, and Mrs. Falconer is obliged to clutch her pochette, and hasten after her fellow females.

"Elspeth is so unobservant," she whispers to me as we cross the hall. "And it was a Jonathan, too — my favourite kind."

In the drawing room there is a moment's silence and then everybody speaks at once.

Elsie asks: "Whatever were you and Dad laughing at?"

Mrs. Falconer begins, "When us girls were all young —"

And Mrs. Loudon says, "Poke up the fire, Hester," and starts pushing chairs and sofas about with fierce and somewhat misplaced energy.

I poke up the fire, which incidentally requires no poking, and sit down beside Miss MacArbin. She looks dreamy and peaceful, and I am in need of peace. I feel slightly battered, and my face is stiff with smiling false smiles and hiding real ones.

"Castle Darroch is beautiful," I tell her. "We had a picnic there one day."

"But it is very sad," she says softly.

Miss MacArbin interests me in spite of her absence of small talk. Her beauty is almost startling. There is something timid, yet proud, in the carriage of her small, exquisitely shaped head, and her eyes are fiery and dreamy by turns. Why, of course, I tell myself suddenly, she is like a princess in a fairy tale, and I feel glad to think I have found such an exact description of her.

"It is the atmosphere of Castle Darroch that is sad," she says, still in that soft silvery voice. "So many strange and terrible things have happened there —"

"I believe I saw a ghost," I tell her with a smile.

Miss MacArbin smiles too, and the smile lights up the wistfulness of her face like a sunbeam. "People often see ghosts when they *expect* to see them," she says lightly. "Perhaps you had read the story of Seónaid just before you went there. I used to play in the ruins when I was a child, but I never saw a ghost."

"This was a woman in white," I tell her. "She was rather like you — now I think of it — tall and slim with dark hair —"

She looks at me strangely. "I am supposed to be like Seónaid."

"Then you think it was the ghost of Seónaid we saw?"

"How can I tell you? I have never seen one."

She does not like the subject, for some reason — perhaps it is because she is superstitious and thinks it is unlucky to speak of ghosts. I look at her hands; they are very pretty, with long, tapering fingers — she has no engagement ring, so I conclude, reluctantly, that Miss Campbell was wrong in her surmise.

"I think you must have a very interesting life," she says suddenly, raising her eyes and looking at me with friendliness. "To move about the world as you do, and meet so many different people, must be very interesting."

"It has its disadvantages."

"Oh yes, but every kind of life has its disadvantages. You get so deeply in a groove if you go on living for ever and ever in the same place, and it is difficult to get out of a groove. It takes courage. I am rather frightened of people," she admits simply.

"People are really very nice."

"Yes," she says. "You would find them so, because you are not thinking of yourself all the time. I think of myself too much."

The advent of the men puts a stop to our conversation, and there is a general reshuffle of chairs. This is the worst of a dinner party — or indeed any sort of party — you have no sooner begun to find out a little about your vis-à-vis, and become interested in her personality, than she is snatched away from you.

354

Mrs. Loudon suggests bridge, and the cards are produced by Guthrie. A great deal of discussion ensues as to who shall play and who shall sit out.

Tony comes over to where I am sitting and says, "It's lovely outside, Hester."

"Aren't you going to play?" I ask in surprise, for Tony Morley is known in the regiment as an indomitable bridge player.

"There is a time and a place for everything," he replies gravely, "and this is neither the time nor the place for bridge."

We therefore go outside, and walk up and down the veranda once or twice, and then sit down in a comfortable friendly silence. If Guthrie were my companion he would want me to walk, down to the gate and wreck my best shoes on the gravel, but Tony is never thoughtless in small matters.

It is lovely here, after the heat and chatter of the drawing room — a few faint, rosy clouds linger above the mountains in a band of pale primrose sky, and a single faint star peeps shyly from behind the jagged outline of a ben.

"*Pâle étoile du soir —*" says Tony softly. "Do you know that thing, Hester?"

"Yes, and I love it. Why is it that one star is so much more beautiful than many?"

"One woman is much more beautiful than many," replies Tony. "And so is one flower."

This idea would not appeal to Mrs. Loudon, and I give Tony a description of my struggles with my hostess

355

in the flower room. It suddenly seems safer to keep the conversation in a humorous vein.

"I want to take you to Gart-na-Druim some day," says Tony suddenly (at least the name sounds like that). "Mrs. Loudon wouldn't mind, would she? It would take us all day. We could lunch there."

"What is there to see?" I ask him with interest.

"The Western Sea," Tony replies. "Small waves lapping softly on white beaches, and small rugged islands and mountains stretching their feet into the sea. It's like no other place in the world, and you really must have one peep at the Western Sea before you go. What about tomorrow —"

"I think I could. Mrs. Loudon wouldn't mind."

"There's a farm that we used to go to when we were children," Tony continues. "I would like you to see it. It's quite a tiny place on the hillside, but it was a sort of Paradise to us. We just ran wild with the farmer's children — spent long days fishing or trekking about the hills. I'd like you to meet Alec — he farms the place himself now that his father is dead."

"Is it a big farm?"

"Oh no — just a tiny croft and the soil is poor. He ekes out an existence with fishing. I never knew anybody so contented with his lot as Alec Macdonald — he's always happy. He was with me in the war. I managed to get him into my company and of course he was splendid — I knew he would be. Even in the tightest place — and we were in one or two pretty tight places together — Alec was perfectly calm and cheerful.

I always go and see him when I am in this part of the world; he likes talking over old times."

The light in the garden is thinning now, the hedges and the trees are lost in gloom, the little white faces of the pansies shine like earthly stars. A moth flies past, and blunders against the lighted window with a dull thump.

"Poor creature," says Tony. "It wanted to get at the light."

"The glass saved its life," I reply.

"But it wanted to get to the light — don't you understand, Hester?"

"It would only have singed its wings."

"Why shouldn't it singe its wings if it wanted to?" asks Tony earnestly. "Don't you think *that one glorious moment* when it feels itself at the very heart of its desire is worth a pair of singed wings?"

Tony is really very puzzling; I never know whether his words have some deep meaning beyond my ken, or whether he is merely talking nonsense on purpose to bewilder me.

"I think it has had a lucky escape," I reply sternly, "and I hope it has learnt a lesson not to go chasing after lights in that idiotic way."

"I hope it hasn't," says Tony Morley softly.

There is a little silence. I can just see the gleam of his white shirt front in the darkness and the fitful glow of his cigarette.

Suddenly Guthrie appears and says they have finished the rubber, and will Tony come and make up another four.

357

Tony replies that he is very comfortable where he is, and that he doesn't much care for bridge. "The only bridge worth playing is three-handed bridge," he adds didactically.

Guthrie, surprised and annoyed at this unusual preference, says that most people consider three-handed bridge too much of a gamble.

"That's what I like about it," says Tony, and I can tell he is smiling by the tone of his voice. "I like a gamble, and I like to gamble on my own. I like playing every hand myself. Partners are such a bore; they don't return your lead at the right moment, or they get fed up if you fail to bid in accordance with some twopenny-halfpenny convention."

"You must be very lucky if you are able to bid for dummy every time," Guthrie says, with cold fury.

Tony replies that he *is* lucky at cards, but not in love, and heaves a ridiculous sigh. "You should not grudge me that poor consolation, Loudon," he adds innocently.

Poor Guthrie turns on his heel, and disappears into the drawing room without another word.

"Got him that time," says Tony with a short laugh.

"I don't know why you're such a beast to Guthrie," I tell him sternly.

"I don't know either," responds Tony thoughtfully, "except that the man has such rotten taste. He's going to have the devil of a life with that girl, and I'm sorry for him, and it annoys me frightfully to be sorry for people."

We return to the drawing room and find the assembled company playing *vingt-et-un*, all except

358

Mrs. Falconer, who says she is no good at arithmetic and never was. Room is made at the gambling table for Tony and me, and we make our stakes. Guthrie remarks that we shall now see whether Major Morley is lucky at cards, whereupon Tony produces an ace and a ten, and rakes in a pile of red counters with an amused smile.

The Bakers are the first to depart. Mr. Baker has been smothering huge yawns for some time, and casting anguished looks towards his daughter. I am thankful when at last she takes pity on him, for I feel that at any moment he may fall asleep in his chair, and have to be carried out to the car by Guthrie and Tony. They could accomplish this feat quite easily, of course, but Elsie would feel the indignity.

Mr. Baker pulls himself together at Elsie's signal, and thanks his hostess with suitable warmth for a delightful evening. "You must come and have dinner with Elsie and me at the hotel," he says earnestly. "The food is first class — just tell the young people to fix a day."

Miss MacArbin says she thinks perhaps they should go home too.

"Well, if you really must —" says Mrs. Loudon. "Dobbie's ready when you are."

They all disappear, calling out that it has been a delightful evening and most enjoyable. Only Tony remains, and he and Guthrie repair to the dining room for a last drink.

"It went off very well," says Mrs. Loudon as we turn out the lamps in the drawing room and make our way upstairs. "Yon MacArbin girl is a pretty creature — I

359

liked her. It's a lonely life for a young thing, keeping house for that brother — did you get any word with him, Hester? A dreigh sort of body, I thought."

"You seemed very much interested in his conversation at dinner," I point out.

"Anything to get away from that Baker man," she replies fervently. "The man scared me. Did you hear him havering on about his income as if it was settlements I was after? And, when I tried to shut him up about that, I declare to goodness he went on as if *I* was to marry *him* — told me I'd be driving him on a snaffle before long," adds Mrs. Loudon with a snort. "The cheek of the man, Hester! And yet it wasn't exactly cheek, either, for he was quite unconscious that he was saying anything wrong."

"Very difficult," I admit.

"Difficult!" she exclaims, as if I had insulted her by such underestimation of her problem. "Difficult! I tell you, Hester, Torquemada's crosswords are child's play compared to my situation with that man."

I feel too tired to discuss the party any further tonight, so I make my excuses to my hostess and retire to my room. I am just on the point of removing my earrings (Woolworth's Oriental Pearl) when I hear the sound of voices in the garden. Guthrie's voice, strangely harsh in tone, announces to some unseen companion:

"I know you think me a fool — I admit I'm no match for you, juggling with words — but I'm not a *cad*."

"What exactly do you mean by that, Loudon?" Tony's voice is smooth as silk.

360

(What a nuisance those two men are! I shall have to delay my undressing, in case it becomes necessary to go down and play the part of peacemaker. What do men *do* nowadays when they quarrel? I can't imagine them hitting each other, but perhaps this is only because I am entirely ignorant upon the subject. I think Tony would get the worst of it, if it came to blows — Guthrie's shoulders are so broad — yet I can't imagine a beaten and humiliated Tony. Somehow or other he would manage to come out on top).

These thoughts fly through my head in a second. I blow out my candle, and lean out of the window. Evidently they are just below me, on the veranda, for the pungent scent of a cigar drifts up through the still air.

"Well, Loudon," says Tony's voice, after a short silence, "I am entitled to an explanation of your words."

There is a strangled curse from Guthrie. "You can always put me in the wrong if you like," he says furiously. "But I don't make love to other men's wives — I don't hang round like a damned lap dog —"

(I realise at once that Guthrie must have discovered some episode of Tony's past — which is said in the regiment to be of a lurid nature — or perhaps there is some lady at the hotel who has captured Tony's vagrant fancy. *I* have heard nothing about it, of course, but the Bakers may have told Guthrie, or he may have found out in some other way. I have often noticed that men have a strange faculty for nosing out this sort of thing.)

To my surprise Tony does not seem very angry. He laughs, somewhat mirthlessly, and says:

"Oh, that's the trouble, is it? You need not worry; the lady is perfectly safe from me. She is hedged about with innocence."

"And if she were not?" Guthrie asks quickly.

"Oh, if she were not I would carry her off like old Hector MacQuill," is the calm reply.

They are now walking down the path towards the Bentley, and the scrunch of gravel drowns what Guthrie is saying, but Tony's answer comes quite clearly to my ears.

"That's my business," he says drily. "If I choose to singe my wings —"

I remember the moth blundering against the window, and the queer nonsense he talked about it — he was thinking of himself, I suppose, and his own affairs. What a strange, incomprehensible creature he is!

I realise that the crisis is past — for some reason they are not going to fight each other tonight. I heave a sigh of relief — for I am very tired — and crawl backwards out of my frock and hang it over a chair.

The Bentley departs, the angry voices have subsided, the night sinks into velvet peace. I kneel at my window and gaze up into the sky — a deep blue, glowing canopy above the dark, lacy branches of the firs. The stars glimmer like tiny yellow lamps. There is no sound save the silver tinkle of the burn, and, far off amongst the hills, a lamb bleats once and is quiet.

Eleventh June

I jump out of bed and poke my head out of the window. There is a thick mist on the ground, and halfway up the hills, above the mist, floats the hilltop, crested with trees, like a fairy island in a lake of fleecy wool.

This is the day of my expedition with Tony, he is to call for me at ten, and the problem which confronts me is this — what am I to wear? It all depends upon what sort of a day it is going to be. Will the mist clear off, or will it thicken and spread? Will it resolve into rain or lift into sunshine?

Guthrie is very cross at breakfast — there is no other word for it. He eats his kidneys with a glowering face, and nearly bites my head off when I enquire what kind of a day it is going to be. Meanwhile Mrs. Loudon smiles to herself as if she has some secret cause for amusement which nobody else may share.

Seeing that my companions are occupied with their own thoughts — pleasant or otherwise — I too relapse into silence, and commune with mine.

After some minutes the silence becomes laden, like the stillness of a storm before it breaks, and, looking up, I see that Guthrie's mood has changed, his eyes are fixed upon me beseechingly — he is sorry.

I feel drawn to experiment with Guthrie — what will happen if I do not speak to this poor young man in a kind manner? Will he blow up and burst into a thousand pieces with the effort to contain his feelings, to keep all the things he wants to say locked up in his poor helpless body? Or will he merely finish his toast

363

and marmalade and walk out of the room? What an alluring experiment it would be! But, alas, I cannot make it, for Mrs. Loudon is looking at me with pleading eyes. "Speak to him kindly," they seem to say. "Speak to him kindly for my sake. For if he should blow up into a thousand pieces, where should I find another son?"

I cannot resist such an appeal, so I lean forward and say very sweetly:

"Are you going to fish today, Guthrie?"

A sunbeam struggles through the clouds. "How can I without my ghillie?" he asks, half smiling, half sulky. "Don't go, Hester; we haven't got many days left. Why do you want to go dashing over the countryside, when we can spend a long day on the loch?"

"Don't be selfish, Guthrie," says Mrs. Loudon, and the wicked woman actually winks at me from behind her barrier of tea cosies. "You can get Donald to row the boat if you want to fish — though you know perfectly well that you'll not catch anything with this mist all over everything. Of course Hester must go about, and see all she can of the country while she's here."

"She won't see much of it today — and I could have taken her if she had *said* she wanted to go. I haven't got a *Bentley*, of course," mutters Guthrie.

The owner of the Bentley now appears upon the scene and asks if I am ready. I reply cheekily that he is far too early, and that anybody who was not blind could see that I am still eating toast and marmalade and drinking coffee.

"Hurry up then, Mrs. Impudence," says Tony, with a smile.

Guthrie glowers.

"What kind of a day is it going to be?" asks Mrs. Loudon, looking up from her paper. "The weather news says — cloudy and unsettled, some mist locally, occasional sunshine."

"It seems a bit thundery to me," replies Tony, with a glance in Guthrie's direction.

At this moment the door opens, and discloses Annie — whitefaced and breathless.

"Miss Betty's gone," she says.

"Gone!" cries Guthrie.

"I left her in the nursery while I took down the breakfast tray, and when I got back she wasn't there —"

"She's hiding from you," Tony suggests anxiously.

"I thought she was at first," Annie admits, suddenly dissolving into tears. "But I've looked everywhere — and her coat and hat's gone too."

Something clutches at my heart, and the room swings round — Betty lost — Betty out alone in this horrible mist.

Tony's hand grips my shoulder. "Don't worry, Hester," he says quietly. "She won't have gone far — we'll soon find her —"

"Pull yourself together, Annie," says Mrs. Loudon in a firm, sensible voice. "It's not the slightest use weeping like that — try to think of something she said that might help us to find her — perhaps she has gone down to Donald's cottage to play with that boy of his."

"It was kelpies she was after," cries Annie, wringing her hands. "She's been talking about them ever since Mr. Guthrie told her that they lived in the streams — and this morning she said, 'Annie, it's just the sort of day to see a kelpie.' "

Guthrie's face is like a ghost. "My God!" he whispers. "What possessed me to tell her such a thing?"

"She'll have gone up the path by the burn side," Mrs. Loudon says.

"I know," he replies.

The two men rush out into the hall and seize their coats.

"Sit down, Hester," says Mrs. Loudon. "You'll only hinder them; they'll be far quicker themselves. Annie, pull yourself together for mercy's sake — tell Dobbie I want him, and send Jean down the garden for Donald and the garden boy —"

The house is full of bustle, and everyone seems to be doing something except me. I wander round the house and stare out of each window in turn. There is nothing to be seen but a thick white blanket of mist; a few branches of trees stick through it in a peculiar manner as if they had no trunks. The fence has disappeared. Oh, Betty, where are you? What will Tim say when he hears I have lost Betty?

Mrs. Falconer comes down the stairs, and corners me in the hall before I have time to escape into the dining room. By this time my nerves are frayed, and I am in no condition to cope with the woman. If she starts making fatuous remarks I shall scream; if she sympathises with me I shall weep. Fortunately for us both Mrs. Falconer does neither the one nor the other, and, for the second time in my acquaintance with her, I wonder whether she is really so foolish as she seems.

"Things always turn up," she says vaguely, more as if we were in the middle of a conversation about lost umbrellas than as if she were condoling with a bereft mother. "I'm always losing things myself, so I know. Why don't you look about yourself, my dear," she adds, peering short-sightedly beneath the hall table, and motioning towards the umbrella stand. "Things never seem so lost when you're looking for them. I remember when I lost my gold locket which I always wear round my neck (it has some hair in it, you know, and I felt quite naked without it — although, of course, I had on all my clothes as usual) I had to keep on looking for it all the time, and I must have looked down the back of the drawing-room sofa at least nineteen times before Susan found it under the mat in the bathroom — but I just kept on looking for it, although I knew it wasn't there, because the moment I stopped looking for it I felt it was so much more lost."

"Yes," I reply, with a slight lightening of gloom.

"So just put on your hat and your raincoat," continues the amazing woman. "You won't need an umbrella because the mist is really lifting a little (there was quite an orange patch in it where the sun is, when I looked out of my window just now), and take a turn around the garden. Poke amongst the rhododendrons with a stick or something — you'll feel *much* better if you just keep on looking —"

367

And the extraordinary thing is that she's right. I poke about the garden, and I feel better; the mist is white and thick, but it does not seem quite such a hopeless blanket as it did when viewed from the windows. So I poke amongst the rhododendrons, and peer over the gate into the woods and I wander blindly into the fruit garden, and shake the gooseberry bushes so that the mist, which has gathered on their leaves like diamonds, falls to the ground in showers.

Hours seem to pass, and then quite suddenly I notice that the mist is thinner — I feel a slight breath of air upon my cheek. Trees, that were invisible before, now loom up like shadows in my path, their dark, dripping foliage spreads above me like a drift of smoke. I grope my way back to the house, and Mrs. Loudon meets me at the door. She tries to smile at me, but her face is grey and drawn:

"There you are, Hester," she says, with a nervous laugh. "I was thinking we'd have to be sending out a search party for *you* next. It's certainly lifting," she adds.

The mist seems to be flowing now, eddying a little round the house; it moves slowly past like pieces of torn cotton wool.

"There," says Mrs. Loudon suddenly. "I thought I heard something — what's that?"

We stand very still, listening, and sure enough a faint shout comes to our ears. I cling to Mrs. Loudon's arm.

"It's all right, Hester," she says anxiously. "They wouldn't be shouting unless they had found the wee lamb — they wouldn't be coming back at all unless they had found her, if I know anything about either of them —"

It is true, of course, but I can't help trembling. She may easily have fallen over some rocks.

We stand there, peering out into the mist for what seems hours, and, at last, two dark figures loom up into sight.

"It's all right," cries Tony's voice. "We've got them; they're quite safe."

I see now that Guthrie and Tony are both carrying children.

"Goodness me, there's two of them!" murmurs Mrs. Loudon as they come up the path.

"It's Ian," says Tony. "They went together to find a kelpie — they're quite safe, only tired and cold —"

By this time Guthrie has bundled Betty into my arms, and I feel her cold, wet hands round my neck. We carry the wanderers into the morning room, where there is a huge fire, and peel off their wet clothes. Everybody seems to be talking at once, but it is all hazy to me. I sit in front of the fire hugging Betty, and nothing matters at all except that she is safe. Mrs. Loudon bustles about getting hot soup and cherry brandy, and telling everybody to drink it up at once. "There's nothing better for keeping out the cold," she says. "But if anybody would rather have whisky, it's here."

"It was rather fun at first," Betty announces, sipping her hot soup, and stretching out a cold bare foot to the fire. "And then we got lost, and it was horrid, and then Guthrie came, and it was all right."

369

"It was frightfully naughty," I tell her in a shaking voice.

"But we wanted to see a kelpie — and Ian took his net to catch it — fancy if we had caught a darling little kelpie, Mummie."

"Someone had better let Ian's mother know that he's all right," suggests Tony. "I'll go, shall I?"

"You will not, then," replies Mrs. Loudon firmly. "I'll send Jean. Drink up your cherry brandy, Ian. Yes, I know it's hot; boys who go looking for kelpies in the mist deserve to get their insides burnt."

"They were up the burn, nearly as far as the Tarn," Tony is saying.

"Near that big heap of rocks," adds Guthrie.

"Loudon found them," says Tony, giving honour where honour is due.

"It was the Major's idea, though —" puts in Guthrie modestly. "Have some more brandy, sir."

"Thanks, I will," replies Tony, helping himself.

The atmosphere is positively genial, which is most unusual, and I only hope it will last. I hug Betty tightly and rejoice silently in the feel of her soft body. She has been very naughty, of course, but I am so thankful to have her back, safe and sound, that I haven't the heart to scold her seriously.

"Major Morley, your feet are soaking," says Mrs. Loudon suddenly.

"I know," he replies. "It doesn't matter —"

"I'll find you some socks," Guthrie says. "My shoes will be too big, but still —"

Tony laughs, but allows himself to be persuaded into changing, and follows Guthrie upstairs.

"Those men!" says Mrs. Loudon, laughing. "They'll be at each other's throats again tomorrow, I suppose."

The excitement dies down in spite of Mrs. Falconer's efforts to fan the flame. By lunchtime everything seems normal, and I can hardly believe that anything has happened. The mist has vanished, and the sun blazes down on to a green and golden world. Betty is none the worse for her adventure, and eats largely of mince collops, a Scottish dish in which she delights.

"I wish we had seen a kelpie," says Betty, with a sigh, as she hands in her plate for a second helping.

Guthrie looks across the table at her with a grave face. "There aren't any to see. There are no such things as kelpies, Betty, so don't you go looking for them any more."

"But you told me —" says Betty.

"I know — but it was all nonsense," Guthrie replies. "I shouldn't have told you — it was just made up."

"No kelpies!" says Betty, her lip quivering.

"No kelpies!" replies Guthrie firmly.

"But we can have stories about kelpies, can't we?"

"Och, let the child be!" whispers Mrs. Loudon.

"No," says Guthrie firmly. "I made up my mind that if we found her safely — I mean I made up my mind out there on the moor that I wouldn't tell Betty anything that wasn't true — never again — and I mean to stick to it. If Betty wants stories we can have stories about dogs, or — or elephants, or something —"

Betty looks at him, and he looks at Betty, gravely, seriously; and it seems to me that in spite of Betty's youth she understands a little of what Guthrie has gone through. Something precious has come into being between those two, something deeper and far more lasting than their former irresponsible friendship.

"I think," says Mrs. Loudon suddenly. "I think it would be a good plan if we all went over to Inverquill this afternoon, to the pictures; it would take our minds off —"

"What about our expedition?" says Tony, looking at me persuasively.

"Goodness me, I'd forgotten all about it!" exclaims Mrs. Loudon. "It's not too late for you to start now. Away with you before the day's any older."

I feel that I would really rather stay with Betty, but can think of no excuse that does not sound foolish. Betty will be perfectly safe and happy to go to the picture house at Inverquill with the others. While I am still wondering what to say, the whole thing is settled — Mrs. Loudon is an adept at arranging other people's affairs, and has a strange compelling force. I can't explain it except by saying that you find yourself carrying out her behests without intending to do so.

Tony and I are hustled off without more ado, and are soon tucked up in the Bentley and flying along the moorland roads like the wind. The day is all golden now, bright golden sunshine pours down from the sky dappled with soft clouds.

"You don't mind going fast?" Tony says suddenly. "We haven't much time, and it would be rather nice to bathe, wouldn't it?"

I agree that it would be lovely. I don't mind going fast with Tony; he is one of those born drivers who give you a feeling of complete safety however fast they go.

He says no more, but fixes his attention on the road. His profile, only, is visible to me as I turn my head in his direction. There is something stern and sad about this view of his face — the straight nose, and the straight lips, compressed into a thin line with the concentration of his thoughts. I realise how little I know about Tony. I know him so well in some ways, but the inward Tony is a mysterious creature; kind and impish, sorrowful and gay by turns, and the mainspring of these changing moods is hidden deep.

The car flies on, over moors, through forests, past lochs which sleep peacefully in the sun; now it lifts over the shoulder of a hill, now it winds along by the side of a river. We seem to have been travelling for hours.

We climb a long, steep hill, and stop for a moment at the top. Far below us lies the sea, shimmering in the sunlit mist. It holds my eyes to the exclusion of all else as the sea always must. The sun is piercing the mist with golden beams, making it opalescent as a rainbow. These shafts of sunlight make pools of light upon the gently heaving bosom of the sea.

Now we are running slowly down the hill to the sea's edge: to our left is a pile of rocks, capped by green turf and a cluster of fir trees; it thrusts its feet out into the sea, sheltering a little bay where the sand is silvery white. Turf of emerald brightness, starred with tiny flowers, edges the bay, and stretches back to the hills, where the young larches stand in patterns of pale green flame against the smoky shadows of the pines. The sea is trembling as the mist lifts and eddies, the gleaming patches of sunlight spread and merge, and their surface is ruffled by a faint breeze from the west. Far off, and blue in the haze, float the tall forms of islands, some rugged and sterile, others crowded with trees to the water's edge. Just at our feet a spit of silvery sand runs out into the shimmering water. It is crowned with reeds which rustle gently in the faintly stirring air. The whole scene is fairy-like in quality, there is something unearthly in its soft beauty, in its stillness, and the delicacy of its colouring; every shade of colour, from the silvery whiteness of the sand to the darkest shadows of the pines is caught and blended into a perfect whole.

"This is my favourite bay," says Tony softly. "Shall we bathe here?"

"I can't believe the sea is real enough to bathe in."

"Oh, it's quite wet, I assure you. There's rather a nice little sandy cave amongst the rocks where you can undress."

He takes our two bundles out of the car and leads the way. I follow in a kind of dream — it is too beautiful to be real.

The sandy cave is a delightful place; it has little pink flowers in its crevices, and tall pine trees leaning over the top. I undress in comfort, and don my bathing suit with the scent of the pines in my nostrils and the murmur of their foliage in my ears.

Tony is waiting for me on the rocks. He has been in already, and his fair hair is streaked with wetness, and shining with little drops of water.

"Come on," he says, smiling happily. "It's cold at first, but glorious —"

The water is almost still. It is very green, and so clear that the sand at the bottom is clearly visible, and a shoal of tiny fish, some silver and red, dart in and out of the gently moving seaweed. We plunge in off the rocks. I let myself sink down to the bottom, and then spring up to the surface for a breath of air.

The sun is quite warm now. We sit dripping on the shore, and watch the seagulls diving for fish out amongst the fairy islands.

"Do you like it, Hester?" Tony asks.

"I like it so much I can't talk about it. It's perfect. I should like to live here always, and sleep in the little cave, and watch the dawn break over the hills, and the sun set in the sea behind the islands."

We slip back once more into the clear water, and become part of its radiant life. It is so easy to float on its cool surface, to turn over like a lazy porpoise, and feel the salty buoyancy of its embrace. The waves are small and timid; they creep along the base of the rocks and fall with tiny splashes upon the white sand of the bay.

I dress in a leisurely manner, and feel the glorious heat rushing through my body and tingling in every nerve.

"Hurry up, Hester," shouts Tony. "Are you dressing for a Drawing Room at Buckingham Palace, or have you lost the feminine equivalent of a collar stud in the sand?"

"I've lost nothing — expect about ten years," I reply, emerging from my lair, and wringing out my bathing suit.

"So you have," agrees Tony, looking at me in what I feel to be a peculiar manner. "You aren't a day older than Betty. I've always thought seven was the most attractive age."

I beseech him not to be foolish, and he replies that he will give the matter his attention. By this time we have stowed the wet bathing suits and the sandy towels in the car, and are walking up the hill to visit the farm. I find it impossible to talk. There is too much to see, and I want to remember it all — every smallest detail — so that I may store it forever in "that inward eye which is the bliss of solitude." Look where you will, a different kind of country opens up before you. Here, in the space of half a mile, you have the sea with its rocks and sands, and innocent shimmer of scarcely moving water; the pine-woods, close and tightly packed together, their foliage like drifts of green smoke above their straight boles; the delicate green of birch and larch; the meadow land, all starred with tiny flowers; and the patchwork quilt of fields spread upon the sloping hills. From the bosom of a meadowy hill, a strong young burn leaps out and rushes seaward; a little wooden bridge carries the path across the water and sets it on its way. There is a wooden rail — grey with age, and yellow with lichen — which we lean upon, watching the silver wave of water as it meets the rocks in its bed, and parts to squeeze between them, or spreads over their rounded surfaces like a fan of clear brown wine.

The little white croft upon the hill is sheltered from the north by a grove of trees. In front is a cobbled yard, and a large green tub of rain water stands by the door. A faint reek of peat smoke rises from the chimney and fills the air with its attractive smell.

"Hullo, hullo! Are you there, Alec?" shouts Tony as we approach.

The door flies open, and a man appears, a tall, broad-shouldered man. He has the brown weather-beaten face and far-sighted eyes of one who spends his time upon the sea, and the earth-engrained hands of a farmer — for Alec is both.

"Och, Major!" he cried. "Is it yourself? It's welcome you are."

They shake hands firmly. "Och, well now!" he says, beaming with happiness. "This is a fery good day."

Tony now introduces me, and I am included in the welcome. "Och, indeed now I would be remembering the captain (or will he be major now?), and it's a proud day for me to be welcoming his lady to my home."

"Oh, of course," Tony says. "I'd forgotten you had met Tim Christie."

"But *I* had not forgotten," Alec replies, with a smile. "It would be a strange thing if I would not be remembering *him*, for we were all together in the worst place I ever was in."

"That farm near Festubert," puts in Tony. "Yes, it was a tight place. Tim Christie was there, was he?"

"He was indeed," nods Alec. "I could be telling you at this moment all the people that were there. Perhaps I have more time for remembering than other people, for when I am out at night in my boat at the fishing I will be thinking again about all the things we would be doing at that time, and all the good times we would be having — for there were good times as well as bad."

"We didn't have much of a time at that farm," says Tony grimly.

"Och well, and I don't know, Major. I wouldn't have missed it now; for it's a grand thing to be thinking about it all, and you safe in your bed, or sitting by the fire, and the wind roaring round. There's times I feel sorry for the young men who are knowing nothing of it all, for it's half alive they are, and not knowing their luck to be that."

"That's one way of looking at the war!"

"Och well, it's my way," he says. "I would often be thinking of the adventure of it all, and the foreign lands, and the strange things that I would be seeing those times —"

"That German soldier you met in the communication trench, for instance," suggests Tony smiling.

"That one," says Alec with an answering grin. "It was a funny thing that. We were both of us frightened of the other one, not expecting to meet each other in that place. A young man he was, with a pleasant face — och, I'd like fine to be meeting him now, that one, and standing him a drink and laughing over the pair of us crawling along that place and bumping into each other — and we scared to death! But what am I doing to be keeping you standing out here? If you would be coming into my house —"

We follow him into the tiny living room, which is spotlessly clean and shining. The walls are whitewashed, and a kettle is singing on the open fire. A small child of about four years old is playing on the hearthrug with a battered wooden train; he gives one loud shriek when he sees us and flies for his life.

"Mrs. Christie must forgive him," Alec says, setting chairs for us. "He sees nobody here, and he is shy. It is a lonely place and —"

"I suppose you will want another war for him in twenty years or so," suggests Tony.

"The Major would be laughing at me," replies Alec, smiling. "But no, I would be wanting no war for him. It is only that I am glad now there was one for me. I was not glad at the time, no, not altogether glad. Wars are bad things, and we want no more of them — but there is good in them for the lucky ones."

"I believe you are right," says Tony gravely.

Mrs. Macdonald now appears, and greets us shyly. She is a pretty young woman with dark hair and quiet eyes. Alec enquires after his son, somewhat anxiously.

"He will have gone to speak to the pig," replies his mother lightly. "There is no need whatever to be troubling ourselves about that one."

So we cease to trouble ourselves about young Macdonald, who has bad taste to prefer the pig's conversation to ours, and settle down to a comfortable chat. I am amazed to find my host so well-informed as to affairs. These people are far from civilization, and cut off from the outer world, yet, in spite of this, Alec can hold his own with Tony, and gives his opinion on current topics — holding to his opinion with respectful firmness when Tony differs from him. They discuss the effect of tariffs, unemployment, and disarmament, while Mrs. Macdonald makes tea, and sets out large plates of scones and crisp home-made oatcakes on a snowy cloth. When all is ready the younger Alec is retrieved from the pigsty, and placed upon a high wooden chair to have his tea. But the tears roll down his cheeks whenever he looks at us, and at last I can bear it no longer and beseech his parents to take pity on him. "Couldn't he have his tea somewhere else?" I suggest.

"Och, he is a foolish boy!" says his mother. "He does not know when he is well off."

"He is not used to taking his tea with company present," adds his father.

"It's proud and happy he should be to be taking tea with a grand lady and gentleman," says his mother. But the younger Alec is so obviously neither proud nor happy that, at last, he is permitted to retire under the table to finish his meal. Alec is full of excuses for his offspring, but Mrs. Macdonald is quite unperturbed, and, having given him his mug of milk — warm from the cow — and provided him with a large, jammy scone, she forgets all about him.

We leave the menfolk to their barren discussion anent disarmament, and discourse together about the more important matters of every day. I am interested to hear about Mrs. Macdonald's life, and she is interested in telling me. Gart-na-Druim is ten miles from the nearest village (or clachan) and the butcher only calls twice a week. Fortunately the farm is practically self-supporting; they have their own butter and eggs, of course, and plenty of fish when Alec can get time to catch them. Yes, it's lonely in the long dark winters — she comes from Oban way, and found it very quiet at first — sometimes the farm is cut off from the outer world for weeks at a time. There was a big snow three years ago, and they ran out of oil and candles. That wasn't very nice, Mrs. Macdonald says, because it was dark at four o'clock, and they just had to go to bed. Wee Alec was a baby then, and everything was very difficult. "But there was fun in it too," she adds, with a twinkle in her eye. "Alec took a bite of soap in the dark, he was thinking it was cheese — och, I'll not forget that in a hundred years! I could not be seeing his face, but I could be hearing what he was saying well enough. Well, after that, I am laying in a store of candles every winter."

"It must be lonely, when Alec is out all day," I suggest.

"Well, it is, then," she agrees. "It is lonely in the winter, but the summer is very nice. Alec's sisters come for their holidays — Alec's sisters are in good positions in Glasgow, they are very nice — and it is a wonder how the time will be flying past with all there is to do. It is just one thing and then another all day long. And wee Alec is a very nice companion now — it is not often he is foolish like today."

381

The men are still deep in talk, so Mrs. Macdonald offers to show me round the farm.

"Don't be long, Hester," says Tony as he sees us depart. "We must start back in half an hour or Mrs. Loudon will be sending out a search party."

I follow my hostess out of the door, and she shows me round with an air, half-deprecating and half-proud, which I find very attractive. She is indeed an attractive creature, with her dark hair and milky complexion. Her voice is low and soft, and she knows when to speak and when to be silent.

I feel that she is a little shy (from being so isolated from her kind) but there is no awkwardness in her manner. She is both simple and dignified, with the reserve of a great lady and the friendliness of a child.

"This is a great day for Alec," she says, as we inspect the dairy, a small but spotlessly clean shed in the shadow of an overhanging rock. "I'll not be hearing the end of this day for long."

Small Alec follows us timidly; he is a beautiful child, and I am able to praise his looks to his mother with an easy conscience.

"Och, he's well enough," she replies, looking down at her son with adoring pride. "He's well enough if his father would not be wasting him the livelong day. His father is thinking there's no child in the world but him, and it's trouble enough I have with the two of them, so it is."

My efforts to speak to Alec, the younger, meet with blank looks, and I conclude that he is still too frightened of me to reply to my blandishments.

"Do not be troubling about him, Mrs. Christie," says his mother. "He is not very good at the English yet; it is the Gaelic we do be speaking to him."

I try him with a bar of chocolate, which I discover in the pocket of my coat, and find, to my delight, that he seems to understand this quite easily and to know exactly what to do with it.

The cows are grazing on a steep piece of pasture land upon the hill, but we inspect their byre. We then move on to another shed, from whence issues a strange smell of burning and clouds of smoke. Mrs. Macdonald opens the door, and reveals rows of fish hanging on lines across a smouldering fire — it is here that she cures the fish ready for the market in the city. I have often eaten kippers and smoked fish, of course, but I never realised that this was the way they were prepared — I never even wondered how they became kippers and smoked fish, though I suppose I must have known, if I had thought about the matter seriously, that they could not have come out of the sea in that condition.

The pigsty is our next stop. There is something about the pink nakedness of a pig that revolts me. I could never extend my friendship to a pig, however sweet its disposition might be. But little Alec is of a different mind. He speaks to it in fond accents quite unintelligible to me, and the pig (obviously a Celtic pig) lifts its ugly snout and grunts back at him.

"Indeed she is all but human," says Mrs. Macdonald indulgently, and I realise, quite suddenly, that this is one of the reasons I don't like her.

It is now my turn to be informative, so we sit down on a log of wood in the warm sunshine, and I try to answer Mrs. Macdonald's questions about life in the army. I tell her about the married families and their communal existence, and how they move from place to place as they follow the drum. I tell her about India — the heat, and the hordes of native servants and the great troopships packed with women and children. She listens with wide eyes, and sometimes she says: "That would be very nice, so it would," and sometimes she says, with a little cry of horror, "Och, that would not be nice at all!" So the time passes very pleasantly, and wee Alec plays round the yard, and falls down and hurts himself and is comforted with strange soft words, and runs off to play again.

Tony and Alec are now seen approaching, and I realise that it is getting late. With great difficulty we refuse more tea — this time with kippers — Mrs. Macdonald declares that she could have it ready in a moment. Fortunately, Tony is clever enough to refuse it without hurting our hostess's feelings, and I feel — not for the first time — that Tony should have been an ambassador; his diplomacy has been wasted as a mere major in His Majesty's Army.

We tear ourselves away, and big Alec walks down the hill with us to see us start. He is going out fishing tonight, for the gulls diving in the bay are indicative of a shoal of fish; he points out his boat, which is rocking lazily in a small cove at the mouth of the burn.

"A good night for it," Tony says. "I wish I could come out with you, Alec."

"I wish you could then, Major," replies Alec fervently.

Once more the sea has changed, and long rollers are coming in from the west, long lazy rollers, with the sun glinting on their glassy slopes. The sky is blue, tinged with palest mauve, and far away behind the islands there is a bank of purple cloud.

"It's blowing up," Tony says.

"It is, then," agrees Alec. "I will be trying for them off the Black Rock tonight — you will be remembering the Black Rock, Major?"

"We always got a basket there."

"Och, those were days! I would like wee Alec to have days like those —"

Tony says: "Well, good luck to the fishing, Alec."

There is a deep undercurrent of feeling beneath the bald simplicity of their words. They understand each other — these two — as only those who have shared pleasures and hardships can understand each other. Memories, grave and gay, bind them together in a comradeship which needs no words, no outward expression; a comradeship more faithful than love, more lasting than life.

Soon we are breasting the steep hill, leaving behind us the sea, the white sands, and the cluster of dark pines. I look back and wave to Alec — a dwindling figure on the white road with the sun shining on his bared head — then we pass over the crest of the hill, and the valley disappears.

385

Today has revealed still another Tony — the Tony that Alec knows and worships — perhaps this is the real Tony at last.

Twelfth June

It is a hot, stuffy, thundery sort of afternoon — too hot to do anything except lie in a deck chair. The ladies have retired to their rooms saying they had letters to write, but I feel convinced they are both dreaming peacefully upon their beds. Only Betty seems to have any energy. She declares her intention of bathing in the loch, and hops off, followed by the faithful Annie bearing bath towels.

Guthrie is reading the Sunday paper, which has just arrived — I look at him, and marvel that anyone can find the affairs of the world so important on a hot Sunday afternoon. Papers are tiring things to read at the best of times, they make your arms ache, and you can usually pick up the most interesting pieces of news from the general conversation.

" 'Organdie has come into its own,' " reads Guthrie solemnly. "How interesting that is! Who or what is organdie, Hester? 'Lady Furbelow wore a charming frock of Old Tile, with a partridge cowl' — good heavens, is it a woman or a bungalow they're describing? — 'The Honourable Mrs. Killjoy had chosen ginger lainage with chestnut trimmings for her ensemble' — makes me think of Christmas. 'The Countess of Nockhem was gowned in foam' — how cold she must have been! — 'She carried an afternoon pochette in Nile rayon. Her daughter was charming in Mallard crêpe with a Sahara cape and gauntlets' — In other words she was a duck in the desert — 'Mrs. Deff Mewte chose sage' — but not onions — 'how lucky she is to be a *true* platinum blonde!' "

I can't help laughing feebly at his disgusted expression.

"But really, Hester," he says seriously. "Who on earth writes tripe like that? They ought to be drowned. It's simply *awful*, and on the next page you read 'Young Girl Murdered on a Yorkshire Moor, Doctor's Examination Reveals —' Ah, hum, yes — very sad —"

I make horrified noises; it is really much too hot to argue with Guthrie. The sun blazes down. Silence falls. Presently the paper, with its curious items of news, slips on to the ground with a soft rustle — Guthrie is asleep and I am not far off it.

Suddenly I open my eyes and see Jean coming towards us across the lawn, followed by a large bulgy figure in white lace — for a moment I think that I am dreaming, but only for a moment. Mrs. McTurk is too substantial to be the figment of a dream. I have only time to kick Guthrie on the shin — perhaps rather harder than I intend — before composing my face into a false smile and going forward to greet her.

Guthrie leaps to his feet with a muffled curse — it is extraordinary how quickly he wakes — and gazes about him in bewilderment.

"Naughty, naughty," says Mrs. McTurk, wagging her finger at me in a skittish manner as she totters up to me on her spike-like heels. "You've been here ten days and never come over to see us. Mr. McTurk is quite hurt."

Guthrie is still in a dazed condition, and evidently imagines that this is one of my bosom friends. "I'm sure if Mother had known —" he says, offering her his chair. "I'm afraid we've been very selfish with Hester — fishing and all that — we've kept her all to ourselves. But you must stay to tea. Mother will be down quite soon, and she will be delighted to see you. We must arrange something — fishing or — or something."

Mrs. McTurk beams at him. "And you must *all* come to dinner at the hotel with Mr. McTurk and I," she says hospitably. "Mr. McTurk will order a special dinner for you — it doesn't matter to us how many of you there are."

This wholesale invitation takes Guthrie slightly aback. He looks at me for guidance, whereupon I immediately signal "washout," still smiling brightly at our unexpected visitor. This signal has proved most valuable to Tim and myself on similar occasions, and I can only hope that the same code of signals obtains in the Senior Service.

"That's very kind," Guthrie says. "*Very* kind indeed, only Mother scarcely ever goes out to dinner nowadays — and we have an old cousin staying with us now," he drops his voice confidentially, "a *widow*, you know — so *sad* —"

"But *you* will come — er — *Captain* Loudon," says Mrs. MacTurk persuasively. "You and Mrs. Christie, and any other young people that you like. Mr. McTurk will send the Rolls for you any evening. We've got to know some cheery people at the hotel, and it really would be a cheery evening. Mr. Stuart Thompson is a real comic — you should see him take off the head waiter, and we can have Miss Baker too — I know *she's* a friend of yours."

It is at this moment, when Guthrie and I are at our wits' end for some plausible excuse, that Mrs. Falconer appears upon the horizon. She looks fresh and bright, and has, quite obviously, had a refreshing snooze. We signal to her like shipwrecked mariners, and she comes towards us, tripping lightly over the grass.

"Oh!" she exclaims. "How very interesting to meet you, Mrs. MacTaggart! I wonder if you are related to some perfectly delightful people — great friends of my parents — who used to live at Brighton. They had a large estate in Scotland, of course, but *he* was rather a delicate man and the doctors advised Brighton. We used to call upon them whenever we went there — which was pretty frequently because Mama found the air so beneficial to her asthma. Mama was not very strong, and was quite unable to chaperon us girls to the balls, so we used to go with Mrs. MacTaggart and her daughters. We were all so amused on one occasion when a gentleman came up to her and asked if we were *all* her daughters. 'There is a great family resemblance, Madame,' he said. *How* we laughed! For of course *we* were not related to her at all. It is so strange that nowadays girls do not require chaperons. I often wonder how they have the courage to walk into the ballroom by themselves. I heard a very ridiculous story the other day about a chaperon and a curate. I can't

389

remember what it was *she* said to *him*, but he replied something about a dodo — comparing her to a dodo. Probably her appearance reminded him of the picture of the dodo in *Alice in Wonderland*. It was an excellent story, we all laughed heartily, I remember. Papa always used to say 'laugh and grow fat' — I dare say *you* are fond of a good laugh, Mrs. MacTaggart," says Mrs. Falconer, with an eye on our guest's ample proportions.

Mrs. McTurk, slightly bewildered by Mrs. Falconer's sudden question, hesitates whether to disown her *embonpoint*, or stand for a sense of humour at all costs. She loses her opportunity of getting a word in edgeways.

"My brother, Edward, once had a fat white bull terrier," says Mrs. Falconer reminiscently, and it is only too obvious what has given rise to this new train of thought. Guthrie dives to collect the scattered newspapers with a strange choking cough.

"It was a most intelligent animal," Mrs. Falconer continues. "Guthrie dear, have you swallowed a fly or something?"

"No, yes," says Guthrie. "At least, I think it was a bull terrier."

"A bull terrier! My dear boy, how could you possibly have swallowed a bull terrier? It must have been a gnat."

I have been watching our guest with great interest; her reactions to Mrs. Falconer's conversation are worthy of note. She was first annoyed, then incredulous, and then utterly bewildered. I can now see her staggering like a torpedoed ship.

390

Tea appears, and with it our hostess, clad as usual in her shabby garments and queenly manner. Her manner becomes even more queenly when she perceives Mrs. McTurk, whom she abhors.

"How do you do?" she enquires stiffly, and is compelled by her old-fashioned notion of hospitality to shake the woman's hand.

Mrs. McTurk, already sinking under the waves of Mrs. Falconer's talk, is in no condition to do herself justice. She replies feebly that she is well, and relapses into silence.

The fortunes and misfortunes of the bull terrier — which rejoiced in the name of Hannibal — are now related to us by Mrs. Falconer with a wealth of detail rarely equalled and never surpassed. We pull it through distemper in 1898, follow it to the seaside with the family in 1899, and finally attend its tragic demise — through eating rat poison — in 1902. Hannibal is buried in the garden with Christian honours beneath the shade of an elm, and his virtues are commemorated by a stone for which the whole family subscribe their monthly pence. From this sad scene we proceed by an agile bound to Mrs. Falconer's recollections of a visit to Madame Tussaud's. Here Mama accosts the wax policeman, and asks him the way to the Chamber of Horrors, while Papa, as usual, improves the occasion with well-chosen aphorisms.

Tea is now over, and we move slowly round the garden to the front drive, where the Rolls is waiting with its mulberry-coloured chauffeur in attendance. Mrs. McTurk suddenly realizes that this is her last chance, and makes a wild effort to gain her hostess's ear.

"Mr. McTurk and I are staying at the hotel," she says breathlessly, and I can see the invitation to dinner is trembling upon her lips, but Mrs. Falconer pounces on the last word like a tiger.

"At the *hotel!*" she exclaims. "I wonder if you have met a friend of Guthrie's who is staying there just now — Major Morley his name is. He is really a very nice man, though a trifle too scurrilous for my liking."

"Scurrilous!" gasps Mrs. McTurk.

"It just means very talkative," explains Mrs. Falconer kindly. "Dear Papa used such *long* words, and us girls got into the habit of saying them, just from hearing *him* — much to Mama's horror. Poor Mama was always telling us we would never get husbands if we used such long words. It was not fashionable to be clever in my young days. Poor dear Mama was always telling us about it. 'Let your conversation be yea yea and nay nay' she used to say. That's out of the Bible, of course, so I've no doubt it is very good advice, but if we all did that, and went about saying 'yea yea and nay nay' we should look rather silly, and there would not be any conversation at all. Papa's views upon the subject were not quite so extreme; he used to say that conversation should never be one-sided. There should be give and take about it, and I think that is so *true*. And that is why I really do not care very much for Major Morley," adds Mrs. Falconer triumphantly.

By this time Mrs. McTurk's eyes are quite glassy, and, when the mulberry chauffeur opens the door of the car, she gets in like a woman walking in her sleep, and is whirled off down the drive without saying another word.

"How very strange not to say 'Goodbye,' " says Mrs. Falconer, peering down the drive after the disappearing Rolls with her short-sighted eyes. "Did you notice that, Elspeth? Guthrie, did you notice? People *are* extraordinary nowadays. Papa always said . . ."

But Mrs. Loudon does not remain to hear Papa's ideas upon the subject — she is already hastening into the house; and Guthrie is making for the woods as if he were fleeing from the wrath to come. I murmur that I *must* write some letters at once, and follow my hostess with all speed. Mrs. Falconer is left standing on the drive, the unconscious victor of the day, in undisputed possession of all she surveys.

I find Mrs. Loudon in the drawing room, sitting on the sofa and giggling feebly.

"Gracious me!" she gasps. "Did you see the poor body's face? I declare to goodness I was sorry for the woman — though I can't thole her! She'll be away back to the hotel with the story that I've a tame lunatic in the house."

We discuss the afternoon's entertainment at length, dwelling on the parts which appealed particularly to our sense of humour.

"Yea yea and nay nay!" exclaims Mrs. Loudon, with a gust of laughter. "Poor Millie, it's a crime to laugh at her, but the thing's beyond me this time."

"How could she help being peculiar with parents like that?" I reply. "Poor Mama was a harmless idiot, of course, but I feel sure I would have hated dear Papa."

"You would not, then," says Mrs. Loudon promptly. "Uncle Edward was a nice, kind, wise-like creature. That's just the odd bit. Millie doesn't exactly tell lies, but she makes everything sound different from what it was. Yon tale about the dog, for instance — I was staying with them when the beast died, and it all happened exactly as she said — and yet it was not like that at all."

"You should have been there when she began the story," I gasp, wiping my flowing tears. "She took one long look at Mrs. McTurk, and away she went — I thought Guthrie would have burst."

"I'm thankful I missed that. It would have destroyed me," rejoins my hostess feebly. "The woman really is exactly like yon bulldog — even to her small beady eyes. I don't admire your taste in friends, Hester."

"I know you don't," I reply with sorrowful emphasis.

"Well, well!" says Mrs. Loudon, rising and blowing her nose with a trumpeting sound. "Well, well, it's been a mad sort of tea party, and I dare say it's very good for us to have a good laugh, but I'll not get any letters written sitting here giggling with you —"

"I thought you were writing letters all the afternoon."

"It was too hot," she replies. "I just sat down by the window with a book, and the next thing I knew it was teatime. And if an old done woman can't take a nap on a Sunday afternoon without people grinning at her like a Cheshire cat I don't know what the world's coming to. Away with you, I *must* write Elinor before dinner. Did you know Elinor Bradshaw, by any chance, when you were at Hythe?" she continues, rummaging fiercely in her desk. "Elinor's perhaps coming up for a few days towards the end of the month."

"Good heavens, are they still there?" I exclaim, pausing on my way to the door.

Mrs. Loudon laughs. "There speaks the wanderer. And why shouldn't they still be there in their own comfortable house? It's not everyone goes trailing over the face of the world like you soldiers' wives. Elinor's still there in the same place, and there's no reason to suppose she will leave it till she's carried out feet first. I don't know why I asked if you knew them, except that they always seem to have a stream of army friends coming and going about the house. Elinor is forever in despair about some bosom friend or other going off to India or Aldershot or some such outlandish spot — and then another woman appears on the scene, and the first one's forgotten in a week."

As usual, Mrs. Loudon has hit off her subject to the life — I can't help laughing at the portrait. How incredible it seems that Elinor has been living there all this time, and I have never thought of her from one year's end to another! I have moved from place to place, borne children, ordered dinners, been happy or intensely miserable, and Elinor has lived on at Hythe keeping house for her brother, with no changes in her life, save the one sad change of growing older. How incredible it seems that the house, with its sunny aspect, and parquet floors, and the garden with its gorgeous roses and queer old sundial, are still the same! Although I have not thought of them for years they have been there all the time —

"But don't you think," says Mrs. Loudon, with a twinkle in her eye. "Don't you think you are a wee thing egotistical, Hester, to be surprised that the poor creatures can go on living unless you think of them occasionally?"

"You're a witch," I tell her, "and a black witch at that." And, with this parting shot, I leave her to write to Elinor, and fly upstairs to write to Tim.

Thirteenth June

Betty and I decide to walk to the village. She wishes to spend a sixpence which she won from Guthrie, who bet her that she could not sit still for two minutes. We set off together very happily across the moor.

"I only did it by wriggling my toes," Betty informs me. "Two minutes is a terrible long time — I suppose it was quite *fair* to wriggle my toes?" she enquires anxiously.

The hill wind is cold, and whips our hair across our faces. The larch trees quiver, and bend their proud heads and shake their glittering leaves. The wind rustles through the pale green bracken, and flows over the moor like a crystal stream. The clouds are racing over the hills, there is movement everywhere today.

Betty finds a glossy-leaved plant with a gold flower — I don't know its name? Never mind, probably it has some long, clumsy, Latin name which does not suit it at all. Flowers should be born with names fitting to their beauty, not labelled by spectacled scientists with collecting tins and dissecting scissors; and those flocks of cloud, like teeming ewes rushing over the hills, they too have long names, according to their shape and density, but, to me, they are a flock of ewes, driven by the summer wind.

Betty runs, and jumps, and springs into the air like a young goat.

"The hills make me full of springiness," she says. "D'you think I shall find something nice to buy at the shop, Mummie? Guthrie says they have everything except what you want, but I don't know what I want so perhaps they'll have it. What do you think, Mummie?"

The problem is beyond me, and I say so with suitable humility.

"I like Guthrie — don't you?" she continues, hopping along on one leg. "But I like Major Morley much better. He's the cleverest, isn't he? Guthrie's rather stupid sometimes. And I like Mrs. Loudon, and I like Mrs. Falconer — *she* said I was to call her Aunt Millie, but I always forget. Why does she want me to call her Aunt Millie, Mummie? And I like Mary, and I like Kitty, but I don't like Jean. Don't you think Jean's got a cross face, Mummie? And Annie doesn't like Jean either. Annie says she gets the sulks."

We reach the village shop without adventure, and Betty turns her attention to the business in hand, while I invest in stamps and darning wool.

"I think I'll buy a postcard for Daddy," she says. "And something for Annie — some chocolate perhaps. Oh, what a darling little pail! That red one — how much is it? Oh, dear, I've only got sixpence! Well, how much is that fishing rod — Oh, dear, haven't you got anything only sixpence? No, I don't want a ball —"

I have completed my modest purchases by this time, and am forced to go to Betty's aid. The shop is ransacked by a patient girl to find something that will appeal to my daughter, and yet be within her means. She seems to have forgotten her altruistic intentions towards Daddy and Annie. Boats, dolls, painting books are all turned down; they do not attract her at all. I can't help wishing that it were not against my principles to buy her a fishing rod — price half a crown — as it would solve all our difficulties in a trice; but I feel that this would be bad training for her character.

At last a wooden hoop is brought to light; Betty greets its appearance with rapture, and demands its price with bated breath. The patient girl replies glibly that it is "chust sixpence with the stick," and all is well.

Coming out of the shop we meet Elsie Baker, attired in the height of fashion, with a red cap on the very back of her head. She says she has been wanting to see me, and can she walk back a bit of the way with me? I reply that she can, and we set off together in a friendly manner, with Betty in front, bowling her hoop.

Elsie takes my arm as we turn up the path which leads over the moor, and says — quite untruthfully — that I have always been so kind to her. "Oh yes, you have, Mrs. Christie — I mean to say you don't try and make me feel small. Look at the other night — I'd have laughed at Mr. MacArbin if you hadn't stopped me. I thought he'd done it for a lark. I don't know much about *Scotch* people, you see."

I reply that I have suffered from the same disability myself, and a fellow feeling makes us wondrous kind.

"I knew you'd done it on purpose," she says triumphantly.

After walking on in silence for a minute or two, Elsie says the reason she wanted to see me was she wanted to ask me something important — don't I think a girl ought to be sure she really loves a man before she marries him? People do make mistakes sometimes, don't they? *She* likes a man with a bit of life about him — "a bit of sauce," says Miss Baker, pinching my arm confidentially. "*You* know the kind. There's a boy up at the hotel, now — why he keeps the whole place in raws. I mean to say he's simply a scream. Now I dare say you thought I was a bit *dumb* — didn't you, Mrs. Christie? Well, I dare say I am, up at Burnside — Guthrie's so serious, and as for the old lady — well, I mean to say she's apt to put a wet blanket on any girl. The funny thing is," she continues, looking up at me very innocently out of her wide green eyes, "the funny thing is, it was just Guthrie being serious and different from the other boys that made me take to him — I was potty about him, you know — but I mean to say it would be too much of a good thing if you couldn't ever have a bit of fun."

I have never liked Elsie Baker so much as I do at this moment — I feel a strange affection towards her. She is being absolutely sincere with me — this is the real Elsie bereft of all her shams. There are tears in the green eyes.

I press her arm and tell her that Guthrie likes a bit of fun sometimes.

"Yes, but it's not *my* kind of fun," she replies earnestly. "And I don't understand it, and he doesn't understand *my* kind of fun. And I mean to say we wouldn't be happy together, I know we wouldn't," says the real Elsie, now weeping openly into a pale-pink handkerchief, which fills the air with exotic perfume.

I squeeze her arm again — it is so difficult to know what to say, and I am so terrified of saying the wrong thing.

"You don't think I'm silly?" she asks.

"I think you are very wise," I reply comfortingly. "One of the most important things in married life is to understand each other's fun."

Elsie scrubs her eyes, and looks up at me earnestly. "I do hope you're happily married," she says.

I forgive the unpardonable sin, because she is ignorant of her transgression, and reply that I am. "Tim and I like the same kind of fun, we do the silliest things together —"

She squeezes my arm. "I do love you," she says, just as Betty might say it. We walk on in amicable silence.

"D'you think Guthrie will be awfully cut up?" she asks at last. This is dangerous ground; I search for some non-committal reply, and murmur that he will get over it in time.

"Life *is* sad, isn't it?" she says with a sigh. "I mean to say you can't *help* hurting people, can you? You can't sacrifice yourself for another person — at least it wouldn't be any good, not if we weren't going to be happy."

"No good at all," I reply fervently.

"I'm glad you think it wouldn't be any good — I mean to say I do want you to see my side. I wish you could meet Stuart sometime," she continues, brightening a little. "You'd like Stuart, Mrs. Christie, I know you would. He'd have you in raws. Why, I'm quite sore today after the way he had me in raws last night. I mean to say I do like a good laugh, don't *you*? Oh dear, I wish you could see his take offs; he's as good as a pantomime, he is really."

This description has a familiar sound, and I feel fairly certain that Elsie's new friend must be the gentleman who made such an impression upon Mrs. McTurk. I enquire tactfully as to his identity and am confirmed in my suspicion.

"Yes, that's him," Elsie says. "Mr. Stuart Thompson — oh, he *is* a scream! He's taking Dad and I to Inverness this afternoon to see Charlie Lloyd in *I Take the Cake*. Have you ever seen it, Mrs. Christie?"

"It sounds very funny, but I thought you were coming to tea at Burnside."

"Oh, that's just it," Elsie says unblushingly. "You see it would be a bit awkward for me, wouldn't it? I mean *you* could tell Guthrie I'm not coming."

I suggest she should tell Guthrie herself but Elsie says I could do it better. "You don't need to tell him

401

where I've gone," she points out. "Just say I'm not coming, and that'll let him down gradually — I mean to say he'll soon find out about Stuart, and Guthrie isn't the kind to be a nuisance."

I realise at once that my companion has had some experience in being "off with the old love," but that her technique differs considerably from the advice of the adage. In fact, the strange creature uses the "new love" as a kind of bootjack.

Betty is waiting for us on the crest of the hill. "How slow you walk!" she says. "This hoop's no good, I can't bowl it over the stones. I wish I had bought that ball, and then Annie and me could have played catches with it. D'you think if we went back now the girl would let me change it?"

I reply that I am quite sure she would *not*, and that we shall be late for lunch unless we hurry.

"Why aren't you hurrying then?" Betty says reproachfully. "Is Miss Baker coming to lunch with us?"

Miss Baker says she must go home to her father, and she is going to Inverness this afternoon to see a talkie. Upon which Betty exclaims rapturously, "Oh, how lovely! Can I come too? Is Guthrie going? Oh, do say I can come."

I entice my daughter away by all sorts of rash promises, and we wend our way homewards.

"You might have let me go," Betty points out. "She'd have *had* to take me if you said I could, whether she wanted to or not."

402

"But you wouldn't want to go unless she wanted you," I suggest, somewhat taken aback at this strange point of view.

"Of course I wanted to go," replies Betty firmly.

Lunch has begun, and Betty and I slip into our places, feeling rather guilty. Mrs. Loudon smiles encouragingly and asks if we have had a nice walk.

"It was lovely," says Betty. "I bought a hoop, but it wouldn't bowl properly over the stones, so now I wish I hadn't."

"I suppose it was the hoop that made you so late," suggests Guthrie teasingly.

"Oh, no, it was because Mummie and Miss Baker walked so slow — Miss Baker was there, you know. She's going to Inverness this afternoon to see a talkie. I wish *we* could go to Inverness," says my irrepressible daughter, hopefully.

Guthrie looks rather puzzled. "But Miss Baker is coming here to tea."

"Oh no, she's not," replies Betty confidently. "She's going to Inverness — isn't she, Mummie?"

I had intended to give Guthrie the message in private, but perhaps this is the best way after all. At any rate he can ask for no details with the glare of the limelight upon him. Thus reflecting I confirm Betty's information.

Everyone looks surprised.

The advent of the postman turns the conversation into other channels. I open a letter from Bryan's headmaster and find that it contains the distressing news that my son has developed chicken pox.

This disaster is received by my companions in various ways. Betty continues to absorb apple tart quite undismayed by her brother's misfortune.

"Poor lad!" says Mrs. Loudon sympathetically. "How will he have got that, I wonder."

"Chicken pox is nothing," Guthrie remarks comfortingly. "Just an excuse for a slack, and lots of fun in the san. I remember when I had chicken pox we had the time of our young lives —"

"Chicken pox!" exclaims Mrs. Falconer. "Us girls all had chicken pox together in November 1900 — or it may have been 1901. I was quite grown up, and I remember being very distressed in case it should leave holes and spoil my appearance. It *must* have been in November, because I remember distinctly us looking out of the window with our spotty faces to see Papa and Edward letting off the fireworks in the garden for Guy Fawkes — or of course it *may* have been for the relief of Mafeking and not for Guy Fawkes at all. At any rate Alice caught a severe cold from being out of bed and not putting on her bedroom slippers. You remember what severe colds Alice used to get, Elspeth? Papa always said if you *breathed* too hard near Alice she got cold at once. That was just dear Papa's fun, of course, because a person breathing near you could not possibly give you cold. I always say if you tie a silk handkerchief round your head at night it prevents you from taking cold. Have you ever tried that, Elspeth? It is a remarkable preventative, but it *must* be silk, of course."

"I scarcely ever take cold," says Mrs. Loudon shortly.

"How fortunate you are!" exclaims her cousin. "Isn't she fortunate, Mrs. Christie? A cold in the head is such a disfiguring complaint, and nobody is the least sympathetic. I declare I would rather have appendicitis than a cold in the head."

"Bryan has colds too," says Betty suddenly. "Doesn't he, Mummie? And now he's got chicken pox — what is chicken pox like? Is it like a cold?"

"Chicken pox is spots," declares Mrs. Falconer. She takes a deep breath, and is about to elaborate the theme, but Betty is too quick for her.

"I had spots at Kiltwinkle," she says breathlessly, "and Mummie thought it was measles, but the doctor said it was indirections of diet. Did you ever have indirections of diet, Guthrie?"

Guthrie says, "Frequently, after a heavy night at sea."

"It's horrid, isn't it? Bryan *never* has it, but then, of course, he's older than me. Sometimes he's five years older than me, and sometimes only four."

Guthrie asks in pardonable surprise how this thing can be, whereupon Betty explains kindly.

"Well, you see," she says, "he used to be eleven, when I was six, and then I had a birthday that made me seven, but Bryan's still only eleven, so he's only four years older than me now."

After a moment's thought Guthrie says that he sees.

All this has little bearing on poor Bryan's misfortune, but when we have finished lunch and are taking coffee on the veranda, Mrs. Loudon returns to the subject and makes sympathetic enquiries about his condition. I

405

answer them from the meagre information contained in Mr. Parker's letter.

"Did you say he was at Nearhampton School?" cries Mrs. Falconer, pouncing suddenly on the name like a kitten on a ball of wool. "How very strange! That is where the Anstruthers' boy is at school — I always thought it such a funny name. You remember Frances Anstruther, Elspeth? This is her grandson, of course — such a charming boy — I saw him once when he was two years old, and he was very big for his age. I must really write to Frances and tell her about it. What a strange coincidence!"

Mrs. Loudon and I discuss the Anstruthers under cover of Mrs. Falconer's flow of talk. She is completely wound up, and seems quite oblivious of the fact that nobody is listening to her.

"I used to know Frances Anstruther well," Mrs. Loudon says. "We were real friends at one time, and then, quite suddenly, the pith seemed to go out of our friendship, and we drifted apart — perhaps you're too young to understand — and now if we meet it's just for the sake of what was, and to repeat, and to remember."

I tell her that I do understand, and that I know Mrs. Anstruther quite well — and am suddenly aghast at the lie. How do I know her? We have met quite frequently, it is true, and discussed the weather, and servants, and the merits and demerits of Nearhampton School. Well, this is one way of knowing a person, I suppose; to know the outline, not the detail; to sit on the veranda and look at the contour of the hill — that shoulder, such a jagged shoulder it looks, running down steeply into the silver water of the loch. I know Mrs. Anstruther in that way — just a few jags, sticking up into the blue sky, just a rounded piece of hill with a few pine trees on it. Some day I may climb the hill and feel the smoothness of the jagged rocks, and find a piece of bog-myrtle in a crevice, or move a stone and see the ants and beetles wriggling amongst the pale roots of grass.

"Dreaming again, Hester?" says Mrs. Loudon, and I can see her smiling at me behind her glasses. "What a dreamer the girl is, to be sure."

"— but in those days," says Mrs. Falconer, evidently finishing a long and complicated story about her girlhood, "in those days nobody talked about being happy, like they do now — nobody minded whether children were happy, the really important thing was that they should be good. But I really think that people were just as happy as they are now, only they never thought about whether they were or not."

Fourteenth June

I receive a letter from Tim at breakfast time, saying that he will travel north on Thursday night, and arrive at Avielochan some time on Friday. This is thrilling news. Mrs. Loudon is delighted too, and says she knew the man would come, and she thinks we had better have another dinner party for him, and asks the MacQuills this time, and perhaps the Farquhars from the Hall.

"I suppose you'll have no further use for *us* after Friday," Guthrie says, looking up from a plate piled with bacon, and running with tomato juice. "Once that

407

husband of yours is here, we lesser mortals will have to take a back seat."

I reply primly that Tim and I are old married folk, and completely inured to each other's charms.

"Look at her, Mother — she's blushing," says the dreadful man with a grin.

"I'm not blushing," I retort indignantly. "My skin is so fair that when I eat tomatoes they show through."

"Tell me when you've quite finished girding at each other," says Mrs. Loudon with asperity. "There's some things I want fetched from Inverness, and dear knows how I'm to get them here. Dobbie says he wants a whole day at the car, the engine's knocking like a riveting machine, and he thinks it's a bludgeon pin or something."

Guthrie says he's sorry to hear about it, but he fails to see what he can do, unless his mother wants him to go to Inverness on Donald's bicycle. It's only a hundred-odd miles there and back, of course, but the bike is tied together with bootlaces — or perhaps she would like him to ride over on the fat pony which is used for mowing the lawn.

Mrs. Loudon retorts that she wants nothing except that he should have some sense, and he had better go and catch fish, as that's about all he's good for.

At this moment Tony arrives and says the Bentley wants exercising, and will I go for a run. Mrs. Loudon jumps at this chance of getting her shopping done, and asks shamelessly if the Bentley would run well in the direction of Inverness. Tony replies that it would like nothing better; we can go one way — by some place with an unpronounceable name — lunch at Inverness, and return the other way.

Mrs. Loudon says, "You really should see it, Hester."

Guthrie says, "Why should she? I can't think why anyone should want to."

Once it is known in the house that I am setting forth upon this expedition, I am besieged by people with commissions to be done. Mrs. Falconer wants some wool matched, and two pairs of black cashmere stockings; Mrs. Loudon has a long list of things — chiefly wine and groceries; Guthrie wants flies and four new casts; Annie requires elastic and buttons for Betty's underwear.

All this takes time, but at last we are ready to start. Tony says would I like to drive. I am amazed and touched at this proof of friendship, but refuse the offer unconditionally — the Bentley is so enormous compared with our small shabby Cassandra that I feel sure it would run away with me, and so disgrace me for ever in Tony's eyes.

Tony says, "Just as you like, of course," and steers carefully out of the gate. We float along rapidly amongst the mountains and the forests, enjoying the lovely breeze.

We have gone quite a long way — I don't know how far — and are rounding a very sharp bend with considerable care, when Tony swerves to the side of the road, and stops suddenly with a jarring of brakes.

"Good Lord!" he exclaims.

The cause of his consternation is at once apparent: a small yellow sports car is leaning drunkenly against a tree at the side of the road. One wheel is buckled and the windscreen is a mass of splinters.

"It's Hector MacQuill's car," Tony says anxiously. "The reckless devil has done it this time with a vengeance. I hope to goodness nobody's hurt. We'd better see —"

I begin getting out, but Tony seizes my arm. "You stay where you are, Hester," he says firmly.

At this moment Hector MacQuill appears from amongst the trees; he looks slightly dazed but appears to be unharmed.

"What's all this, Hector?" cries Tony in a relieved tone of voice. "You seem to have smashed up the Yellow Peril successfully — I knew you'd do it some day."

"I wish to goodness I had chosen some other day," replies the young man gloomily. "I don't care a blow about the car — the thing is we're in a frightful hole —"

"I can see that," Tony says facetiously.

"Perhaps I could speak to you for a minute," says Hector, with a glance at me.

Tony follows him over to the car, and they discuss something in low voices — I can't help wondering what it is all about. The car seems to be completely wrecked, and I see nothing for it but to go to the nearest garage, and send a breakdown lorry.

After some minutes' conversation, Tony comes back to me, his eyes sparkling with mischief.

"You'll never guess what's happened," he says mysteriously. "Here's our friend Hector running off with Miss MacArbin. Who said Romance was dead?"

410

"Miss MacArbin!" I exclaim.

"None other," responds Tony. "He has a precedent for the deed, of course. I confess I did not think her wildly exciting, but there's no accounting for tastes. Perhaps the explanation lies in the fact that forbidden fruit is always the sweetest — anyway, here they are, and lucky to be alive — I don't know what happened. Hector is in such a state that he doesn't know himself."

"But where *is* Miss MacArbin?"

"Hiding in the trees and awaiting our decision," replies Tony dramatically. "Shall we bind them with the towing rope and deliver them to their respective families, or shall we drive on, and leave them to their fate, or shall we risk the wrath of both their clans, and further love's young dream by taking them to Inverness and putting them in the train? These are the three courses open to us, as far as I can see."

"But are they — do they —" I stammer.

"Apparently they are, and do," he replies gravely. "They have been meeting secretly for some time, and are quite convinced that they wish to follow the example of their notorious forbears."

"Well, I suppose they know their own minds —"

"I suppose nothing of the kind," says Tony with a twinkle in his eyes. "And it is quite against my principles to help anybody to marry anybody else. I am convinced that marriage is an overrated sport — except, of course, in exceptional cases. These two young people will probably live to curse our names — unless Hector succeeds in smashing himself up before the year is out. However, it's none of our business —"

"You *will* give us a lift, won't you, Mrs. Christie?" says Hector, himself, coming forward and putting an end to Tony's unseasonable dissertation. "We don't want to get anybody into trouble, but —"

"Of course we're going to help you!" I exclaim.

"I say, it's awfully good of you," he says, his brow clearing. "I'll just get hold of Deirdre and tell her the good news."

Tony is now busy unstrapping the suitcases from the back of the ill-fated Yellow Peril, and transferring them to the luggage grid of the Bentley.

"It's rather fun, isn't it, Hester?" he says. "But we shall have to be careful not to get mixed up in it — there's going to be an unholy row when it's discovered."

Miss MacArbin now appears from her hiding place looking more ethereal than ever, and I feel glad that the Fairy Princess has got a Prince worthy of her beauty. They make a splendid pair.

"You know Mrs. Christie, don't you, Deirdre?" says Hector, putting his arm through hers and gazing at her with adoring eyes.

"Of course I do," she replies.

"We met at the dinner party, didn't we?"

"And once — nearly — before that," says Miss MacArbin with her sunlit smile. "I was the White Lady at Castle Darroch."

"And you thought she was the ghost of Seónaid," cries Hector boyishly. "By Jove, that was a near thing. I thought some of you saw me running into the wood when the rain came. Deirdre and I found the ruin a

412

good place to meet — there is a secret passage from the tower which we found useful on more than one occasion."

"Well, jump in — if you've finished talking," Tony says. "And you had better cover yourselves with the rugs when we get near Inverness — Mrs. Christie and I don't want our throats cut by Clan MacQuill, nor our bodies thrown into Loch-an-Darroch by Clan MacArbin —"

"The whole thing is awful rot, isn't it?" says Hector, helping his fellow runaway into the car. "If Father could only *see* Deirdre —"

The Bentley's pace precludes any further conversation with our passengers. The miles flash by, and it seems but a few minutes before we are running through the streets of Inverness. By this time, however, Tony has outlined a plan which seems to me a feasible one. Deirdre and I are to be dropped at the entrance to the station, we are to take two tickets to Edinburgh, and make our way to the platform. Tony will park the car, and he and Hector will take two platform tickets and meet us at the train. Hector and I will then exchange tickets, and the runaways will get into different parts of the train. In this way the two victims of the feud will not be seen by anybody in each other's company — a circumstance which would at once give rise to talk and conjecture.

The plan is carried out without a hitch. Deirdre meets a friend on the way to the booking office, but, as her companion is merely an innocuous female, no suspicions are aroused. I find her a comfortable seat in the train and wish her the best of luck.

"I do hope we'll meet again," says Miss MacArbin.

"We must," I reply firmly.

She does not burden me with thanks, for which I feel suitably grateful.

"I'm rather frightened, Mrs. Christie," she says suddenly. "It's such a plunge — do you think they'll ever forgive us?"

"Of course they will — and even if they don't he's a perfect dear," I tell her comfortingly.

So I leave her and walk down the platform to meet the others. Tony is bubbling with mirth. "We've just seen old Brown," he says. "The biggest gossip of the district — if only he knew what was afoot —"

Hector is grave, and I like him for it. "I shall never forget what you have done for us," he says as he shakes hands. "Once the train starts I shall go and find her. She'll be feeling rather scared, I expect."

We wish him every happiness, and leave him to his fate.

"Well," says Tony. "I don't know what you feel about it, but I'm simply starving — it's frightfully late."

We repair to a small hotel and order lunch. Tony is in splendid form, and full of amusing comments on our adventure. He is a most entertaining companion when he is in this mood.

By the time we have finished it is nearly teatime. Tony says it is too much trouble to move, and he thinks we should stay where we are and order tea. The waiter, who has just brought the bill, looks somewhat surprised at Tony's remarks, as we have both eaten enormously of veal-and-ham pie and various other substantial dishes. After a certain amount of byplay for the waiter's benefit, Tony is persuaded not to order tea at present, and I manage to drag him away.

The drive home is accomplished in record time.

"Not a word about today's doings to *anyone*, if you value your life," says Tony as we turn in at the gate, and I realise with a thrill of excitement that he is only half joking. This elopement is bound to cause a tremendous stir in the neighbourhood, and the consequences are wrapped in the mysterious veils of the future.

Mrs. Loudon has heard the approach of the car, and comes out to meet us, and, at the sight of my hostess, I suddenly remember that I have done none of the important commissions which were entrusted to me before starting. I have brought back from Inverness neither wine nor groceries, neither wool nor flies. What an awful thing! I would give five pounds — ill though I could spare it — if, with a wave of magic wand, the car could be filled with the required number of parcels — but, alas, the days of miracles are past.

I look at Tony and Tony looks at me. I can see that he has just remembered too.

"Good Lord!" he exclaims. "We've done it this time."

Mrs. Loudon is surprised when she sees no parcels in the car, and even more astonished when I confess that I forgot all about the shopping.

"Oh well," she says. "I suppose we'll have to manage somehow — never mind about it. You enjoyed yourself, I suppose, and that's the main thing."

415

Mrs. Falconer is less forgiving; she treats me to a homily on the subject of memory, in which Papa comes out very strong. "Papa was very anxious that us girls should all have good memories," she says. "So he engaged a man to come and teach us the right way to remember things. This man had a system — quite infallible it was. Say you wanted to remember seventy-four, you had to think of seven apples and four bananas on a dessert dish. But one day when he was going away he forgot his umbrella, and Mama — who had never liked the man, he was very good-looking, of course — said that a man, who forgot his umbrella was not fit to teach anyone how to remember things. So that was the end of it, and we never learnt any more."

Guthrie says: "It's easy to remember things unless your mind is full of something else."

I have no idea what he means, as he can't possibly know anything about Hector and Deirdre MacArbin.

Fifteenth June

Awake with a feeling that something exciting has happened, and decide that it must be the result of yesterday's adventure. The breakfast table is buzzing with the news of the elopement — brought to the house with the milk. I listen to it all in silence, and find great difficulty in concealing the fact that I know more about it than anyone else.

Guthrie says he didn't think either of them had so much spirit, to which Mrs. Loudon replies that those

416

quiet people are always the worst — and anyway she hopes this will be the end of that ridiculous feud.

"It wasn't last time," says Guthrie. "I mean when old Hector went off with Seónaid, it made the feud worse than ever."

"My dear Guthrie, this is the twentieth century," replies his mother tartly.

"But is it?" Guthrie says, waving his hands in the effort to explain. "We're living in the twentieth century, of course, but are *they*?"

Mrs. Loudon's answer is a snort. She has no patience with ideas of this kind.

"Don't you see," says Guthrie, elaborating his theme with complete disregard of his mother's scornful attitude, "don't you see if you go on living in the same house — like the MacQuills — for hundreds of years, you are bound to develop at a slower rate than people who move about the world and see things with their eyes? Castle Quill was at its zenith in the sixteenth century, or thereabouts, and its atmosphere is thick with ghosts. Anybody living in Castle Quill is living in the sixteenth century."

"Perfect nonsense!" says Mrs. Loudon, rising from the table and collecting her letters. "And anyway that doesn't account for the MacArbins."

"Oh, the MacArbins!" says Guthrie racking his brains for an answer to this. "The MacArbins take their sixteenth-century atmosphere with them wherever they go —"

We finish our breakfast in peace after Mrs. Loudon's departure, and Guthrie asks if I will walk over to the hotel with him this morning to call on Elsie Baker, who has not been seen nor heard of for two days. I gather that Guthrie has written to her, and sent the letter over by the garden boy, but that he has received no answer. All this does not surprise me in the least, as I realise that it is part of Elsie's plan to "let him down gradually."

"You had better go by yourself," I tell him, for I have no wish to be present at the interview. "I should only be in the way."

Guthrie is so downcast at my refusal, and so insistent that I shall accompany him, that, in the end, I am obliged to go.

"You see, I think the poor little thing must be ill, Hester," he says, as he opens the gate for me. "You could go up and see her in bed, couldn't you?"

I am pretty certain that Miss Baker is perfectly well, and, far from languishing in bed, has probably been touring the countryside in "Stuart's" car. Every step of the way I feel increasingly regretful that I have come, and send up silent prayers that Miss Baker may be out. I have no experience in delicate situations of this kind, and no wish to be involved in one.

"Poor little thing!" Guthrie continues, working himself up into a passion of pity for Elsie's imaginary sufferings. "I wonder who looks after her when she is ill — she has no mother, poor child! I can't bear to think of her lying there, day after day, with nobody to take care of her."

"Don't think of it, then," I reply lightly. "Wait and see whether she requires any pity before you waste it on her."

"You're awfully down on Elsie," he says reproachfully. "I never thought *you* could be so unsympathetic."

"I shall wait and see if any sympathy is needed."

"Poor little thing!" Guthrie continues. "She has never had a chance. Once we are married she will be able to stay with Mother while I am at sea —"

"You are most certainly at sea if you visualise Elsie Baker settling down with your mother at Holmgarth," I reply brutally.

"I thought you liked Elsie!" he exclaims.

"I do quite like her at times," I reply, with strict regard for the truth. "But your mother doesn't — and Elsie doesn't like your mother. They would be bored to death with each other in two days. It means choosing between them, and the sooner you realise that the better."

"I have chosen," Guthrie replies sulkily.

This conversation has raised my spirits. I feel so annoyed with Guthrie for his obstinacy and stupidity that I don't care whether he gets hurt or not. Yes, you have chosen, and so has she, I think to myself, reflecting with cruel satisfaction that the coming interview — if interview there be — will give my self-satisfied young friend the shock of his life.

My prayers for Miss Baker's absence from home are not answered by an all-wise Providence. We find her stretched upon a deckchair on the terrace in front of the hotel reading a novel, and exposing quite a thrilling

419

amount of very creditable leg, encased in Elephant Brand silk hose, at eight and eleven a pair.

"Elsie, have you been ill?" asks Guthrie anxiously. "No, don't go away, Hester."

"No, don't go away, Mrs. Christie," echoes Elsie. "Guthrie will bring another chair for you."

Can it be that she is slightly nervous? Perhaps she is not quite so experienced in matters of this kind as I imagined. I sit down, unwillingly enough, and ask what she has been doing with herself.

"Oh, we've been all over the place," says Elsie, with studied carelessness. "Mr. Stuart Thompson has been taking Dad and I for spins in his car."

Guthrie looks extremely taken aback at this news, but manages to control his feelings. "That was very nice," he says. "But you could have gone for spins with me, if I'd known you wanted to. I thought you must be ill or something — did you get my letter?"

"Oh yes — but I really hadn't time to write — we've been ever so busy with one thing and another."

"Well, I'm glad you weren't ill," says Guthrie in a far-from-glad tone of voice. "What about this afternoon — would you like to come to tea, and fish afterwards?"

"I'm rather off fishing just now — I mean to say it's a bit slow. Besides, I've promised to go to Inverness this afternoon with Stuart," replies the lady candidly.

At this moment I see a large, fat shape — clad all in green — emerge from the hotel, and realise that it is Mrs. McTurk. For once she appears to me in the guise of an angel. I murmur that I simply *must* speak to her for a minute, and dash off, leaving the disillusioned lovers to their fate.

Mrs. McTurk is delighted to see me, and welcomes me warmly. She evidently bears me no ill will for her discomfiture on Sunday. (I had nothing to do with it, of course, but I feel that it is magnanimous of her to be so pleased to see me.) I ask breathlessly after all her relations, and am immediately involved — as I had hoped — in long descriptions of their various conditions. We stroll round the hotel garden in amicable conversation.

"I had no idea," says Mrs. McTurk suddenly, "that Mrs. Loudon had a sister living with her —"

"Cousin," I murmur.

"Oh, it's a cousin, is it? Does she always talk like that?"

"Yes, always," I reply firmly.

"Dear me — it *must* be trying. Is the poor thing quite all right, Mrs. Christie?" asks Mrs. McTurk with an upward movement of her brows.

"Oh, *quite* all right," I reply hurriedly.

"Well, well, she'll be quite harmless anyway, I suppose," says Mrs. McTurk, evidently unconvinced by my assurance, "or Mrs. Loudon would scarcely risk having her about. You've seen no *dangerous signs*?"

"Oh, no."

"Still, there's no *knowing* with anybody like that," says the good lady anxiously. "They might go off suddenly, Mr. McTurk says, and then where would you be? Such a strange way she had of talking — I declare it made me feel quite queer. I hope you lock your door at night, Mrs. Christie. I know I would. But anyway when I told Mr. McTurk about it, and we had talked it over, we came to the conclusion that *it wouldn't do to have her here*."

"To have her here?" I repeat in amazement.

"To have her to dinner," explains Mrs. McTurk. "People talk so in an hotel — you know the way they talk, Mrs. Christie — and Mr. McTurk and I feel it wouldn't do — unless you could come without her, of course —" she adds hopefully.

"Oh, we couldn't possibly come without her," I reply firmly. "She would be so dreadfully hurt — but of course I quite understand your feelings —"

"It's very disappointing," she says sadly. "But Mr. McTurk is very strong about it. It was lucky I said nothing about it to Mrs. Loudon. I shouldn't like her to be disappointed — and it seems a bit inhospitable somehow. You didn't mention it to her, did you?"

I comfort her as best I can, and assure her that Mrs. Loudon knows nothing of the projected dinner, and therefore will not be disappointed when it does not materialise.

"Well, that's one mercy," she says, more cheerfully. "I was afraid you might have said something."

Guthrie is waiting for us on our return; he seems dazed, and has to be reminded that he has the pleasure of Mrs. McTurk's acquaintance.

"Oh yes, of course," he says. "How stupid of me! I don't know what I can have been thinking of."

I know exactly what he has been thinking of, but naturally refrain from saying so.

Presently Guthrie and I find ourselves walking home across the moor. He is very silent, and somewhat morose, and I can't help wondering what has happened — in other words has he definitely got the boot, or is he still in a state of suspense?

"Hester," says my companion suddenly, "I can't understand Elsie at all. I'm afraid this man she has been going about with has not a very good influence over her — you can't think how queer she was today."

I reply lightly that ladies have the privilege of changing their minds.

"You mean she has changed her mind about *me*?" he asks incredulously, and he looks so like a little boy who has offered somebody his cake and has had it thrown back in his face that I have to laugh.

"It looks a little like that," I gasp.

"But — but he's the most awful bounder — I *saw* the fellow — it's all very well for you to laugh at me, Hester, but he really is."

"I can well believe it," I reply, as soon as I can speak. "From the various accounts I have had of Mr. Stuart Thompson I had visualised a bounder of the most bounding proclivities — but, all the same, Elsie will be much happier with him than she would ever have been with you — and I'm not laughing at *you* so much as the queer way things turn out in this queer world."

"Well," he says, "you're not very sympathetic, I must say."

"You've already said that to me this morning," I reply. "And my answer is the same as it was last time — I keep my sympathy until it is needed. Elsie did not

423

require my sympathy, and neither do you. Accept my congratulations instead."

"What *do* you mean?"

"You know perfectly well what I mean, Guthrie. It would have been the greatest mistake for you to marry Elsie. It would have resulted in misery for you both, and for Mrs. Loudon as well. Fortunately Elsie has realised that you are not the right man for her, and has been trying to convey the fact to your slightly obtuse intelligence."

"You are pretty scathing, aren't you?"

"I'm a perfect beast," I own cheerfully.

"But it's all for your good, my dear. Buck up and look a little more cheerful. You know as well as I do that this is the best thing that could have happened."

"I can't understand it at all," he says in a bewildered manner.

Sixteenth June

Guthrie comes down just as Mrs. Loudon and I are finishing breakfast.

"I suppose you are remembering that you are going over to lunch with the MacKenzies at Inverquill," says Mrs. Loudon, with an eye on Guthrie's oldest and most disreputable trousers.

"Oh, I put it off," replies her son, helping himself to porridge and cream with a liberal hand. "I thought we'd fish here —"

"Well, you can't then," announces Mrs. Loudon firmly. "At least you can fish here, but there will be no lunch."

"No lunch!"

"No. Mary's away to Inverness for the day — I promised the creature a day in Inverness, and she's meeting her cousin, and going to the pictures."

"But what about you?" demands Guthrie, not unreasonably. "I suppose I can share your bread and cheese, or whatever you're having."

"We're lunching at the hotel," replies Mrs. Loudon. "You need not look so surprised, both of you. I worked out the whole thing in bed last night, and it's all settled, so there's no more to be said. Hester will enjoy lunching at the hotel; she must be tired of seeing nobody but her host and hostess day in and day out. It will be a change for her, anyway."

"Hester will hate it," replies Guthrie gloomily, and I can't help feeling that he is probably right. Difficult situations will probably arise from meeting the Bakers and the McTurks, and the presence of Tony will not make things any easier.

"It's Hester's last day, too," adds Guthrie.

"It'll be *your* last day," replies his mother tartly, "if you look at Hester like that when her husband's here. If you want to come over with us to the hotel, you can, but you would be far better to go over to Inverquill, and fish with Ian."

"I believe I would," agrees the wretched man. I really feel very sorry for him, and when Mrs. Loudon has departed, jingling her housekeeping keys,

425

I beseech him to go to Inverquill, or Timbuctoo, or, in fact, anywhere except the Avielochan Hotel.

"Oh, I'll go to Inverquill," he says in martyr-like tones. "Ian will be quite glad; he said I could leave it open, but I thought we could have a nice long day on the loch. You can tell Mother I've gone."

It seems strange that I should always be saddled with messages which people don't want to deliver themselves. I try to believe that it is because my nature is sympathetic, but have an uncomfortable suspicion that it is because I am too weak-minded to refuse the job.

The morning flies past with incredible speed, and it is not until we are ready to start that I find an opportunity to give Mrs. Loudon the information.

"It's just as well," she says, in a relieved voice. "I'd never have thought of the hotel with Guthrie. We would have had that goggle-eyed Baker girl tacked on to us the whole time. Where's Millie? It's time we were away."

We walk slowly over the moor. Mrs. Falconer's legs are less active than her tongue. She stops every few minutes to admire the view, and to inform us what Papa would have said if he had been here. Thus delayed, it is after one o'clock when we reach the hotel, and most of the visitors have gone in to lunch.

"We'll have cocktails first," announces Mrs. Loudon surprisingly. "I've never tasted the things, and I've often wondered what they were like."

426

"You'll do as you please, of course, Elspeth," says Mrs. Falconer, sinking into a cane chair with a groan of fatigue. "I, for one, shall not risk it."

"You'll take sherry, then," says Mrs. Loudon firmly. "It will do you good." She summons the waiter in her queenliest manner, and orders two cocktails and one sherry.

"Yes, madame." He bows, and reels off a string of the different kinds obtainable at the hotel. The list is long enough and peculiar enough to daunt a stout-hearted man, but Mrs. Loudon rises to the occasion nobly.

"I'll have a Broncho," she says gravely. "What about you, Hester? Two Bronchos, please. I don't know why you are laughing, Hester, but if it is a good joke you might share it with us. Good gracious, there's the Baker man!"

"The baker man!" echoes Mrs. Falconer, peering round short-sightedly.

Mrs. Loudon is not listening. "He hasn't seen us," she announces in a relieved voice. Personally I feel sure Mr. Baker has seen us, but, not having sufficient aplomb to deal with the situation created by his Elsie, has shirked the issue by pretending to be stone blind.

We drink our cocktails peacefully, and enter the dining room, where Mrs. Loudon's manner procures us the instant attention of the head waiter and a delightful table near the window. I look round and find to my satisfaction that all our neighbours are complete strangers. The McTurks are at the other end of the room near the band, and the Bakers are giving a luncheon party to their friends at the large centre table.

427

Elsie is looking very pretty in flowered voile; she talks and laughs in an animated way, and seems to be enjoying herself immensely. The young man on her right with the fair wavy hair and the Adam's apple must be Guthrie's supplanter. She is so enchanted with his wit that it is not until the luncheon party is nearly over that her eye falls upon me.

I should like to have to record that she turns pale, and that the laughter dies on her lips, but nothing of the sort occurs. She merely looks a trifle surprised, and smiles at me in a friendly manner.

Meanwhile Mrs. Loudon has seen Elsie and her entourage. She gives no sign of recognition, but her mouth hardens and her thin fingers pluck at her bread.

"We'll go when you've finished, Millie," she says quietly.

"But we haven't had the ice!" exclaims Mrs. Falconer, who enjoys her food. "Don't you want the ice, Elspeth?"

At this moment Tony appears through the swing doors. He sees us at once, and comes across the room to our table.

"Well," he says, smiling gravely. "This is an unexpected pleasure. Has Burnside been burnt to the ground or what?"

"What," I reply instantly.

"Ah, I'm glad it's what," he says. "Burnside is too pleasant a place to go up in smoke. May I sit down at your table? — and how does the Cannibal Feast strike you, Mrs. Loudon?"

"I don't understand it," replies Mrs. Loudon, moving her gloves and bag from the chair to make room for Tony.

"It's difficult, isn't it? Why should a Cannibal Queen fall for an Adam's apple? And the answer is because however tired an elephant may be, he can't sit down on his trunk."

"I'm afraid I don't follow you," says Mrs. Falconer helplessly.

"I like you all the better for it," replies Tony. "I simply can't bear being followed. If you knew what I had been through before the Adam's apple appeared on the scene and took the hotel by storm, you would understand my feelings."

Mrs. Falconer gives up the unequal struggle, and falls to with a will upon the large pink ice which has appeared before her as if by magic. She is obviously afraid that "Elspeth" will drag her away before she has finished it.

The McTurks now descend upon us, and invite us to take coffee in the lounge — an invitation which can hardly be refused without rank discourtesy. They wait politely until Mrs. Falconer's ice has disappeared, and then we all file into the lounge. Tony and I are the last through the swing door. He holds it open for me, and whispers, "It's frightfully amusing, but I really don't know why."

Seats are found for us beneath the spreading branches of a palm tree, and Mr. McTurk orders large cups of "special coffee" for the whole party. He induces Mrs. Loudon to try a Benedictine, and my poor friend

429

is so bewildered at finding herself in this galley that she has not the strength to refuse. Mrs. McTurk has seated herself as far away from Mrs. Falconer as possible, and keeps a wary eye on that harmless lady in case she should "go off suddenly."

"I suppose you've heard about the elopement," says Mr. McTurk, turning to me with a beaming smile.

"It's the talk of the hotel," adds Mrs. McTurk. "I must say we've been lucky in our visit to Avielochan this year. It makes a difference if you've got something to talk about when you're in an hotel like this. It makes it so much more exciting on account of the feud — it's a real Highland feud, you know, Mrs. Christie."

"Yes, I know," I reply feebly.

"Mr. MacArbin was here last night — or no, it was the night before — looking for his sister. It was quite exciting. And then who should walk in but Sir Hector MacQuill, looking for his son —"

(I look at Tony for confirmation of this, and he nods imperceptibly, and whispers "Frightful, wasn't it?")

"And we've made such a lot of nice friends this time," says Mr. McTurk, continuing the saga.

"Indeed we have," agrees Mrs. McTurk. "Mr. McTurk and I were just saying this morning what a lot of nice friends we had made. Mrs. Loudon and Major Morley — and Captain Loudon, of course — and the Bakers, and Mr. Stuart Thompson. Everybody is sure that they're going to be married — I mean Elsie and Mr. Thompson — quite a romance it's been. I declare it's just like a book —"

430

Mrs. Loudon looks at me in a dazed manner. Her misery is apparent, and I wish that I could get her away and explain everything to her; but we can't do these obvious things in civilised society; we must sit and smile at the right moment, and sip our "special coffee" until the correct time for departure arrives.

If it were not for Mrs. Loudon's misery I should be enjoying myself, for it is a pleasant party, and the McTurks are on their best behaviour. I realise that it is only because they have accomplished their object, and that they have used me in a shameless manner as a means of getting to know Mrs. Loudon; but they are so kind and hospitable, and are trying so hard to be nice that I can't help liking them. I can hardly believe that these are the same people who were so rude to us at Kiltwinkle — so snobbish and vulgar and selfish.

The Baker party now bursts into the lounge, laughing and talking with gay abandon. Mr. Stuart Thompson is giving one of his famous "take offs," to the intense amusement of his friends. Some of them are doubled up with mirth, others have the strength to beat him warmly on the back. They have evidently partaken of an excellent lunch at Mr. Baker's expense, and the champagne has been poured forth like water.

"Mr. Thompson is impersonating the manager," Tony whispers. "It is always the manager when he walks with his chest well forward like that. I believe his 'take off' of me is very lifelike, and chiefly consists of remarking, in a strange high-pitched voice, 'Haw haw — don'tcherknow.' Have you ever heard me say 'Haw haw — don'tcherknow,' Hester?"

I reply that it is a well-known fact that majors in His Majesty's Army are in the habit of saying "Haw haw — don'tcherknow" at every opportunity.

"Well, you ought to know what you're talking about," says Tony, with a sigh. "The remark seems somewhat fatuous to me, I must say."

"Now don't you worry about what Mr. Thompson says," Mrs. McTurk adjures him, bending towards him with a fat smile creasing her face. "It's just his fun, and he doesn't mean anything nasty. Why, he took off Mr. McTurk the other day, and Mr. McTurk didn't mind a bit —"

She breaks off, and looks up in time to see Mr. Baker come through the swing door. He has been left behind — obviously to tip the waiter and sign the bill. He stands there alone, looking for his guests, but his guests have vanished. They have no use for Mr. Baker except to foot the bill, and the little man is aware of the fact. He is a lonely, dejected figure and I can't help feeling sorry for him. Does he approve of Elsie's change of heart, I wonder; has he offered Mr. Thompson a partnership in that comfortable little business at Portsmouth; or does he realise that a man so inimitable at "take offs" might make but a poor partner in a serious concern?

Mr. McTurk, who has quite a kind heart, calls to Mr. Baker and invites him to join us, but the little man is too frightened to accept. He bows politely to the whole party — with a special obeisance to Mrs. Loudon — and trails away after his daughter and her friends.

432

"What's the matter, Hester?" enquires Tony. "Are you breaking your heart over Mr. Baker?"

"I am rather," I admit. "They are so horrid to him, and he's really rather a dear."

"You're too soft-hearted," Tony says. "He'll be as happy as a grig — whatever that may be — when the grandchildren begin to arrive. I can imagine Mr. Baker with a grandchild on either knee, jigging them up and down, and singing 'The fox is off to its den — oh.' "

I can imagine it too, and the vision is comforting. Tony is an astounding person.

At the correct moment Mrs. Loudon rises, and we say goodbye and are whirled home to Burnside in the Bentley. Mrs. Falconer is delighted with her "ride," and confesses that she never was a great walker, and, even when she was young, preferred to go in the carriage with Mama than to walk with the other girls. "But we always took it in turns," she adds with a sigh. "And there were so many of us that my turn did not come round as often as I could have wished." I commiserate with her — somewhat half-heartedly I fear. "Yes," she continues, "dear Mama liked to take us girls to pay calls with her — only one at a time, of course. She considered it an important part of our education to know exactly how many cards to leave at each house, and to learn to take part in cultured conversation."

Mrs. Loudon follows me into my room when I go to take off my hat, and I am not at all surprised, for I know she has been boiling with bewilderment and wrath for the last hour.

433

"Well!" she says, sitting down on my bed and looking at me. "Well, of all the blatant hussies! Guthrie will have to be told — it's beyond everything —"

"Guthrie knows," I tell her briefly. "I'd have told you before, but I didn't want to say anything until it was absolutely settled —"

"Guthrie knows that she's carrying on with that frightful-looking man?"

"She told him yesterday — at least she tried to tell him — Guthrie found it hard to believe —"

"Then it's off," she says. "Thank God the boy has come to his senses — and thank *you*, Hester. For I believe you had a lot to do with it, and I'll never forget it as long as I live — *Hester?*"

She holds out her arms and I hug her tight. I try to tell her the truth of the matter, and point out that it was none of my doing, but simply because Elsie had the sense to see that Guthrie and she were unsuited to each other, but Mrs. Loudon does not listen. She is convinced that I — aided and abetted by that nice Major Morley — have saved her son from the clutches of a harpy. "I'll never forget it as long as I live," she says again. "If ever there's anything I can do for you — but there won't be — there never is, when you want there to be. There's the gong for tea, I declare. Come away, and get something to eat — I don't believe I ate much lunch, it seemed to choke me. Anyway, I'm starving now."

We go down to tea, arm in arm.

At tea Mrs. Loudon is as gay as a girl; she teases Mrs. Falconer, and crosses swords with Guthrie and me. But I notice that sometimes she looks at Guthrie when his attention is directed elsewhere, and there is a radiance in her face that is wonderful to see. She loves him so dearly. Her dry manner covers a very tender heart.

Guthrie has come back to her, and it is almost as if he had come back to her from the grave.

Dinner is over. We are all comfortably settled in the drawing room, and Guthrie and I have started our usual game of chess. Guthrie is an extremely careful player, and ponders long over every move; he considers me rash to the verge of insanity, but has only managed to beat me once, so far. I will admit to the sacred page of my journal — though never to Guthrie — that my dashing moves are more often matters of pure luck than well-thought-out maneuvres.

"There's a car coming up the drive," says Mrs. Loudon suddenly.

"Can it be Tim?" I cry. It would be just like Tim to arrive before he was expected. Nothing pleases him more than to surprise people like that.

But our visitor is not Tim, it is Tony Morley. He comes in, smiling cheerfully, and is warmly welcomed by Mrs. Loudon. I notice that Mrs. Falconer and Guthrie greet him with perceptibly less warmth — he is no favourite with either of them.

"I wondered if any of you would like to come up to the fair," says Tony. "It's such a lovely mild night. There's a fair over at Inverquill — quite a good fair, with roundabouts and things. I could run you over in the car."

"What an extraordinary idea!" remarks Guthrie (moving his queen without having considered the matter with his usual care.)

Tony is in no way dashed. "I thought Hester might like to see a real Highland fair," he says persuasively.

"So I should," I reply (taking Guthrie's queen with my last remaining knight, who has been lying in wait for her for some time). "I should simply love to see a real Highland fair."

"There's no real Highland about it," Guthrie says, pushing the board away crossly. "All fairs are exactly the same wherever they are — sordid shows with a crowd of dirty people shoving their elbows into your ribs —"

"Well, there's no need for you to go," says Mrs. Loudon. "Hester can go with Major Morley. I'd go myself if I were ten years younger, but it's not for an old woman like me to go gallivanting off to fairs at this time of night."

"Oh, if Hester wants to go, I'll go too," says Guthrie quickly. "I don't suppose she'll enjoy it when she gets there —"

I rush upstairs to change into warm clothes — tweeds will probably be best, and my thick grey coat with the fur collar, and a red tammy. I reflect, as I hastily powder my nose, that the evening will not be without its difficulties. Guthrie will take every opportunity of being rude to Tony (he is already in an unpleasant frame of mind) and Tony will retaliate by making a fool of Guthrie, which seems to give him untold pleasure. Why can't they be friendly and pleasant, as they were that dreadful morning when Betty was lost? How difficult life is! Difficult enough without people going out of their way to make things awkward for themselves and all around them.

For a moment I wish that I had refused to go, and then I look out of the window, and the night calls me. The sun is setting now, and, above the hills, the sky is aflame. It will soon be dark — and darkness is ideal for a fair. The lights flare so gaily in the darkness and throw dancing shadows on the jostling throngs. It will be fun. My spirits rise with a bound, and I feel ready to cope with anything.

Betty calls to me from her room, next door. "I can't sleep, Mummie," she says. "The sun's so glowing bright. It's making my room all red." There is a patter of bare feet, and Betty stands beside me. "You'll get cold," I point out, but only half-heartedly, for it seems impossible that anybody could get cold tonight. "No I won't," says Betty. "You can't get cold when it's quite warm." She kneels up on the window seat, and the setting sun turns her yellow curls to gold. "Mummie," she says thoughtfully. "Where is the sun's nest? I think it's just behind Ben Seoch, don't you? I think it's going there now, very slowly, because it's tired. I'd like to peep over Ben Seoch and see the sun settling down all warm and cosy in its nest —"

I pick up my daughter and carry her back to bed. "You settle down warm and cosy in *your* nest," I tell her, as I tuck her in. "I'll tell you about the sun tomorrow."

"Darling Mummie," she says sleepily. "Daddy's coming soon. How lovely that will be —"

My two cavaliers are waiting for me in the hall. They are a handsome enough pair to look at, for both are tall, and Guthrie is broad in proportion, but handsome is as handsome does, and it remains to be seen how they will behave themselves this evening. We climb into the Bentley and are off like the wind; it is a lovely sensation flying through the gloaming. All the light seems to have drained out of the woods, leaving them black as pitch; but, on the road, and over the open moor, there is still a ghostly sort of radiance, and the sky is not yet dark, but darkening fast. The Bentley makes short work of the twenty miles or so which stretch before us to Inverquill, and soon we hear the distant sound of the organ in the roundabout, and see the lights from the booths flaring in the twilight.

First we visit the shooting gallery (in spite of Guthrie's repeated assurances that the coconut shies are infinitely more amusing). It is situated in a wooden shed, full of flaring light and a strange smell of humanity.

"Three shots a penny," yells a small man in an ancient khaki jacket which, I feel sure, saw its best days during the war. "Three shots a penny; only a penny for three shots, and win a brooch for your young lady, if you get 'em all bulls — come along, gentlemen, three shots a penny and win a brooch — make way there for the gentleman —"

438

A burly farmer hands his rifle to Tony with a wink. "If you would be aiming high left every time you might be getting a bull," he says confidentially. "For my part I'm better with a gun than one of these toys."

Tony thanks him and takes careful aim. At first his shots go rather wide, but after several pennies' worth, he settles down to it and gets three bulls without apparent difficulty. The khaki man congratulates him warmly upon his achievement, and invites him to take his pick of the brooches on the tray.

"I hope they are real," Tony says gravely. This is considered a splendid joke by the khaki man — and indeed by all who hear it.

"Oh, they're real enough," he says, winking slyly. "This is Bond Street, this is. You won't find no sham julry on *my* tray."

Tony chooses one with two gold hearts transfixed by an arrow, and hands it to me with great solemnity.

By this time Guthrie has had enough of it — he has been shooting farther down the gallery — he returns to us, and says it is just as he thought, the rifles are all doctored, and the whole thing is an absolute fraud. I conclude that he has not been so successful as Tony in his shooting. He eyes my brooch — which I have pinned on to my coat — with scorn and disgust (it might be a black beetle from the way he looks at it), and suggests that we should have a go at the coconut shies.

I feel that it is Guthrie's turn for a little consideration now, so we make our way in that direction. Here Guthrie displays tremendous prowess, and sends

439

coconuts flying in all directions, much to the disgust of the coconut man and to the delight of all the onlookers. Tony and I are completely out-classed at this sport, but we share in his reflected glory, and back him up loyally in his argument with the owner of the stall, who tries to do him out of his hardly earned spoils. We leave the place in triumph, Guthrie carrying four large coconuts which are a perfect nuisance to him for the rest of the evening.

So far we have seen nothing the least different from any other fair. In fact most of the people in the booths have undoubtedly come from south of the Tweed. Guthrie points this out to Tony in a somewhat sarcastic tone of voice. Tony replies that we are only just starting, and the night is yet young. He seizes hold of a hurrying man, and asks what that crowd is "over there."

"If you're quick you'll see Jock Sprott," replies the man. "He's at it now."

"And what is he at?" asks Tony in dulcet tones.

The man glares at him indignantly. "Have ye never seen Jock Sprott throwing the hammer?" he enquires, and is gone before his rhetorical question can be answered.

"Come on, we *must* see Jock Sprott," Tony says, dragging us along at a tremendous pace. "Here's your chance to see something really Highland at last."

I demand breathlessly who he is, and why he throws hammers about.

"Oh, he's a Scotch relation of the man who could eat no fat," replies Tony glibly, "and he throws hammers about for a living — it's quite different from throwing

440

them into the corner because they have hit you on the thumb when you were trying to knock in a nail."

We push through the crowd and arrive just in time to see the contest. A huge hammer is lying on the ground — it is the sort of hammer that a giant in a fairy tale might be proud to own. It is such an enormous hammer that to me it does not look like a hammer at all.

Jock Sprott now appears from a small tent — Tony whispers that he has been in there, eating beefsteaks to make him strong, but I don't believe all Tony says. He is a huge Highlander in a kilt. He strides up to the hammer, spits on his hands, and takes the shaft in a firm grip — a whisper like the sound of rustling trees goes through the crowd. The moment has come; he lifts the hammer (his muscles bulging beneath his cotton shirt) and twirls round and round, and at every twirl the hammer rises higher and higher in the air. At last, when it is level with his outstretched arms, he lets go of it and away it goes down the field . . .

The throw is evidently a good one, for the crowd applauds loudly, and two solemn-faced umpires appear with tape measures, and discuss its merits. Jock seems to have a number of staunch backers in the crowd, and these push forward and question the umpires' decision, and make themselves disagreeable in various ways.

We watch several other broad and hefty men trying their skill and strength with the hammer, but they have not the same air of confidence as Jock, and have therefore fewer admirers and nobody to tackle the

441

umpires on their behalf. Jock Sprott is proclaimed the victor amidst loud applause.

Guthrie says this is poor sport compared with tossing the caber, but, of course, we shan't see them tossing the caber at a rotten little fair like *this*.

We are pushing our way out of the crowd when suddenly we are confronted by a tall man in Highland dress — it is MacArbin. My first instinct is flight, and I believe that Tony feels the same almost overpowering impulse; but Guthrie — who, of course, has no reason to avoid him — presses forward and shakes him by the hand, and we are involved in talk with the unhappy man. I am quite shocked at the difference in him, which, I suppose, is due to distress over his sister's elopement. He seems years older, and his glossy self-confidence has completely gone.

"Have you heard from your sister, sir?" asks Guthrie, rushing in where angels might fear to tread.

"I have no sister," he replies — not dramatically, but just as if he were stating a sad fact. "No sister," he repeats, and, bowing to us with something of his old-time grace, he passes from us and is lost in the crowd.

"Good Lord!" Guthrie says. "I seem to have put my foot in it with the old chap. Who would have thought he would have taken Deirdre's marriage so much to heart? Hector's one of the best fellows going — I suppose he's still chewing away at his silly old feud."

Tony and I say nothing — perhaps he is as shocked as I am at the change in the proud Highlander — at any rate he lets Guthrie's tactlessness pass without comment, which shows that he is not feeling quite his usual self.

The roundabout is encompassed by a crowd of gaping children, the horses prance gaily in their red and gold trappings, and the organ blares forth a pot-pourri of popular tunes. All around is the darkness of the night and the silent hills, but here there is light and gaiety and noise.

"In eleven more months and ten more days I'll be out of the calaboose," shouts Tony, elbowing his way through the crowd. He has suddenly gone quite crazy, and his mood is infectious. I feel on for anything that's going, and squeeze after him through the lane he has made. We have lost Guthrie by this time, but perhaps it is just as well — I have already decided that it is a frightful mistake to come to a fair with two swains in attendance.

We mount two fiery-looking steeds and prance round and round — I have no idea how many turns we have. The flaring lights, the rhythm of the organ, and the hot happy faces of the riders melt into a sort of blur. Just in front of us is a fat woman who screams delightedly and waves to various friends in the crowd of watchers. Behind us a farm boy and his sweetheart hold hands and smile at each other in excited bliss. Tony's eyes are shining with a strange light, he has lost his hat, and his fair hair is standing on end. I can't believe that this is really the reserved and cynical Tony Morley. Surely there is some madness abroad in the June night that has got into his blood!

At last we decide that we have had enough, and climb down. I can hardly stand, and cling to Tony's solid arm like a drowning man.

"Giddy?" he enquires, looking down at me with smiling eyes. "I'm a bit giddy myself — feel as if I wanted to do something silly. Look here, Hester, I've got a grand idea — let's treat all these kids to a ride — shall we?"

I realise afresh how lovely it must be to be rich, and nod my head emphatically.

The owner of the roundabout — who is of a suitable build for his profession and possesses a shining red face — is delighted with Tony's offer, and agrees that ten shillings will give all the children a good ride. He therefore climbs on to a convenient tub and announces through a megaphone that a kind gentleman is giving a free ride to all the children present. "Come along all of ye," he shouts. "Walk up, children — free ride for every one of ye."

For about half a minute nobody moves. The children are utterly incredulous of their good fortune . . . and then there is an absolute stampede. We are almost swept off our feet by the rush, and the roundabout man only saves himself from disaster by jumping nimbly off the tub and clutching Tony's arm.

"We've done it now, sir," he says, looking at the juvenile avalanche in dismay. "There'll be murder done — and 'ow on earth 'ull I ever get them children off those 'orses again?"

Tony evidently shares the fat man's views. He presses a pound note into the grubby hand and drags me away.

"For God's sake let's get out of this, Hester," he says. "I had no idea we were going to let Bedlam loose in the place."

Bedlam is loose indeed. The children have stormed the roundabout, and are fighting like demons over the horses. The air is rent with the battle cries of the victorious, and the shrieks of the fallen. A few fond parents are pushing through the throng and calling wildly for their young.

We fly from the scene, hand in hand, pursued by the noise and the commotion — from afar we hear the fat man shouting through his megaphone in despairing tones, and beseeching his young patrons to refrain from dragging each other off the horses and hitting each other on the nose.

"You'll *hall* get a free ride if you comes quiet," he bellows. "Hevery one of ye — stop it now, do. 'Ow can I start the 'orses if ye keeps on fighting?"

The booths are almost deserted, everyone having been drawn to the roundabout by the noise. Tony and I have ample leisure to stroll round and make our purchases. The booths are lighted with flares, as all booths should be; there is something mysterious and exciting about flares. The wind plays with them, blowing them this way and that, so that they almost vanish, and then leap up with renewed energy. The shadows dance and waver on the eager faces of the stallholders as they bend forward over their wares; so that at one moment a man's face seems all nose, with two dark caverns below his temples for eyes, and the next moment he seems quite an ordinary little man

445

with nothing remarkable about him. Two girls lean together, whispering, and the dancing red light makes them beautiful and hideous by turns. One of them laughs, throwing up her head, and her hair is like a red nimbus round her pallid face. I catch Tony's arm and tell him to look.

"It's queer, isn't it?" he says. "They live in their own world, just as important to them as ours is to us. We have never seen them before, and we shall never see them again, but tonight, just for a moment, our two worlds touch."

"Let's speak to them."

"No, it would spoil it," says Tony. "It's perfect as it is, and they probably drop their aitches — I wish I could paint."

I feel it would not matter if they dropped their aitches, it is the girls that interest me, not so much the picture they make. How do they live? What are they talking about? But at the same time I realise they couldn't tell me what I want to know, even if they would; so we leave them and stroll on.

"I want a gingerbread man," Tony says suddenly. "I simply must buy a gingerbread man. Do you mean to tell me you haven't got a gingerbread man?" he says to the girl at the sweet stall. "With gilt on the outside that you can lick off — no? Hester, I'm sorry, this isn't a real fair at all. They haven't got a gingerbread man."

The girl is quite frightened and offers him a gingerbread horse, but it has no gilt and Tony looks at it with scorn.

"How can we go on saying '*That* has taken the gilt off the giner-bread' if there never was any gilt on it?" he demands. "You see my point, don't you? Unless, of course, this horse was covered with gilt, and someone has licked it off already —"

The girl indignantly repudiates the suggestion.

"Oh well!" says Tony sadly. "Another illusion gone west . . ."

At the toy stall I buy a doll for Betty, and Tony buys her a monkey on a stick. I also invest in fairings for Mrs. Loudon, Mrs. Falconer and Annie. Tony shows me a small India rubber frog — green, with goggling yellow eyes — and says he is going to give it to "our dear Guthrie" and don't I think it is a speaking likeness. I reply quite frankly that I can't see the smallest resemblance, which damps Tony's spirits for about twenty seconds.

We are passing a tent, covered with mystic signs and black cats, when the flap is suddenly thrown back, and a tall burly figure emerges from the gloom. It is the long-lost Guthrie, and he looks somewhat sheepish when he sees us.

"I've been looking everywhere for you," he announces.

"Have you really?" says Tony kindly. "What bad luck! But you'll know another time not to look for us in the fortune teller's mystic abode. Hester and I make a point of never having our fortunes told."

"You probably do something far sillier," replies Guthrie, guessing right for once. The effect of his pronouncement is marred by the wretched coconuts, which escape from his clutches and roll in all directions. We collect three of them with some difficulty, owing to the darkness, but the fourth has gone forever.

"Never mind," Guthrie says. "Three is enough to make all the birds at Burnside thoroughly ill."

I feel we have been rather neglectful of Guthrie, so I enquire in my friendliest manner what the fortune teller said to him. He responds at once to slight encouragement, and replies:

"Oh, just the usual rot. I am going a long journey over the sea, and I must beware of a girl with golden hair; and a brunette is going to save me from danger, and alter my whole life — what *is* a brunette?" asks Guthrie.

"Hester is," says Tony wickedly. "By the way, Loudon, the sybil didn't tell you that a tall man with a kind face was going to give you a frog, did she? Well, I don't think much of her then," and so saying he takes the frog out of his pocket and presents it to Guthrie with a low bow.

Guthrie looks at it with suspicion. He cannot make up his mind whether it is some new and deadly insult, or whether it is merely a joke.

"What on earth is *this* for?" he asks.

"For your bath," says Tony gravely. "And to remind you of me when we are far apart and the seas divide us."

"I think I had better give it to Betty," Guthrie says. "When I'm in my bath there's not much room for frogs."

I feel relieved and pleased at the way in which Guthrie has taken the joke, and congratulate myself upon the fact that they have actually spoken to each other without being rude.

"There seems to be the devil of a row going on at the roundabout," Guthrie says suddenly. "Let's push on, and see what's happening."

Tony and I refuse firmly, with one accord, to go near the place.

"It looks like a free fight," Guthrie continues, turning round and gazing at the roundabout with interest and animation. "Let's go over and have a look at it. We needn't get mixed up in it if Hester is nervous."

"It's nothing, absolutely nothing," Tony assures him. "They always go on like that at roundabouts."

"Rot," says Guthrie. "There's a row on, and I'm going over to see what it's about — you needn't come if you're frightened."

"I'm simply terrified," Tony replies. "But I'll try to be brave if Hester will stay with me, and hold my hand. Give my love to the roundabout man," he calls out to Guthrie's retreating back, "and meet us at the car if you get out of it alive."

The whole place is now beginning to close down. At some of the booths the flares have been extinguished, and the occupants are busy packing up their wares and taking down their tents and wooden stalls. Huge vans have appeared upon the scene, and men in shirt sleeves are busily engaged in packing them. We accost a small dirty youth and ask him if the fair is moving.

449

"We'll be on the road in twa hours," he replies briefly.

"What a life!" ejaculates Tony.

"Aye, it's a fine life," echoes the boy. "Ye get seeing the wurrld in a fair."

All mystery has departed from the fortune teller's tent; it is merely a heap of dirty canvas. A large, fat woman with greasy black hair, and a red shawl pinned across her inadequately clad bosom, is dancing about with a flaming torch in her hand, directing operations in a shrill shrewish voice.

"Guthrie's sybil!" says Tony sadly. "I'm afraid we've stayed too long at the party."

"I think it is rather fun," I reply. "I like seeing things that I'm not meant to see — besides, it's not really very late."

"Mother said I was to be home at six to have my hair washed," says Tony in an absurd treble.

I tell him he's a perfect idiot and we walk on laughing.

"Here you are!" exclaims Guthrie, pouncing on us suddenly — so suddenly that we both nearly jump out of our skins. "Look here, you simply must come over and see the fun — people are knocking each other down — there's a funny little fat man with a megaphone — I want to get hold of him and find out all about it."

"I'm sure he knows nothing," says Tony untruthfully, "and if he did he wouldn't tell you. We're going home now, Hester's tired."

"But surely you can wait ten minutes."

450

"Not one minute. Do come on, Loudon. The show is all over now; Hester wants to get home."

"I don't know why you're in such a hurry all of a sudden," says Guthrie pettishly. We take no notice — neither Tony nor I have the slightest desire to renew our acquaintance with the roundabout man.

Guthrie follows us reluctantly, murmuring at intervals that he doesn't know why we are in such a hurry all of a sudden.

The Bentley is now reposing in the car park in solitary state. We pack in, and soon we are buzzing homewards through the darkness, with two bright shafts of light streaming out before us like the beams of a lighthouse. The trees and hedges look a peculiar artificial shade of green in the glare of the lamps, and the white road runs smoothly backwards beneath our wheels.

Tony sets us down at the gate. "Goodbye, Hester," he says, "and thank you for being such a dear. Give my love to old Tim when he rolls up, won't you?"

"But you'll be coming over to see him," I point out. "We'll be here until Tuesday, you know."

"I may — or I may not. It all depends how strong I feel," replies Tony cryptically. "But tell him from me he's a lucky devil."

"Do come on, Hester," says Guthrie impatiently. "I thought you were in such a terrific hurry to get home."

"But now she *is* home, so there's no need to hurry any more," explains Tony kindly.

"I don't know what you're talking about, and what's more you don't know yourself," exclaims Guthrie furiously. "You seem to think I'm half-witted —"

"No, no — not half-witted."

"What do you mean?"

"Think it over when you get into bed," Tony advises him in a soothing voice. "You are bound to understand it in time if you persevere. Just lie flat on your back, and breathe easily through the nose —"

Guthrie turns on his heel with a muttered curse and strides up the drive like a grenadier. I am thankful to see him go without bloodshed.

"What a peppery little fellow he is, to be sure!" exclaims Tony. "Always taking the huff about something, isn't he?"

"It's entirely your fault and you know it," I tell him sternly. "You could wind Guthrie round your finger if you liked — why can't you be nice to him, like you are to me?"

"I'm nice to you, am I?" he enquires in a strange voice.

"Frightfully nice," I reply.

"Well!" he says, "I suppose that's something," and, so saying, he lets in his gear and is gone in a flash.

I follow Guthrie up the drive, and we let ourselves into the quiet house as silently as we can. I can't help smiling to myself, for the darkness and silence of the house remind me of that night when Guthrie and I laid our plans to capture the burglars, and discovered the treasure seekers instead. Guthrie remembers it too, for

I see him glance at the warming pan on the wall with a strange expression on his face.

"What are you thinking of?" I whisper as we creep up the uncarpeted stair.

"Bones," he replies solemnly, and the tone of his voice bodes no good for that lanky individual.

We part at my bedroom door.

"This is the last night, Hester," he says sentimentally. "You won't want me after tomorrow."

I tell him not to be a donkey, and he goes away sorrowfully.

My undressing is soon accomplished, for I am very tired, and I slip into bed and blow out the candle; but for a long time sleep eludes me. Tonight is, in a way, the end of my leave. I am longing to see Tim, of course, but I can't help being sorry the fortnight is over. It has been such a complete change from my ordinary life — almost a change of soul. Instead of thinking all the time of my family, and my household affairs, I have been able to think of myself for a whole fortnight — to *be* myself, not just Tim's wife, and the mother of Bryan and Betty. It has been a lovely thing to find that people like me for no other reason than just because they like me.

Is it really only a fortnight since I left Kiltwinkle? It seems years. I have done so much in the time, seen so many beautiful places, and made so many new friends. Mrs. Loudon I knew before, of course, but my feeling for her has grown and deepened; we shall never lose each other now. I love her downright manner and her uncompromising attitude towards life. Guthrie is a new

453

friend well worth having, his simplicity is endearing. (I hope Tim will like Guthrie; somehow I think he will.) I have learnt to know Tony Morley in a different way during these two weeks, to appreciate his real goodness of heart, though I cannot always understand him. Even Mrs. Falconer is nice. Strange as she is I like her, and I know she also likes me. And Deirdre, my Fairy Princess, what of her? Shall we see each other again? I hope so greatly, for she interested me, and I feel that we would be friends if we had the opportunity. I shall always remember, and be glad that I helped her to marry her Fairy Prince.

A score of bright little pictures stand out clearly as I look back over my time at Avielochan. I pick them out and smile over them one by one. My first morning in the garden — the bright, bright sunshine, and the crystal clearness of the air; Guthrie and Elsie fishing on the loch (how hard poor Guthrie struggled to reconcile the rival attractions of love and sport!); Castle Quill party where I first heard the story of the beautiful Seónaid; the visit to the laundry (I can see the lines of snowy garments dancing in the breeze and hear the soft tones of Miss Campbell's gentle voice); Guthrie's burglars; the picnic when we saw the ghost of Seónaid which turned out to be Deirdre; the dinner party; Betty's adventure in the mist; my expedition with Tony to Gart-na-Druim with its pleasant memories of our welcome and the beauty of the Western Sea; the elopement of my Fairy Princess; and lastly the fair (a jumble of impressions from which our adventure at the roundabout stands forth as the highlight).

Dawn is breaking now, and its pallor creeps in at my open window and spreads like water over the polished floor. Somehow the coming of the new day turns my thoughts to Tim. The page is turned; it is a page of bright colours which will live for ever in my memory. Tim will be here tomorrow — no, *today*. At this very moment he is rushing towards me in the train. The same dawn which is creeping in so slowly at my window is breaking over Tim as he rushes through the sleeping land. Dear old Tim — how lovely it will be to have him here! He will enjoy it all so much — the mountains, the forests, the lovely clear air. We shall go fishing together, perhaps we shall climb the hills. We shall laugh together at Mrs. Falconer's rambling stories and Betty's quaint sayings. What was it that Mrs. Loudon said: "Never the time, and the place, and the loved one all together." Lucky me, for I shall have them all!

The light brightens and fills the room. A little bird chirps outside my window, and another wakens and answers. Suddenly a perfect choir of little birds bursts into song.

Also available in ISIS Large Print:

Miss Buncle Married

D. E. Stevenson

Marriage to her publisher, Arthur Abbott, has done nothing to stop Barbara Buncle from involving herself in the lives of her neighbours. The only difference this time is that she's trying to avoid writing about them too.

After leaving Silverstream and moving to London, Barbara and Arthur are enjoying their newly-wedded bliss, but not the city life. The only solution to their problem? Returning to the country. Silverstream is out of the question, but Barbara eventually finds the perfect candidate in the town of Wandlebury. After falling in love with the town, and the run-down Archway House, the Abbotts move in and make it their home. Barbara doesn't intend to get mixed up with those around her again, but can't help falling into those scrapes, often with humorous consequences!

ISBN 978-0-7531-8554-4 (hb)
ISBN 978-0-7531-8555-1 (pb)

Henrietta's War

Joyce Dennys

Spirited Henrietta wishes she was the kind of doctor's wife who knew exactly how to deal with the daily upheavals of war. But then, everyone in her close-knit Devonshire village seems to find different ways to cope: there's the indomitable Lady B, who writes to Hitler every night to tell him precisely what she thinks of him; flighty Faith who is utterly preoccupied with flashing her shapely legs; and then there's Charles, Henrietta's hard-working husband, who sleeps through a bomb landing in the neighbour's garden. With life turned upside down, Henrietta chronicles the dramas, squabbles and friendships in a community of determined troupers.

ISBN 978-0-7531-8602-2 (hb)
ISBN 978-0-7531-8603-9 (pb)